WISECRACKER

WISECRACKER

The Life and Times of

WILLIAM HAINES,

Hollywood's First Openly Gay Star

William J. Mann

VIKING

VIKING
Published by the Penguin Group
Penguin Putnam Inc., 375 Hudson Street,
New York, New York 10014, U.S.A.
Penguin Books Ltd, 27 Wrights Lane, London W8 5TZ, England
Penguin Books Australia Ltd, Ringwood, Victoria, Australia
Penguin Books Canada Ltd, 10 Alcorn Avenue,
Toronto, Ontario, Canada M4V 3B2
Penguin Books (N.Z.) Ltd, 182–190 Wairau Road,
Auckland 10, New Zealand

Penguin Books Ltd, Registered Offices:
Harmondsworth, Middlesex, England

First published in 1998 by Viking Penguin,
a member of Penguin Putnam, Inc.

3 5 7 9 10 8 6 4 2

Frontispiece courtesy of the collection of Sergei Troubetzkoy

LIBRARY OF CONGRESS CATALOGING-IN-PUBLICATION DATA
Mann, William J.
Wisecracker : the life and times of William Haines, Hollywood's
first openly gay star / by William J. Mann.
p. cm.
Filmography: p.
Includes bibliographical references and index.
ISBN 0-670-87155-9 (alk. paper)
1. Haines, William, 1900–1973. 2. Motion picture actors and actresses—
United States—Biography. 3. Gay men—United States—Biography. I. Title.
PN2287.H172M36   1998
791.43'028'092   97-39665
[B]—DC21

This book is printed on acid-free paper.

∞

Printed in the United States of America
Set in Cochin
Designed by Kathryn Parise

For Wulfgar

Contents

• • • Contents • • •

Photographs follow page 156.

Foreword

I'd come to ask her about William Haines, but there was much she wanted to say first.

"Have you seen my performance in *Our Dancing Daughters*?" Anita Page's elegantly penciled eyebrows rose. "The critics said it was my best work."

I told her yes, I had seen it—in fact, I'd seen it several times. I added that I agreed with the critics' assessment. Her performance withstood the test of time.

She smiled. It was the same smile I'd seen up there on the screen, sweet and innocent, but wistful, too, a little sad. I was honest in my appraisal: She *did* turn in a wonderful performance as the drunken, slatternly daughter, the foil to Joan Crawford's good girl. In truth, however, I *was* attempting a bit of flattery. I understood well the delicate idiosyncrasies of silent stars, those rare creatures of shadow and light, an exotic endangered species as we approach the end of the millennium.

My search for Billy Haines—one of the biggest of the silent stars, although few remember him now—began that crisp January day in 1996, having lunch with Anita Page at the Hollywood Roosevelt Hotel. I insisted on calling her "Miss Page" despite her much-younger entourage's habit of calling her Anita. She had been one of

Billy's most frequent costars, and one of the very few still alive. I knew that to find Billy—who'd died more than twenty years before—I'd need to look into the eyes of another time, eyes that had seen a world few of us today could appreciate.

"Miss Page?"

We both looked up. An elderly gentleman, natty in tweed jacket and bow tie, timidly approached our table. Behind him a woman, presumably his wife, hovered a bit.

Anita Page sat up straighter in her chair. The eighty-six-year-old silent-screen star lifted her eyes, heavy with mascara, and grinned broadly at the man. There was a sudden alertness, a sparkle in the eyes, the same I'd noticed when I first introduced myself—a summoning of something very deep within her, something very old, something from another time, a magic, a magnetism, a luminescence.

"Oh, Miss Page," the man gushed, and I had the eerie sense of finding myself plunked down in the middle of *Sunset Boulevard*. "I am *so* happy to see you out and about. I had thought you—"

He didn't need to finish. She'd apparently heard it before. She graciously held out her hand to be kissed. Her manager instantly retrieved an eight-by-ten glossy of Miss Page from his briefcase. Of course the photo was from sixty-odd years ago: Anita Page, MGM starlet, in an off-the-shoulder dress. But it was that young woman who the man wanted, who he remembered, who indeed he saw sitting at the table—who Anita Page, too, still believed herself to be.

When I began my search for Billy Haines, I was cautioned that there would be few who remembered him in his prime. There were few who could tell me what kind of a man he was, or who remembered that lost era of glittery abandon, the days of champagne-filled bathtubs and free love, the days before repression settled over Hollywood like a heavy black tarp, snuffing out the fires of the Flaming Youth.

Anita Page remembered. Somewhat hard of hearing and just a trifle confused at times, she remains a lovely, effervescent woman. For her those gilded days have not ended. She is still a movie queen, a silent-film goddess. With Gish and Swanson, Pickford and Garbo,

Bow and Davies all gone, Anita Page has become, by default, the greatest silent star alive.

Once her admirer was gone, she returned her attention to me. Her lipstick was painted over and above the top of her lip, creating that bee-stung look she was famous for a lifetime ago. "You wanted to know about Billy Haines," she said. She patted my hand. "His star is right outside the front door here. Would you like me to show it to you?"

Of course I would. First, she insisted, we must take a peek inside the ballroom, where sixty-seven years ago the very first Academy Awards ceremony had taken place. "I was here with Billy," Miss Page told me. "How *handsome* he looked in his tuxedo."

The room is small. There are few adornments, no stage, nothing opulent like the Dorothy Chandler Pavilion, the site of today's awards. Yet here walk the ghosts of Mary Pickford and Charlie Chaplin, Janet Gaynor and Emil Jannings, Louis B. Mayer and William Haines.

But ghosts could not tell me what I needed to know. I had to believe there were those still among us who remembered the handsome, all-American wisecracker I was searching for—a man whose life, I was convinced, still had something to offer us today.

"He was the biggest of the big," a rotund old man had told me at a Hollywood movie-stills store. I'd just bought their entire paltry collection of William Haines stills. "I'm probably the only one left alive who remembers him when he was big."

Not quite, but close. William Haines was the number one box-office star in the country for just one year—1930—but he was in the top ten for another five, from 1926 to 1931. A calamitous time for Hollywood: the Talkie Revolution, the establishment of the Production Code. Somewhere in the midst of all the upheaval the public forgot about Billy Haines. One recently published account of the transition from silent to talking pictures calls Billy "a second-echelon star" usually paired with bigger names. In truth, Billy only costarred once during his peak years, with Marion Davies in *Show People*, and that was to give the beleaguered Davies a box-office boost. In the late 1920s, very few were bigger than William Haines.

I was certain there was a story to this man's life, a story worth telling more than sixty years after his heyday and twenty years after his death. There were all sorts of legends: how he'd been fired by MGM for refusing to give up his boyfriend, how he'd dared to live as an openly gay man in an era when such a concept didn't even exist. How he'd helped shape the image of his good buddy Joan Crawford. How he'd gone on to establish the very *look* of Hollywood itself in his second career as screenland's premier interior decorator.

By now, I'd seen most of his films, at least those few that remain extant. I could understand why he'd been such a favorite. Handsome. Breezy. Cocky. A kind of antihero for the 1920s. No gentleman like John Gilbert, hardly romantic like Ramon Novarro. "A new day has dawned in comedy," wrote Warren Colby, film reviewer for the *Evening World*, in 1929. "For every custard pie that's thrown nowadays there are ten that are eaten." He gave the credit to William Haines. The whole joy of a Haines picture was seeing him fall flat on his face and eat—in the slang of the times—"humble pie" before he finally won the girl. "A hero?" Colby asked. "Well, hardly. Your pet heroes don't go out and get drunk while they're in training for football, nor do they turn yellow at crucial moments and say the devil with dear old alma mater."

If Billy had a prop, it was the smart aside, the wisecrack—first seen in subtitles, then tossed out of the corner of his mouth with just the hint of his good-old-boy Virginia accent. He wore his cracks as cockily as Chaplin wore his derby. Many of these witticisms were his own invention, ad-libbed on the spot. In a famous speech at the University of Southern California in 1929, MGM production chief Irving Thalberg called Billy Haines the perfect leading man for the times. "The idealistic love of a decade ago is not true today," Thalberg said. "William Haines, with his modern salesman attitude to go and get it, is more typical."

The image I had of him was surprisingly contemporary. Standing in the ballroom at the Hollywood Roosevelt Hotel with Miss Page, I tried to picture Billy Haines strutting into the hall, slapping friends on the back, being rushed by reporters and photographers, his equally handsome lover, Jimmie Shields, at his side.

"He really *was* the most popular actor of the time," Miss Page sighed, as if reading my mind. "It can't be that people don't remember him anymore."

I assured her that it was so.

"Oh, my, that's terrible. Why, Billy Haines—*everyone* knew Billy Haines. He was so handsome, so witty, so friendly, so—"

I asked her if she would say courageous.

She paused. Despite being shorter than I am, she managed to meet and hold my gaze. "Why, yes," she said. "I would say he was *quite* courageous."

Anita Page, even in her eighth decade, retains the childlike wonder that she projected so magically on the screen. She still prays for the soul of Joan Crawford, her onetime MGM archrival, and she still believes that Ramon Novarro just never met the right woman. Yet, she knew what I meant when I asked her if William Haines was courageous. Anita Page holds the distinction of being the only woman Billy Haines ever asked to marry—and for that alone, I knew I had to meet her.

"Yes," she repeated, her eyes still holding mine. "Courageous he certainly was."

Although the general public may no longer recognize his name, William Haines remains something of a fascination for film buffs. They love to tell the stories about him—of the supposed raid at a Hollywood gay bar that netted both Haines and Constance Talmadge; of the alleged tryst with a sailor at the YMCA (or was it Pershing Square?); of the famous final confrontation with Louis B. Mayer, where Haines reportedly told the belligerent studio chief that he'd give up his boyfriend only when Mr. Mayer gave up his wife.

In the swirl of time, after all the ground-shifting—both literal and figurative—that has gone on in Hollywood since Billy Haines was its top star, stories have a way of growing quite pat, of becoming the legends we want them to be. The truth—as always—is far more fascinating, and considerably more complex. It's perhaps anachronistic to call Billy Haines "openly gay," when such a term had not even been *conceived* sixty years ago. The social constructs of homosexuality were not what they are today, or even what they would become thirty years later, with the founding of the first American homosexual rights group. Nonetheless, it took courage to refuse to play the Hollywood game of arranged marriages and photo-op dates— Anita Page notwithstanding. There was no gay movement in 1930, no political imperative to identify in the public arena as homosexual. While Billy Haines might have refused to take seriously publicity linking him to Pola Negri, he also never introduced Jimmie Shields in the pages of *Photoplay*. Such was simply not part of the consciousness of the times.

Yet he lived a completely authentic life. In the more permissive days of the 1920s and early 1930s, being homosexual was simply something that *was*—at least within Hollywood. There might have been no such animal as a "public identity" of a gay man in those days, but Billy Haines came close. He was a man perfectly suited for his times.

A hero, then? Some gay activists have suggested as much, but how do we reconcile his later friendships with Hollywood conservatives? At the very time when then-governor Reagan was blanketfiring his homosexual staffers, Ron and his wife, Nancy, were frequent dinner guests at Billy and Jimmie's home. More than one friend has insisted that Billy wanted nothing to do with "Gay Liberation," the birth of which he lived just long enough to witness.

And yet William Haines *is* a kind of hero for the ages. In researching a biography, one looks for the hidden lines that too often are airbrushed out of a public image. Billy Haines had his share of lines, as we all do. However, that word—"courageous"—kept coming up again and again, in interview after interview. Most remembered him only from his later career as Hollywood's premier interior decorator. Even these people kept emphasizing the same things: Principle. Integrity. The courage to be truthful. "That in itself is remarkable," said one of his clients. "Especially in this town."

While he lived a life uniquely his own, when his story is set in context with his times, it takes on even greater implication: It is, in fact, a mirror of the gay experience in Hollywood. It resonates today not because of the glamour and style of his life (of which there was plenty), but because he was a vital part of the stunning upheaval in the early 1930s that so dramatically altered the course of motion pictures—the arrival of the Production Code, which had a far more profound and lasting impact than even the coming of sound.

The story of William Haines is, in many ways, the story of a march backward, of a community closing in on itself, repressing its own, stifling its own creativity. It's the story of how the closet came to be the paradigm for a town overrun with gay men and lesbians, of how a long-ago era of tolerance and openness came to a sudden and conspicuous end.

The story of William Haines is also one of personal triumph. He was a "wisecracker," his own (and the media's) cute code word for queer. Through such wit, through his sheer force of personality, he was also a survivor. Ramon Novarro became an alcoholic hermit; Cary Grant embarked on a disastrous string of heterosexual marriages; Billy Haines and Jimmie Shields celebrated nearly fifty years together. Joan Crawford called them the "happiest married couple in Hollywood." When Billy died, it was not in obscurity, as so many of his contemporaries found themselves. Rather, he died with the respect of a community known for turning its back on outcasts and misfits. And he won that prestige not just for his craft, but for his courage in being himself.

In the course of researching his life, in talking to those who knew and loved him, I came to many observations, many conclusions. They are presented here and they are my own. Every biographer ultimately recognizes that he or she alone bears authorial responsibility to interpret the evidence. If Billy were living, he'd probably question why the one decade during which he was a movie star is the primary focus of this book, while his three decades as a decorator—his life's true calling—are reduced to just two chapters. Billy found personal satisfaction in his later career and rightfully considered his work in the design field to be of greater achievement than any of his pictures. In the reverse of most biographies of movie stars, however, it is not Billy's *work* that makes him historically important—it is his *life*. His *personal* life—how he conducted himself in private, among his friends, his community, his colleagues, and his employers. This was a man who played by rules of his own design, and that, in Hollywood, is extraordinary enough.

Still, I have attempted to be as careful as possible in not applying contemporary definitions or attitudes to the historical record. Billy saw himself as homosexual, to be sure, but it's very possible that he never actually used the word to identify himself, or anyone else, for that matter. Such terms as "out" and "closet" have no meaning in describing the situations of the era. Even "gay" and "lesbian" carry no particular historical weight; both were used, but not in the common, self-identifying parlance of today. (I have used "gay" throughout this account to describe and identify those individuals who were predominantly homosexual in orientation, if not always in behavior. They tended to know one another and often formed social cliques.) There was no "gay community" to speak of—at least no sense of a larger, politically identified population of people—but there *was* a definite grouping of those who had such inclinations versus those who did not. The full account has yet to be told, but Billy's story shines, for the first time, an important beacon on gay Hollywood during the Golden Age.

As it turned out, Anita Page never showed me Billy's star on the Walk of Fame. I left her regaling a crowd of young admirers at a table in the lounge. I found Billy's star on my own, just as the sun was setting and the long purple shadows of palm trees stretched out in front of me on the sidewalk. There it was, just a few feet from the front door of the hotel, the only monument to William Haines left in a town where he'd once been king. Even most of the decors he created in his second career have been destroyed: David Geffen gutted the magnificent Jack Warner estate; new owners tore out the finely crafted interiors of George Cukor's house. This is all there is: a simple gold star, covered with dried wads of gum.

I was startled by a man with a long shock of white hair and a ruffled pink shirt who came up behind me.

"Do you know him?" he asked. "Do you know William Haines?"

I explained I was writing a book on his life.

"Ah," the man exclaimed. "He is well worth it. I remember when this street was crammed with people and automobiles for the premiere of *Tell It to the Marines*. He was a very bright star, very bright indeed."

The old man's eyes sparkled. I couldn't resist. So, I asked, would he also say *courageous?*

The old man grinned. "Like none since," he said, and winked.

The next day, I continued my search for Billy Haines.

WISECRACKER

1

WINE OF YOUTH

1900-1915

It's a central fact of his life that Billy Haines rarely told a lie, but he did have his ways of making the truth fit the situation at hand.

"I'm a true child of the twentieth century," he often boasted, cocking his head, jutting out his chin, his thumbs behind his lapels.

In fact, he was. Born at midnight on the first day of the first year of the new century, William Haines was, from the start, a man both ahead of and perfectly in step with his times, a model of modern sensibilities. But was the midnight at which he actually first entered the world the witching hour between December 31, 1899, and January 1, 1900? Or that between January 1 and January 2?

Billy, of course—along with his studio publicists—always claimed the January 1 date. It's such a romantic scenario, after all, sustaining his image as the ideal contemporary hero: "A true child of the twentieth century." How eminently disappointing it would be to enter the world one minute *after* the first day of the first year of the new century, which is precisely what the sexton of Trinity Episcopal Church in Staunton, Virginia, recorded on the occasion of Billy's baptism, eight years after his birth. There, in faded old ink, in the spidery script of another time, is scrawled January 2, 1900.

No birth records exist for Staunton for the period, so it's impossible to know for certain on exactly what date Billy Haines was born.

"I was born the night of January 1," he always said, enigmatically—
not so much a lie as a creative use of the truth. Billy Haines knew
how to be honest, brutally so—just ask many of his decorating
clients—though brutality in any form offended his keen sense of
what was beautiful, what was real, what was right. How much better to be honest with a little flair, with a little chinoiserie around the
fringe, than to demean oneself with the starkness of truth or the
absolute certainty of lies.

William Haines—matinee idol, box-office champ, renowned decorator, friend of the rich and famous, and pretty rich and famous
himself—started life as the third child (and the first to survive in-
fancy) of a struggling Virginia cigar maker, George Adam Haines,
and his wife, Laura Virginia Matthews.

Both his parents hailed from old, respected Virginia families. No
matter how far he traveled, no matter how comfortable he became in
the sea breezes and smog of southern California, no matter how flat
he managed to hammer his accent, there was always something distinctly Southern to Billy Haines. "There was a graciousness to Billy,
a genteel sensibility," remembered his longtime friend Bob Shaw.
"He could be pretty outrageous, but there was always that sense of
Southern hospitality just below the surface. You could imagine him
as the perfect country squire."

Staunton (pronounced STAN-ton) is nestled in the heart of the
Shenandoah Valley. Settled during the 1730s as one of the first Virginia towns west of the Blue Ridge Mountains, Staunton became a
major trading center in the 1850s with the arrival of the railroad. It
was through Staunton that many pioneers began their journeys west
to settle new land.

To drive into Staunton today is to journey into the past. The hills
roll alongside the highway, blue fading to purple in the distance.
Everywhere, too, there is the lush green of cornfields and cow farms,
bales of hay stacked for the winter. It is not the Old South, and
never was, not really: Virginia has always been among the most en-
lightened of Southern states. A strong antislavery movement had developed after the slave rebellion of 1831, and the state had the lowest

lynching rate in the South. Representatives from Staunton to the state assembly twice voted not to secede from the Union, and there were, years before the war, many free blacks living in the region. William Haines himself grew up in a fairly integrated neighborhood, even if the servants his family employed were usually black.

Still, the town is a changeless kind of place, despite its shopping center and spiffy new library. It remains much as Billy Haines would have known it; indeed, his grandparents would still recognize it today. An architecturally rich town, most of the buildings from the nineteenth century still stand. It is a city built on hills, with steep, often narrow streets, surrounded by the omnipresent Allegheny and Blue Ridge mountain ranges. Reaching the summit of the street where Billy grew up, one can see a panorama of the town enclosed by the mountains—a captivating if somewhat claustrophobic observation.

Billy certainly would have heard the old-timers, his grandfather among them, tell the tales of "them thar hills." At the crest of the county line, remnants of Confederate entrenchments still mar the earth, where Stonewall Jackson repulsed Union troops in five fierce hours of bloody fighting in the second major battle of the Shenandoah Valley campaign. During the Civil War, Staunton served as an important supply depot. It proved a vital rail link between the "breadbasket of the Confederacy" and the rest of Virginia.

After the war, Staunton experienced rapid growth, its population nearly doubling from its prewar numbers. It was the largest town in the region by the end of the nineteenth century, boasting more than seven thousand citizens. Beginning in 1891, famed architect T. J. Collins designed more than two hundred buildings in town. At the time, mule-drawn streetcars operated on five and a half miles of track throughout Staunton. In 1896 they were converted to electricity. It was a lively, bustling little center of industry and commerce by the time Billy Haines was born, and his family had played a large part in its success.

Later on, West Coast friends of Billy Haines would insist that he was the scion of a grand Southern clan, a family of affluence and great social prestige, conjuring images of plantations, columned mansions, and aristocratic men on horses. "He was from Vuh-gin-i-uh, suh!" one friend drawled, nose in the air.

When asked if Billy's family ever expressed surprise or seemed a little dazed after he imported them all to California, showering upon them the largesse his Hollywood success allowed, another friend shrugged off the question. "You must understand," this friend said. "The Haineses were one of *the* families of Virginia."

Well, maybe. It depends on how one defines *"the."* Certainly during his later life, when Billy moved among the jet set of the Annenbergs and the Bloomingdales, he did not discourage the prevailing notion that his family was Virginian aristocracy. But in truth, the Haines family was comfortably middle class. For each of the three generations before Billy Haines, the family had moved from place to place. They were apple farmers, then merchants and factory owners, not the landed gentry.

Charles Edward Haines, Billy Haines's grandfather, was born in 1841. Until his death in 1912, two generations of Haines men would grow up in the shadow of this extraordinary man. In 1861, not yet twenty years of age, Charles enlisted in the Confederate army as a private in the Fifth Regiment of the Virginia infantry, known as the "Bloody Fifth." It was organized as a volunteer militia and received its baptism by fire along with Stonewall Jackson's First Brigade at the Battle of Falling Waters on July 2. He was an eager young soldier devoted to the Southern cause, a fierce advocate of the Confederacy and states' rights. He was a musician with the regiment's band, which also served as a medical unit, rescuing wounded soldiers from the field and treating their injuries. So impressed with their service, Stonewall Jackson himself recognized them, rechristening the troupe the Stonewall Brigade Band, a name they have kept to this day.

At the Battle of Cedar Creek in October 1864, where eighteen hundred Confederate troops were killed or wounded, Charles was taken prisoner by Union forces under General Philip Sheridan. He was not released until the end of the war the following April. But there wasn't complete rancor at the North among the Stonewall Brigade Band: At the Appomattox surrender, Union General

Ulysses S. Grant allowed them to keep their instruments, a gesture that was appreciated and not forgotten by band members.

After the war, Charles settled in Staunton, marrying Rosa Lee Armentrout, the sister of his army buddy James Armentrout, who also got him involved in the tobacco business. Rosa Lee was a quiet, dignified, gentle woman, the antithesis of her ambitious husband. She would watch quietly from the kitchen as her husband and brother outlined their new business and managed the postwar Stonewall Brigade Band, the two great passions of Charles's later life.

As determined to succeed as ever, Charles quickly specialized in cigar making, the most profitable area of tobacco. By the 1880s, the Haines Cigar Company was doing big business, producing such brands as Nosegay and Cock of the Roost. Although Staunton was not in the tobacco-raising part of the state, it benefited from Virginia's rich tobacco-growing history. Charles traveled the state and into Pennsylvania to purchase the finest leaves, with the demand for tobacco products mushrooming in the years after the war. "We were drop-shipping cigars all over the South," recalls Henry Haines, Charles's grandson and Billy's younger brother.

The business was located on the corner of Beverley and Augusta streets in downtown Staunton, which came to be known as "Haines's corner." The "factory," located above the store run by Armentrout, consisted of little more than a couple dozen workers seated at long tables rolling tobacco into cigars. It was quiet, tedious work. Charles, who seems to have had show business in his blood, brought in musicians to enliven the monotony for his workers. Sometimes he'd even hire readers or actors to perform scenes.

Such showmanship served him well when he succeeded Armentrout as the third president of the Stonewall Brigade Band. After the war, the troupe took on new vigor, playing not only on the town green of Staunton but all around the state as well. Resplendent in their uniforms and with Confederate flags flapping, they performed whenever a veteran was buried, and in 1877 traveled to New York to play at the funeral of Ulysses S. Grant. They had not forgotten his kindness to them at the end of the war. In 1897 they returned for the dedication of Grant's Tomb.

"Charles Haines was well known for his participation with the band," says Staunton historian Sergei Troubetzkoy. "They would rouse the town, singing patriotic songs. He would put on great shows at the Beverley Theatre or in Gypsy Hill Park, music and reenactments. He was a terrific showman. It's clear where his grandson got it from."

Charles Haines was a larger-than-life citizen, one of the grand elder statesmen of the town. By the late 1890s, as the president of the Staunton Chamber of Commerce, he was responsible for the lively street fairs and carnivals that rolled through the town's streets. The young Billy Haines would have watched in fascination the vaudeville acts and traveling circuses, the streets packed with people, all with Charles Haines as the ringmaster. Did he envy the spotlight, the drama? Did he look upon his grandfather as some kind of magician? Whatever the young boy's impressions, Charles Haines would be a big act to follow.

Certainly Billy's father felt that way. Charles had great plans for his children, and by 1890, he had seven of them. Rosa Lee bore her husband three daughters, Julia, Fanny, and Mary; and four sons, Harry, George, James, and Alfred. Mary would become Billy's godmother and favorite aunt. George, Billy's father, was born in 1874.

By this time the family employed two live-in servants, testament to Charles's standing in town. One, Cornelia Palmer, was a white nineteen-year-old cook; the other, Sophia Bags, was a black eighteen-year-old nursemaid. For twenty years, Charles also employed "Aunt" Lila Tucker, a devoted elderly nursemaid to his children and grandchildren.

The original Haines homestead stood at 129 New Street, an affluent neighborhood of physicians, lawyers, clerks, and merchants. Most families on the block had at least one live-in servant, usually a cook or a maid, more often than not black. By 1900 Charles Haines had done well enough in his tobacco business to own his home free and clear of any mortgages. It was a large house, spacious enough to allow his son George and George's wife to live with them for a time.

Charles fully expected his children to follow his lead. At least three of his sons became members of the Stonewall Brigade Band, including George; all four of his sons would at one time or another work in the family tobacco factory. There appears to have been at least some discontent among his offspring. His eldest son Harry (actually named Charles in honor of his father, but who preferred his more original nickname) left town, abandoning the family business to work as a bookkeeper in New York City. Harry had been among the most talented and ambitious of the Stonewall Brigade Band's younger members, yet he seems to have had a burning desire to break out and try his fortunes in the big, northern city. Such a desertion must have piqued his father, who resettled his hopes and ambitions on his next son.

George Adam Haines had similar difficulties living up to the illustrious examples set by his father. Quiet where his father was gregarious, the young George nevertheless possessed a quick, often cutting sense of humor—a trait passed on to his son. He needed it, one imagines, to survive in a family of seven and with a father as bombastic as Charles.

In 1896, at the age of twenty-two, George Haines married Laura Virginia Matthews. Born in 1878, she was barely eighteen when she married George. Her middle name reflects her family's pride of place: She, too, came from an old Virginia family, one of some prominence in Staunton. Her father, William A. Matthews, was a contractor, responsible for many of the new buildings erected in Staunton during the boom years of the 1890s. Her mother was Annie Irving, originally from Culpeper. For George and Laura, there was struggle and heartache in the first years of their marriage. Living with George's parents and numerous siblings, there was no privacy and little chance to escape from Charles's rigid direction. During this time, too, Laura gave birth to two children who died shortly after birth.

Soon, however, their fortunes changed. Renting a house a few blocks away from George's father, at 311 New Street, they, too, employed live-in servants, a twenty-six-year-old black cook named Mary S. Anderson and "Aunt" Lila Tucker, who moved over from the elder Haines's residence after Billy was born. The house, which still stands today, is a simple two-story midcentury dwelling, with a small yard, and built close to the road. A couple of doors north stands a black Baptist church, designed by the famed T. J. Collins. Billy would have seen, after 1904, the congregation gather every Sunday for services.

The neighborhood had its share of black families, and while there remained segregation in social activities, Billy grew up with black children playing along his street. Certainly he must have befriended some of them, forging his curious hybrid of Old South and twentieth-century thought on the matter of race relations. On the one hand, Billy had a great appreciation for black culture and hardly a prejudiced thought in his head. On the other, he remained Charles's grandson: The dividing line between black and white was natural, not to be questioned.

He'd been named Charles William Haines, for both his grandfathers, but was called Billy almost immediately. Whether that was on Charles's instigation or whether he viewed it as a slight is unknown. Certainly it was better for Billy, who as "Little Charles" would have had an even greater burden of living up to the image of the old man.

Billy's birth was quickly followed by others. Lillion Juliet Haines was born in 1902; Ann Fowkes Haines in 1907; and George Adam Haines, Jr., in 1908. At each new birth, Billy clung more tightly to his mother, desperate not to lose her affection and attention. His uncle James Haines would recall that as a boy of five or six, Billy would stand on the front steps whenever Laura would leave the house: "He'd come as far as the front steps and holler his head off." The farther away she got from home, the uncle said, "the louder William would holler."

Standing in front of Billy's house today, one can picture the scene. The street into town rises to the top of a hill and then quickly descends. Laura would have climbed that hill, probably turning around repeatedly to reassure her son, who would have watched from the front porch until she reached the crest and disappeared over the other side.

"The hills of Staunton, it seemed to me, were higher than any other place in the world," Billy wrote. "The trees grew larger, and nowhere else were the distances so great."

He was an easily frightened child. "When I was little, it was my duty to go every evening to the coal shed back of the house and bring in fuel for the stoves," he remembered years later. "I was scared to death of the dark." Sister Lillion, two years younger but infinitely more brazen, would jump out at him and yell, "Goop!" Billy would invariably spill the coal all over the walk.

He was baptized on March 27, 1908, at age eight in the Trinity Episcopal Church. He was confirmed there as well on April 13, 1913. The family wasn't particularly religious, but they played by the rules. "In the South, if you weren't an Episcopalian," Billy would remember, "you didn't go to heaven." From a young age, he sang in the choir, but, he said, "Like most children, I didn't pay much attention to the sermon."

George finally bought his own home for the family on March 5, 1907, a two-story house with a three-arch portico at 315 North Coalter Street. Also still standing today, the house sits directly across from the Staunton Military Academy. Later reports said Billy would sit in his front yard and "watch the cadets in all their activities."

Interestingly, the North Coalter house was bought (and later sold) in Laura's name. By now George was running the tobacco factory for his father, and business was slowing down. Putting the house in Laura's name may have been a safeguard should the business go bankrupt, but the act also reflects Laura's commanding position in both the family and their marriage. Unlike George's mother, she did not sit idly by as her husband made the decisions. Indeed, George seems to have been somewhat of a retiring character, and Laura the motivating force.

Billy adored his mother. He remembered her as "lovely and aristocratic—everything that a boy could wish of a mother." Laura Haines was indeed a finely featured woman, with a delicate face and small frame. Billy would inherit his height from his father; his handsomeness was clearly a gift from his mother.

She worked as a dressmaker, helping to support the family as the tobacco business waned. At least twice a year she would visit New York to keep up to date on the latest fashions. At one point, she employed as many as five dressmakers working in the parlor of their house, and enjoyed a reputation throughout the area as a superior craftswoman.

Billy's relationship with his mother dances along the stereotype for a young gay boy. He said he was "willingly tied to her apron strings." While his brother and sisters played outside, Billy preferred to sit with Laura and her dressmakers, sharing local gossip while they taught him to sew. Billy prized his talent to make doll clothes for his sisters, using snippets of fabric discarded by his mother.

His mother and Aunt Lila also taught him to cook. "He could cook very well," one dressmaker recalled. "He learned the art from constant association with his mother. He used to don cap and apron and work around the kitchen table. The first thing he did when he came home from school was to beg his mother to let him have things for making candy."

From a very young age, he delighted in beautiful things. He was enchanted with architecture and the style of homes, an appreciation gleaned perhaps by the wealth of design Staunton offered. The more than two hundred houses architect T. J. Collins had built in town offered a variety of styles, many of which Billy would later employ in his career as an interior decorator. The Eakleton Hotel showcased the high mansard roof of the Second Empire Style; a building on East Beverley Street was done in Venetian Revival; and right on Billy's street Collins had designed a row house in a striking example of Elizabethan architecture. Billy's maternal grandfather, William Matthews, was also a contractor; perhaps his young grandson accompanied him on jobs, gaining an early appreciation for the craft of building and designing structures.

"Bill's sense of design goes back to when he was a boy in Staunton," says his brother Henry. "You should have seen his room. He redid it in the Virginia colors, all orange and blue. It was very spectacular."

Charles Haines, despite his reputation as a showman, disdained such frivolity in his young grandson. As a very young boy, Billy had enjoyed the affection of his grandfather, but as he grew older, ex-hibiting preferences for decidedly "unmanly" pursuits, Charles lost patience with him. "He'll never amount to anything," he told anyone who'd listen, including Billy's parents. "He never thinks of anything but silk pajamas, silk underwear, and good clothes! And the way he decorates his room! Pictures of all kinds, and everything fancy!"

While his grandfather clucked his disapproval, Billy's father was more tolerant of his son's eccentricity. George appears to have been a rather distant parent, but Billy was fond of him. "I liked him tremendously," he wrote later, "not just because he was my father, but because he was a good scout." It was George who introduced Billy to the beauty of antiques (although George collected Ameri-cana and Billy preferred European), and it was George who fine-tuned Billy's sharp wit. "Dad would crack a lot, just like Bill," says Henry Haines. "My sister had a boyfriend with a long, long face. Dad would greet him with, 'Hiya, horseface,' but of course, it was all good-natured."

Perhaps Billy's favorite male relative was his uncle Harry, who'd forsaken the whole lot of them and headed for New York. Harry's visits back home must have made an impression on the young Billy, who admired his bachelor uncle's sophisticated Northern airs. So, too, must Harry's early death have affected him: When Harry's body was sent home by railroad for burial in 1908, dead from unknown causes at the age of thirty-five, the world beyond those encircling hills must have seemed not only fascinating, but decidedly frighten-ing, too.

By the time Billy was old enough to dream of the future, Staunton had begun its long slow decline. The boom years were over, and the enthusiasm that had once prevailed among the citizens faded slowly as the new century progressed. The city's motto, adopted a few years later, sums up the town's new character: *Moderata durant* — "Modera-tion endures."

Such a worldview proved stifling to a boy such as Billy. "It was not a happy childhood," says his friend Francie Brody, whose house he decorated in Los Angeles. "I'm not sure exactly why, but that's the impression I always got. He was not happy as a boy." His rest-lessness manifested itself in mood fluctuations. He'd go from pulling the girls' pigtails and being sent to detention hall to long periods of inactivity, sitting with his chin in his hands and staring out into space.

He'd describe himself later in the third person: "The William Haines who went to school in Staunton was a dreamer, moody, sub-ject to despondency. He had a temper like a skyrocket, and then for-got what he was mad about as quickly as the skyrocket flares up and dies."

Later, after Billy had entered the movies, a family friend told a re-porter: "I always said William would be one of two things, either a great actor or a great scamp. He was eternally up to tricks of every conceivable kind, not mean tricks, but those full of real mis-chief and fun."

During a school presentation of *The Mikado*, Billy played the role of a flower, "all dressed up in Dennison crepe paper," as he remem-bered it. When the three young divas of the cast regaled the audi-ence with their rendition of "Three Little Maids from School Are We," an envious Billy stood in the wings and "accompanied them in a voice that ranged from bass to soprano." The dramatic coach grabbed him by the seat of the pants and tossed him out into the alley.

He called himself "the black sheep of an otherwise respectable family." He played hooky. He swiped candy from the general store. He outraged his grandfather. Some of his hijinks have a curious ho-moeroticism or gender play. One summer, he got a job painting bed-steads for $6 a week at the Staunton Military Academy, across the street from his house. "The students used to forget shirts and under-clothes," Billy wrote. "I would snatch them and take them home and wear them."

His clothing play didn't stop there. "One day," he wrote, "my teacher, a prim and precise old maid, reached the end of her pa-tience. She locked me in the clothes closet for an hour. When she fi-nally opened the door, I had improved each shining moment by getting rigged out in her tight-fitting raincoat. She was fond of Queen Mary inverted soup-bowls for hats, topped off with birds and gee-gaws. I had on the hat at a rakish angle, and clutched an efficient-looking umbrella in my hand. I should have been punished, but she laughed instead."

No amount of time in detention halls would change him. "The teachers always despaired of me," Billy remembered. "I would sit in the schoolroom gazing years into the future, romancing about myself and never hearing a word of the lecture." He admitted to liking history class, however, "because there's *drama* in history."

Apparently there wasn't enough of it in Staunton. The last big celebration in the town was the visit by President-Elect Woodrow Wilson, who'd been born in Staunton. In December 1912, the town bedecked itself in red, white, and blue finery to welcome Wilson, who spent the night in the house where he was born, just a few blocks from the Haines's home on North Coalter Street. The Stonewall Brigade Band performed, of course, and fireworks, performances, and music played throughout the town for an entire weekend. Billy was certainly there, enjoying the spectacle and drama.

The days of Charles's street festivals and carnivals were now largely past. To compensate, Billy spent much of his time in Staunton's theaters, where both live acts and one- and two-reel moving pictures frequently played. At the New Theater downtown, Billy thrilled to the exploits of Pearl White, laughed at John Bunny and Flora Finch, and imagined himself to be Mary Pickford and Blanche Sweet. Each day a different program was presented, and contemporary accounts of the theater praised its orchestra for "always rendering the latest musical selections."

The movies offered the young Billy Haines his first glimpse of life beyond the Blue Ridge Mountains. There was no specific desire on Billy's part to become a movie star, but there *was* a hankering to find his way to the world the movies so tantalizingly revealed—a world of big-city streets, sophisticated people, gracious living, and elegant homes.

On April 9, 1912, Charles Haines died at age sixty-eight after an illness of about three months. His death was announced in large type on the front page of the *Staunton Leader*. "In the death of Charles E. Haines, Staunton loses one of its most public-spirited men," the paper editorialized. "Year in and out, he planned and worked for his city. No movement looking to the public good was ever too great or too small for him to enter into with the spirit which characterizes the useful citizen. He was a man who always held the general good above all else, and who was never too busily engaged in his own affairs to lend a helping hand to his fellows. Staunton has too few citizens like Charles E. Haines."

The funeral was a huge affair. The Stonewall Brigade Band and a delegation from the Workingmen's Fraternal Association provided honorary escorts of the casket through the streets of Staunton. Magnificent floral tributes covered the grave site at Thornrose Cemetery, and two buglers from the band played taps as his body was lowered into the ground. He left the family house in five equal shares to his surviving children, with the provision that Rosa Lee be allowed to remain there for the duration of her life. She lived until 1924, just long enough to see her grandson make his first halting attempts in motion pictures.

Although he'd been retired from active leadership of the cigar factory for a number of years, Charles had continued to provide the business with a guiding hand. Without his acumen and with the increased pressures of competition, the Haines Cigar Company faltered. George must have felt the pressure to follow in his father's large footsteps even more acutely after the old man's death. He began suffering from a deep depression, characterized by a moodiness not unlike his son's. Laura stepped up her dressmaking as the cigar business declined.

Billy, meanwhile, now on the cusp of his teenage years, was continuing to be a headache. His attendance at school became increasingly irregular. George collared him to work in the factory, where Billy began smoking, a lifelong habit. Since smoking was not then widely considered a health hazard, and because to-

bacco was the lifeblood of the family's income, he was actually encouraged to do so. He would routinely supply cigars and cigarettes
to classmates.

One of the more fascinating of his factory co-workers was Willie
Teagle. Even today, there are folks in Staunton who remember
"Miss Willie"—a mustachioed, cigar-smoking fellow who sashayed
through town "like a woman," wearing false bosoms. He seems to
have been generally accepted, and as long as he didn't parade
around in a dress the police had no reason to detain him. It's notable
that George kept Miss Willie in his employ, certainly a message of
some tolerance for the young Billy Haines.

He was eager to grow up. He was impatient with the silliness of
other young people, and was precociously anxious to become an
adult. His sister Lillion was one of his few companions near his own
age. "There were never very many," he said, "chiefly because I did
not care for other children. I preferred to be with people much older
than I."

One of these was his English teacher at Robert E. Lee High
School. He'd show up at her house, banging on the door, begging
her to accompany him to Highland Park, where a dance pavilion
was a popular attraction. A single lady, she usually consented, dancing the afternoon away with her teenage pupil, always going home
exhausted. "When I was ready to go home," she'd recall years later,
"William would beg me to dance just one more time."

He was different from the other boys, a child keen to be rid of
short pants. At age thirteen, entrusted to buy a pair of dress
trousers, he ran up a huge charge on his mother's bill, outfitting himself in dark coat, black derby, and walking cane. Laura Haines was
astonished to see him stride jauntily back into the house, and despite
her initial protestations, she allowed him to keep the clothes.

He was good-looking, very pretty for a boy, no matter that he
was tall and lanky. He grew fast: By the time he was fourteen, he
was nearly his full adult height of six feet. It must have been unbearable towering over the other children; it set him even further apart
from them. And yet despite his physical size, he never played sports.
The other boys would taunt him when they stumbled upon him,

sitting on a rock near a lake, his chin in his hands, dreaming dreams no one around him could understand.

It's not hard to conjecture what must have been going on in his adolescent mind. Staunton, with its deeply rooted sense of history, offered no surprises and little inspiration for him. Here, Billy Haines was the heir of a good family, the grandson of a Civil War hero and the leader of the Stonewall Brigade Band. That very tradition must have chafed at his restless spirit, his unorthodox view of life. And with the onset of puberty, with the strange stirrings in his mind, heart, and loins, Billy likely felt suffocated by his conservative small town. Echoing across the decades, Billy's misfit childhood seems achingly familiar, a telling commentary on the universality of the gay experience.

When he was fourteen, he ran away from home. "Black sheep always run away," Billy would later write, the only explanation he'd ever offer.

He was bored with school, tired of having to face his parents after his latest scrape with the authorities. He was weary of being taunted by the boys in his class, dispirited by the moderation Staunton so prized. He strained under the pressure of being the eldest son, much like his uncle Harry. Billy resisted the idea that he was expected to dutifully follow in his father's footsteps, one day taking over the cigar factory. Nothing could have been further from his dreams.

There were other forces compelling Billy Haines in 1914. "My life before the age of fourteen does not interest me particularly," he'd later write. "The things that happen after one is fourteen are so much more important. After that age, one is sex-conscious, and it is always an important discovery."

Reading between the lines, it is possible to imagine that this is when Billy's first sexual experience occurred, and it was likely with another boy. Immediately following his observation about becoming "sex-conscious" at age fourteen, he wrote that he and "a boyfriend" ran away together. Even if there was no sexual relationship between the friends, Billy's choice of words is significant. This was likely someone who had captured his heart as well as his imagination.

Just who the boy was is unknown. He and Billy eventually ended up in Hopewell, Virginia, a notorious boomtown on the James River south of Richmond. Staunton historian Sergei Troubetzkoy interviewed one of the town's oldest residents, Felix Kivlighan, who as a boy was a neighbor of Billy's. Kivlighan recalled two boys who'd gone to Hopewell with Billy: Charlie Teabo, age eighteen in 1914, and George Powers, age fourteen, the same age as Billy. Might either have been Billy's first lover?

The *Staunton Leader* would later provide an accounting of the local men and boys working in Hopewell. Billy's name topped the list; neither Teabo nor Powers was mentioned. Among the boys closest to his age were James Dore, Jr., whose Irish-born mother ran a lodging house in Staunton; Frank Bergin, whose father, also born in Ireland, worked in the town's coal yard; and Ralph Henry, whose Virginia-born father was a railroad inspector. Billy was the youngest on the list, and from arguably the "best" family. The rest were primarily Irish and Russian-Jewish immigrants, all working-class. Likewise, George Powers's father was a salesman. This little window on Billy's world suggests that his friends and associates—and first lover—would probably have been considered beneath his social class by his family. It makes sense: The friends Billy would have felt most comfortable with would have been other boys who were outsiders, somewhat different from the others. It's also ironic, given how aggressively class-conscious Billy became later in his life.

Enamored with his new boyfriend, Billy reached out in a desperate attempt to subsidize their adventure. "I unceremoniously appropriated a diamond fichu pin and pawned it for expenses," he later admitted. "I couldn't have chosen an article that my mother cherished more deeply. The little jewel was old at the time of the Civil War, and was one of the few things saved when my great-grandmother fled from the approaching army of the North."

This is hardly an action one might expect from a boy who "adored" his mother. Yet Staunton had become unbearable for Billy. More accurate, the crush of feelings inside him had become excruciating. His friend paid his share by stealing some old coins, and together they headed out over the mountains.

They hit the road sometime in the late fall. Both Billy and George Powers performed in *The Mikado* at school in October, so their departure took place perhaps shortly after. What feelings propelled Billy as he finally made his way over the hills and out of Staunton can only be imagined. They headed first to Richmond; Billy left no details of how they got along once they were there. The money from the fichu pin might have paid for a week's worth of meals and a few nights' lodging, but after that they were at the mercy of the streets. In any event, they spent only a short time in Richmond and then followed reports that promised jobs and adventure in the Sin City of the South, Hopewell.

"A big, ugly, sprawling town" is how Billy would describe it years later, "not the best environment for fourteen-year-old boys." The tiny hamlet of City Point, with its excellent railroad and deep-water transportation possibilities, had been purchased a few years before by the E. I. Du Pont de Nemours Company and rechristened Hopewell. Du Pont began construction on a large dynamite plant at the site, but when World War I broke out in Europe in the summer of 1914, the demand for greater explosives increased dramatically. The factory was expanded and thousands of workers were brought in. Hopewell became the largest supplier to Britain (and later to the United States) of nitrocellulose, commonly known as "guncotton," the ingredient necessary for smokeless powder. Ten huge smokestacks towered over rows of stark brick and wooden factories, where sulfuric and nitric acids were stirred into roiling life. It was a dirty, grimy, foul-smelling place, but tremendously efficient: A billion pounds of guncotton were produced at Hopewell during World War I.

The city stood on the other side of the tracks from the factory. It had been built by Du Pont for its workers from the ground up in a matter of months. Nearly thirty thousand employees crammed into rows of wooden tenements by early 1915 (triple the size of the entire population of Staunton). Apartments were rented by shifts to accommodate the overflow. A rowdy city life sprang up to entertain the workers, almost all of whom were men without their wives looking to make fast money at the prosperous plant. Floating brothels like the *Bo Peep* made their way up and down the James River. A saloon beckoned in every block, and shootings and murders became commonplace. The town was a haven for thieves, gamblers, and prostitutes, as there was no local police force. County officials, accustomed to lazy Southern town life, were unequipped to deal with such lawlessness. Hopewell had sprung up almost literally overnight, leaving much of Virginia aghast.

The town's wickedness was precisely the draw for two spirited, restless youths. Hopewell had none of Staunton's tradition. Families had not lived there for generations. Names were not known at the post office; faces were not recognized on the street. Billy and his boyfriend got jobs at the Du Pont plant, making the astonishing salary (for the time and for boys their age) of $50 a week. They were soon living a life of excess.

"Work in the factory was hard and dangerous," Billy remembered. "In the fumes of the nitroglycerine [*sic*], my hair turned as blond as Gwen Lee's."

It was clearly not work that Billy Haines, a lover of fine things, would tolerate for long. If life on his own these past several months had taught him anything, it was how to be resourceful. He watched as the salons and brothels did smashing business all around him, catering to the tired and lonely workers. He and his friend got a brilliant idea: Open a dance hall and rake in the cash. "I hadn't yet reached the age of fifteen," Billy recalled, "but there was little I didn't know or didn't think I knew."

That's for sure. To survive in a place like Hopewell, Billy would have had to grow up pretty quickly. Which he undoubtedly did: He was handsome, available, and very young—then as now three very attractive traits to older men who've gone without sex for any length of time. Although Du Pont built some family housing for its workers, the majority of the tenements were dormitories for single men. The dance hall idea likely didn't emerge out of thin air, but was arrived at after much experience with lonely, amorous men.

In a world of con men and pimps, prostitutes and gamblers, young Billy Haines, his hair "as blond as Gwen Lee's," took tickets from factory workers while his boyfriend played the drums at their dance hall. "The factory workers earned good money and they were not averse to spending it recklessly," he recalled. The (no doubt) drunken workers would stagger in and pay their dollar a dance. Since the ratio of women to men in Hopewell was exceedingly disproportionate, many of the men must have danced together, or with Billy and his friends. "Dance hall," of course, is often used as code for "brothel."

There was at least some music involved. It might not have been the Stonewall Brigade Band, but Billy put together a handy little ensemble. His boyfriend played drums, accompanied by a redheaded Irish pianist and a Chinese violinist—"the strangest combination one could imagine," Billy would say years later.

"If there were not two or three fights during the evening, we thought things were pretty dull," he wrote. One night he got into a scuffle with an Italian boy—he doesn't reveal about what—and was knifed with a stiletto. He carried a long scar across his chest for the rest of his life. "It was all to be expected," he wrote. "All part of the game."

And Billy Haines was becoming a master at how it was played.

Meanwhile, as might be expected, George and Laura were distraught back in Staunton. They had called the police, who finally tracked Billy down in Hopewell. Confronted by a police investigator, he refused to leave his dance hall, getting his foreman at the Du Pont plant to intercede. It was made to appear that Billy was vitally needed at the factory and that he stood to make a good deal of money if he stayed.

The policeman relayed the news to Billy's parents, possibly with the promise that Billy would begin sending money home. Laura, quite understandably, wanted to see the conditions in which her son was living and made the trip down to Sin City herself. She was no doubt appalled by Billy's lodgings and the general mayhem of the town, but she did not order him to return with her. "I've always admired her for the stand she took," Billy recalled years later. "She did not try to force me to return to Staunton. She put me in a boarding house near the factory, the best surroundings she could find in the town. She knew that if she compelled me to go back with her that I would not stay. I would only run away again."

For a son as devoted as Billy Haines, causing such anguish to his beloved mother must have been terribly conflicting, and yet he couldn't abide returning to Staunton. By leaving his parents bewildered for months as to his whereabouts he surely must have felt some guilt, some strain for what he put them through. Something more than simple discontent must have triggered his leaving, and then his refusal to return. Could he have been discovered with his boyfriend? It would seem as if only something that traumatic could have induced him to cause his parents—and particularly his mother—such heartache.

Nevertheless, the visit with Laura rekindled some kind of filial responsibility, some sense of duty as the eldest son. He did indeed begin sending cash home to help his financially strapped family. It was a pattern that was to remain for the rest of his life, and the specter of his actions of 1914–1915 would remain with him. Although he would continue to keep his independence from them, he increasingly assumed the yoke of responsibility for his family's welfare.

His dance hall thrived through 1915, and Hopewell, subsidized by the slaughter in Europe, spiraled into a dizzy, inebriated hedonism. Its fate could have been predicted by religious zealots, and probably was: It was destroyed overnight—even more quickly than it had sprung up—in the blinding glare of purifying flames.

The fire began at about one o'clock in the afternoon on December 9, 1915, in a three-story wood-frame Greek restaurant on Appomattox Street. It was a cold, dry, and very windy day. Gales up to thirty-five miles an hour swept the flames quickly down the block, and within instants entire buildings were engulfed. The hastily constructed wooden structures burned like paper in the immense heat, and there was no adequate water supply in the town to sufficiently fight the conflagration. Press reports say, "The wildest excitement prevailed throughout the afternoon." Understandably so, since wide-eyed, terrified residents stood helplessly as the furious flames went unchecked, consuming everything they touched. The fire destroyed the hospital, the restaurants, the hotels and saloons, as well as most of the tenement housing. Billy's dance hall was not spared.

He would later say that the fire burned on for days, but it was actually contained late that same evening when the flames burned themselves out at a lumberyard near the railroad. Of course, the worry throughout the day had been the Du Pont plant: An explosion there would have obliterated everything in a several-mile radius south of the river. Fortunately, the plant, separated from the town by the railroad and several yards of flat, barren land, was not affected. In fact, when officials realized the fire was under control that evening, they ordered their workers back on the job for the eleven o'clock shift. This despite the fact that most of them had just lost their homes, their belongings, and their entire savings.

Billy spent the night in a barbershop that had been protected from the flames. Scattered fires still played themselves out in various parts of the city, and the danger had not yet fully passed. His statement— "During those red nights, I slept in a barber chair and went hungry"—is unquestionably an exaggeration. He may have gone without eating that night—many did—but by the morning relief crews had brought food and water to the survivors and most were put on trains to Petersburg.

His little enterprise had been wiped out. Press accounts say that men sat on their pitiful saved belongings all through the night with rifles, on alert for looters. One man was lynched when he was caught carrying off clothing from a burning store. If Billy had managed to save anything, he'd have had to fight to keep it.

Although practically no building was left standing when the flames were finally extinguished, there was, miraculously, no reported loss of life. It was, however, impossible to determine the damage with complete accuracy, since so many residents spoke no English. Many workers had been transients without next of kin to report them missing. The cause of the blaze was never determined. Briefly there was talk of sabotage from German agents, but in the end, it was more likely that an errant spark and the town's slapdash construction had been its undoing.

The news of the fire made headlines in every newspaper around the country. The *Staunton Leader* listed the names of the workers from the area, and surely Laura and George spent yet another day of anguish wondering about their son's well-being. Once they got word that he was all right, they hoped he'd return to Staunton. He'd been away from home for a little over a year now. Maybe, so his parents hoped, he'd gotten whatever it was out of his system. Maybe the disaster in Hopewell had taught him a lesson. Maybe now he'd return home, go back to school, follow in George's footsteps at the tobacco factory as George had followed in Charles's.

Billy, however, preferred to follow another example: that of his uncle Harry. "With our dance hall smoldering in its ashes, I went north," he said. Not back to Staunton—that would never do, not now. Fifteen years old, wise beyond his age to the ways of the world, he journeyed even farther north: to New York, and whatever fate might await him there.

2

THE THRILL HUNTER

1916-1922

Looking back years later, Billy wrote: "I suppose every youngster at one time in his life has a desire to carve out some sort of career in New York." No, not every youngster—only those who burn with a peculiar restlessness, who struggle to individualize themselves in a world defined by Episcopalian priests and staunch heroes of the Confederacy. It is these youngsters who often dream of the anonymous, permissive city. And the New York that the young William Haines first encountered early in 1916 was a city of limitless options, where boundaries were indistinct and permeable. As wave after wave of immigrants crowded into blocks of tenement housing, New York became known as the "city of bachelors."

For Billy, there was a special mystique about New York. Here was the place where Uncle Harry had dared to come, defying Grandfather Haines and all Confederate tradition, coming north and so forfeiting his place in the family business, not to mention the family patriarchy. It was here, too, that Uncle Harry had *died*— a young man, only to be brought back to Staunton for burial in Thornrose Cemetery, next to his Haines kin and the Confederate dead, laid to rest with a final dirge played by the Stonewall Brigade Band. No doubt there was an element of fear mingled with his excitement as Billy stepped off the train and looked up at the

tallest buildings he'd ever seen, shuddering just a moment in the chill
winter air.

It's unlikely that he made the journey from Virginia alone.
Whether or not his Staunton boyfriend accompanied him is unknown; at any event, we hear no more mention of him. Quite possibly a number of Hopewell workers had traveled north. Although Du
Pont was rapidly rebuilding the town, many of the dispossessed
were already on their way, in search of their next adventure, their
next dollar. Besides, state officials were clamping down, promising a
more law-abiding, patrolled city. How much fun was the new
Hopewell likely to be?

According to Billy, upon his arrival he took a job with the Kenyon
Rubber Company, making $14 a week—quite a comedown from the
fast and easy bucks he piled up at Du Pont and his dance hall. Still,
this was New York, and suddenly even the glamour of Sin City, Virginia, seemed provincial. Billy didn't reveal what his duties were at
the Kenyon company, or even what kind of rubber goods it produced or sold. There's no company by that name listed in the city
directories of the period. Probably the company's actual name
was Kenyon Roto Ink, makers of rubber stamps, with offices at
165 Broadway. George W. Kenyon, the president of the company,
was also president of Motor Mart of New York, Inc., which had
offices at 1876 Broadway and may have sold rubber tires.

Billy's work was most likely in the factory. The process of vulca-
nization—the treatment of rubber to give it strength and elasticity—
was and is a complex process, involving the addition of sulfur and
heat. The heat is applied through steam-heated molds or by hot air
or water. Once again, Billy was sweating in a steamy, malodorous
workshop, the only major difference this time being that his hair
didn't turn blond.

For a boy with such a preference for beautiful things, his early
factory jobs seem unlikely choices. Given the limited options for a
boy his age, the dirt, grime, and foul odors were no doubt worthwhile trade-offs for the glamour, excitement, and intrigue of living in
the heart of a large, cosmopolitan city.

There's no evidence of exactly where Billy lived during this first stay in New York. He likely took a room in a boardinghouse with friends, one of those long, narrow tenements in the fifties west of Eighth Avenue. After his year in Hopewell, he would have gotten used to waiting in line every morning for the one toilet offered in rooming houses, and wolfing down the strong, bitter coffee put out by the houses' owners, most often middle-aged widows. There was a jostle of humanity in these places, a cross-section of classes, cultures, and ethnicities. Billy would have elbowed his way among card-sharps, gamblers, and ex-cons. He was just sixteen, not so far away from the frightened young child who cried after his mother and was scared by his sister in the dark. Much of that fear surely still lingered within him, cleverly masked with bluff and bravado, an attitude of "there was little I didn't know or didn't think I knew."

And yet no matter how streetwise he became, he was still a boy among men. Billy was no longer a simple rube from the Shenandoah Valley, but he could easily have been taken advantage of by the less scrupulous characters he no doubt encountered. While he was probably still too young to completely self-identify with the gay sub-culture that was even then quite visible in several areas of the city, Billy always alluded to the sexual freedom he enjoyed in New York, even as a very young man. "He was young and lusty," says his long-time friend and colleague Ted Graber of Billy's New York years. As in Hopewell, there were no doubt men who both helped and took advantage of their younger, less established fellows—especially ones as good-looking as Billy.

George Chauncey, in his groundbreaking study *Gay New York*, writes of the various gay identities that emerged in the city's prewar years. Chief among these were the fairies, "the obvious, blatant, made-up boys whose public appearance and behavior provoke oner-ous criticism," according to one gay artist of the time. In the public mind, the fairy was the image of the homosexual man—the preening, effeminate fellow with tweezed eyebrows and daringly red necktie. Billy Haines certainly must have known his share of fairies (one po-lice report at the time said the city was "teeming" with them) but he was—emphatically—not one of them. Despite public perception, most gay men, especially those from middle-class backgrounds like

Billy, did not assume the fairy persona. "It was," Chauncey writes, "above all, a working-class way of making sense of sexual relations."

More likely, Billy at age sixteen fell into the category of "punk," a term he often used to describe himself later on. In the parlance of the street, a "punk" was a younger man or boy who exchanged sex with an older or stronger man (called a "wolf") for cash, protection, or some other type of support. Chauncey writes: "The punk's sexual character was ambiguous . . . he was regarded by some men as simply a young homosexual, by others as the victim of an aggressive older man, and by still others as someone whose sexual subordination was merely an aspect of his general subordination to a dominant older man."

Whatever Billy's particular situation was during the early months of 1916, by the end of the year he would have been sharply aware of the potential fate of many in his generation. The World War, raging for the past two years in Europe, was reaching closer to home, with many predicting America's involvement to be imminent. There was growing sentiment in support of the war against Germany, despite President Wilson's isolationist policies. Billy would surely have heard the drunken warmongering over raised mugs of beer in saloons. His own personal thoughts about the war are unknown, although given his distaste for grime and chaos, it isn't likely that he was one of those raising his mug. Indeed, just about the time when war was finally declared in April 1917, when thousands of young New York men were rushing to enlist, Billy Haines was getting on a train and heading back home.

"I loved the noise and the rush, but my first stay [in New York] was cut short," he later wrote. He had received a telegram from his mother, probably the latest of several communications over the last year bearing increasingly dire news from back home. In early 1916, Billy's father George had suffered an emotional breakdown and was briefly committed to a mental hospital. Around the same time, he also declared bankruptcy, signing over the Haines Cigar Company to his brother James. Whether the breakdown or the bankruptcy came first isn't known; either could have contributed to the other.

George had been growing steadily more depressed over the last few years. The death of his father and the decline of the family business weighed heavily on him. There may have been other factors contributing to his emotional state. His eldest son, like his elder brother, had forsaken the family. Billy had been a trial since at least his first year in high school; then he had dropped out and taken off with friends George could scarcely have approved of. Might Billy's sexuality have been discovered at this time, too? George was certainly distraught when Billy was found working in Hopewell, and the fact that it was Laura who made the journey down to see their son may be evidence of George's already fragile state of mind. The subsequent fire and then Billy's decision to head to New York—where Harry Haines had died—could not have made George rest any easier. Within months of Billy's move to New York, George Haines suffered his breakdown.

It would be unfair to blame Billy for his father's illness. While his actions couldn't have helped, there is certainly no evidence to suggest they were the only or even the primary cause. George's many years of trying to live up to his father's example and the eventual decline of the thriving family business would be enough to set off bouts of depression. Henry Haines says that George had at one point wanted to sell the business to the American Tobacco Company, but the move had been prevented by Charles. Had he been successful in his effort, the Haines family would likely have enjoyed a considerable period of prosperity.

Instead, George filed bankruptcy on May 18, 1916; the petition was granted by the court on May 20. Strapped for cash, George also sold his share in a family property on Market Street to his sister Mary Haines Fifer for $250. It's clear she did this as a way of helping out her brother. On September 28, Laura sold their house on North Coalter Street with the stipulation that they could remain until January 1. This allowed them time to find a new place.

Laura was now the sole breadwinner for the family. The other children were still too young to work: Lillion was fifteen, Ann ten, and George Junior nine. Because of Staunton's continuing economic decline, Laura felt she could do better in Richmond, the state capital, where she could sell dresses to large stores like Thalhimer's and the Cohen Company. The bankruptcy and breakdown—so much more scandalous in those days—also figured heavily in their desire to move.

Still, through all of this, Billy did not return home. Whether Laura kept him deliberately in the dark, whether she stubbornly insisted she needed no help, or whether she asked and he refused, is not known. The last scenario seems the least plausible, knowing Billy's character. It was probably a combination of the first two, with Laura playing down the family's troubles while maintaining she could manage on her own. In truth, she did remarkably well. In Richmond, in addition to making dresses, she took in boarders at their rented home on 314 East Franklin Street. Gone were the servants and the cooks; Laura, with the help of Lillion, did it all. Then, in what must have been a shock that staggered her, she discovered— after nine years—that she was pregnant again.

"I was the surprise of the family," Henry Haines says today. That's quite the understatement. In fact, it was not until late in her pregnancy that Laura clued in other family members (like her mother-in-law). It's possible that Laura, a very proud and capable woman, wanted no pity and no family interference. She was also smart enough to realize she'd need some help.

So in the spring of 1917, she asked Billy to come home. George, although obviously somewhat improved, was still receiving treatment, and eventually Laura would have to stop working and care for her newborn. Perhaps recalling the anguish he'd caused her two years earlier, Billy didn't hesitate when his mother asked. "Doctor bills took most of the money and things were in a serious condition," he remembered. "To make matters worse, there was to be another baby. It was absolutely necessary that I go back and help with the support of the family." In November, Henry Haines was born, nine years younger than his next-eldest sibling.

That this family crisis coincided with America's declaration of war also had the effect of keeping Billy out of the European conflict. In the spring of 1917, he was still too young to be drafted: The Selective Service Act of that year had required all males age twenty-one to thirty to register. One year later, the age limits were extended to eighteen and forty-five. Had Billy not been supporting his family, he'd very likely have been called to serve in early 1918. There was surely some part of him grateful for this unexpected family obligation; he'd remain in Richmond with them through the end of the war in November 1918.

That's not to say Billy was happy being back in Virginia. He barely knew his younger siblings, having been away for much of the past three years, and he had an extremely difficult time finding work. He eventually landed a job as a floor manager for the Cohen Company department store on West Broad Street, making the paltry sum of $7 a week. That was half of what he made at Kenyon in New York, although the higher cost of living in the city needs to be considered. Still, he was miserable. Living back home under his mother's roof and careful eye must have been intolerable after the freedom he'd experienced in New York.

Billy would later recall his two years in Richmond as a nightmare. He was, he said, "constantly unhappy, restless all the time." He'd been on his own as a youth, but now, just as he was becoming an adult, he was back with the clan, holding down a boring job and turning over almost all of what he made for the family's welfare. The Eighteenth Amendment also took effect during this period, forbidding the manufacture, sale, or consumption of alcohol; what little nightlife there was in Richmond was forced underground, and Billy yearned for the greater possibilities New York offered. "The South now seemed very narrow and provincial," he said. "After one brief taste of a big city, I wanted nothing else."

By early 1919, however, it appeared his wish might come true. Laura was hired as chief of the dressmaking division at Thalhimer's. George, too, found work, as he gradually recovered from his breakdown. A Richmond cigar company had snapped him up as a salesman, impressed by his expertise. (Henry Haines says his father could take one look at a tobacco leaf and tell you in which county it had been grown.) But George wasn't happy with the work; tobacco had been his father's passion, not his own. He moved over to another job, with a building supply company, selling paints and varnishes.

Whatever his job, the fact was that George was well enough to support his family again. Billy felt comfortable bidding them all a fond goodbye once more, promising to send money home to help them out just as soon as he found work.

This time, however, Laura wasn't going to let him just run off with no plan, with only his youth and good looks to carry him through the streets. She thrust a card at him as he left the house, bright-eyed and eager to get back to the city. On the card was the name of a man, the husband of one of her dressmaking clients. Billy was to call him upon his arrival in the city; Laura had already written him, telling him to expect Billy's call. The name on the card was Orison Swett Marden.

In the 1910s and 1920s, the name Orison Swett Marden was synonymous with the idea that where there was a will, there was a way; he was the Dale Carnegie of the early twentieth century. Since publication of his book *Pushing to the Front* in 1894, his particular brand of American idealism had been used as the gospel of motivation by thousands of businesspeople and educators. His was an optimistic message: The *will* to succeed—not brains, not connections, not investment capital—was the single most important factor in one's eventual success.

He published *Success* magazine from 1897 to 1912 before suffering financial reversals. Then, adhering to his own philosophy, he pulled himself up by the proverbial bootstraps and remade himself, restarting *Success* in early 1918. He moved from Boston to New York, buying a farm at Glen Cove, Long Island. In 1919 he published his two latest books (there were more than fifty in all), called *Ambition and Success* and *You Can, But Will You?* Laura Haines knew exactly what she was doing when she directed her aimless son to contact Mr. Marden.

Marden was sixty-nine years old in 1919. He was a literate, articulate man, holding a degree from Harvard. He had edited the ten volumes of the Consolidated Encyclopedic Library and knew something about nearly everything. He was also wealthy. The farm at Glen Cove rolled on for several acres, watched over by a Spanish superintendent. His wife was the former Clare Evans of Louisville, Kentucky. Just how long she had known Billy's mother is unclear, but in 1919 she had an eighteen-year-old daughter named Laura.

Billy didn't call Marden right away. Upon arriving back in New York sometime in the spring of 1919, he may have used his connections or experience at Cohen's to secure a position at a similar store. As a salesclerk in the linens department, Billy found many opportunities for mischief. He'd make faces at pompous ladies and weave elaborate fabrications about the merchandise. "I rattled off sales talk about Madeiras and imports from Ireland," he remembered. "I spent too much time talking to the women customers. I made quite a lot of dates that way. The Lonesome Clubs aren't the only places where a young fellow can get acquainted in the city."

Such a recollection—given to a movie magazine in 1929—was obviously meant as a bone to the hungry wolves of the press, always anxious to link him with some woman. As always, he allowed the reader to do the work, allowing implications to be made without any lies being told. No doubt Billy *did* spend too much time talking with the women customers. No doubt, too, he made several dates by being so loquacious—but he never says the dates were with the women themselves. Some of them might have been—Billy had learned to be on the lookout for wealthy patrons, male *or* female—but other dates may have been with the men he encountered on the job. Surely, then as now, a high proportion of the men in the service industries—and those who shopped in linen departments—were gay.

No matter whom he was dating, however, the job itself was brief. Billy was fired for flirting too much while on the job. It was probably at this point that he pulled out the crumpled card his mother had given him. Why not give this guy Marden a call?

Marden's office was located at 1133 Broadway. Billy trekked up there, dressed in his one spiffy suit, his hair properly parted in the middle and plastered down on his head. Marden was extraordinarily welcoming and generous. Billy was just the type of energetic young man of whom he enjoyed making an example. Did Billy want to make it rich? Of course, Billy told him. Did he have drive, ambition, a will to succeed? Billy laughed. Sure, he said. He had all that. What he didn't have was a job.

It's likely that Marden helped him land an office-boy position at (in Billy's words) "the eminently respectable" bond house of S. W. Straus and Company. It's not known what else Marden did for him, except that Billy always felt a debt of gratitude toward the man. It's possible that Billy left Marden's office that day loaded down with his books—maybe the two most recent, and maybe *Cheerfulness as a Life Power* (1899), *Character: The Grandest Thing in the World* (1899), and *How to Get What You Want* (1917). Certainly such a determined optimism became Billy's stock-in-trade from this point on: There would be no more smelly factories or seedy dance halls. Billy would find that his will to succeed was matched only by his charm. He might not have a Harvard education, he realized, but there were other ways of getting what he wanted.

He lived in a boardinghouse at 207 West 56th Street run by May F. Stuart, a fifty-year-old divorcee, and her two children, Nathalie, age twenty-eight, and Fargo, twenty-three, a salesman for an export house. According to the 1920 Census of New York City, taken in January, there were four other lodgers in the house besides Billy, all salesmen. Ralph F. DeClaremont, a twenty-eight-year-old California transplant, sold thread; Wallace Clark, twenty-three, originally from Connecticut, sold tobacco; Frank Kurz, twenty-six, also from Connecticut, sold cakes; and Clyde Lurvey, twenty-two, born in Massachusetts, sold chemicals.

Billy was the baby of the house, just twenty that year, the same age as the century. Given his youth, there was probably some teasing from his roommates and extra favors from his landlady. Of the roommates, only Clark seems to have stayed in New York for any length of time. The census provides a simple snapshot of a moment in time, those who happened to be in the house in January of that year. It's an illustrative one: It was a house of transients, young men trying to make a living in the big city. Indeed, Billy himself moved rather soon after the census was taken. There's a listing for a William Haines, clerk, renting at 4 West 104th Street in the 1920–1921 city directory. Perhaps he moved uptown for a short period.

By mid-1920, Billy was pulling himself up out of the ranks of clerks and itinerant salesmen. At S. W. Straus, he was rather quickly promoted from office boy to assistant bookkeeper. Clearly he had learned from Marden's philosophy. "They must have liked me, in spite of my faults," Billy would recall of his bosses at the bond house. "I stayed there for more than a year, but I can't recall a single instance when my books ever tallied. A trifling thing like a balance never troubled me."

Billy was learning that a little charm and an energetic drive went a long way. Still, he couldn't have been incompetent. S. W. Straus, established in 1882, was a leading firm at the time, offering "safe 6% investments" on first-mortgage real-estate bonds. Serial bonds were secured by a first mortgage on the "highest class of improved, income-producing city property." They claimed no investor had ever lost a dollar on any security purchased under the "Straus plan."

With offices located at 150 Broadway, S. W. Straus allowed Billy to move among a class of people he had not known in his previous positions. He made a decent salary: $20 a week, significantly better (even with the increased cost of living) than the $7 a week in Richmond. He may have had some help in the form of advice from his father, who had found a new career as an investment broker, becoming as adept with figures as he'd been with tobacco. Billy's success at Straus must have reassured his parents, but he was still as much of a rascal as he ever was. It was not a job that could have satisfied him for long: He was as restless in front of his ledgers as he had been behind his school desk in Staunton.

His new friends may have been more genteel, but they still danced along the social edge. These were children of affluence, boys and girls who dared to break away from their families' dominion to carve out lives for themselves in the bohemia of postwar New York. Many of these young people were themselves veterans of the World War, the bloodiest conflict in history, the War to End All Wars. Witness to unprecedented atrocities, they were disenchanted with their parents' world upon their return to civilian life. Many made their way to the city of bachelors, where they pursued lives unencumbered by middle-class mores. Many, like Billy, held down "respectable" day jobs, but evenings and weekends could be found in the city's burgeoning speakeasies and cabarets. Among Billy's crowd were still gamblers, con artists, and prostitutes, although only the most honest among them would admit to it. Attired in the finest fashions and sipping the most expensive bootleg liquor, Billy's new friends would become the youthful spirit of the Roaring Twenties.

It was at this time that Billy moved into an apartment in the heart of Greenwich Village. What had been a sleepy, remote neighborhood populated mostly by artists and the working class had undergone a transformation in the years immediately following World War I. Construction of the subway line along Seventh Avenue suddenly made the Village easily accessible to those working elsewhere in the city. The neighborhood's notoriety as a hub of bohemia attracted those with a particular social bent, creating a carnival-like atmosphere along Sheridan Square. Tourist traps like the Pirate's Den came complete with clanking chains and patch-eyed buccaneer waiters. Middle-class men looking for women known as "free-lovers of the Greenwich Village type" went slumming in the neighborhood's speakeasies, and college men and "flappers" strolled arm in arm past sidewalk artists selling paintings to tourists.

That wasn't all. As Chauncey writes, "The Village's reputation as a center of unconventional behavior—particularly of unconventional sexual behavior—had made it a beacon not only for rich slummers but also for increasing numbers of disaffected youths [who] wished to escape the constraints of family and neighborhood supervision." He observes that the Village "took on special significance for lesbians and gay men around the country, and disaffected New Yorkers were joined in the Village by waves of refugees from the nation's less tolerant small towns." What resulted was a vibrant—and visible—gay subculture that flourished throughout the 1920s. A half century before the Stonewall riots touched off modern gay liberation, Greenwich Village was already an established and fully conscious center of gay life, with the contemporary sociologist

Caroline Ware noting the neighborhood as the "home of 'pansies' and 'lesbians' " and that "dives of all sorts featured this type."

Billy Haines's life was fundamentally shaped by the two years he lived in Greenwich Village. It wasn't so much that he learned how to buck convention. He'd been doing that all along, and as the years passed, he didn't so much buck convention as shape it to his own purposes. What his experience in New York taught him was how to get what he wanted, and that nothing—not even those things most forbidden by society—was beyond his grasp. In the Village, an artist could draw naked women without fear of reprisal. Alcohol could be consumed with impunity. One could even dare to love without the sanctions of marriage. Billy's sense of himself was grounded in this early experience in the Village, in which a self-definition of homosexual was not only acceptable but could even be respectable.

Billy would have been familiar with the area's gay speakeasies and tearooms. On the corner of Christopher and Gay streets stood the Flower Pot, and the Red Mask was a popular gathering place on Charles Street. At Paul and Joe's, on the corner of Sixth Avenue and Ninth Street, female impersonators like Jackie Law and Jean Malin performed outrageous parodies of Gloria Swanson and Theda Bara. The Liberal Club's balls at Webster Square on East 11th Street near Third Avenue attracted scores of gay Village residents, most done up in sensational drag. Competing with the more flamboyant Harlem balls, the Liberal Club balls also proved a popular spectator sport for heterosexual city residents.

What made the gay presence in the Village so striking was its visibility in a distinctly middle-class milieu. Despite its bohemian rejection of bourgeois edicts, the Village was predominantly white and largely populated by youths like Billy: wayward children of middle-class families. In the working-class world of the Kenyon rubber plant, Billy's status as a "punk" among "wolves" was a fact of life; the "fairies" and men with red ties were accepted as fellow parts of the toiling masses. In the years after the war, gay life suddenly manifested itself visibly in middle-class enclaves like the Village, and for the first time in modern history it was not only tolerated, but integrated.

This experience, this grounding in a self-identified, affirming, even bourgeois gay culture, set the tone for the rest of Billy's life. "The gay history of Greenwich Village," Chauncey writes, "suggests the extent to which the Village in the teens and twenties came to represent to the rest of the city what New York as a whole represented to the rest of the nation: a peculiar social territory in which the normal social constraints on behavior seemed to have been suspended and where men and women built unconventional lives outside the family nexus." Although it was not a paradise, the Village came close: Women danced together at predominantly lesbian tearooms; men walked arm in arm along the neighborhood's streets. The memory of such visibility in the 1920s became cloaked by the repression of later decades, but for those who lived through it, the experience of the Village fundamentally shaped how they saw the world — and themselves.

It's not known exactly where Billy lived in the Village, although it wasn't far from Washington Square. Compared to his previous apartments, this was a spacious walk-up in a brownstone building. Since rents were rising quickly in the suddenly chic Village, he shared the place with three other young men — "every one of us," he remembered, "as improvident as the devil."

Two of the roommates were Mitchell Foster and Larry Sullivan. The identity of the third roommate is unknown, but he'd served in the war and been wounded. When he collected his indemnity from the government, the boys had, in Billy's words, "a hilarious month."

Foster and Sullivan were destined to play more lasting roles in Billy's life, both in New York and in Hollywood. Foster proved a mentor in more ways than one. Tall, handsome, cultured, he was a decade older than Billy and entirely comfortable in his identity as a homosexual man. Sullivan, who was Billy's age, was Foster's lover. From Foster, Billy acquired an appreciation for antiques and the theater, but he also gained something else: a fundamental dignity and self-definition as a gay man.

"Mitt Foster and Larry Sullivan made no secret of the fact that they were a couple," recalls longtime friend Michael Pearman. "There were some who were like that, who never hid anything. They didn't announce it to the world, but then again, perhaps they did— just by not doing the other [pretending to be straight]."

Such was the particular freedom and character of the Village. Certainly that's what attracted both Foster and Sullivan to the place. Although they may have met in Boston, hometown to both, it was in the easygoing atmosphere of the Village where they coupled, as unlikely a duo that ever paired off. Foster was the son of a prominent Brookline family; Sullivan's father ran a candy store in East Boston. Their commitment to each other (their union lasted some four decades) left an impact on Billy. He developed a surprisingly modern attitude about same-gender "marriage"; it might not be like his parents', but it could be just as stable and enduring.

It's unclear how they all actually met. Possibly Billy knew Mitt Foster first. At the start of 1920, Larry Sullivan was still living with his parents and four brothers and sisters in Boston. His parents were hardworking, second-generation Irish; there was little to offer Larry, their second son, in the way of work. So he took off for New York, a slight, awkwardly effeminate, eighteen-year-old boy.

Mitt Foster, on the other hand, was a tall, sturdy, deep-voiced, masculine man. Born Alfred Mitchell Foster in 1889, he was the son of Alfred S. Foster, a wealthy manufacturer. The Fosters were a prominent old Ipswich clan, with roots dating back to the seventeenth century—the Yankees that Charles Haines had fought in the Civil War. Growing up, the young Mitchell (so called for his mother's family) was tended by servants and coachmen. While Billy also grew up with family cooks and the occasional nursemaid, the Fosters were far more affluent. Their homes—first on Chiswick Road in Boston and later on Chaplin Road in the tony suburb of Brookline—were showcases of antiques and fine craftsmanship. Alfred S. Foster was known throughout the country for his work in the shoe industry. Around 1880 he helped pioneer rubber footwear— known today as sneakers—and worked with the Converse Rubber Shoe Company. He later supervised his own plants in the production of athletic shoes.

The senior Foster seems to have suffered some financial reversals; in any event, his son Mitt wanted no part of the family business. After serving in World War I, he set up a life in Greenwich Village that was in complete antithesis to his father's values. He first roomed on West 4th Street with three artists and a theatrical director—two men and two women. Living next door was the noted interior designer Judson Bard, still single at age forty-four. By 1920 Mitt was selling clothes for a living (possibly at the same department store where Billy worked). He retained the trappings of his class, however: an extravagant wardrobe, a taste for fine wine, and a devotion to the theater.

Billy idolized Mitt. Here was a man he could emulate: He wasn't effeminate, and yet he wasn't like the coarse factory workers Billy had encountered, either. Mitt enjoyed the camp and theatricality of the drag queens at Paul and Joe's, but would never consider tweezing his own eyebrows. His relationship with Larry Sullivan gave Billy a model he'd copy in his own long-term partnership with Jimmie Shields; Billy, like Mitt, was the "man," the "top." There was likely no sexual dalliance between Billy and Mitt; in their worldview, two masculine men were meant to be friends, not lovers.

Billy had become, by the age of twenty, a strikingly handsome man, and one who embodied the "manly" ideal. He was six feet tall, with broad shoulders and a deep, commanding voice—one that he no doubt trained in the resonance of Mitt's. The Virginia twang was softened, and although Billy later teased starlets for doing precisely the same thing, he began to affect an indefinite Boston accent in his quest to remake himself.

His beard was so heavy that barbers despaired of shaving him. It grew so quickly he had a five o'clock shadow around two. Because his whiskers were so rough, he'd go without shaving as often as he could, sometimes bearing three days' growth. He parted his black hair severely down the middle, as in the fashion of the times, and slicked it back with heavy oil. To modern audiences he looks more attractive (and younger) when his hair tumbles down onto his face, but for 1920, the slicked-back look was a mark of virility. He cared little for clothes, but under Mitt's tutelage he began to sport some flair for fashion. Since they were about the same size, Mitt often insisted that Billy wear one of his coats or vests.

It was through Mitt that Billy began to make friends in the world of art and the theater. One of Mitt's former roommates was Jeanne Carpenter, a director of stage shows, and she no doubt introduced them to popular performers of the day. Billy, Mitt, and Larry were also frequent patrons of Village nightlife. "What a grand time I had when I finished at the office," Billy would write years later. He'd race home and change out of his drab work clothes, although there weren't many other options in his closet. ("I came up from Virginia with a shabby suit and a wide-brimmed hat," he'd recall, "everything but streamers.") Mitt would be there, offering a pair of fancy trousers and fur coat, which Billy accepted gladly.

"With all my borrowed fine feathers, I splurged into nightlife," Billy said. "I didn't have any money, but then I didn't need any. There were parties with chorus girls, and the girls were always the most generous with money 'lifted' from visiting firemen and butter-and-egg men from the country."

How many of those chorus girls (remembered for a fan magazine much later) were, in fact, *girls* is open to question. It was during this time that Billy first made the acquaintance of Jean Malin, the noted female impersonator. Malin was a popular act at Paul and Joe's, which by now was being called the "headquarters for every well-known Lesbian and Queen in town." In many ways, the Village operated like a small town: People knew one another and the gossip flowed as freely as the booze in the area's speakeasies. It would have been highly improbable for Billy *not* to have met Malin, or any of the other performers of the time, especially with Mitt Foster's theatrical connections.

Mitt had befriended a number of entertainers (possibly through Jeanne Carpenter) that he introduced to Billy and Larry, all of them socializing together at various clubs. Several friends recall Billy talking about meeting Elsie Janis and Sophie Tucker during this time; he was certainly acquainted with Frank Fay. Billy later said his longtime friendships with George Burns and Jack Benny began during their youth in New York. Burns at the time was a struggling vaudevillian in search of an act, not yet paired with Gracie Allen. Benny was somewhat more successful by 1922, at least in terms of defining an act: He was one of the new breed of "monologists," like Fay. "Gone were the funny clothes and aggressive style of the old clowns," wrote Burns biographer Martin Gottfried. "These were gentleman-comedians wearing suits and ties. They stood at stageside with one hand in their trousers pockets, and spoke with casual confidence in well-modulated voices." Billy's own style as an urbane wit follows this model.

Rumors of Benny's homosexuality were even then whispered among entertainment circles, despite his reputation—often emphasized in biographical accounts—as a notorious womanizer. Certainly Benny was familiar with the gay scene; he adopted the campy mannerisms into his act to great effect. One of his biographers, Milt Josefsberg, vehemently denounced the idea that Benny was gay, but according to friends, Billy always insisted on clarifying that it was Benny's *wife* he was referring to when he said "Mary Benny."

Another acquaintance was Charlie Phelps, also known as Charlie Spangles, then appearing at the Metropole Club in an act called "Josephine and Joseph." He wore the costume of a hermaphrodite, with a beard on half his face and lipstick and rouge on the other. It was a wildly popular show, playing up the Village's gender ambiguity for tourists. He lived in a loft apartment with two other young men: a twenty-three-year-old painter from Australia, Jack Kelly, and a seventeen-year-old vaudeville performer from England, Archie Leach. Both would become famous under different names in Hollywood: Orry-Kelly and Cary Grant.

Billy formed quick friendships with both of them. There may have even been a romance with Kelly, a beautiful, slightly effeminate young man with dreamy eyes and a well-toned, stocky body (which also described Jimmie Shields). However, Kelly was in love with Archie Leach, and Billy settled into a platonic friendship with the two roommates. Archie was younger than most of their circle, but Billy admired him for his drive and determination, qualities Billy recognized in himself. Archie had left home even earlier than Billy had, surviving among a company of performers since the age of six.

Also like Billy, Archie and Jack accepted their sexuality with the nonchalance particular to the Village in the 1920s. Archie had come to America as part of the Pender Troupe of Giants, an acrobatic group now appearing in the revue "Good Times" at the Hippodrome, one of the nation's largest theaters. He was a handsome, breezy youth, with a devilish grin and flashing eyes. He attracted attention from everyone he met.

Billy liked Archie, but when the younger man went off on tour with the Pender Troupe in the spring of 1921, it was Jack Kelly with whom Billy developed the closer bond. Jack drew subtitles for use in motion pictures, but what he really wanted to do was design clothes. He worked as a tailor's assistant in the garment district, with fierce ambitions to be much, much more. Most of his friends owned neckties hand-painted by Kelly; according to George Burns, Archie Leach had been known to hawk them in the street to make a few extra dollars for the household.

Billy would have understood Kelly's drive. All of them—Billy, Jack, Mitt, Archie—had that in common. None had much money or connections, but they had the *will* to make it, Marden's first requirement for success. Jack Kelly also had another important characteristic: a killer wit, honed sharp in the fast and cutting world of the Village. Billy was inspired by Kelly's quick tongue, learning how to put an edge to his own repartee, developing the wisecracker persona for which he'd become famous. In fact, many in his gay circle of the 1920s were "wisecrackers." It was part of their characters, an identifiable trait as much as the tweezed eyebrows of the "fairies." It was, in many ways, the origins of the "camp" so common among a later generation of gay men.

Also at this time Billy may have met another man with determined ambitions: George Cukor. Later, when Cukor came to Hollywood, Billy was one of the first to take him under his wing, suggesting an earlier connection, one that some longtime friends believe to be accurate. If Billy and Cukor did meet at this time, it was likely in the fall of 1920, when Cukor was working as a doorman at the Criterion Theater. He'd been an assistant stage manager in summer-stock productions and had returned to New York, his hometown, for the winter. His middle-class family had wanted him to become a lawyer, but Cukor was determined to have a career in the theater. If he met Billy, it was probably through Mitt and his higher-brow theatrical friends; Cukor wouldn't have been friends with the likes of Jack Kelly and Archie Leach at this time. He also struggled more than they did with his own homosexuality; he often made fun of gay men and gay life, using the German slang for "fag," *schwel,* as a put-down. Yet he was also drawn by the fact that the world of the theater was populated by homosexuals, even welcoming of them. If Cukor met Billy at this time, a real friendship didn't yet blossom: He wasn't quite ready for Billy's particular brand of wisecracking self-affirmation.

Much later, Billy would tell friends that he looked for and found "patrons" to help him maintain his standard of living. In an interview in 1969, he admitted, "I was kept by the best men and women in New York City."

He was twenty-one years old, rascally handsome and devilishly funny. No doubt he was very popular. He was often seen on the arms of well-to-do visitors to the Village. His most lasting "patronage" came from a woman he met through Mitt Foster in late 1920 or early 1921, some twenty years his senior. "It was at this period of my life that I met the woman who played so important a part in molding my existence anew," he later recalled. "There have been three women I shall always remember—the ones who have meant the most. The first, of course, was my mother. This woman was the second." (Barbara La Marr would be the third.)

There is no one left alive who remembers her, no records to indicate who she was or the exact nature of her relationship with Billy. What we are left with are only Billy's reminiscences and some tantalizing clues. She had known Mitt in Boston, Billy recalled. She "came from a family high in Boston Back Bay society." She may have shared Mitt's rebellious spirit, turning her back on her family's expectations as Mitt did his, following him (or preceding him) to New York, where she carved out a new life for herself.

In 1920 Mitt was living with two women: One was Jeanne

Carpenter, the theatrical director, and the other was Charlotte W. Remington, an artist. Neither was born in Massachusetts, but both were the right age for the woman who became Billy's patroness. Carpenter was listed as "married" in the 1920 Census, although there's no husband in sight. The kind of luxuries Billy describes his patroness as having might make more sense for a divorced (or at least separated) woman than one who had never married.

Whoever the woman was, she held great interest for Billy, despite his preference for men. "She had charm and culture and a keen sense of the beautiful," he later said. "I was twenty and she was nearing forty, but the difference in ages made no difference." They were casual friends for several months, then became lovers.

In the Village, such fluidity to one's sexuality was common: There were many reports of heterosexual men and women "exploring" relationships with others of their own gender. Chauncey has unearthed press reports of "pseudo-lesbians" who'd get drunk, forget their resolve, and dance with men. If straights were dabbling, so were gays. And Billy—in search of a way out of poverty and his boring, soul-numbing job—welcomed the life this woman was offering.

"It was she who instilled in me the love of beautiful, old things," he remembered fondly. Her apartment on lower Fifth Avenue was furnished with priceless antiques, paintings by the masters, and exquisite old china. "From her I learned of good literature, fine music. She took me to the opera. A new and different world opened to me."

The days of seediness were over. Gone were the stinking factories and dirty overalls, the cramped boardinghouses and shared bathrooms. Billy left the apartment he shared with Mitt and Larry and moved in with this woman. He might have been a school dropout, but she gave him a crash course in the necessary requirements to move among the upper class. While never as "cultured" as Mitt— classical music bored him, for example—Billy did develop an appreciation and unerring eye for taste. His benefactor taught him what he came to consider a simple, fundamental truth, and one that would become his life's adage: "A person could be forgiven for illiteracy, but never for the lack of good taste."

She indulged him. He wrote that he lost his job at Straus while "spending so much time with her." Why bother to work at that tedious job when she could support him and provide him with the finer things he'd been struggling for? When he admitted to being "kept," he wasn't exaggerating.

He loved her, he wrote. And quite possibly he did, as many young men love older women who nurture them. It was apparent she wanted more, and the relationship grew strained. "I don't know why the romance didn't last," Billy wrote, rather disingenuously, years later. "Constancy may not be one of my virtues. Anyway, I was restless." Just who he was being restless with may have been at the heart of the woman's objection.

It's not difficult to imagine the scenario. Billy, ensconced in the lap of luxury, nonetheless needed diversion—diversion in the form of Mitt Foster, Larry Sullivan, Jack Kelly, and other gay friends. Might he have tried to impress a male date by bringing him up to the swanky apartment on Fifth Avenue? His comment that "constancy" wasn't one of his virtues is intriguing: Although monogamy was never part of his lifestyle, not even with Jimmie Shields, "constancy" certainly was. He remained loyal to Jimmie for decades. The kind of loyalty he was willing to show this woman was evidently—and perhaps understandably—not enough for her.

Just how long they were together is unclear. Probably for several months, maybe close to a year. She likely gave him the boot sometime in late 1921. He slumped back to Mitt and Larry, but the quality of life he'd become used to would be difficult to maintain. "It wasn't so easy getting along in the interval that followed," he said. "Still, I had a good time, did things that interested me and was with people who interested me." Might he be alluding to a return to the gay scene?

Mitt suggested he pick up some extra cash by posing for advertising photos and illustrations. Professional models referred to the practice as "doing animal crackers." Billy pulled on the best suit his patroness had bought for him, slicked back his hair, and made his way over to a photographer's studio. "I'd been told I could make a career on my face," he said. "Now I was going to see if they were right."

There are various stories about just how William Haines came to be a movie star. His wasn't the typical Hollywood story, of the starry-eyed youth who dreams of becoming another Valentino or Mary Pickford, who boards a train and sets out for Hollywood with nothing but pluck and a smattering of talent. He seems to have paid little attention to the movies, beyond attending the shows in Staunton and cavorting with actors and artists (like Jack Kelly) who'd done some work in the field. "I had never before given a thought to the stage or screen," he recalled of the moment just before destiny caught up with him—in the person of a Hollywood talent scout with the unlikely name of Bijou Fernandez.

Bijou Fernandez was forty-four years old in late 1921, a former musical-comedy actress, a crusty Broadway and vaudeville veteran. She'd appeared on stage as a child with James O'Neill in *The Two Orphans*, and later in Augustin Daly's company of *A Midsummer Night's Dream*. As an adult she'd appeared in *Man and Superman*, but now she was following in the footsteps of her mother, Mrs. E. L. Fernandez—the first female theatrical agent in America—and working as a promoter for Goldwyn. She'd been entrusted with the much-ballyhooed campaign to find the "New Faces" of 1922.

Legend says Fernandez spotted Billy walking down Broadway and stopped him. "I like your face," she said.

"So do I, but it ain't mine," he told her. "I'm breaking it in for a friend."

A pretty story. Very much in keeping with Billy's image after he became a star. He's suitably witty, and besides, fans love stories of chance discoveries. It made them believe it could happen to them, too.

Another story may contain more truth. In this one, Billy was at a photographer's studio, and a fellow model (identified in some stories as Eleanor Boardman, but that's likely more Hollywood fluff) asked why he didn't try out for the movies. Intrigued, Billy said he'd give it a shot. In this version, he borrowed some of Mitt's clothes, sat for a series of portraits, and sent them over to Goldwyn's New York offices, without Fernandez ever seeing him on the street (although from all accounts, she does appear to have been an early booster of his career).

This seems more likely. By this point, Billy had become a regular in photography studios. He'd surely have heard about Goldwyn's "New Faces" contest: It was on the lips of models throughout the city, most of whom hoped to be "discovered" by Hollywood. The contest was one of those publicity-driven campaigns that the Hollywood studios, giddy with their own success, loved to foist on the public. By plucking an unknown out of the teeming masses and pledging to make him or her a star, the studios perpetuated the myth of Hollywood. It was just like the myth of America—where anyone could make it big—except it was even more grand and glamorous. Making it in Hollywood didn't simply turn you into a successful capitalist; Hollywood, with a wave of its magic wand, turned you into a god or goddess.

The Goldwyn studios were, at the moment, in the midst of a power struggle. Samuel Goldwyn had founded the company in 1916, but his temperament had made it difficult for his partners. In particular, the ambitious Frank J. Godsol had designs on the top spot himself. The two partners were dissimilar in manner—"Joe" Godsol was handsome and stylish, even ostentatious, while Sam Goldwyn was homely and rumpled, given to making obtuse quotations. Both were canny wheeler-dealers, however—shrewd operatives who wrestled for control of the company.

Goldwyn was still at the helm when the "New Faces" contest was authorized in the fall of 1921. Casting director Robert E. McIntyre was put in charge of selecting the winners. At a stockholders' meeting in March 1922, Godsol was persuasive in blaming Goldwyn for the studio's all-time low profits over the past year, and the pioneer producer was voted out of the company that bore his name.

It's not clear exactly when the contest results were decided by McIntyre, but it was certainly before Goldwyn's ouster. It was probably in December 1921, as Billy would later write he waited three months before leaving for Hollywood, and we know his first day at the Goldwyn studios was in March 1922. Out of more than a thousand entrants in the male category, Billy had been selected as the winner. On the female side, Eleanor Boardman, also working as a model in New York, was chosen.

One story—certainly apocryphal—has Billy getting the call from Bijou Fernandez just as he was getting ready to return to Richmond for Christmas. He couldn't come down for a screen test, he told her, as he had a train to catch.

"But this is a great opportunity," countered Fernandez.

"I have my tickets," Billy supposedly insisted. "The holidays are coming and I'm going home. I can't be bothered."

This is patently absurd. McIntyre would have dropped him like a hot potato, picking up the next photograph in the pile. Again, it was part of the image nurtured by publicists for Billy: the wisecracking, down-to-earth fellow who never really wanted to be a star.

That much may be true, as far as it goes. Billy had no particular ambition to be a movie actor (or an actor at all, for that matter), but winning that contest was truly fateful, and he knew it. Had the movies not discovered Billy Haines, who's to say what kind of life he might have led? He might have had some success modeling, but such work wouldn't have opened the avenues to him that the movies did. For a young man in search of the finer things in life, who wanted the kind of existence he'd tasted so briefly on Fifth Avenue, Hollywood provided the perfect opportunity. He had no skills, no ambition to succeed in any particular thing—just the ambition to *succeed*, period. Winning the "New Faces" contest was the deus ex machina solution to his dilemma.

He never made it home for Christmas. He took a streetcar over to Goldwyn's New York office, met with Fernandez and McIntyre, and made the screen test. It apparently proved satisfactory, as he was given a contract that started him at $40 a week. This was considerably more than he'd ever made before (except for his Hopewell days). Billy was suddenly feted around the Village as a star-in-the-making. He made grand promises not to forget his friends, vows they certainly took with grains of salt. But Billy was a man of his word. To his family, too, he promised that if he made it in Hollywood, they'd share in his success. He had every reason to think that this just might be the break he'd been looking for, the fortune he always expected he'd find.

The weeks between signing the contract and getting the call to board the train west seemed interminable. Billy continued to pose for pictures and made friends with his cowinner, Eleanor Boardman. "Perhaps the fact that we came into pictures at the same time created a bond between us," he would later write of his lifelong friend. "We had the same early struggles, the same heartaches and disappointments. I admire her tremendously. She's such a real person."

Boardman was born in 1899 in Philadelphia. A few months older than Billy, she was as precise about her career as he was lackadaisical. She had a canny agent, Murray Philips, and an ambitious agenda, landing the plum job of chief model for the Eastman Kodak company by the time she was twenty. She was a strikingly lovely girl, with a beauty that stopped passersby with its sheer naturalness. Her face became well-known to New Yorkers, adorning advertisements for soap, hats, and coats. Philips booked her on the Keith vaudeville circuit, and her big break came playing opposite Laurette Taylor in *The National Anthem*. During one performance, so the story goes, the plucky Eleanor lost her voice, but somehow managed to keep the show going by the use of pantomime, good practice for a career in silent film.

Philips would later claim he arranged the Goldwyn job for her. If so, then the whole "New Faces" contest could have been a hoax, with agents wheeling and dealing for the coveted assignment. Billy had no agent; other than the maternal hand offered by Bijou Fernandez, he had no particular advocates in this new venture. Eleanor, a bit wiser to the ways of the entertainment industry, lent her friendship and advice as well as her sense of frivolity. If she or the studio publicists had any designs for a romance between the two of them, Billy squelched the idea. He and Eleanor were *pals* from the start.

It was in March 1922 that the tickets finally arrived with orders that they report to the Goldwyn studios within a matter of weeks. An upper berth had been reserved for Billy on a westbound train. He was leaving a cold, damp winter on one coast and heading for the warm spring of another. "Coming across the continent I caught a terrific cold," he remembered. "A beautiful boil burst into bloom on my nose." The alkali dust of the long train ride across the country also irritated his skin. The corners of his mouth were chapped. By the end of the journey, when he stepped off the train into the bright sunlight of Los Angeles, he looked horrible.

No one was at the station to greet them. "The Los Angeles Chamber of Commerce doesn't exactly send bands to the train to meet contest winners," Billy recalled. "They're as common as coal miners in Pennsylvania." He and Eleanor took a cab directly to the Goldwyn studios in Culver City. Riding through town, they marveled at the sudden change of scenery: instead of brownstone tenements along narrow streets and the bare gray limbs of maple trees, they were greeted by wide avenues lined with Spanish-style haciendas and vibrant, swaying palms. The studio, too, must have made an impact. It was one of Hollywood's most elaborate, with massive Corinthian columns along Washington Boulevard. Once on the lot, they would have noticed the large swimming pool with its wind-whipping devices to create the illusion of the sea, as well as the massive dressing rooms that lined the property. If they turned one corner, they would have felt they were back in New York, with a replica of Fifth Avenue extending past them. Turning another, they were in nineteenth-century London. Billy, despite how jaded he may have become in the last few years, was fascinated.

He'd barely had time to run a comb through his hair. "I've often thought what a disappointment I must have been when they were expecting a Valentino," he recalled of the moment he was ushered into the studio executives' office. "My knees were knocking together with fright, but I bolstered up enough courage to be flippant." With his chapped face and boil in full blossom, he announced to the assembled moguls: "I'm your new prize beauty."

Later, he'd recall meeting with Goldwyn himself. If so, there was only a small window of opportunity for such an encounter. Goldwyn was certainly still head of the studio when Billy was hired, but was out by March 10, 1922. Billy would write on a *Photoplay* questionnaire that he'd entered films on "March 18," which would mean he would have missed the big man by about a week. March 18 may have been the date he first stood in front of a camera; Goldwyn may have still been around for a few days upon Billy's actual arrival at the studio.

The story itself has a ring of authenticity. Billy recalled being summoned to Goldwyn's office. The room was about "two miles long," he said, with Mr. Goldwyn seated up on a mahogany plateau at the end. "I started down the two miles feeling like a Ziegfeld chorus girl advancing down the runway to the footlights," Billy remembered. "Finally, I arrived, a little out of breath." Goldwyn had him walk across the room so he could see his profile. 'That is all," the producer said, and Billy was escorted out, feeling as if he'd just "tried out for a track meet or something." If the story is true, Goldwyn would have been ousted just days later; Billy would likely have had to make an encore presentation to Godsol and his cronies.

Immediately he was outfitted with $1,500 worth of new clothes. A publicity story in 1924 said the "down-to-earth Bill" simply shipped them all off to his father. He *was* regularly sending money and gifts to his family, but after knocking around New York in one good suit, he no doubt appreciated some finer threads. He was a young man in search of good and beautiful things; this first gift from the studio was the harbinger (he hoped) of more to come.

Whether it was his boil, his general lack of experience, or the turmoil in the front office, the Goldwyn studios seemed unprepared to make use of their new find. Eleanor, more conventionally ambitious, was quickly placed in her first film, *The Stranger's Banquet*, by the important director Marshall Neilan. It was a substantial part, but Billy found himself buried in crowd scenes in a number of forgotten titles. The publicity machine kicked into high gear for Eleanor: She was called the screen's great new actress, "a superb talent." Conversely, after some initial hype—in August, columnists wrote that "youthful William Haines is regarded as the find of the year"—Billy was left to fend for himself.

He lived in a hotel on Hollywood Boulevard during these first months. Despite his inactivity, he must have been excited by the sudden change in his lifestyle. Sun, warm weather, nice clothes, movie stars. Tagging along with Eleanor, who quickly charmed her way into the movie colony, Billy marveled at a town waking up to its own self-importance. Hollywood's rash adolescence coincided with the prosperity of the postwar years. Just a little more than a decade before, the town had been merely a collection of farms and itinerant moviemakers operating out of storefronts. Now magnificent studios sprawled over acres of old orange groves; on Hollywood Boulevard, ornate theaters and opulent Spanish stucco homes defined the town's emerging excess. More money than most of these folks had ever imagined was now theirs to spend recklessly and extravagantly. Already movies stars like Gloria Swanson and Rudolph Valentino were building outrageous castles to their absurd fame. Prohibition held no meaning here—champagne, beer, and more illicit drugs were easy to obtain—and studio chiefs like Sam Goldwyn and Jesse Lasky wielded more power than the local police force. If any town was designed for the sensibilities of Billy Haines, it was Hollywood in the Roaring Twenties.

After the grim and dark streets of Hopewell, Richmond, and New York, Billy reveled in the very *look* of Los Angeles. Rows of bunga-lows in festive pastels lined the avenues. In particular, he was in-trigued by the palm trees, some as tall as buildings in New York. A handsome Mexican boy on a bicycle, shirtless in March, was one of Billy's earliest and fondest memories of Hollywood. Here, as no-where else, not even the Village, Billy felt he fit in. Hollywood was a town fueled by ambition—often vague, indefinite ambition, where success mattered more than the vehicle for achieving it. Nearly everyone who populated the colony, from established stars to the hordes of young men and women arriving daily on trains and coaches, shared a similar worldview. They weren't content to work as salesclerks or waitresses or housewives or bond salesmen. They harbored dreams and aspirations of success, some of them clear-cut and defined like Eleanor's, others more enigmatic like Billy's. Here was a place Billy could finally make good: "I was lonely and poor in a strange, confusing business," he'd admit years later, "but I made up my mind that I would succeed."

Sometime during 1922, encouraged by his win, Billy's mother and sister Ann traveled out to Hollywood and stayed with him at the hotel. He delighted in showing them around town, pointing out Gloria Swanson as she whizzed down Hollywood Boulevard in her leopard-interior convertible as if she were a great and dear friend. Ann, then sixteen and maturing into a stunning beauty (she much resembled her brother), expressed an interest in acting. Billy had yet to obtain a real role in any picture himself, however; and by the end of the year, mother and daughter were back in Virginia.

He spent the spring learning to move in front of the camera, to take direction, to apply makeup. Trade papers, when they mentioned him at all, reported he was "undergoing a thorough training" and "learning cinema technique." How many scenes in how many films of 1922 hold glimpses of a young Billy Haines is impossible to determine. Then, in July, he was presented with a prized assignment, one that surely must have made him dizzy with anticipation. He'd been selected to join the *Passions of the Sea* company on their trip to Tahiti. It was planned as a big movie, directed by Raoul Walsh, then a rising director, and starring House Peters, the English-born Broadway star. It was also a racy melodrama of white slavery and island natives, an excuse for beautiful actors like Pauline Starke and Antonio Moreno to take off as much of their clothing as the censors (who were then pretty lax) would allow.

These were the first big movie stars Billy worked with on a close basis. He liked Moreno and found Starke lovely and fragile, but had no fondness for the company's aloof leading man. Billy doubled for Peters, rolling around in the mud in long shots so the urbane actor wouldn't have to soil his breeches. "I always called him Out House," Billy recalled. "He was in all probability a perfectly decent man, but I resented having to double for him."

Still, it was the penultimate moviemaking experience. The distracted student who once sat dreaming at his desk in Staunton was now wading in the warm, crystal-clear waters off Tahiti, sunbathing on white sand as soft as crushed velvet. It wasn't all glamorous, of course: He was also standing in the brutal sun for hours at a time while Walsh herded his crowd of extras—both natives and

Americans—from scene to scene. And there was a price to be paid for the nightly rum-drinking and cavorting with the islanders, easily impressed by all the commotion. "Cast and crew collected many splendored souvenirs," Billy remembered wryly years later. "This was before the days of penicillin."

The film was eventually released in February the following year, retitled *Lost and Found on a South Sea Island*. Billy, lost in the crowds of extras, received no billing. In his next film, he also went uncredited: He played Norman Kerry's butler in *Brothers Under the Skin*, which was released in November (before the South Seas picture).

Despite the excitement of the trip to Tahiti, Billy was becoming impatient. By the end of the year, after nearly seven months in Hollywood, he'd played no significant part in any picture. Eleanor Boardman, meanwhile, was climbing the ladder fast, already linked romantically in the trade papers with Charlie Chaplin (a publicist's clever maneuver). While Billy could write home to Richmond and to his friends in the Village about his wondrous Tahiti trip, there was still no "William Haines" on the nation's marquees. Back in New York, many of his old friends predicted Billy would find a suitable sugar daddy or mommy and that would be finis to any ideas about an acting career.

In fact, it was just about this time that his former patroness from Fifth Avenue arrived in Hollywood, determined to regain Billy's affections. He was not happy to see her: By now, he had found a crowd of young, happy comrades, all possessed with that fire peculiar to youth. Billy's ex-lover, on the other hand, was a woman closing in on middle age, desperate to rekindle the spark with a man much younger than she was—not to mention one with an interesting job and a fascinating circle of friends. She could offer him wealth, and undoubtedly did, but he was no longer as hungry as he once was. The studio salary of $40 a week had recently been raised to $50, and there were perks even she couldn't dangle before him. On Eleanor's arm, he could attend parties at the homes of Chaplin and King Vidor; as far-fetched as it seemed, he could still hope to become the next Valentino, or Barthelmess, or, at least, Charles Ray. As much as she tried, the woman from New York could not fit in with

Billy's new friends. "It was a most unhappy association," he later wrote. "We got on each other's nerves." When she discovered the house she was renting on Alvarado Street had been the site of the murder of noted director William Desmond Taylor, this "terribly superstitious" woman packed and left town the same day. Billy, no doubt, gave a long sigh of relief.

He was, by now, a very different young man than he had been even twelve months before. He didn't know if he'd make it in pictures, but he knew something more important: He had found a home. The warm breezes over the orange groves were only part of what made Hollywood so attractive. This was a place where he could put Marden's maxim to the ultimate test. Could he make it here without any particular skill at acting, or directing, or anything else? Could he make it here without the connections that would guarantee his name up on there on the screen? Here, in the magic land of Hollywood, Billy determined he *would* make it: on looks, charm, and *will*—along, of course, with a little bit of luck.

3

THE GAIETY GIRL

1923-1926

A curious phenomenon happens among ambitious people, especially ambitious people in creative fields. There are those at the top — those who've made it — and those who are still struggling, still toiling away toward that elusive goal of success. Both envy the other. The strugglers want what the successful have, but the successful walk precariously along the tightrope of fame and fortune, well aware of how easy it would be to fall. They envy those below them for their youth, their energy, their unrealized dreams. For it is the young and the struggling who set the tone, who cut the edge, who — in the parlance of today — define what it means to be hip.

The biggest stars of 1923, as determined by the annual Quigley Publications poll of the nation's exhibitors, were Norma Talmadge and Thomas Meighan. Both, although exceedingly popular in America's heartland, could hardly be described as "hip." Talmadge had been a star since 1910; her vehicles were soggy melodramas that only armies of housewives could love. Meighan was of that generation of stolid, dependable leading men, noble in their sacrifice and devoted to their leading ladies. He was forty-four in 1923; Billy, already known for mocking the older and "stuffier" generation, may well have viewed Meighan the way he'd viewed House Peters.

Billy's crowd was the young, trendy set. Some were famous, others were simply fast and fashionable. The parties they threw were more lively and more popular (if hardly as influential) as the galas at Pickfair. Billy and his friends were the up-and-comers, the next generation of stars. They were careless, noisy, and gay—before that term came to mean anything other than frivolous and happy-go-lucky.

Of course, many were gay in the modern sense, too, but in Hollywood, Billy mixed with a wide swath of people—Fitzgerald's Flaming Youth, that generation of driven young people determined to make up for the deprivations imposed by World War I. Their energies were devoted to dismantling the conventions of their Victorian parents. Women had won the right to vote. Modern technology was freeing women from the home and men from mindless labor. There was an energy, an optimism, that had not existed before, born out of despair as well as hope. Fitzgerald wrote that the Flaming Youth had found "all gods dead, all wars fought, all faiths in man shaken." What was there left but to have a good time?

This was the culture in which Billy Haines—as true a child of the twentieth century that ever lived—came into his own. The "new morality," as it would be called, allowed Billy's generation to break down gender roles: Women could be friends with men, smoke with them, drink with them, have sex with as much independence as men. And if women could reject the rigid gender codification of the old century, so could men. The new male star of the era was Rudolph Valentino, hardly the virile type who had dominated the screen a decade before, the days of Francis X. Bushman and William S. Hart. Men could now afford to be "pretty," indulging in luxuries and finery once considered feminine. Valentino in *Monsieur Beaucaire*, foppish in silk tights and powdered wigs, and John Barrymore in *Beau Brummel*, gorgeous in satin smoking jacket and ruffled shirts, were the new images of male beauty. In such a culture, homosexuality became less a taboo and more an exotic indulgence.

Of course, Prohibition was the order of the day, but in Hollywood—where the Flaming Youth burned brighter and hotter than perhaps anywhere else—alcohol came easily. Billy imbibed with gusto; nondrinkers were social pariahs. These were young people just beginning to sense the wonders of the new century. Their fates appeared limitless, their options eternal. America was, for perhaps the only time in its brief history, a happy country. And nowhere was that more evident than in its youth, and in particular, the youth who played in the town of myth and magic.

Many of them ultimately went nowhere: names now forgotten, hopeful young actors, writers, and artists out to conquer Hollywood just as Billy was in those crisp clear early weeks of 1923. Some of them made it, and it's those whose names come down to us today.

Claire Windsor was a strikingly beautiful girl, who'd played an important supporting role in *Brothers Under the Skin* with Billy. Her big success—with Douglas Fairbanks in *The Thief of Bagdad*—was still a few years in the future.

Paul Bern had been the scenarist on *Lost and Found on a South Sea Island*. He was a shy, soft-spoken writer with a small, pinched face, receding hairline, and severe inferiority complex—the reason being an underdeveloped penis, so small, it was said, he could not have traditional heterosexual intercourse. Throughout his life, Paul Bern fell obsessively in love with beautiful women, but he was also sexually drawn to men. Through Bern, Billy probably first met Irving Thalberg, then just twenty-three and vice president in charge of production at Universal Pictures.

Bern also likely introduced Billy to the sultry actress Barbara La Marr. Bern was devoted to La Marr, one in a long line of women with whom he'd fall madly in love while finding sexual gratification with men on the side. By early 1923, Barbara La Marr was on her way to becoming a major star. She had been memorably lovely in *The Three Musketeers* (1921) with Douglas Fairbanks, and even more stunning opposite Ramon Novarro in *The Prisoner of Zenda* (1922). Publicists liked to say that audiences gasped when they saw La Marr's close-ups, but she really *was* that beautiful: great liquid eyes, a delicate nose and chin, pouting lips.

Of course, Billy was still good friends with Eleanor Boardman, who in 1923 was being promoted to full-fledged stardom in Rupert Hughes's *Souls for Sale*. Billy was still doing walk-ons. Discussing the contest that had brought the two of them to Hollywood, one press notice opined that Eleanor had "fully justified Mr. McIntyre's judgment." Left unsaid, of course, was that Billy had not. Now, as the first anniversary of the New Faces contest approached, his particular new face was still unknown to movie audiences.

Billy can't be faulted for his long apprenticeship. When McIntyre hired him, it was clear that he had no acting experience, no performing background. Eleanor had been quite successful as a professional model in New York, and the roles she was now being given required little more of her than to stand around looking pretty. It was something she did very well—and Billy could have, too, of course, but male parts demanded something more. "What type are you?" casting directors would ask him. He'd shrug and crack, "Latin lover?" They'd just wave their hands and look at the next boy in line.

He tried to keep his chin up, rushing about from set to set, doing a bit here, a walk-on there. Writer Charleson Gray remembered Billy from this period, bounding into a tailor shop near his rented apartment, a bundle of energy and high spirits. A number of underemployed movie folk had their suits pressed at the shop. Billy had a large outstanding bill, but the tailor liked him. "Watch out for that fellow," he told Gray. "He's going to make the grade someday."

He now lived, as many of his friends did, in "downtown" Los Angeles, if such a thing can be said about a city with such fluid borders. He rented a cramped "two-by-four apartment," as he called it, at 1026 Ingraham Street, a turn-of-the-century structure with at least five other apartments in the building. Here he would entertain his new friends, singing raucous tunes late into the night, sharing their disappointments, exchanging gossip about the stars and the studio heads.

He was a strapping lad, always in motion, rocking back and forth on his heels as he talked, jingling the coins in his pocket. He was easily distracted, as if his ears were always attuned for the next call, the next opportunity, the next good time. Among his circle of friends it was Billy Haines who had the most energy, pulling faces, cracking jokes.

The frivolity often masked an edge of desperation, a feeling of failure. Might drive and charm and the will to succeed *not* be enough?

In Hollywood, connections were all-important, and although Billy had some—Thalberg, for instance—he wasn't as fortunate as Eleanor, who'd soon be dating the leading director King Vidor. Billy might have tried that route: A number of top stars, writers, and directors were known to be gay. Edmund Goulding, with whom Billy did form a friendship later on, had been prominent since scripting the megahit *Tol'able David* in 1921. Although his biggest hits were past, J. Warren Kerrigan, a matinee idol since 1912, was the star of one of 1923's biggest pictures, *The Covered Wagon*. Eugene O'Brien was a very popular star that year, often teamed with the top-polled Norma Talmadge. Although their sexualities were known and even accepted among Hollywood power brokers, their "sponsorship" of a young man, as Vidor was sponsoring Eleanor, would have had to be much more clandestine. Besides, Billy was contracted to Goldwyn, and if he was to find a mentor, he would have had to find him on the lot. And of the men in positions of power there, none were known to be homosexual.

Of course, Billy might have looked to a powerful woman as his patron, as he had in New York. In Hollywood, however, with the exception of a few key stars like Pickford or Swanson, or writers like Frances Marion or Anita Loos, there weren't many women of influence. Despite the greater popularity of female stars on the whole, and despite how many gay actors and directors gained acceptance and success, Hollywood was (as it has remained) a heterosexual male town. Then as now, producers were nearly all men, nearly all straight, and they aimed for the broadest possible audience. Billy did not have the options Eleanor had: her route to success was more clearly delineated. That she had talent helped, but such things were not prerequisites. Billy would have to just keep up his will to succeed, and pray hard to Lady Luck.

It was in this atmosphere that his friendship with Barbara La Marr intensified. "I met her when I was discouraged and most unhappy," he recalled. "She encouraged me and made me believe in myself. She was a wonderful woman."

Some have suggested he began dating La Marr as a way to fit into the straight boys' club. That may have been an ancillary benefit, but Billy's friendship with La Marr seems authentic and mutual. They were smitten with each other: both beautiful, vivacious people, eager for success and good times. Billy was mesmerized by her, by the way she moved, the way she laughed, the way she widened her extravagant green eyes and threw off an unwanted suitor as casually as she tossed back her ebony hair.

Barbara was four years older than Billy, yet in reality the age difference between them was much greater than that. While both laughed easily, staying out on the town until dawn, there was a weariness to Barbara La Marr that had not yet settled in on Billy. La Marr had seen and done much in her relatively young life, and by 1923 she was searching for something very different from what she'd had.

Billy adored her life story, full of the kind of drama and intrigue he'd left Staunton to find. Although some accounts place her birth in Richmond, Virginia, which would make an affinity with Billy easy to understand, she was actually born in North Yakima, Washington. She was forever changing her background: For a while, she and her publicists insisted that her father was an Italian count and her mother a descendant of Napoleon. Mr. and Mrs. W. W. Watson of North Yakima had just been raising her while her real parents traveled the world.

The Watsons were indeed her flesh and blood. She was born Reatha Watson in 1896. She was a deeply driven girl, ambitious and full of spirit. She shared that restlessness with Billy. When she was fourteen—the age at which Billy said life begins—Reatha slipped out to Los Angeles. It was then a sleepy city of only a few thousand, but with enough dance halls and taverns to make life infinitely more interesting than North Yakima. The movie people were just moving into nearby Hollywood, people like Colonel William Selig, David Nestor, and Al Christie, hard-drinking, hard-playing pioneers who after a long day of turning the crank on the camera looked forward to a night on the town. Reatha quickly made a name for herself among the city's nightlife, despite (or perhaps because of) her very tender years.

She landed in juvenile court. After all these years, the exact charge has become obscured, but likely she was caught with an older man and was asked her age. In the kind of ironic twist that only happens in Hollywood—where screenwriters need only look around them for ideas—the reporter assigned the juvenile court beat for the *Los Angeles Herald* was Adela Rogers St. Johns, later the noted journalist and Hollywood columnist.

St. Johns would remember, "I entered just as Judge Monroe from the bench was saying, sternly: 'You are too beautiful to be allowed alone in a big city. You are too beautiful to be without constant protection.' The old judge was not a man easily fooled. If he said this girl—I could only see her back—was too beautiful, then she could stop traffic. She did. As she turned, I lost my breath." The newspaper ran a three-page gallery of pictures: "Reatha Watson, The Too Beautiful Girl."

Although she had been remanded back into the custody of her parents, now living in Fresno, Reatha didn't stay long. Out there in the wild country, she met a cowboy named Jack Lytell, several years her senior, who got her father's permission to marry her and whisked her off to his ranch. Reatha tired of him rather quickly, ran back to Los Angeles, and had the marriage annulled, telling the court Lytell had tried "cave man stuff" with her.

Husband number two came when she was seventeen, a dashing and brilliant attorney named Lawrence Converse. The morning after their marriage Converse was charged with bigamy. He had a wife and three children before he fell under the spell of the too-beautiful Reatha Watson. In his cell he banged his head repeatedly against the bars calling Reatha's name, causing himself to black out. He never regained consciousness.

Then came Phil Ainsworth, a popular dancer with whom she made a splash at the 1915 World's Fair in San Francisco. She determined she would become a great dancer, and she and Phil a magnificent partnership. Like both her previous husbands, Ainsworth came from a wealthy family, and Reatha demanded the best clothes, the finest jewels, the latest automobiles. She got them, too, until Ainsworth passed one check too many and ended up in San Quentin.

She really was, apparently, just too beautiful—or at least, so went the legend of Barbara La Marr. "They say if Cleopatra's nose had been an inch longer the history of the world would have been different," Adela Rogers St. Johns wrote. Reatha told her bitterly after her husband went to jail, "I wish my nose was as long as the elephant child's."

In 1918 she married for a fourth time, to Ben Deely, another dancer. Together they performed at various road shows and county fairs. Touring the Orpheum circuit, Reatha changed her name to Barbara La Mar (she added the second "r" for the movies) and was part of the dance team Carville, La Mar and Carville. It was during this period that she was chosen by Douglas Fairbanks to play Milady in *The Three Musketeers*. She drew good notices, more for her looks than any great talent.

By this time, she and Deely had separated. He had moved to New York, and it was as if she had never been married, not to him or to any of the others. When Billy Haines met her in late 1922, she was poised for a huge career. And—world-weary—she saw in this eager, good-natured youth from Virginia something refreshing: a man who liked her not so much for her physical beauty as for her company, her wit, herself.

They made one film together, *Souls for Sale*, a snappy comedy-drama of backstage movie life directed by Rupert Hughes, based on his novel, in 1923.

Eleanor Boardman was set for the lead. On February 10 a notice in the trades said William Haines was getting his "first real opportunity" in *Souls for Sale*. It wasn't much of an opportunity: He was on-screen for a total of four and a half minutes. He played the part of the assistant director to a troupe of actors filming in the desert. Billy must have had a ball making the film with pals Eleanor and Barbara, along with Aileen Pringle, who became another friend. In one scene, he's seen laughing in the background at some antic or another: His fun looks genuine, slapping a fellow player on the back. The all-star (or soon-to-be-star) cast collectively turns in good work: Mae Busch is a hoot as the self-absorbed starlet; Dale Fuller is outstanding as the lonely, swindled spinster; and La Marr turns in a fabulously melodramatic death scene.

As for Billy, there's not much to say, except he looked great in his knickers.

Nevertheless, it was announced that he would next appear in King Vidor's *Three Wise Fools*. After more than nine months at the studio, Billy was finally being given a part—however small—in a major production by a top director.

The publicity department began building him up to audiences and exhibitors. "A new juvenile actor, handsome enough to contest the laurels of the long established favorites, will be introduced by the Goldwyn Company in *Three Wise Fools*," said one notice. Another reported that although William Haines had been in pictures for only a year and had no previous screen experience, he had "risen rapidly in his chosen profession."

Nothing, of course, could be further from the truth. The publicity machine had finally kicked in for Billy, pumping out press releases and eight-by-ten glossies and sending them out to newspapers and fan magazines. There were a few "blind items" planted by the studio about his friendship with La Marr, but Billy, despite his ambition to "make it," found all the publicity silly. When a reporter asked him if he was involved with anyone, he could have corroborated the La Marr story; after all, they *were* most likely lovers as well as friends by this point. But a wisecrack seemed a better comeback than a half-truth or distortion. "Of all the fair ladies of Hollywood," the reporter noted of Billy's response, "it's Kate Price, who's fat and fifty, who's his favorite." It was the beginning of a long tradition of refusing to play the game.

Billy Haines always liked women. Preferred them, in fact, to men—but as friends, confidantes. After wisecracking about Kate Price, he actually met her and adored her, inviting her to dinner and posing for photographs with her. She was indeed fat and fifty, but he saw her as a delightful conversationalist, a fellow jokester, a live wire. Who could have predicted the friendship between the handsome twenty-three-year-old Virginian and the stout, matronly Mrs. Kelly of the popular *Cohens and Kellys* comedy series?

With La Marr there was, most likely, sexual passion as well. "Oh, yes, I think so," says Ted Graber. "She was a great, great beauty. There was something between them for a while. He always spoke highly of her."

Still, the affair clearly meant very different things to both. In early 1923, La Marr adopted a baby and declared she wanted a family; nothing could have been further from Billy's plans. Certainly he cared for her, but he could no more settle down with her than he could have with the woman in New York—than he could, in fact, with any woman. It's generally believed today that the baby La Marr adopted was her own—placed in an orphanage in an elaborate ruse to deceive the press and avoid a scandal. It's interesting to speculate who the father might have been; not Billy, as nine months earlier they did not as yet know each other. What Barbara La Marr wanted by 1923 was love, family, and stability. The height of screen stardom was within her grasp, but after everything she'd been through, it didn't seem to matter quite so much anymore.

Love and family might also have been hers to have, but not with Billy Haines. Paul Bern remained as devoted as ever, and he often accompanied Billy and Barbara out on the town. (Some claim a distinct resemblance to Bern in later photographs of La Marr's son.) La Marr felt only bemused tolerance toward the homely little man. According to Adela Rogers St. Johns, when La Marr turned down Bern's proposal of marriage, he made a pathetic attempt at suicide by putting his face in a toilet and flushing repeatedly. Another time, having been stood up by La Marr at a party, Bern tossed the diamond bracelet he had planned to give to her into the bushes and stalked off. Guests searched for it for hours without any luck.

Part of the reason La Marr was so cavalier in her treatment of Bern was, of course, Billy Haines. It was Billy to whom she turned for affection and support. He was likely the first surrogate father for her son, whom she named Marvin. She told the press: "When people ask me why I adopted a baby, I often wonder if they have any idea how lonely is the life of a woman like me. . . . They call me a vampire on the screen. But you see, you can't tell where you will find mother love. It doesn't belong exclusively to any little circle of women who look blonde and spiritual and perfect. But I'm not willing to admit that because I've got black hair and green eyes and what they call beauty, I'm not going to make a good mother to my son."

For a span of a few months, they must have made a surprisingly modern alternative family: the flamboyant Barbara, her little son, and an army of uncles who no doubt showered the child with gifts and attention.

Meanwhile, her career—unlike Billy's—was on the fast track. She was signed for a major costarring role opposite Lionel Barrymore in *The Eternal City*. Still, La Marr wanted more, and she wasn't finding it with Billy Haines.

Their friendship ended in a "quarrel," Billy would later write. Three days later, on May 6, she married Jack Dougherty, a Universal comedy actor, and never spoke to Billy again. Although more than seventy years later it is impossible to unearth the details of their quarrel, it is not hard to imagine what might have happened. She had fallen in love with him, but he could only return those feelings in a partial, mostly platonic way—certainly as unsatisfying to her as it was for his older patroness back in New York.

"Perhaps it is strange that we did not meet" after that, Billy wrote, but it's not so difficult to understand. Her marriage to Dougherty collapsed less than a year later. Barbara told the press: "Men—bah! I am sick of men. The admiration of men. The so-called love of men. Men's love is most unsatisfactory, the most disillusioning thing in the world. If you happen to find love—real love—that is different. That is heaven-sent. [But] it has been denied me."

"She was the woman who meant most to me during my years in Hollywood," is all Billy would ever say about the relationship. Certainly he must have missed her camaraderie and support, especially since he felt he'd been "turned out to pasture" by the studio. "Nobody paid any attention to me," he lamented. "I played bits and extra parts and more bits. I thought they had forgotten I was here!" Now, in the wake of the breakup with La Marr, he seriously contemplated heading back to New York.

Even that might not have been possible. He initially made around $2,500 a year at the Goldwyn studios. "It seemed like an awful lot of money," he wrote, "but then I had to buy clothes, and pay rent. In addition, I was sending money home. I hadn't saved a sou, and wouldn't even be able to get back to New York."

His small part in *Three Wise Fools*, however, brought him some notice. Eleanor once again had the lead. Billy played her suitor. The picture was classic Vidor: direct, straightforward, elegant, and honest in its simplicity. It's not surprising that Billy would enjoy working with Vidor, or that in their four films together the director would extract telling, restrained performances from the usually extravagant young actor.

In this film, Billy wasn't even aware of how good he was. "I had to wear a high silk hat," he remembered, "and I had to wear it while I did my most dramatic scene. I'd never had one on before, and it takes a good actor to be emotional in a top hat. I was just as conscious of it as I would have been without my pants. I was terrible, awful."

When *Motion Picture News* called his selection for the role "excellent," the Goldwyn publicity machine began kicking in at full throttle. Much about his earlier life was fabricated. A report appeared that he had been educated at the Staunton Military Academy, which must have made him laugh. Ignoring earlier reports that had acknowledged his lack of experience, suddenly he was a serious thespian, "much interested in the college theatricals" at the military academy. One report said he had pursued dramatic work as a "diversion" while working in New York, that he'd been dissatisfied at Straus, "feeling the urge for expression without knowing it."

He was reportedly offered leads in four different pictures after that. "He wants to play them all," according to a notice in *Photoplay* on June 25, "but it's difficult for a young man to be in four places at once." This appears to have been a publicist's hyperbole, for no leads materialized. He was loaned out to Fox in October, however, to play his first substantial role, a western called *The Desert Outlaw*, directed by Edmund Mortimer. Although technically not the leading man (defined as who gets the girl), the plot revolved around him. He plays Tom, an innocent cowboy charged with murder. He has to flee from a posse, but Buck Jones—then in his early days of popularity as a western star—saves the day.

Even this first chance at stardom would have to wait. During location filming in Santa Barbara, Billy fell ill during the last week of October and underwent emergency surgery at Carnegie Hospital in Los Angeles. Press reports don't reveal the nature of the operation, but he was convalescing during the early part of November. His brother Henry Haines suspects it was a routine appendectomy. It's unclear when Billy was well enough to finish shooting, but the film would not be released until August of the next year, after several other pictures had made Billy a more bankable name.

It may have been this delay that caused Billy to forget the film. When the cinema journal *Filmograph* compiled a filmography of William Haines in 1972, Billy told them he'd never made *The Desert Outlaw*. Although the film itself has apparently been lost, ardent fans unearthed a copy of *Boys' Cinema*, published in England and dated January 17, 1924, that showed three clear photos from the film of Billy in cowboy hat and chaps. "I can't be expected to remember every picture," Billy said. "In the early days, they all ran together."

There was more "running together" of projects throughout late 1923 and early 1924. He returned to Goldwyn for a series of small parts, some in notable pictures, others in minor titles, but at least now he was working regularly with screen billing. His part in *Three Weeks* (released in March 1924) was negligible, as a curate at the church where Conrad Nagel gets married. This was an important production, based on the notorious Elinor Glyn best-seller of 1907. Besides Nagel, it starred Billy's chum Aileen Pringle as Glyn's distinctly modern heroine. The film, like the novel, dared to reverse the conventional heterosexual dynamic: The woman is the sexual aggressor, and unapologetically so. The man is the prey, and her conquest of him is taken for granted. In 1907, *Three Weeks* scandalized a generation. In 1924, as the Flapper Era shifted into high gear, it was perfect for the screen.

Billy must have loved the story, although he despised Elinor Glyn. Ever since "Madame" had arrived in Hollywood a few years earlier to write screenplays, the film colony had flocked around her, humbly awaiting her cues on manners, mores, and most everything else. The wrinkled dowager wore absurdly comic false eyelashes, dyed her hair scarlet, and clicked her ill-fitting dentures as she talked. She ruled over Hollywood society in the 1920s like some dotty empress, done up in bizarre costumes and issuing outrageous pronouncements. "Why do people pay her so much attention?" Billy would lament. "She's absurd."

Yet pay attention they did: Even Gloria Swanson, the reigning queen of Hollywood, fell at her feet. "She smelled like a cathedral full of incense," Swanson would recall. "Her British dignity was devastating. She took over Hollywood. She went everywhere and passed her fearsome verdicts on everything. 'This is glamorous,' she would say. 'This is hideous,' she would say."

Billy should have loved her outrageousness, but her air of infinite superiority put him off early. When she visited the set with her retinue of ladies in waiting, a studio janitor leaned over to Billy and asked him who the grande dame was. "Her?" sniffed Billy. "That's Baby Peggy."

Although he had another small part in Goldwyn's *True as Steel* (released in April and again starring Aileen Pringle), it took another loan-out to give him a chance to prove his mettle. "Harry Cohn was a life-saver to me," Billy recalled. The Columbia chief asked Goldwyn for a leading man for a series of five pictures, and Godsol gave him Billy. "They must have been glad to get me off their hands for they fell joyfully on his neck."

Columbia was a minor studio, with few actors under contract. The picture they had in mind to start the series would star Elaine Hammerstein, who was then nearing the end of her days of major stardom. She was about as big as they came: From the Broadway theatrical family, she had entered movies in 1915 and was top box office for years. Now she found herself freelancing at Columbia, a comedown from her days as the star of Lewis J. Selznick productions.

Still, for Billy Haines, the chance to star opposite an established, bona fide star as a leading lady was a terrific opportunity. The film was *The Midnight Express*, directed by George W. Hill. "The picture was made for a dill pickle and a cold fried egg," Billy would say with a laugh, "but it was my first success."

He played Jack Oakes, whose father disowns him for being too shiftless to ever make good. Taking a job in his father's railroad yard, he falls in love with Hammerstein, the daughter of the engineer of the famed Midnight Express. Jack finally proves himself when his quick thinking prevents a freight train from colliding with the Express. "I had one of those actor-proof roles, a young engineer who races to the rescue of something or other," Billy said. "I was popular. Naturally, I was happy."

One writer on the film would recall years later seeing Billy in the lobby of the theater after the film's premier in May, "a happy, bright-faced youth with the applause of the audience still ringing in his ears."

The reviews were excellent. *Exhibitors Trade Review* said, "William Haines can swing a mean fist and do the heavy melodrama heroics with the best of 'em." Although the *New York Times* quibbled that his face was "invariably a little too clean when he is working in the sweat shop," *Variety* selected him as "the outstanding member" of the cast, saying, "He looks to have everything a leading man of the screen should have." In fact, the review observed, Columbia had a sure star on their hands "if they can hold him."

Harry Cohn did indeed try to keep Billy on the Columbia lot. "When my studio found out that somebody else wanted me, they became coy," Billy said. Godsol asked for $20,000 for Billy's contract option, scaring Cohn off. Billy returned to his home studio and more bit parts.

At some point in 1924, *Screenland* magazine interviewed socialite and occasional actress Peggy Hopkins Joyce. She offered that in her opinion, the best screen kiss she had ever seen was given by William

Haines to Elaine Hammerstein in *The Midnight Express*. Goldwyn publicists went wild. This was perfect. Joyce, renowned for her beauty and poise, would make a sensational mate for Billy in the fan magazines. For an up-and-coming young star, a link to Peggy Hopkins Joyce could accomplish wonders.

It's a good example of the hypocrisy of Hollywood publicity. No publicist in his or her right mind would dream of Peggy Hopkins Joyce as an ideal mate for a rising juvenile star. *Modern Screen* would later write of her: "All the world loves a lover, but certainly not a lover who is using love as an excuse to get her name in the papers." She was twenty-nine years old, five times divorced, laden with diamonds and years of experience. A former Ziegfeld Girl, she had been the toast of New York and Paris. Already, one man was rumored to have killed himself over her. When she arrived in Hollywood in 1922, she began a torrid affair with Charlie Chaplin. Nude photos of the two of them frolicking on the island of Catalina had somehow made it to the underground market.

If Billy had been serious about her, studio publicists would have done everything in their power to discourage the match. Because he wasn't—and because, quite possibly, they knew he would *never* be serious about a woman—a few well-placed items in the fan magazines would titillate the public and establish Billy's heterosexual credentials.

A meeting was arranged by Howard Dietz, head of Goldwyn publicity. A trip may have even been set up, for Billy would later recall traveling with Joyce on a train. "What a technique!" he'd recall. "No wonder she has a million dollars in diamonds. I can understand how she fascinates so many men. She makes a life work of keeping them interested. I remember she bought all the fan magazines to read up on things that would interest me."

It didn't work. Any hint of a romance fizzled out. Billy, perhaps still smarting over the Barbara La Marr affair, did not encourage Joyce's fantasy. In fact, he appears to have taken some pleasure in rebuffing her advances. Whether she was able to discover if his off-screen kiss was as good as the one she'd seen in *The Midnight Express*, no one knows. One thing is certain: Billy's first Hollywood-arranged pairing was a big bust, because he just couldn't be bothered to play the game.

Big changes were afoot at the studio. Since January 1924, Frank Godsol had been negotiating with Marcus Loew of Metro Pictures Corporation about a merger. Metro had just lost its chief star when Rudolph Valentino had refused to renew his contract. The two struggling companies, it was reasoned, could survive better together.

To run the new conglomerate, Godsol and Loew approached Louis B. Mayer, whose small, efficient production company impressed both of them. Mayer had recently hired Barbara La Marr away from Goldwyn, possibly through the influence of Paul Bern, who was also now on Mayer's writing staff. When Loew toured the lot, he met La Marr with Ramon Novarro, with whom she was making *Thy Name Is Woman.* By an interesting twist, La Marr found herself back at the same studio with Billy Haines that spring, when Mayer trucked over his actors, his sets, and his property, which included the animals of the famed Selig Zoo.

Billy would laugh and say, "Louis Mayer came over with his troop of trained animals and Norma Shearer and Ramon Novarro and the rest of them."

In March, Godsol was out: Loew took over his $750,000 worth of Goldwyn stock. He also offered William Randolph Hearst, the newspaper mogul who had started his own film company, Cosmopolitan Pictures, a large share of the new studio. The decision was to base operations at the Goldwyn lot in Culver City, the most elaborate and efficient space. The melding of three studios—Metro, Goldwyn, and Mayer, along with the somewhat autonomous addition of Cosmopolitan—created overnight a major force to be reckoned with in Hollywood.

Billy would remember seeing Mayer rushing about in those early months of 1924, before the merger was official. Mayer had an office on the lot starting in January, but he did not concern himself with the films then in production. Billy thought him a funny little man, with his round face and round glasses, neatly tailored, impeccably groomed and manicured, talking nonstop without pausing for breath. Mayer would hardly have noticed Billy: The face of William Haines did not stand out among the sudden accumulation of so much star talent under one roof. From Goldwyn came Eleanor Boardman, Conrad Nagel, Aileen Pringle, Mae Murray, Blanche Sweet, and John Gilbert. From Metro came Ramon Novarro, Alice Terry, Buster Keaton, and Viola Dana. From Mayer came Lon Chaney, Norma Shearer, Renée Adorée, and, of course, Barbara La Marr.

On April 26, a gala celebration on the front lawn marked the opening of the new studio. Fred Niblo, one of Mayer's top directors, served as emcee. The dais was hung with a giant American flag and an enormous portrait of Marcus Loew, while ten Army and Navy airplanes passed by in formation overhead, littering the lot with roses. Three hundred naval personnel, sharply attired in white dress uniforms, were led by the commander of the Pacific Fleet.

Mayer, moved by this great orchestration of glamour, glitz, and Old Glory, could barely choke back the tears. "I hope that it is given me to live up to this great trust," he intoned before the assembled crowd of actors, politicians, directors, and technicians. "It has been my argument and practice that each picture should teach a lesson, should have a reason for existence. With seventeen of the greatest directors in the industry calling this great institution their home, I feel that this aim will be carried out. . . . This is a great moment for me. I accept this solemn trust and pledge the best that I have to give." Thus was born Metro-Goldwyn-Mayer.

It was just the kind of speech Billy would have said was full of corn—no, worse than that: full of air. Hot air. Billy Haines had nothing but bemused contempt for Mayer from the start. Born Eliezer Mayer in Minsk, Russia, in 1885, the new chief of MGM was a hustler of the first magnitude. He relied on intuition rather than intellect, and in the course of just a decade went from being an impoverished theater owner in Haverhill, Massachusetts, to the head of the most powerful and influential movie studio of all time. He could be petty, vindictive, and cruel, but he had an unerring skill in charting his ship through often very rough waters.

Part of that skill was in choosing the right first mates. In all of

Hollywood history, there have been few who have rated such esteem as Irving Thalberg, who was by now vice president in charge of production under Mayer. As loved as Mayer was loathed, Thalberg was a sickly, high-strung intellectual, and a young man not yet twenty-five already being called a legend. Such fulsome praise did not, however, go to Thalberg's head: He was far too driven to indulge in complacent self-congratulation. Even more than Mayer, Thalberg breathed life into the new enterprise, encouraging quality directors and prodding them along to new heights—while at the same time lording over them to make sure their pictures came in under budget and on time.

Mayer also brought with him another important lieutenant: producer Harry Rapf, a generation older than the boy wonder Thalberg but no less intuitive in sniffing out quality. The triumvirate of Mayer, Thalberg, and Rapf would forge a studio like none other in the history of cinema, and standing on the front lawn of the old Goldwyn studios that day in April 1924, they seemed to sense their destiny.

Among the stars who gathered on the dais behind them were most of the aforementioned. John Gilbert jockeyed for position with Conrad Nagel; Norma Shearer, even then, was whispered to have her eye on Thalberg. Billy was near the back; Barbara La Marr was closer to Mayer's side. No words were spoken between the former friends, but Billy did catch the roving eye of Ramon Novarro. While Mayer preached the noble theme of meaningful pictures, his stars were all angling over who would take whom to bed.

While the merger was still being settled, Billy was loaned out to Universal for *The Gaiety Girl*. Again he had the leading male role, this time opposite Mary Philbin. *The Gaiety Girl*, however, was a trifle: Billy plays a wealthy Briton who saves the family castle and wins Philbin in the bargain.

Back on the home lot, King Vidor again chose Billy for a small part in his latest drama, *Wine of Youth*. The picture started under the Goldwyn banner; it was released as one of the first MGM productions. It must have been humbling for Billy to play leads during loan-outs, only to be handed small, supporting parts at his own studio. He welcomed the opportunity to work again with Vidor, and his part, if not large, was at least memorable.

In *Wine of Youth*, we see the first flash of the onscreen Billy Haines character that he would create over the next few years. He plays Hal, one of two suitors of Eleanor Boardman. Hal is brash and conceited; his rival, played by Ben Lyon, is quiet and devoted. Unlike the formula of later Haines films, in which the braggart eats humble pie and wins the girl, *Wine of Youth* ends predictably, with Boardman choosing Lyon.

The film, based on Rachel Crothers's play *Mary the Third*, offers a glimpse of the raucous social life of the times—a window on the parties Billy and his friends were throwing in real life. There's dancing on tops of pianos, lots of liquor being swilled, and girls and boys kissing passionately on sofas. The film is a prime example of the freedom with which filmmakers could work in the 1920s. A decade later, after the introduction of the Production Code, such a scenario could never have been filmed. In one party scene a drunken girl's blouse gets caught on a nail. It unravels as she walks until she is completely topless, although we see her only from the back. Later, when the young people go off unchaperoned, Ben Lyon asks if they're doing the right thing. "We're doing the *glorious* thing!" Eleanor insists. "The world's asleep and we're running away from it!"

Billy, again, was memorable mostly for his appearance. In a swimming scene, he looks terrific in a bathing suit: small waist, not an ounce of body fat, well-developed (but not overdeveloped) pectorals, biceps, and thighs. He was certainly leading man material, and he was envious that Ben Lyon had the sympathetic part. William (Buster) Collier, Jr., who had another small part in the film and who would go on to become a good friend, predicted that Billy would someday be the bigger star.

He began knocking out a new film every couple of months. The parts were all insignificant. He played a fellow partier with the wild Mae Murray in *Circe the Enchantress*; the loyal brother of Boardman in *Wife of the Centaur*, another Vidor film; and a war hero in *The Denial*, directed by Hobart Henley and released in March 1925. For the last, *Moving Picture World* actually singled out his role as Claire

Windsor's sweetheart who dies in the war, calling him "capable." He might have uttered something about damnation with faint praise.

As usual, he had better luck with loan-outs. Continuing his five-picture deal with Columbia, he made three more pictures there in rapid succession, starting with *A Fool and His Money*, filmed in late 1924 and released in January 1925. Directed by Erle Kenton, *A Fool and His Money* featured Billy as the new owner of yet another castle. He finds the wife of the previous owner (Madge Bellamy) hiding in the attic, and plays knight to the rescue when her demented former husband (Stuart Holmes) returns. All in all, a neat little thriller, with *Variety* commenting that Billy, "although stiff once or twice, has a Harold Lloyd-like face that suits the role."

His next two films on the Columbia lot — *Who Cares?* and *Fighting the Flames* — costarred Dorothy Devore. Both films gave Billy ample opportunity to play the hero, and in *Fighting the Flames* we see again a hint of what was to come: Billy as the irresponsible, wisecracking youth who learns his lesson and redeems himself just before the final fade-out. The picture had a simulated fire scene that necessitated firemen standing around the set with hoses ready. *Exhibitors Trade Review* gave him good marks: "William Haines is highly pleasing. . . . He looks the part he portrays, and renders a sympathetic performance."

In all, his Columbia experience was a happy one: He got to play leads, and the smaller, cozier atmosphere at the studio was refreshing after all the high-handed goings-on over at MGM. Despite Harry Cohn's reputation for unscrupulous behavior, Billy felt he'd been treated well. For Christmas, the studio distributed simple, homey Christmas gifts to everyone: Billy got a bathrobe. "It created a friendly spirit," Billy remembered, although he was probably one of the few actors to ever make a film at Columbia who would have used that particular adjective.

Success, to Billy, was defined as being able to live in the manner he chose. Certainly part of that was measured in opulence, even excess. He'd seen the way his wealthy friends had lived in New York, and he was beginning to live the same way himself in Hollywood. By now he was making considerably more money: The new studio paid significantly better than the old Goldwyn company. By early 1925 he was making $250 a week. The money was a rush in those pre–income tax days. He still sent a good chunk of his salary back home to Richmond, allowing Laura to quit her job and the family to buy their own home once again. That still left a good amount for Billy to use on himself.

The increased income allowed him to move into a larger, more elegant apartment at 729 North Western Avenue in Hollywood. It was a Spanish-style complex built around a courtyard, and Billy occupied a suite of rooms on the second floor. The trolley line ran not far from his door. He'd breeze out jauntily in the morning, twirling a cane and spiffed up in his newly bought, impeccably tailored clothes, whistling as he rode to the studio in Culver City.

He was never really interested in becoming a great actor. He'd landed in this Shangri-la by lucky accident, and he was determined to make the most of it. As a movie star, he could suddenly afford to buy the fine things and fine clothes he'd grown up wanting. He could discover the kind of high-spirited, jazz-baby friends who liked the same things he did: fun, frivolity, and finery. "I like the domestic life pictures permit one to live," he'd relate just a few years later, describing a Los Angeles that once was. "I like being able to go to my comfortable home every night and to drive through the cool, pure California air which still retains some vestige of perfume from flowering shrubs."

It was more than just living large that Billy sought. Being a star permitted him that independence he first experienced in Greenwich Village, the freedom to live an authentic life. In the Hollywood of the 1920s, unlike later decades, lifestyles were undisguised and rarely apologized for. Radical politics, drug use, heterosexual cohabitation, and homosexuality were all parts of the scene—integral parts, no more or less unusual than anything else. Certain things weren't acknowledged in public, of course, but in a world that both denied and decried their existence, those who lived on the social edge found Hollywood offered authenticity that would have been difficult to achieve anywhere else.

"Billy cared more about living the kind of life that allowed him to be who he was than any of the trappings of being a movie star," says one longtime friend. "Yes, part of that was being able to live as a stylish young man who liked nice things. Part of that was also being able to live as a homosexual man in a relatively open way."

He'd never had to hide who he was, not in Hopewell, not in the Village, and not now, in Hollywood. Just as there was no such thing as an "openly gay" person in those days—such a definition of one's public self, based on one's sexuality, did not yet exist—there was also no such thing as the "closet." While certain performers—Jack Benny, Rudolph Valentino—may have chosen to deny aspects of themselves both to friends and to strangers, many other gay men and lesbians in Hollywood lived lives of relative openness. The great star Alla Nazimova enjoyed titillating the press and the public with hints of lesbianism. Although she pretended to be married to a man, she was quite open in her relationships with women. Columnists wrote of her "mannish" suits and "all-girl" poolside parties at her house; she told *Photoplay* most of her friends were young girls. Most recently, her girl had been Natacha Rambova, the wife of Rudolph Valentino. Eugene O'Brien's homosexuality was common knowledge; the producer Joseph Schenck would encourage his casting opposite Schenck's wife, Norma Talmadge, because he knew no romance would arise out of their love scenes. Billy had every reason to expect such treatment himself. Even his cavalier relationship with the press didn't concern him, since even his publicists seemed to laugh at his wisecracks about Kate Price and his disdain for Peggy Hopkins Joyce. Being gay just wasn't a big deal in 1925, and there were few indications that that would ever change.

His career was given a major boost that year. After his string of leading loan-outs, he was finally rewarded with a leading male role at his home studio. The picture was *Mike*, originally called *Patsy*, and it commenced shooting in February 1925. It was directed by the highly regarded Marshall Neilan, whose career, even then, was on the decline. Neilan was a victim of his own drinking and incorrigible playboy nonchalance, but he had been an important director since

1915. His name still carried prestige, and Thalberg supported him at the studio, giving him plenty of free rein.

Mike was pure hokum of the sort Neilan was good for. Sally O'Neil, the latest Metro ingenue being groomed for stardom, plays the title role, a feisty Irish lass who learns of a gangland plan to rob her father's mail train. Again, Billy plays the part of the down-on-his-luck suitor, who proves his mettle by foiling the robbery. In a scene obviously inspired by his *Midnight Express* success for Columbia the year before, he rescues Sally and her family — trapped on board a caboose in the path of a fast-approaching passenger train — by jumping into a nearby engine and pushing the caboose out of the way.

The picture was filmed at El Cajon Pass near San Diego, and some later scenes were done near San Bernardino. The cast and crew lived for the duration in three Pullman cars on a siding off the main line of the Santa Fe Railroad. In the cast as Mike's young brother was a lively, freckle-faced eight-year-old named Frank "Junior" Coghlan. Although he'd made other films, this was his first important screen credit at a major studio. He made $75 a week for the roughly six weeks it took to make the picture.

Although he'd finally played his first real lead in an MGM picture, Billy would have to wait a year for its release, due to a feud between Neilan and Mayer. Meanwhile, he accepted a secondary part in *A Slave of Fashion*, directed by Hobart Henley and costarring Norma Shearer and Lew Cody. It premiered in August, and there was little reviewer comment on Billy's part.

So well known was Billy's sexuality by mid-1925 among the young Hollywood crowd that he could even dabble in the occasional heterosexual fling without his partner getting any false hopes. George Cukor, later a close friend of Billy, maintained that Billy had an affair with Norma Shearer, although he said the affair occurred *after* Norma had married Irving Thalberg. That's highly unlikely, since Thalberg was not only Billy's boss but his friend, and a very necessary ally against a hostile Louis B. Mayer.

"Bill Haines most certainly had an affair with Norma Shearer," says Shearer's biographer Lawrence Quirk, who knew both Billy and Cukor, from whom he heard the story. "That doesn't mean he was any less homosexual. He was just one of those guys who was narcissistic enough [to have an affair] if a woman came on to him by telling him he was attractive. . . . And I believe Norma understood that."

The affair most likely occurred during the filming of *A Slave of Fashion*, when Billy and Norma were often seen together around town. Norma's mother gave the pair her blessing, according to Anita Loos, because she considered Billy both amusing and *safe*. Several columnists mentioned the twosome, although no romance was hinted at. That's because there wasn't one. The affair was for one reason and one reason only: sex. Cukor, who was in a position to know (even if he got the date wrong), insisted that Billy had told him that Shearer was the "one woman who really got a *rise* out of me, and for *me*, that's saying a *mouthful*."

If heterosexual dalliances are difficult to substantiate, the homosexual ones are next to impossible. At around the same time Billy was slipping between the sheets with Norma Shearer, he may also have been involved in a much more significant relationship with Ramon Novarro.

William Haines and Ramon Novarro. They are the two best-known gay actors of the silent screen. Mention one, and someone's bound to ask about the other. That they would know each other and socialize with each other should come as no surprise. Both worked for MGM; both were young, beautiful, unattached, sexually adventurous, and comparatively open about being gay. If they *didn't* have an affair, it would be surprising. And the relationship, much more so than the tryst with Shearer, might even appropriately be called a romance.

"He was very fond of Ramon," says Lawrence Quirk, who knew both men. "Yes, they indeed had an affair. Ramon eventually got around to everyone. He had an obsession for good-looking young men."

Billy certainly would have told Cukor or other gay friends, but the vow of silence that so many of the crowd later imposed upon themselves would not permit repeating such a story. Cukor could feel free to reveal the decades-old affair with Shearer, but he—like so many others—would clam up the moment any direct question of homosexuality was asked.

During 1925 and 1926, Billy and Ramon were often photographed together, appearing in the fan magazines as widely grinning "buddies" with their arms draped around each other's shoulders. In the 1970s, author Jane Ellen Wayne interviewed an unidentified former MGM technician, gay himself, who recalled Billy and Ramon as a pair, saying that it was common knowledge the two of them went out on the town together. Billy would often mention Ramon in interviews—there's a famous line of his in which he quipped that he and Novarro "sang in the same church choir."

Novarro was born José Ramon Gil Samaniegos in Durango, Mexico, in 1899, to a large and socially prominent family. They moved to Los Angeles in 1914. Ramon was a delicate, sweet-natured, generous boy. His dream was to become a great opera singer, and indeed his voice was strong and melodious. He sang in some vaudeville revues that toured California, danced in the company of choreographer Marion Morgan, and to make some extra money he posed nude for art classes at the J. Francis Smith School of Art in downtown Los Angeles. His body was perfectly natural, and naturally perfect.

He became friends with a handsome young Italian actor by the name of Rodolpho di Valentina, born Guglielmi, who was then working as a supporting player in such films as *A Society Sensation* and *Eyes of Youth*. Later, of course, he'd become Rudolph Valentino, and his carefully constructed "Great Lover" persona would be plagued by whispers of homosexuality. In 1917–1918, however, rumors didn't bother him, and the two exquisitely beautiful Latin boys reportedly enjoyed a brief but memorable romance.

Ramon followed Rudy into films. By 1920 he was working frequently as a bit player at a number of studios, although his goal remained the opera. The next year, Rex Ingram pulled him out of a line of extras to give him the lead in *The Prisoner of Zenda*, and he became an overnight success. Roles followed that showed off his swashbuckling skills and, more important, his physical assets. In *Where the Pavement Ends*, he was practically naked, causing one reviewer to scoff that he was "almost too beautiful to be taken seriously." With the release of *Scaramouche* in 1922, he became a serious rival for his old lover Valentino's throne. Mayer was quick to give him a contract, but he could barely tolerate him in person: Novarro's effeminacy offended Mayer's sense of masculine propriety. Still, by 1925, Ramon Novarro was one of the biggest stars on the Metro lot, and more than anything else, Mayer respected good box office.

That Novarro was one of the studio's most valuable assets underlies Mayer's rage when a scandal in the making was brought to his attention, a scandal involving both Ramon and Billy Haines. During the filming of *A Slave of Fashion*, Billy and Lew Cody, who had the lead, got into a war of words. There were few actors whom Billy didn't like, or at least pretend to like—but Cody was one of them. Billy called him a stuffed shirt; pomposity without any self-conscious humor was the one characteristic Billy couldn't abide. Cody promptly stormed off the set and marched straight to Mayer's office to tattle. He'd heard stories about Billy and Ramon frequenting a male bordello on Wilshire Boulevard, and he just thought that Mayer might want to know.

The story originates, as so many of them do, with Anita Loos, who wasn't yet on the Metro lot but who seemed to know everything that went on in Hollywood, and was usually fairly accurate. According to Loos, it was Billy who "got called on the carpet," as Mayer refused to believe the more soft-spoken Novarro had been the ringleader. Hal Elias, who was working in the publicity department at the time, said it was genuinely believed by the studio brass that star misbehavior—straight or gay—"could scuttle the ship." Mayer wanted to fire Billy right then and there. This was prevented, Loos writes, by William Randolph Hearst, although the timing seems a little early for his friendship with Billy. More likely it was Thalberg who intervened, saving Billy's head from the chopping block. Nonetheless, it's the first recorded clash between Billy and Mayer. The outraged MGM chief, according to Loos, pulled strings with police to close down the brothel, and ordered Novarro never to see Billy Haines again.

Harry Hay, a young actor at the time who went on to become one of the founders of the gay rights movement, remembers the area along Wilshire Boulevard well. Most of the houses were three- and four-story mansions owned by some of the city's most prominent families. "A number of those old mansions, when they had been inherited by younger folks, had been redivided into living quarters with separate wings [and] separate studios," Hay says. Some housed "newfangled" hair salons, but Hay doubts that a fully operational bordello could have coexisted in such a setting. The affluent, influential families living nearby would have "run them all out of the county."

Still, he doesn't dismiss the story. One of those subdivided mansions, inherited by a "temperamental" son (the word sometimes used in 1920s Los Angeles for "homosexual"), could easily have been employed for such purposes. "A male brothel [on Wilshire Boulevard] would have had to have been a *veddy proper* Society Establishment, superintended by a dutiful younger son," Hay surmises. In such a place, Billy and Ramon could have entered through the front door, shared a cigar in the parlor and maybe a glass of sherry, before ascending the stairs to try out the wares.

Clearly neither Billy nor Ramon paid much attention to Mayer's edict that they not see each other again: Henry Haines recalls seeing Novarro at Billy's beach house in Santa Monica in the late 1920s. All suggestion of a romance or an affair disappears after this episode, however. They would remain friendly for a number of years, until Ramon, haunted by personal tragedy and unfulfilled ambition, retreated deeper into reclusiveness and alcoholism. In the end, these two stars—sharing so much in common in 1925—couldn't have become more dissimilar.

Billy's friendship with Shearer continued through their next film together, *The Tower of Lies*, filmed during the late spring and released in October. This was a major film, starring box-office champ Lon

Chaney and helmed by the renowned Swedish director Victor Sjostrom. Chaney has the top-billed part as a debt-ridden farmer. He imagines his daughter (Shearer) to be a prostitute and drives her out of the house. Billy has the secondary role as Norma's faithful childhood sweetheart, whom she marries in the end.

It was not a pleasant collaboration for Billy. "Sjostrom, being Swedish, had a chilly exterior and never took the trouble to look inside," he'd recall. "However, he was treated with the elegant respect accorded a Viking god by Mr. Mayer."

Sjostrom's reserve and Mayer's fawning only served to intimidate Billy, who for the first time seemed genuinely concerned about his talent in front of the camera. It had been more than three years, after all, and he had watched Boardman, La Marr, Shearer, and Aileen Pringle improve their techniques and get rewarded for it.

"I felt everything depended on this film," Billy said. 'This time it was do or die." So anxious had he made himself that he became violently sick — ironically, in the middle of a love scene with Shearer — and was sent home to bed by Sjostrom. "I told the director it was just a touch of ptomaine. I couldn't tell him the real truth." According to his own account, he spent the rest of the day in bed crying.

Something more was going on here than mere nerves. Many would attest to Billy's often jarring mood swings. "There's no middle ground with Billy Haines," said one magazine article, "he's either laughing or depressed."

Time and again, there is the suggestion of a manic-depressive personality. Billy fits the profile: high levels of energy, often outlandish behavior, followed by periods of despondency and quiet. Yet he remained highly functional; there are no reports of any serious bout with depression that left him unable to work.

It would appear that after the run-in with Mayer, Billy realized he needed to safeguard the lifestyle he so prized by making himself more valuable. He may have also realized that a top star salary could buy much more in the way of fine clothes and furniture. Although he'd gotten yet another raise, Chaney and Novarro were making $3,000 a week to Billy's $400. Norma Shearer made $2,000, Eleanor Boardman $1,500, and Aileen Pringle $750. Such disparity in income must have been a motivating factor in both his determination and his dissatisfaction.

He reported back to work on the set of *Tower of Lies*. "I argued the thing out with myself," he recalled. "Why should I be afraid of the camera? It was an inanimate object and couldn't reach out and bite me on the chin. It had the faculty of photographing thought as well as features. I made up my mind that I would think more of what I was doing, to try and live the role."

It was sound advice, and he repeated it to his new friend, Joan Crawford, who could have given him a crash course in ambition. She'd arrived on the lot in the early months of 1925, having been brought out from Kansas City by Harry Rapf. She had the godawful name of Lucille Le Sueur, and she'd stand wide-eyed, freckled, and fiercely determined in the wings watching Norma Shearer or Eleanor Boardman emote. At night, she'd hustle herself back to her little apartment to reenact the scenes in front of her mirror. Billy, meanwhile, had spent his first three years in Hollywood just having a gay old time.

Such was the difference between them, and maybe it explains why it took so long for Billy Haines to reach the heights, whereas it took only a matter of months for Lucille Le Sueur to become Joan Crawford and elbow her way to the front of the pack.

Of all Billy's new Hollywood friends, none would prove more loyal, more devoted, more enduring than Joan Crawford.

Her new name was chosen by a movie magazine contest when the new head of publicity, Pete Smith, decided quite wisely that Lucille Le Sueur would never do. But she wasn't sure the new name was any better. "Joan *Crawford*!" she whined to Billy. "It sounds like 'Crawfish.'"

"Crawford's not so bad," he told her. "They might have called you 'Cranberry' and served you every Thanksgiving with the turkey." Turkey, of course, was Hollywood lingo for box-office flop. The name stuck: He called her "Cranberry" for the remainder of their decades-long friendship.

If anyone was responsible for Crawford's stardom (other than the indomitable lady herself), it was Billy. Although she arrived in Hollywood with an impetuous determination to learn the craft, it was Billy who explained the other side of being a star. "Let me give you some advice," he told her, in a story that is certainly apocryphal but nonetheless illustrates the truth of their early friendship. "You've got to draw attention to yourself. There are fifty other girls trying to get roles in pictures, and the producers don't know one pretty face from another. You've got to make yourself *known*. Get yourself some *publicity*. Go to dances and premieres. Let people know that Joan Crawford is *somebody*." There is a certain symmetry in the fact that a gay man—and one as open as Billy—helped create a phenomenon like Crawford, a quintessential gay icon.

She and Billy would dance the night away at the Montmartre or the Coconut Grove, located in Hollywood's Ambassador Hotel. She also began dating a series of men, several of whom won dancing trophies with her at the nightclubs. She became the queen of the Charleston, swinging her beaded skirts with near-manic fury as she shimmied the sexy dance on the tops of tables and pianos. Louella Parsons wrote, "It was remarkable to watch the abandon with which she threw herself into the dance."

Billy and Joan clicked immediately. He adored her energy, her gritty determination. For her part, Joan found Billy's irreverence a beguiling balance to her self-conscious ambition. She could be coarse and crude as well as highbrow and sophisticated. She was also voraciously sexual: While preferring men, she was also attracted to women, and that essential bisexuality was another link to Billy.

In one interview, Billy said he and Eddie Goulding (who by 1925 was an MGM director) took Joan under their wing because so many had been put off by her broad Oklahoma accent and undisguised ambition. There's a story that someone in the front office— Thalberg, maybe—suggested to Billy that Joan would make a good wife, since she was so understanding of his sexuality. But Billy rejected the idea categorically. It would have destroyed a beautiful friendship.

They really *were* best friends, and remained so for almost fifty years. "They 'grew up' together in Hollywood," says Joan's daughter, Christina Crawford. "She was fiercely loyal [to Billy] because he knew her when she was young." In later years, as the finely edged Crawford persona became manifest, Billy was one of the few still around her who remembered the wide-eyed kid just off the train from Kansas City named Lucille Le Sueur. As such, he was permitted liberties—like slapping her butt in public—that no one else would dare to try.

Billy had other pals as well—all women. There was Hedda Hopper, a brittle, bristly character actress who'd made *Sinners in Silk* with Eleanor Boardman and *The Snob* with Norma Shearer. Old enough to be Billy's mother, Hedda did indeed play mother confessor to the younger actors on the lot, learning all their secrets and uncovering their skeletons. Despite their trust in her, she wasn't averse to using such information for her own advantage, or passing on particularly juicy stories. It was a habit that eventually lost her several friends, but served her well in her second career a decade later, as Hollywood's most shrewish gossip columnist.

Hopper gathered around her a clique of younger males. That some of her young admirers were gay didn't faze her in the slightest, but she usually urged them to marry some girl who "understood the situation." Billy just laughed at the idea, and Hedda didn't press the issue. She was far too enthralled with the life they all were living to push her point. Despite her protestations of propriety, Hopper swore like a sailor and refused to go gracefully into sedate middle age. She wore flashy clothes and eschewed friends of her own generation to spend evenings with her twentysomething crowd. While she personally was never known to take a lover, she thrilled to the amorous exploits of the younger Hollywood set, both gay and straight.

Among that younger set, Constance Talmadge blazed like a gilded butterfly. She was witty, straightforward, and devil-may-care, and she and Billy Haines became particular chums. How he met her is unclear, since she didn't work for MGM—and Metro players, in Billy's own words, "looked down our noses at actors from other studios." It's possible—perhaps likely—that he was introduced to her by Irving Thalberg, who was actively pursuing her at the time. Billy had consented to escort Thalberg's sister Sylvia to various functions, and Irving, pleased to see his sister treated so well, was grateful to Billy. He invited him to accompany the Thalberg family to their resort at Lake Arrowhead. On several occasions, Billy piled into the backseat of the Thalberg car with Sylvia and Thalberg's mother, while Irving and his father rode up front. Billy found the bickerings of the tight-knit but querulous family amusing, and this made him consider bringing his own clan out to California if he ever made enough money.

Despite their friendship, Thalberg may have harbored some resentment toward Billy. Irving had pursued Peggy Hopkins Joyce without success a year before, just at the time her crush on Billy Haines was the talk of the town. And now the blossoming friendship between Billy and Constance Talmadge may have given Thalberg pause.

Affectionately known as "Dutch" to her friends, Talmadge had been making films since she was a teenager in 1914 and showed no sign of slowing down. High-living, free-loving, and drop-dead gorgeous, the sassy, saucy heroines she played on the screen were no match for her real-life personality. Billy adored her, and their hijinks left the obsessed Thalberg out in the cold.

Screenwriter Anita Loos would recall, "Every night Irving used to hide in the shadows across from the Talmadge residence in Beverly Hills and wait, just to watch Dutch return at dawn with the slaphappy young comedy star Bill Haines. . . . In one sense, Irving couldn't be jealous, because Bill [was] as gay as a jaybird. But it was true that Dutch preferred laughing it up with [Billy Haines] to making love to Irving."

What set the friendships with Talmadge, Hopper, and Crawford apart from the relationship with Barbara La Marr was the simple fact that they did not fall in love with him. Part of the reason may be Billy's greater openness about himself. Although La Marr certainly knew of his homosexuality, they were also probably lovers, which left her hoping he might be "converted." Billy seems to have learned a lesson from the La Marr affair: There was no ambiguity to his friendships with Dutch and Cranberry. In the parlance of today, such women are affectionately referred to as "fag hags."

"They were like a couple of girlfriends," one longtime friend recalls of Billy and Joan Crawford, but the same could be said about a number of his close female buddies. There was a comfort, a camaraderie, but most of all, an honesty between them. They knew his story; he knew theirs. There would be no such "quarrels" as the one that ended his relationship with La Marr.

After his experience during *Tower of Lies*, Billy applied himself to acting. He wasn't sure how much talent he had, but he determined to do his best. That didn't mean he slowed down his revels outside the studio. He remained the party boy, but he now gave as much attention to his work as he gave to play.

He landed the opportunity of a lifetime in *Little Annie Rooney*, released by United Artists. His costar was the most popular actress in the world: America's Sweetheart, Mary Pickford. She had liked Billy in *The Midnight Express*, and specifically requested to borrow him from MGM. Such generosity did not translate into friendship, however. "Miss Pickford was at the height of her career," Billy recalled, "and the rest of the cast and crew were treated with the respect shown an unwanted relative."

Pickford had her reasons to be testy on the set. She hadn't had an unqualified hit in three years; she was damn sick of playing little girl parts; and a plot to kidnap her had just been uncovered. A bodyguard was posted on the set, and Little Mary walked around with a Colt .45 in her dress pocket. The conspirators were finally caught, but Mary remained jittery and antisocial with her costars.

Based on the sentimental old song, *Little Annie Rooney* is the sentimental tale of a young girl out to avenge the death of her father, a New York City cop. "Get out the rubber boots, Mary has got to cry," called director William Beaudine on the day of Mary's big scene. Getting second billing under Pickford, Billy plays Joe, a ruffian with a heart of gold whom Annie loves and who gets falsely accused of the murder. Pickford's acquiescence to her fans paid off: *Little*

Annie Rooney turned out to be her biggest smash in years, restoring her to the top of the box office. It also helped bring notice to the career of William Haines, despite his rather standard, thankless part. The *New York Times* called him "effective."

Back at MGM, he again played leading man—this time to three leading ladies. The story of three showgirls and the various choices they make, *Sally, Irene and Mary* premiered December 27, 1925, starring Constance Bennett, Joan Crawford, Sally O'Neil, and William Haines (in that order). Sally (Bennett) is the brassy, self-assured chorine in search of a sugar daddy. Irene (Crawford) is romantic and easily seduced by con men. Predictably, she dies tragically. Mary (O'Neil) is the true heroine, leaving all that sordidness behind to settle down with Billy, playing yet another upstanding young man, this time a plumber.

He was friendly with all three actresses, although Bennett, the most established of the three, had little time for socializing. He'd made *Mike* with O'Neil—it still wasn't released—and of course, he enjoyed making his first picture with Cranberry Crawford. It was with director Edmund Goulding that Billy had the most interesting relationship. Goulding, a sensitive, dedicated craftsman, was pretty open about his homosexuality, although, like most gay men in screenland, he was married. He was known for orgies at his home, in which both men and women would cavort in all-night revelries. It's possible, perhaps likely, that Billy participated; it would certainly not have been out of character.

There was another, more important connection: Goulding was an actor's director, attuned to actors' concerns and struggles. A former actor himself, Goulding sensed Billy's growing attempt to define himself as a performer, and took particular care with his part. It's unfortunate that they never worked together again. For the most part, Billy's pictures would be charted by competent but pedestrian directors, offering little in the way of creative inspiration or encouragement.

A notable exception was John M. Stahl, who directed Billy's next film, *Memory Lane*. It's not surprising that Billy turns in his best performance to date in this picture, as Stahl was a master at eliciting strong emotion in his intensely passionate, personal melodramas. He had signed with Louis B. Mayer before the merger, and Mayer adored his work, filled with the themes of family love and domestic devotion that he so prized.

Memory Lane is a gorgeous film: superbly lit, carefully edited, sensitively scripted. Once again united with Eleanor Boardman, Billy plays the man she has loved since girlhood. Finding him unavailable, she settles for Conrad Nagel, a decent, if less than passionate, husband. The film is a careful study of the three principal characters, building to the emotional climax of Billy's return. Eleanor's married to Nagel by this time, but her heart still belongs to Billy. She is nervous and edgy awaiting his arrival, and when he appears, he shatters her dream: he has become boorish and inconsiderate. Her fantasy of what might have been is replaced by a loathing of the jerk he has become, and Nagel suddenly seems far more appealing in her eyes.

But wait: Stahl has a surprise in store. For after Billy leaves the house, with Eleanor securely in Nagel's arms, he falls back against the door in a sudden collapse of emotion. He had been putting on a front, of course, designed to wipe his haunting image from Eleanor's mind and allow her the freedom to find happiness with Nagel. In that one instant, Billy Haines supersedes all his previous work: He is utterly convincing, and heartrending.

"We all thought at the time that *Memory Lane* was an outstanding picture," Billy recalled. "It suffered, though, for lack of exploitation." Stahl was still fulfilling a commitment to distribute his pictures through First National, which meant Metro-Goldwyn-Mayer offered little support to *Memory Lane*. Mayer tried his best, but ultimately, neither studio promoted the film with much vigor. It premiered on January 17, 1926, to favorable reviews. *Motion Picture News* said it was "a tale that tugs at the heart strings. . . . Conrad Nagel and William Haines do exceptionally well as rival suitors."

With the exception of one more film with King Vidor (*Show People*, in which he agreed to take a backseat role to Marion Davies), Billy never again worked with a director of the caliber of Stahl or Goulding. Which is a shame: As an actor, William Haines never developed much beyond the two-note role he played in *Memory Lane*—the noble young man and the boorish cad. While effective here, he was never given the opportunity to explore the finer shadings of such characterizations. While his greatest days as a movie star still lay in the future, his last shot at becoming an actor of sophistication and skill ended the day John Stahl called his final "cut."

The picture that finally established William Haines as a top box-office star was 1926's *Brown of Harvard*.

There was considerable advance publicity surrounding the picture. Jack Conway was set to direct, and its star was Jack Pickford, Mary's brother and a talented actor in his own right. MGM had signed him for a two-picture deal, but Jack was on his way out: At age twenty-nine and already a rapidly declining alcoholic, he hardly looked the part of the collegiate hero. Still, Pete Smith was banging the drums loudly for *Brown of Harvard*. Several newspaper accounts detailed Conway's search for an authentic college kid to play Tom Brown, Pickford's roommate (and the title role). Conway tested scores of athletes at UCLA, USC, and Harvard. He eventually told the press that college boys simply "do not act collegiate enough," so he had to resort to an actor.

Much of that was probably hype, although several weeks passed with Tom Brown still uncast. Billy waged an all-out campaign to win the part. The part of the wisecracking, conceited college hero — who gets his comeuppance at the end, winning the audience's sympathy—seemed tailored to Billy. "I determined that no one but William Haines would play the role of Tom Brown," Billy said. "The executives were just as determined that anybody *but* William Haines would play it."

Conway, a hard-edged, straightforward director who had gotten his start as an assistant to D. W. Griffith, was adamantly opposed to Billy Haines as Tom Brown. There was no personal animosity: Despite the director's aggressively heterosexual posture, he had no personal bias against homosexuals, having long enjoyed the friendship of playwright John Colton and others. It was simply that given Billy's résumé, there was little to recommend him. Tom Brown, despite the ostensible star Jack Pickford, *carried* the script. Conway saw nothing in Billy's previous work to convince him he had the power to work that magic.

So Billy went to Thalberg, who backed him up. It was through his intervention that Billy was cast, and Conway could do little but shrug and accept it. These were still the days when producers rode roughshod over directors, where casting decisions and running length and final script approval still came from the front office. Conway cautioned Billy: "Don't think you can steal the picture from Jack." Billy just grinned.

The story would evolve into the classic Haines formula: Billy's character starts out as a rude, conceited oaf but transforms into a noble hero. At Harvard, Tom Brown, a cocky, smart-aleck athlete, is idolized by his frail roommate, Jim, played by Pickford. There is a good deal of conscious or unconscious homoeroticism in *Brown of Harvard*. Jim loves Tom far more than Tom loves Mary (played by Mary Brian), the ostensible love interest. Tom is devoted to Jim as well. The director Ernst Lubitsch said he'd jacked up the underlying homoeroticism in *The Student Prince* when he realized Ramon Novarro was gay; Conway may have done something similar here. *Brown of Harvard* is, bottom line, a love story between Tom and Jim.

Billy certainly performs naturally enough. "I thought and planned for that role," he remembered. His inspiration came from the once-great star Charles Ray, who had specialized as the backwoods yokel dropped down in the middle of the big city. Although Ray's star had dimmed by 1926, Billy had loved his pictures in the past, especially the scenes where the brash city slickers try to do him in. Ray was a strikingly handsome lad—and many had commented on Billy's physical resemblance to him. "So I determined to take a Charles Ray character, turn him inside out and make him the freshest punk that ever drew breath."

It worked. In that single burst of inspiration, Billy had created a new screen type—and for the next couple of years he practically owned the patent on it. He bounced off of Jack Pickford with such zest and speed that at times Pickford seems stunned, unable to volley back. Word of mouth spread quickly that Billy was doing just what Conway had said he couldn't: stealing the picture right out from under Pickford's nose. Witty subtitles written by the famed humorist Donald Ogden Stewart helped propel the humor along; some were inspired by Billy's own ad-libbing on the set.

He knew he'd succeeded when he overheard Conway telling an assistant to watch "that young punk put the scene over." At first he thought Conway referred to Pickford. "Then I realized he meant me — Pickford was in bed asleep and couldn't be doing much emoting. That was the first I realized that I was good."

Brown of Harvard was shot in just over three weeks. Billy then shuttled over to Columbia to fulfill his five-picture deal. He played an author mistaken for a king in the farce *The Thrill Hunter*. It caused little comment, although *Variety* said Billy gave a "nice Harold Lloyd performance."

Conway, meanwhile, screened *Brown* for Thalberg after it had been cut and printed. Thalberg, who was often surrounded by yes-men, brought several of his assistants to watch the film. Confident of Billy's performance and Stewart's witty titles, Conway was stunned when the opening reels didn't produce so much as a snicker from the producer. "I was dying," he recalled. "It didn't seem possible. Suddenly the film broke and the lights came on. Irving was sitting down in front of all of us; he hadn't moved or made a sound. But now he turned around and said very slowly, 'Jack, if the last reels are as good as those we've seen, we've got the comedy hit of the year!'"

The moment had arrived. After four long years, William Haines was suddenly a star. Upon the film's release in April, reviewers practically ignored the rest of the cast. *Variety* said, "Haines is corking in the name part. He not only looks collegiate and like a halfback, but paces his performance to a nicety, in which glib subtitles are more than the usual help . . . an outstanding performance by Haines."

Moving Picture World agreed. "The work of the various players does much to forward the interest [but it is] William Haines well to the fore in the name-part."

Even more important, *Brown of Harvard* was a smash at the box office. It cost $164,000 and made $276,000, a significant profit of more than $100,000. Such figures even enticed Louis B. Mayer to shake Billy's hand and clap him on the back.

Even with all of the praise ringing in his ears in the spring of 1926, Billy could not drown out the news of the tragic death of Barbara La Marr.

Over the last few years, she'd continued to drink heavily and had developed an addiction to cocaine. She ate until she became fat, seeming determined to destroy any last vestiges of her beauty. Her doctor ordered a crash diet; according to legend, he prescribed sugar-coated tapeworms that ate out her insides.

Then, in October 1925, she collapsed on the set of her last film, *The Girl from Montmarte*. She was diagnosed with galloping tuberculosis. Her once-repudiated father—the one who'd had to take a backseat to a fictional Italian count—rushed to her side. "She is very, very ill," Mr. Watson told the press. "She couldn't stand the strain. It was too much for her."

That's as apt a eulogy as any. Her father permitted no one to see her. If Billy even tried—which is doubtful—he would have been rebuffed. Barbara La Marr, the girl who was too beautiful, wasted to a pitiful skeleton and died on January 30, 1926, around the time Billy Haines was completing the performance that would finally make him a star.

At her funeral, forty thousand fans filed past Barbara La Marr's casket. It is not known if Billy was one of them. They had both traveled a great deal away from each other in the last three years. Billy had survived: growing up, dedicating himself to the task at hand, staying true to himself. Barbara La Marr, never quite sure of what the truth really was, died as she had lived: a lonely, frightened little girl.

4

FREE AND EASY

1926-1928

During the years when he'd been struggling, when it seemed as if his whole move to Hollywood had been a joke, Billy vowed never to return home to Virginia until he'd made it. He kept that vow. Shortly after completion of *Brown of Harvard*, but before its release, Billy took a well-earned vacation, boarding a train to Richmond.

His name was well-known enough now that when Virginia newspapers ran ads for his films, he was referred to as "the Staunton boy." *Brown of Harvard* had yet to be released, so there were no marching bands to greet him at the train station. George and Laura were there, however, and Billy was delighted to see them. George Haines was doing better now as an investments broker, but the check that arrived regularly from Hollywood was still a big help. The black sheep who'd run away at fourteen hadn't forgotten the promise he'd made to them all those years ago.

His parents took him to the Cohen Company, where he glad-handed his former colleagues. George and Laura stood back and watched him: They must have wondered who this self-assured, outgoing young man was. He was not the shy, introspective Billy Haines of Staunton. This was a man who had blossomed, who had discovered his identity apart from them, who had defined himself according to a model outside of their experience. They seem to have accepted their son's transformation with equanimity, if not yet with full understanding. Of course, they had every reason *to* accept it: Billy's Hollywood earnings had made all of their lives better, and they were now glimpsing a world they never would have known had it not been for the adventures of their son.

That he had changed significantly from his Staunton days was no doubt the impetus for Billy's insistence to his parents that they visit the old hometown. "To tell you the truth," he recalled later, "I expected to stir up a little bit of a flurry." Which high school bullies might he have hoped to impress upon his return? Which teachers who had discouraged him in his dreams did he want to prove wrong? In fact, the proprietor of the New Theatre had made George Haines promise that the next time Billy came home, he'd bring him by for a special appearance. Billy, with a grin even wider than usual, agreed.

He had not seen his hometown in nearly a decade. "Somehow the hills were no longer so high," Billy wrote of the place where he first dreamed his dreams. "The trees looked like any other trees . . . and the buildings, which once had seemed to tower into the sky, now looked small, and the bank windows needed washing. The illusion was lost, and one can never recapture an illusion. It is never wise to go back to the past. One should always go on in life."

There was no flurry, as he had hoped. Billy found he could walk along the streets without attracting much attention. Local historian Sergei Troubetzkoy tells of old-time Staunton residents who remembered Billy's first visit home. One man in his eighties recalled being a teenager, sitting at the soda fountain and raising his mug to Billy, who was spotted across the street. Billy came over and shook his hand. While no throngs clawed at Billy's clothes, a respectable crowd did turn out to welcome him at the theater, and a couple of his films were screened.

One former neighbor recalled seeing Billy strolling with his mother nostalgically past their old house on North Coalter Street. "I saw this young man all dressed up, derby, white gloves, spats, and cane," she said. "He fooled me for the moment, but I instantly recognized his mother. It flashed across my mind that this was no one but little Billy Haines. He threw his arms around me and kissed me just as he used to do. He was the same old Billy."

He hardly knew eight-year-old Henry, who looked up at his movie-star brother with quiet awe. Sister Ann had married James Langhorne, the son of a distinguished Virginia family, and sister Lillion had moved to New York with her husband, James Stone. Ann had a baby son, named after his father, who was just two at the time of Billy's visit. Life had gone on. While he could not have functioned within the conventional constructs of his family and life in Richmond, he nonetheless longed for a sense of stability, a sense of family and home that his high life in Hollywood, for all its freedom, failed to provide.

From Richmond he headed to New York, to visit with his other family: Mitt Foster, Larry Sullivan, Jack Kelly, and the rest. It would turn out to be a momentous trip: If he was feeling just a trifle lonely, a little unsettled (he was, after all, twenty-six years old and still unattached), all that was about to change.

In early 1926, Billy met Jimmie Shields, the one great love of his life.

Their first encounter was hardly auspicious. "I think Billy picked him up on the street," says Arch Case, who became a friend in the 1950s. "There was always talk that was how they met," echoes another longtime friend, Bob Wheaton. Jimmie was a sailor, and there were dozens of public parks and bathhouses in New York where men met each other. Both Billy and Jimmie would have stood out from the crowd: young, attractive men, their eyes locking through the darkness. Jimmie was handsome, with a strong jaw and classic profile. Shorter than Billy, he was nonetheless well-muscled, freshly twenty-one, and eager.

Names aren't usually exchanged in parks and bathhouses. Often there is very little dialogue at all. Somehow Billy and Jimmie connected, and they arranged to get together again. Whether Jimmie knew right away that this was the star of *Little Annie Rooney* and other pictures is unknown. Perhaps his time at sea had left him unfa-

miliar with the latest movies. Still, he would have discovered it soon
enough, and within days, Billy was rarely seen without the handsome young Jimmie at his side.

Jimmie had been born James Shields Fickeisen on May 24, 1905,
in Pittsburgh, the son of Irwin Marquis Fickeisen and Ida Belle
Shields. Named for his maternal grandfather, Jimmie would drop
the Fickeisen after his parents divorced, although he never legally
disowned the name. His mother was a strong-willed matriarch,
known throughout her life to all in the community as "Aunt Ida." After Fickeisen gambled all their life savings in a failed hotel venture,
Jimmie's father left his family, only to lose even more money in
the Crash of 1929. Ida secured a divorce and remarried Joseph
Haselden of Kentucky, her former husband's business partner. The
family, including Jimmie's two sisters Margaret and Virginia, then
moved to Daytona Beach, Florida. Later, another son was born from
her second marriage, named Joseph after his father but always
known as "Bunny." The family became well placed in Florida society. The elder Haselden would later serve as mayor of the town of
Holly Hill.

Jimmie, however, did not stay in Florida long. In 1924, just before his nineteenth birthday, he enlisted in the Navy. It may have
been at the urging of his stepfather, who wanted to make a "man"
out of the too-pretty, effeminate teenager. He served as a pharma-
cist's mate, third class, on the S.S. *Newport, Rhode Island*. Not a year
into his service he came down with meningitis and was horribly sick
for a long period with high fevers, severe headaches, and convul-
sions. Miraculously, since so many died from meningitis at the time,
he survived, and was honorably discharged in November 1925.
Rather than return to Florida, he chose to live with his uncle
Howard Fickeisen in New York, at 445 West 124th Street. He met
Billy just a few months after that.

It was a brief, whirlwind romance. Billy had to return to Los
Angeles—*Brown* was about to be released and he was set to start another picture—and he urged Jimmie to follow, promising him extra
work. Jimmie agreed to come. He convinced his sister Virginia—

who, as Miss Florida, had won a dancing job at the Paramount Theater—that this was their big chance. Larry Sullivan, too, was headed west: Billy had offered him a job as his private secretary. Mitt planned to joined him later. Together, Jimmie, Larry, and Virginia boarded a train for California.

Billy, true to his word, found Jimmie work at MGM as an extra and stand-in. Their romance continued, and it wasn't long before they viewed themselves as a committed couple. Billy had Mitt and Larry's example in establishing the relationship; there was every reason to think he could enjoy the same commitment they had. Jimmie (along with Larry Sullivan) moved in with Billy on North Western Avenue. Virginia Fickeisen roomed with Joan Crawford for a period, working as an extra in some of Crawford's pictures. By all accounts, Jimmie was dazzled by the world he had so fortuitously stumbled into: lunching with Joan Crawford and Eleanor Boardman, being driven by chauffeurs, dressing in fabulous costumes to wear in front of the camera.

Like many people who come from modest means, Jimmie reveled in his sudden affluence. Billy indulged him, surprising him with flowers and gifts of jewelry. This would remain the pattern for their entire relationship. As the steady boyfriend of movie-star William Haines, Jimmie took himself quite seriously—ironically affecting the kind of attitude Billy loathed in others. "Jimmie's real name was Fickeisen," says longtime friend Michael Pearman, one of the few still living who knew Billy and Jimmie during the MGM years. "I'd always tease him, calling him Chicken Fricasee. He didn't think it was funny. He didn't really have any sense of humor."

Jimmie wasn't all superficiality. He was forever giving his friends presents, and never failed to tip waiters and bellhops generously. He also had a soft spot for beggars and charity drives: It was as if he felt he needed to share his unexpected fortune with as many people as possible. His family adored him, much as Billy's adored him. Like Billy, Jimmie was generous with his family back in Florida. "Jimmie was quite bountiful throughout his life," says his nephew, Charlie Conrad. "He loved very good things and I received many beautiful items from him." Jimmie never threw out his clothes; after he'd wear

them for a year or so, they'd be shipped out to his nephews back
east.

Jimmie may have enjoyed being spoiled by Billy, but Billy relished
even more the act of spoiling him. Despite all his close friendships, what had been missing for Billy in the midst of all his Hollywood revelry was a sense of family. Jimmie gave him that. At
age twenty-six, a time when most young men had already settled
down into domesticity, Billy decided he had found the man he
wanted to spend the rest of his life with. That in itself—in a time
when homosexual relationships were rare even in tolerant communi-
ties like Hollywood—is a radical act. Billy's fiercely determined
commitment to the union is even more iconoclastic. In Hollywood,
many actors had already been married, divorced, and married
again by the time they were Billy's age. Billy would never have any
serious affair that would threaten his relationship with Jimmie. Although their relationship would remain open sexually, prompting
occasional tension, there was never the kind of disruption that
marred the marital lives of such friends as Joan Crawford or
Eleanor Boardman.

Billy had found something with Jimmie that many couples—gay
or straight—never find: contentment. When he came home from the
studio, there was someone waiting for him, someone to whom he
could devote himself. "Spoiled rotten" was how more than one
friend described Jimmie. Billy loved spoiling him as much as Jimmie enjoyed being spoiled, and so they were, despite any external
differences, the perfect pair.

Once *Brown of Harvard* was released, Billy found himself a full-
fledged star. He couldn't quite believe his fortune: He'd sneak off
to theaters on the outskirts of Los Angeles, turn his collar up, and
slink into the back row. He'd watch and listen in awe as the audience laughed and applauded. Each time, he was staggered by the
experience.

He told the story of encountering a couple of hecklers at one
showing. "Look at the mouth on it!" one of them called when Tom
Brown got his comeuppance and starts to cry.

"Well, you're no Helen of Troy yourself," Billy huffed, but the hecklers paid him no mind.

The second one chimed in, "Will you look at that great big guy crying like a woman! He ought to be moving pianos."

"Moving pianos don't pay so well," the first heckler said, and they both laughed.

Billy told that story—or some version of it—many times, as if by acknowledging the "softness" of motion-picture acting he was somehow justifying his experience with it. Not that he had any compulsion to move pianos—and indeed, his telling of the story was certainly his own dig at conventional American masculine culture. Still, there remains something in the story that hints at some level of personal insecurity, as if he were still trying to prove himself to the bullies who taunted him back in Staunton. While his father, mother, and brother toiled away in Richmond, Billy was earning his living— and a quite comfortable one at that—making funny faces in front of the moving-picture camera.

Mike was finally released in April as well, so there were two William Haines features playing in theaters simultaneously. While his part in the earlier film was not nearly as showy as the one in *Brown*, *Mike* nonetheless was a tremendous hit, pulling in almost double the profits of *Brown of Harvard*.

Billy would admit later that the publicity that followed in the wake of *Brown* and *Mike* was intoxicating. "I got the swelled head, an awful case," he said. "I was good, and boy! No one knew that better than William Haines."

Within months, he was receiving more mail on the Metro lot than any other male star except John Gilbert. The studio publicity kicked into gear. A challenge went out to the fans to come up with just 150 more pieces of mail to top Gilbert. "Can't the girls do something about it? Rah! Rah! Rah! for Brown of Harvard!"

But the camera stops for no man, no matter how popular. Billy was required to report to work on a Bessie Love vehicle directed by King Baggott. It was little more than the kind of "boy next door" part he'd "aw shucked" his way through in *Mike* and *Little Annie*

Rooney. The film was *Lovey Mary*, a desperate attempt by veteran star Bessie Love to stay on top of the box office.

Clearly, Billy's assignment to the film took place before Thalberg had fully gauged his impact in *Brown*. In fact, Billy isn't even on-screen until the picture is about half finished. The result was tepid box office (hastening Love's retirement before her comeback in talking pictures) and a much-needed deflated ego. "I still put my fingers to my nose when I think of myself in that one," Billy said later. "It took the wind out of my sails completely."

There would be no such squandering of Billy's newfound star power with his next feature. *Tell It to the Marines* was touted as his blockbuster follow-up to *Brown of Harvard*. He was reunited with Lon Chaney from *The Tower of Lies*, but this time he wasn't some lowly supporting player. In fact, although Chaney received top billing and turns in a superb performance, Billy's part, as written, was the pivotal one, around which all the others turn. Eleanor Boardman was cast as his leading lady. It's interesting to watch her play second fiddle to Billy, when in all of their previous films together, hers was the more central part.

Opening-day ceremonies were held on the MGM lot in June. It was a grand production with a squad of Marines under the command of Major J. P. Wilcox. Mayer, flanked by Thalberg, Rapf, and director George Hill, accepted a flag from Wilcox, whereupon it was raised as a bugler blew "Colors." Both Billy and Lon Chaney looked resplendent in their well-tailored uniforms at the event.

The plot of *Tell It to the Marines* would become a Hollywood staple: A reluctant, irreverent young serviceman learns about life and values from a gruff but caring sergeant. Billy plays "Skeet" Burns, who enlists in the Marine Corps just to get a free train ride across country so he can bet on the horses in Tijuana. Apparently he loses bigtime, for he returns to the base looking forlorn. With nowhere else to go, he decides to honor his enlistment. In a scene made even more amusing when one knows Billy's true story, the major who swears Burns in asks him if he's ever been married. "Who, me?" Burns responds, shaking his head and laughing uproariously. "No," he says winking. "I'm America's Sweetheart." One wonders if director George Hill, who certainly knew that Billy was gay, was playing the scene for a little Hollywood in-joke.

In fact, Billy's development of the wisecracking city slicker—in *Marines* and in subsequent films—owes much to the mannerisms of the urban dandy, who was often identified as homosexual. Billy's wisecrackers flip their hands dismissively at ruffians. They wink over their shoulders and walk out of rooms in huffs. In *Marines*, when he sits for his first haircut, he bats his eyelashes and requests "sheik style on the sides and long and fluffy on top." When Chaney asks if he can drive a car, Billy responds: "Brother, I can drive anything, from a bargain to a battleship."

Many of Billy's quips in his pictures were picked up by the screenwriters from his own parlance around the set. And on *Marines* he had a new, more confident sense of his own screen style. "I was determined to stand up to Mr. Lon Chaney," he remembered many years later, "who was a superb actor but who took himself quite seriously. [He was one of] many actors who should have been hanging in the smokehouse."

The picture took nearly three months to film, almost the entire summer of 1926, Billy's longest production yet. (*Brown of Harvard* had been completed in three *weeks*.) It premiered at the Embassy Theatre in New York on December 23 and went into general release in January 1927. The reviews were exuberant in their praise of Billy. "Lon Chaney is starred as the sergeant," wrote *Variety*, "but William Haines really takes it away from him because his role is built up as strong as the hero." *Motion Picture News* called Billy's part "a well-nigh perfect characterization." And *Photoplay* opined, "This picture is going to do a whole lot towards making a star of William Haines."

Tell It to the Marines proved his success in *Brown of Harvard* was no fluke. He was now one of the hottest properties at the studio, his name bandied back and forth about proposed films. He had only three days off before starting his next picture, *A Little Journey*. It was announced that the highly successful team of Chaney and Haines would reunite for *Span of Life*, based on the play by Sutton Vane. Pauline Starke was set to costar, but nothing materialized of the project.

With fame came not only glowing notices from the critics; the spotlight, when turned full upon someone, makes hiding anything difficult. Suddenly no detail about a star's life is too small, and everything takes on compelling interest to that vast and powerful entity, the public.

Hollywood's great fan magazine tradition was just beginning to flower in 1927. Although fan magazines had been around since 1911, it was not until the late 1920s that their influence began to be felt, both by the studios and the public. For by then, movies and movie stars had transcended mere popular entertainment. By the late 1920s, movie stars were gods and goddesses, and Hollywood their Mount Olympus. The burgeoning movie press was an integral part of that mythology, helping to shape it and share it with the lowly mortals who lived far beyond the glittery palaces of the film colony. Without the fan magazines, how would audiences have known about Gloria Swanson's furs and sunken bathrooms, her marriages to European royalty, her custom-designed automobiles with their leopard-print interiors?

It was a cooperative effort all around, a uniquely designed four-pronged formula consisting of the studios, the stars, the press, and the public. In developing stars, the studios worked closely with the fan magazines, providing access to their actors in an attempt to create the myths that the public was desperate to believe. A whole motion-picture press arose from the need to create and sustain these myths. Gossip columnists, Hollywood reporters, star profile writers—none had existed in the world of journalism before. Now they were vital: They played their part as much as the studio publicists did, as much as the public played its part. The public's role was simply to *believe*: believe the myths that were being spun about the gods on high. In 1927 everyone benefited from such a balance.

Illusions are fleeting. And times change. What may have worked in 1927 might not work just a few years later. Accommodations made willingly in the beginning would become increasingly difficult for everyone involved. The press would begin to sense its own inherent power, outside of studio publicists' machinations. And the stars themselves would also begin to chafe under the barrage of studio-generated untruths. The balance was extremely precarious, and everyone must have known that, even as early as 1927.

In no small part, it was the homosexual actors who threatened most to overturn the apple cart. Lawrence Quirk, whose uncle, Jimmy Quirk, was the founder of *Photoplay*, said the fan magazines knew who was gay and protected them. Sometimes they'd engage in studio-generated stories of heterosexual dalliances; other times, they'd use code words like "loner" or "independent" (or "wisecracker") to describe gay and lesbian stars. Jimmy Quirk was especially fond of Billy Haines; he allowed Billy free rein in *Photoplay* stories to wisecrack, evading the truth without ever really lying.

Other gay stars were more problematic, both to the press and to the studios. Ramon Novarro shied away from reporters; his interviews were rare, and always vague. Nils Asther, who'd recently arrived in Hollywood from Sweden, was antagonistic, resentful of publicity departments: Press reports always called him "moody." Valentino, despite his best attempts to appear manly, was often snickered at by reporters who dared to push limits. His death the year before had come not long after an editorial in the *Chicago Tribune* had castigated him for "debauching" the masculine image in America, dismissing him as a "pink powder puff."

Over the next few years, the "pink powder puff" image haunted studio publicists whenever they were given the job of promoting a gay star. Unlike a decade later, when the sexualities of stars were often unknown (or at least unconfirmed) even to their studio publicists, most gay and lesbian actors in the 1920s did not go to any great lengths to deny themselves. Some, like Edmund Lowe and Lilyan Tashman, forged convenient marriages, but their real lives were well-known throughout Hollywood. The "twilight tandem"—the union of a gay man and a lesbian—became relatively common: Everyone but the public understood them for exactly what they were. Cedric Gibbons and Dolores Del Rio were another such pair: several fan magazines referred to their separate bedrooms in their elaborate home.

If Billy had been heterosexual, chief MGM publicist Pete Smith might have found his job a little easier, but not by much. Certainly straight stars like John Gilbert and Mae Murray, with their myriad affairs and temper tantrums, posed their own publicity problems. Being gay was just one more factor to be considered in an actor's résumé. Smith's assistant Katherine Albert became friendly with Billy and Joan Crawford, often accompanying them to clubs and parties. There was no request that Billy restrain himself in his private life, for in the 1920s there was still a clear distinction that a star *had* a private life separate from his public image.

"We had our Bill Haineses and our Ramon Navarros," said Hal Elias, another of Smith's assistants in the publicity department. "Those are the people who were discussed. Not negatively exactly— their so-called transgressions were considered important, but not in a negative sense exactly. They weren't condemned for it, let me put it that way."

At its height, MGM employed more than one hundred people in its publicity department. It was an incredibly organized, efficient system. An indiscretion on the part of a star wasn't necessarily a secret from the press; it was, however, carefully restructured or defused by a well-oiled publicity machine that held out carrots to the press with one hand while sweeping garbage under the rug with the other. The press, accustomed to the game, understood their livelihoods depended on the largesse of the publicity departments. It would have been going against their best interests to challenge the official word of the studio.

Still, it was tricky. How does a reporter frame questions for (and print responses from) an obviously gay star? The best of the Hollywood journalists—such as Louella Parsons, Ben Maddox, and Herbert Howe—weren't hacks. They were thoughtful, determined writers who, despite their maintenance of the game, tried not to rely simply on studio press releases. They knew Billy's true story. In fact,

Katherine Albert later became a head writer at *Photoplay*. Their challenge became finding a way to present the truth in such a way that the whole house of cards didn't come tumbling down.

Some articles succeeded at this better than others. Writing about Valentino was an exercise in futility if a reporter had even the faintest desire to be truthful. Valentino, who was likely not exclusively homosexual but who certainly transgressed traditional gender and sexual boundaries, lied repeatedly and allowed his wife, Natacha Rambova, to lie for him. Billy, however, was different. If one asks how a writer dealt with reporting on a gay star, one must also ask how that star presented himself to the writer. Valentino lied. Novarro hid. William Haines, however, came up with a completely different tack: He wisecracked.

He gave an interview to Dorothy Spensley of *Photoplay* shortly after *Marines* was completed. It was one of the first depictions of the down-to-earth, let's-have-fun William Haines persona. "I like people who are themselves," he told Spensley. "As soon as they begin to get famous they forget to be natural."

Such "naturalness" was certainly in evidence that day. In the midst of the interview, he was interrupted by Aileen Pringle, who had been away for several months from the studio. He jumped up from his seat, let out a whoop, and pounced on the exotic star, proclaiming "Mother of God!" and smacking her playfully.

"Bill is most catholic in his affection for femininity," Spensley observed coyly. "It would seem that he loved them all."

It was an accurate statement: Billy did indeed love a great number of women. It was also a statement that would satisfy *Photoplay*'s army of largely female readers that their new hero was indeed a ladies' man.

"There are two little extra girls whom I like," Billy volunteered. "Of course," he added hastily, "I don't see them often. But when I do I'm always glad to talk with them. They are themselves. No sham. And you get plenty of sham in Hollywood."

Of course, the very article might be called sham. Spensley's enigmatic phraseology—"most catholic in his affection for femininity"—

was the beginning of a unique partnership. If Billy had lied—if he had married Barbara La Marr—the press would have lied right along with him. Because he refused to, his interviewers followed suit. The trick became how to tell the truth without telling all of it, to write so that those who knew would get it, and those who didn't, wouldn't.

"Handsome male stars usually fete lovely ladies of the stage when they wander west," Spensley wrote, "but Bill is the only actor I know of to tender a dinner to two of Hollywood's dearly beloved character women—buxom Kate Price and Polly Moran."

Only one interview was unearthed in which Billy actually played the game: an undated, unsourced magazine article in the New York Public Library collection from this period. Entitled "My Ideal Girl" and purportedly written by Haines, it was likely a studio-generated puff piece to make him more appealing in the wake of his *Brown of Harvard* and *Tell It to the Marines* successes. Once he learned how to flex his considerable box-office muscle, however, never again did he allow his name to be used for this type of publicity. The article has him writing: "I suppose every young fellow has a mental picture of the perfect girl . . . to me the ideal girl is almost beyond realization yet I know that should she pass in a crowd I would recognize her instantly."

There is the oft-repeated story that the studio attempted to link him to exotic actress Pola Negri, even distributing photographs of a king-size bed that they would use upon their marriage. In not one article in the exhaustive clippings files of both stars at the Academy of Motion Picture Arts and Sciences, the New York Public Library, or the Museum of Modern Art does such a photograph appear. The story originated with MGM story editor Samuel Marx, who did not arrive at the studio until 1930. Still, there must be some basis to the story: In several contemporary articles, Negri is reported to have once been romantically linked to William Haines.

Probably it was Billy himself who started the rumor, raising the image as a wisecrack. Pola Negri was about as much the opposite of Billy Haines as any actress could be: pompous, pretentious, overblown. She was a Paramount star, not an MGM player, making the idea of a studio-generated romance even more unlikely. They shared one important trait in common, however. Both transgressed conventional sexual definitions. Billy, clearly privy to such information, probably linked himself to Negri in the same sort of in-joke as his quip about singing in the same choir with Ramon Novarro.

In 1923 Negri had also been linked to tennis star "Big" Bill Tilden, another homosexual. And she made much of her supposed romance with Valentino, melodramatically fainting at his funeral in August 1926. In between that event and her marriage to Prince Serge Mdivani in early 1927, she may have been amused to see herself paired with Billy Haines, the amiable star of *Brown of Harvard*. Billy would recall a few years later, "I was attracted to Pola Negri. I met her first in the Coconut Grove at the Ambassador. Pola was a great scout. I call myself an alumnus of the Pola Negri Finishing School for Young Actors."

It was precisely in that way that he could turn any suggestion of romance into a wisecrack. Dorothy Spensley of *Photoplay* said he possessed "a darting, daring, ever-alert wit that shoots with the rapacity of a machine-gun and the keen, cool thrust of a rapier." Warren Colby of the *Evening World* quipped, "You can cut everything Billy says in half and still be far from the truth."

There is a telling exchange between Haines and Samuel Richard Mook of *Picture Play* that exemplifies his relationship with the press. Mook reports that he requested an interview, only to find Billy in a playful mood.

HAINES: Fix up something yourself for me to say. You know as much about this game as I do.

MOOK: Like fun I will. Why should I rack my brains for something to make you appear clever? I'm as dumb as you are.

HAINES: Really? I didn't think writers were ever dumb. I thought I was being generous. They never write what you tell 'em, anyhow.

MOOK: True, but when they don't, the actors still get the breaks.
HAINES: Yeah? You break the best of them.

And then, in an aside to his readers, Mook exclaims: "Ingrate!"

Of course, Mook would have every reason to call Billy an ingrate, even if Billy's belligerence was tongue-in-cheek. For, indeed, the press *did* give Billy a break. It was part of how the game was played.

Still, some reports had more sting. Fan magazine articles, written by reporters who had personal relationships with the studio's publicists and stars, were easier to control. The increasing number of gossip columns and Hollywood "inside reports" in the nation's far-flung newspapers were a different matter. An item in the *New York News* on September 30, 1926, said all it needed to say: "William Haines, who is perhaps the most eligible film bachelor of them all inasmuch as he has never been married though he's 26 and handsome, will star in a new film."

It was inevitable that the marriage question would be directly posed to him at some point. Of course, Billy was indeed "married" to Jimmie, and most of the Hollywood reporters knew that fact. That wasn't something shared with the legions of movie fans out in the hinterlands. More than the lavish parties, more than the opulent homes and leopard-lined automobiles, the public wanted to know about a star's love life. It was the crux of the myths: Zeus and Hera, Hercules and Iole, Eros and Psyche. Without romances, the stars wouldn't have been gods and goddesses, rending heaven and earth with their ferocious passions and acrimonious splits.

At some point in 1927, a very prim young woman from a Boston newspaper arrived on the Metro lot to interview William Haines. She was quite unprepared for Billy's personality, and this particular day he was full of hijinks. Heady with his success, he felt cocky. Until now, most reporters had willingly played along with him. They were insiders, Hollywood people. They knew the story. They'd write things like "catholic in his affection for femininity." This rather naïve out-of-towner was much more plain: "Are you planning to get married?" she asked, and waited implacably for his answer.

In true fashion, Billy didn't hedge. He wisecracked. "Yes," Haines told her. "I am engaged to Patricia Moran. She's one of the Morans of Virginia—one of the very best families from that state."

"I don't believe I know them," the reporter murmured.

"No," Billy grinned. "You wouldn't."

She scribbled the name furiously on her pad.

"It's bound to be a happy marriage," Billy continued. "We have so much in common. We can ride to the hounds together. We enjoy the same things when we're away from the studio. We're only waiting until she's finished her contract and saved a little more money before we marry."

By this time, the reporter had figured out that he was talking about the homely comedy actress Polly Moran. Yet, in her naïveté, she believed him. When the article appeared, the Hollywood press corps had a big laugh—as did, presumably, Polly Moran, who had recently struck up a close friendship with Billy. Pete Smith was not so pleased. It would not do to have their strapping All-American star engaged to a horse-faced comedienne more than ten years his senior. Although MGM issued public denials, the story circulated for years.

Polly Moran became one of his closest friends. He credited her with helping him develop his on- and offscreen humor. She taught him the fine art of the double take, the broad pantomime of screen comedy. She assured him that being a comedian was every bit as acceptable as playing the romantic hero, and much more fun.

In dozens of articles, she provided the distraction to any real questions of romance. Polly was the loving butt of Billy's romantic jokes. She laughed along good-naturedly, even writing a piece called "Me and the Boyfriend" for *Film Fun*, presenting herself as a naïve, lovesick older woman getting conned by a younger man. " 'Darling,' I murmured to Bill as I sat there holding his hand (to keep him from socking me), 'why do you love me?'

" 'Sweetheart, I'll tell you why,' he shrieked. 'It's because of your seething, sizzling, shocking sex appeal!' "

Accompanying the article was an extremely ungainly photograph of Polly being pushed on a swing by Billy—and Ramon Novarro.

She may really have been in love with Billy. The image that emerges is one of a lonely, bucktoothed woman in her fifties who spent all her time with young gay men, enduring their kidding and playing along with their games. Most of her time was indeed spent at Billy's house; he was her escort to nearly every Hollywood function. That she married hastily after her friendship with Billy ended—and to an abusive, dominating man—lends support to the idea that her time with Billy was not all the fun and games he liked to imagine it.

Still, there was genuine affection between them. Billy respected her talent and her experience. She'd had a long career in vaudeville and musical comedy, boasting that she'd crossed the Atlantic fourteen times to play on European stages. Her best friend was Fanny Brice, and the two share many similarities: homely girls with self-deprecating humor. Polly started in films with Mack Sennett, and made her MGM debut in 1927. Her pairing with Marie Dressler in *The Callahans and the Murphys* started a whole new career for her.

She was more willing to twist the truth than Billy himself. At the height of the publicity about her bogus romance with Billy, she told an interviewer: "Someday when Bill has made his pile and quit pictures, he'll pick out some nice young girl, marry and settle down. Just about that time I'll be donning my black alpaca dress and wrapping up the birdcage for my trip to the Old Ladies' Home."

Billy just wisecracked, "Sure, I'd marry Polly. It's her girlish figure!"

Billy's quips became legendary in Hollywood. They also allowed him to live his life as he chose, and get away with it.

"The wisecrack is my shell, my protection," Billy would write. "At heart, I am not a wisecracker. William Haines, the wisecracker, came into being in Hollywood."

Wisecracking allowed him to walk the line. On the one side were his fans, the adoring public, who wanted to know all about the private life of Tom Brown and Skeets Burns. On the other were his friends, his parties, and, of course, Jimmie. Billy understood, however, that it was a fine line he walked. How much easier it would have been to simply get married, to play the game in its conventional way. He could have found a lesbian to marry, as Valentino, Edmund Lowe, and Cedric Gibbons did. He knew that as a single man—and one who was gregarious and visible—his world would be easier to puncture than someone like Novarro's, who drew the gates around his home and let no one inside.

Billy didn't hide, but he *was* cautious. "I never go to premieres anymore," he told one interviewer. "I avoid them like the measles. One night I was behind all the mobs at the Chinese Theater. I heard some of the cracks made about the stars. That cured me of wanting to go. Neither do I believe in personal appearances. It destroys an illusion. The public may find out that you have liver spots and halitosis. Not that I have either, as far as I know, but they say that your best friend won't tell you."

The author of that article, Marquis Busby, would have understood the liver spots and halitosis reference. So would everyone "in the know" in the film colony. Wisecracks like that allowed the vast public out there in Little Rock and Cincinnati to stay happily in the dark.

Every article written about William Haines commented on his wisecracking. One reporter wrote that an actress, flirting with Billy on the lot, blushed furiously when he came back with a racy retort (which, unfortunately, went unreported). The actress' companion chided her: "Don't you know better than to ask Billy Haines a question in public?"

It was hardly a "gentlemanly" response to innocent flirtation, hardly the kind of response one might have expected from Billy's chief rival for fan mail, John Gilbert. "Life, to Bill, is just one huge, hilarious joke," wrote *Picture Play* in 1928. One of the publication's photographers grew frustrated trying to get him to sit still. "I'm a wreck," she said. "He won't be quiet. He gets up and does absurd dances . . . and he wisecracks and wisecracks!"

The wisecrack was more than just a cover for his gayness. It also helped propel him into the kind of social life he'd desired ever since coming to Hollywood. By playing the joker, he made himself indispensable to the film colony's nightlife. Dorothy Spensley reported in October of 1926 that several hostesses had postponed dinner parties while Billy Haines was out of town. "You know, my dear," Spensley quotes one of them as saying, "we just *couldn't* give a dinner party without Bill. He's better than cocktails and things."

Around this time, Adela Rogers St. Johns wrote a fascinating piece for *Photoplay* on the topic of gossip. "Gossip never hurt anyone's career," she insisted, facing down conventional wisdom. "Gossip actually helps. It makes people sit up and take notice."

St. Johns was one of the wise women of Hollywood. Fully cognizant of her own part in creating and maintaining the myth of Hollywood, she understood that gossip was essential in the making of the myth. She knew that for the public to believe in its celluloid gods, there needed to be the kind of romantic sagas once attached to the denizens of Mount Olympus. Ordinary people did not expect Gloria Swanson or John Gilbert to live as they did. They expected them to live in palaces and wear exotic clothes. They also did not expect them to share the same mores or even hold the same values. A three-time divorcee would be looked upon suspiciously in most American towns, run out on a rail in many. In Hollywood, however, divorce was commonplace. Gossip about one star having an affair with another was exactly what the public demanded, even if the affair was fabricated. When the star was married, it caused greater concern, but even that, St. Johns argued, was not really damaging.

Scandals, she added—*real* scandals, like the kind that had destroyed Fatty Arbuckle, Mary Miles Minter, Wallace Reid, and Mabel Normand—were different. An authentic scandal was gossip gotten out of hand, and whether there was any substance to the scandal or not, once it had progressed to a certain point, it would inevitably upset the carefully constructed balance between studio, star, press, and public. At that point, there would be no going back: A star was destroyed, and nothing studio publicists could do would revive his or her career. The press, then, had only one option: to jump on the story and ride it out, playing it for whatever it was worth, since this would be the last opportunity to squeeze out any copy from the unfortunate actor.

Cases in point: Fatty Arbuckle and Mabel Normand. Arbuckle, a beloved comedian for several years, was charged in the brutal death of a young starlet, Virginia Rappe, at a party in September 1921. No publicist in the world could put a positive spin on an arrest for rape and murder. As the lurid details of the party emerged—the 266-pound actor in ripped pajamas wearing Virginia's squashed hat on his head while she lay bleeding on the ground behind him—the public turned ferociously on Arbuckle. After two mistrials, he was found not guilty, but in the court of public opinion, he was a murderer. And a *fat* murderer at that. His girth was now seen as obscene rather than amusing. He became the target of the early reform movement, demanding that Hollywood clean up its act and force its players to behave.

On the other hand, there was no evidence of guilt in the case of Mabel Normand, but the public still turned its back on her. Or perhaps the studios turned their backs on her in *anticipation* of the public doing so. It was hard to tell which came first. The fact that Normand had been the last to see director William Desmond Taylor alive on February 1, 1922, the night he was shot to death in his home, was enough to convict her by association. Although both Normand and Arbuckle attempted comebacks, few in Hollywood dared to work with them, and both died young and miserable in obscurity.

Such scandals were still fresh in the minds of the studio heads. There was little concern about a performer's sexual preferences; it was what he or she might do in *conjunction* with those preferences that unnerved them. Billy could be gay without issue; it was patronizing a bordello or some other public exhibition that could snowball into a real, authentic scandal. What if the charges—like Arbuckle's—turned out to be too serious for even the influence of Louis B. Mayer to dismiss? Some historians allege that Paramount, William Desmond Taylor's studio, had gone so far as to plant Mary Miles Minter's panties at the scene of the director's murder to throw detectives off the trail of Taylor's homosexuality and the wild lot of boys with whom he associated. If true, it suggests Hollywood honchos feared a gay scandal more than a straight one, that publicity surrounding an unprosecuted murder was preferable to headlines about homosexuality.

Screenwriter Frances Marion, a close friend of Billy's, recalled in her memoirs that around the time of *Tell It to the Marines*, Billy got into some trouble with the top brass, and there was talk of tearing up his contract. Although she wasn't specific, it could only have meant that he'd been caught by the police in some raid: A story circulated for years that Billy had been caught having sex with a sailor in Pershing Square, a popular Hollywood cruising spot for gay men. There is no record of an arrest for Billy (or Jimmie) in the Los Angeles County Superior Court criminal files, but outdoor cruising *was* an activity both of them enjoyed for some years, sometimes together, sometimes on their own. "It was really Jimmie who had the hot pants in the family," says Arch Case, and he's backed up by numerous friends who insist Jimmie was the one more likely to be out cruising the streets. "I wouldn't be surprised if it was Jimmie who got Billy into a few of those scrapes at MGM," says Bob Wheaton.

Marion might also have been referring to the incident with Novarro at the bordello. Whatever the nature of the incident, it landed Billy in Mayer's office for a showdown. The studio had gotten the charges dropped, and as repayment, Mayer expected complete servitude. Billy was "independent as a tomcat," says Marion, and "refused to kowtow" to Mayer.

Although his friendship with Thalberg had continued, Billy's relationship with Mayer had grown more antagonistic. He knew Mayer had antipathy toward homosexuals. He also knew the threats to dump him were merely bluffs: *Marines* was the biggest hit of the year and Thalberg was already planning a series of starring vehicles for him.

Because of Billy's box-office value, Mayer tried to dissuade him from any behavior that might jeopardize his star status. Billy later recounted the story of Mayer throwing his arm around his shoulder and saying, "Oh, my son. I never had a son. I always wanted a son."

He'd do this often, Billy reported, after which Mayer would always start to cry.

"I finally found a way to stop Mayer's tears," Billy remembered. "I'd start crying too."

Such theatrics only made Mayer dislike Billy even more. Billy took too many liberties, pushed the envelope too far. And in truth, it may have been that Billy, used to the collaboration of the press, grew a little too complacent, a little too cocksure. He pressed his luck, trusting that the general regard in which he was held by the press and studio publicists would keep him from any scandal. Such peace of mind, however naïve, nonetheless allowed him to lead as authentic a life as any gay man ever lived in Hollywood. Certainly no figure, before or for many years since, was ever so out, so completely honest about himself, in the world of myths, magic, and make-believe.

He had found a spouse. Now Billy wanted a home.

"I always longed for the day when I would have money enough to build a home in Georgian style and furnish it exactly as it should be," he'd later say. He'd been given a raise after *Brown's* success, a spectacular jump from $400 a week to $1,000. In 1997 dollars, this is roughly equal to about $12,000 a week, or $624,000 a year. Remember, too, that there was no income tax and that combined other taxes averaged no more than four percent on high incomes. It was a rush of affluence he couldn't possibly have imagined. Any dream he harbored was now within his reach.

In September he bought a house at 1712 North Stanley Drive, just off Sunset Boulevard, from Charles and Bettie Kimble. While most of the movie elite was moving into Beverly Hills, Billy opted to stay right in the heart of Hollywood. He paid $12,500 (along with a trust deed of record for $8,000) for the plain, two-story Spanish home. Billy was determined to transform his house into a showplace.

Ever since his days in New York, when his Fifth Avenue patroness had taught him to appreciate fine things, he had collected furniture, buying the odd antiques at auctions and flea markets. He had spent many days since coming west staring into the display windows of various antique dealers, wishing for certain pieces that caught his eye. Not only could he ill afford them, there was no room in his small flat for all the treasures he desired. Now that had changed. Now he approached the redesign of his house with more enthusiasm and dedication than he ever brought to acting.

One of the older homes in the area, 1712 North Stanley was built soundly, with deep foundations and heavy timbers. Such solid construction had attracted Billy, as it could withstand significant structural changes. He and Jimmie moved in and began taking measurements, drawing up rough floor plans. He abhorred the mishmash of historical styles that so characterized Hollywood architecture of the time, especially the pseudo-Spanish style that had been the rage of the 1910s and early 1920s. Indeed, he shuddered at many of Hollywood's gaudy mansions. Alongside her Ming vases, Clara Bow had lamps that looked to one reporter as if they'd come from five-and-ten-cent stores. Valentino's piano was draped with the shawl of some Spanish infanta, and he was often photographed reclining on velvet sofas behind heavy velvet drapes. Most houses, Billy complained, were so dark that one needed a guide dog to get through. He was determined to set a new trend.

This new trend was not just in the style of his residence. Without any fanfare, without any thought for "permission" from the studio, Billy and Jimmie set up house together. This was far more meaningful than sharing a rented flat. Forget for a minute that they'd only known each other for less than a year. Youth rushes headfirst into situations, and in this case, their impetuousness was vindicated by their long years together. What makes their cohabitation significant is that, in 1926, it wasn't. Just a few years later, when the political and social climate had changed in Hollywood, it would have been unthinkable for a top Hollywood star to live openly with his male lover — or, if straight, with an unmarried lover of the opposite sex. In the 1920s, mores were very different. The same month Billy and Jimmie moved in together, so did Greta Garbo and John Gilbert, without any eyebrows being raised in MGM's front office, despite Mayer's personal moralizing and judgmental attitudes. No magazine article was going to "expose" their lifestyle: In fact, in his first months as a proud new homeowner, Billy ushered several members of the press through the house, with Jimmie serving tea in the dining room.

Construction on the house began sometime late that year, continuing through to 1927. Billy and Jimmie went back to the apartment while work was being done. Best of all, they went on a marvelous, thrilling, head-rushing buying spree: scouring the entire county for antiques, obtaining rare pieces Billy could only have dreamed about back in his days in New York. Federal beds, Chippendale chairs, Sheraton tables, a Hepplewhite secretary, Aubusson rugs, original artwork by eighteenth-century masters. He was preparing for his most important role, one far removed from the screen's favorite wisecracker.

The year 1927 opened auspiciously for William Haines. He was at the top of the world. He was reveling in the design of his house. He was deliriously happy spoiling Jimmie. And everywhere, *Tell It to the Marines* was breaking box-office records. It was far and away MGM's biggest hit of the 1926–1927 season, pulling in a spectacular profit of $664,000.

His next film, *A Little Journey,* was released in January, directed by Robert Z. Leonard. As its title implies, *A Little Journey* is a simple story, a journey of the heart. Billy plays well against his old pal Claire Windsor and the popular character star Harry Carey. The film pleased both audiences and critics. *Motion Picture News* said, "William Haines gives a corking performance as the irrepressible and impressionable youth, showing considerable skill in the lost art of flirting."

The *New York Times*, however, had a small reservation, sounding a note that would become a refrain in Billy's reviews: "The picture jogs along merrily and one is not annoyed even by Mr. Haines' fondness for keeping his face in action, although it is obvious that a little more restraint would improve his characterization and make it more natural."

Restraint was hardly in sight for his next film, *Slide Kelly Slide,* released on March 12. Directed by Edward Sedgwick, it's a fast-paced, tightly scripted film that nonetheless allows Billy to run wild with his characterization. This time, he's a small-town rube, Jim "No Hit" Kelly, coming to try out for the New York Yankees, but he's as much a smart aleck as his city-slicker impersonations. Once again, there's a little play with sexual ambiguity: Sally O'Neil (his costar from *Mike* and *Sally, Irene and Mary*), done up in cap and pants, is mistaken for a boy at the post office. Immediately in strides Kelly, who, still thinking she's a boy, winks and says, "Hello, cutie." Later, on the field, Karl Dane takes one look at Kelly, all done up in spiffy jacket and carnation in lapel, and smirks, "Can I smell your sunflower, Pansy?" Of course, it squirts him when he bends over for a sniff.

Slide Kelly Slide firmly established the Haines formula: Conceited jerk thinks he can wisecrack to his heart's content and that he knows all the answers. Then enters true love. In this case, it's not so much O'Neil as the little street urchin played superbly by Junior Coghlan, who'd also appeared in *Mike*.

"Bill Haines was one of the nicest, friendliest, and wittiest people I have ever worked with," Frank (Junior) Coghlan says today. "I had a wonderful time making the picture with him." Indeed, their rapport comes through in the film: Kelly's gentleness with the boy stands in marked contrast to his arrogance toward his teammates. Billy may have been thinking of his brother, Henry, about the same age as Junior, back in Virginia. In one scene, they pray together in a vignette that could have been maudlin, but turns out quite natural and poignant.

It's ironic that the film established Billy as a sports star. In several subsequent films, he'd portray top athletes, despite the fact that he had never been athletic and was bored silly by competitive sports. Still, he grinned through a publicity trip to New York to meet and pose with Babe Ruth and Lou Gehrig at Yankee Stadium. Real pitchers taught him how to throw a ball so he'd look convincing onscreen.

The *New York Times* called his performance "capital," and *Photoplay* said: "William Haines gives a performance calculated to add a great deal to his popularity."

Perhaps because he played them onscreen, and perhaps because he had allowed success to go briefly to his own head, Billy had no tolerance for egomaniacs. He chided actresses for their "California British" accents that seemed to emerge only after they'd had one qualified hit. The reason he got on so famously with Hollywood's top players was that most of them were nouveau riche like himself, girls like Lucille Le Sueur from Kansas City and Dutch Talmadge from Brooklyn.

That didn't mean they were gauche: They were just natural. In fact, the truly tacky—like Elinor Glyn—were as much the targets of his scorn as the "ice cold" blue-blooded society dames. Anyone with pretensions was an insufferable bore.

Garbo was one star he had little use for, failing to see beyond her reserve into her fear and vulnerability. They were hardly compatible people: the outgoing Billy with his cracks and pranks, the sullen, withdrawn Garbo with her air of mystery and reclusiveness. Yet they shared some mutual friends—Eleanor Boardman, Edmund Goulding, and, later, George Cukor—and there should have been a *simpático* understanding of each other's lives: Garbo, after leaving Gilbert, made little pretense of her relationship with Mercedes de Acosta. Despite having a dressing room directly beneath hers, Billy had never received so much as a hello from the aloof star. "I can hear the water running when she washes up, yet I've never met her," he told reporters.

Garbo was the only one of MGM's top female stars—Crawford, Shearer, Boardman, Marion Davies—with whom Billy was unable to forge a friendship. When she walked past his dressing room, Billy would call out, "Hello, Gret." He never got an answer, so he stopped expecting one. Instead, he began answering for her: "Hello, Billy," he'd say, within earshot of Garbo. "How are you? You're looking well today." In fact, he told reporters, he had whole conversations with Garbo in this way.

If anything, he had grown more handsome with the passing years, maturity giving his still boyish face added charm. He was twenty-seven, as old as the century and as filled with life. He had boundless energy, except for those brief spells of melancholy, which continued to plague him periodically. What struck most people upon meeting him was how big he was, even bigger than he appeared onscreen. He carried his six feet well, and his shoulders were broad.

Clothes always made him uncomfortable, because he didn't think he wore them well. He eschewed neckties, preferring a white silk scarf tucked into his collar. Not only was it more of a style statement, it was far more comfortable. His clothes tended toward quiet, sub-dued tones — dark grays and serge blues — but every once in a while he threw on red-hot sweaters and belted-leather jackets. He absolutely despised garters and suspenders, and refused to wear them. Despite the latest fad, he never wore a straw hat.

At home, Billy tended to lounge around in old sweaters, sporting a three-day growth of beard because his tough whiskers made shaving such a bother. Jimmie was the opposite: always impeccably groomed, with a wardrobe that filled several closets. Already his jewelry collection, courtesy of Billy, was growing: Cartier watches, diamond-and-emerald rings, gold bracelets. Jimmie managed the servants and the house, and saw to it that Billy had a passable meal when he came home from the studio. For guests, however, it was al-ways Billy who supervised — and sometimes participated in — the cooking. He began collecting cookbooks, trying out new recipes, creating surprisingly gourmet dishes to impress his friends.

All of this while he was also seeing to the renovation of their house. In the spring of 1927, it was finally done — or, at least, the first phase of it was done, as he'd continue to shape it for nearly his entire time there. Billy and Jimmie moved in, pleased with the work, delighted to see how Billy's ideas had come to life. The "Haines cas-tle," as it came to be known, was one of the monumental Hollywood homes.

Reporter Samuel Richard Mook described a tour of the house af-ter it had been completed. From the outside, Mook wrote, the long, narrow, white stucco house could have belonged to anyone; but once you stepped inside, it was clear that only "a person of uncommon taste" lived there. The elegance of his home took many people by surprise, so accustomed were they to Billy's irreverent manners and screen image.

The house had been transformed from the Spanish style into a unique blend of colonial New Orleans and eighteenth-century England. The walls were entirely replastered and reconfigured, leaving only the foundation intact. The interior reflected the simple elegance of an English manor house with its low wainscotings, high ceilings and exquisite chandeliers. Wide fireplaces had been added and intricate moldings had been carved to highlight particular rooms.

The house seemed so much larger than it appeared from the outside. To enter, one walked up a shallow flight of brick stairs through a white-paneled door with a knocker of solid brass. Past the door was the formal drawing room, with walls and woodwork painted a cool Georgian green and carvings in gold leaf. Billy used the room as an eighteenth-century lord of the manor might have: A drawing room was for those guests not intimate enough to penetrate deeper into the house. The furniture combined the simple Louis XVI and the more elaborate Venetian styles. With its high ceilings, it was an imposing room, as Billy wanted it to be.

The dining room was accessed by walking down four low black marble steps. Here the space was enlivened by Zuber pictorial wallpaper of palm trees in natural colors, a tan Aubusson rug partially covering a parquet floor. Raspberry-satin draperies set off the high-gloss Sheraton table and Directoire chairs.

Upstairs, there were three bedrooms, each with four-poster beds, highboys, and Sheraton chairs. Displayed with great care in the master bedroom were a couple of Bohemian glass perfume bottles and a huge decanter handed down from Billy's great-great-grandmother. The Zuber wallpaper here was bright, gaily arrayed with flowers of many colors. The carpet was taupe velvet, the windows draped in green and gold taffeta. The dressing table was Chinese Chippendale topped by an American Colonial mirror. An exquisitely carved William-and-Mary walnut cabinet stood out against the plain ivory wall.

The house's most famous room was the upstairs sitting parlor, done completely in knotty pine. "Bill was one of the first designers to use knotty pine," remembers Henry Haines. "When he did that room, he said the knotty pine wasn't knotty enough. So he had an artist draw more knots, to get just the look he wanted."

The room blended several periods into a harmonious whole. The floor was covered in a plush carpet of eggplant velvet. Glazed chintz chairs stood at either side of a large fireplace at the end of the long room. The draperies were also chintz, flowered in an array of colors. A Chippendale couch and a priceless Hepplewhite secretary stood opposite each other. Set into the walls were elegantly carved cabinets—bought from Edgar Graber, a local cabinetmaker Billy much admired and whose son, Ted, would become Billy's friend and associate. The Graber cabinets held rare porcelain and china.

Escorting Mook around the house, Billy beamed like a kid showing off his treasures. A set of sixteen miniatures were his pride and joy, but he'd hung only a few. "He didn't believe in sticking them up just because he had them," Mook wrote.

"When you do a home," Billy told the press, as if he were an old pro at it, "you must do it with the feeling that it has been lived in for years. The rooms must look as if there might be a pair of carpet slippers beside a chair, and a pipe or two on the table."

Such were not the musings the press and public had come to expect of its wisecracker. He was very serious about this house business, and he quite clearly knew what he was talking about. Irving Thalberg was stunned the first time he entered Billy's new home. "Who did this?" he kept asking.

"I did," Billy said simply.

Of course, he had architects, and Mitchell Foster (who had recently joined Larry Sullivan at the North Western Avenue apartment) no doubt helped. But the fact remains that it was Billy's vision that created the house. It was his own sense of style and design that produced the finished product. He was extraordinarily proud of the achievement, as he had reason to be. Much more than any film role, the design of his house satisfied him, both emotionally and artistically. He felt affirmed by the amazed reaction of his friends. His sense of accomplishment was exhilarating.

To run the household properly, however, he needed help. Like his family before the financial reversal, Billy hired a staff of live-in servants, all black. Impeccably mannered, they impressed the Hollywood folk. "He had the most wonderful colored servants," remembers Michael Pearman, "the best in town." One of them was a plucky young woman in her late twenties named Beulah Brown. His chauffeur was a former Pullman porter (some reports say he was a Staunton native like Billy). A favorite story of the movie magazines was that Billy had met him on the train that brought him out to Hollywood in 1922. Having no money to tip him, Billy promised that if he ever found success in the movies, he'd find him and give him a job. Reporter Constance Blake observed in 1932 that Billy still had the same servants as when he first opened his house, a testament to his integrity and decency. Keeping one's help, Blake wrote, "is, after all, a better test than keeping the same friends."

Earlier that year, Billy's mother Laura had arrived from Virginia. A notice in the *New York Telegraph* called Billy "the happiest chap in Hollywood" now that his mother was living with him. The fact was that Laura Haines had fallen ill, and Billy insisted that she join him in California. "Bill and his mother were very, very close," Henry Haines says. "When she became ill, Bill wanted her near him." Laura was diagnosed with hypertension, with symptoms of nervousness, dizziness, and headaches. She may have already been suffering from some form of kidney disease as well. It was agreed that the California sunshine might be best for her, so she packed up and headed west. George and the rest of the family planned to join her later.

Living in Hollywood, Laura had to deal directly for the first time with Billy's homosexuality, as Jimmie was right there under the same roof. Seventy years later, all who knew them insist that there was complete harmony between Billy's family and Jimmie, and certainly that is what emerged. One suspects that like most mothers, even today, Laura Haines experienced some discomfort in accepting and integrating Billy's life into her own vision of the world. Around his mother, Billy was always the devoted son and proper gentleman. Particularly raucous behavior from his friends—whether it be Jimmie or Larry Sullivan or Polly Moran—was discouraged in his mother's presence. Still, it had to have been an adjustment.

When Billy's house was unveiled at a gala dinner party that summer, Laura acted as a gracious hostess. Despite her illness, she was charming and aristocratic welcoming Billy's guests. Expecting a more boisterous affair, many Hollywood colleagues were startled to be received formally in the drawing room. They were surrounded by thousands of gardenias and orchids, infusing the house with a deep, hypnotic fragrance. Softly flickering candles added to the elegance of the occasion. They were all escorted into the dining room for a sumptuous meal, and those fortunate enough to be asked to stay later—Crawford, Thalberg, Eleanor Boardman, King Vidor, among others—were treated to an after-dinner liqueur in the upstairs sitting room.

Billy's soirees became coveted invitations, and they were renowned not only for their elegance but for their egalitarianism. Dorothy Spensley described a dinner party at his house where Hollywood society matrons sat alongside movie extras. "Bill reigned as supreme host over them all," she gushed.

He recalled, "I do like to give parties, and how I mix crowds! I remember one party at which I entertained some very down-at-the-nose society people. Polly [Moran] was there and she had a swell time horrifying the proper dames. I had an ex-pugilist valet, probably the world's worst valet, but he was funny. Polly always called him Meadows. 'Meadows,' she said in a broad English accent, 'will you be so kind as to pass me some of those little sandwiches? Why, I cawn't take *that* one. It looks as if someone had nibbled on it and put it *back*.' And she glared suspiciously at everyone."

Billy's dinner parties became legendary. At one party he provided necklaces made of gardenias for all the female guests. Among his frequent guests were also reporters, guaranteeing that they'd continue to treat him kindly. Constance Blake, Katherine Albert, Samuel Richard Mook, and Ben Maddox were all guests in his home. With the exception of Louis B. Mayer, there weren't many people who disliked Billy Haines in Hollywood. In 1927, he had the town eating out of his hand.

It's not clear exactly when and how Billy's friendships with Marion Davies and William Randolph Hearst first blossomed. It may have been through Eleanor Boardman; Marion had hosted the wedding for Eleanor and King Vidor in September 1926. By the time Billy and Marion became tight, she was in the midst of a career low point: Of her four pictures in 1927, only *The Fair Co-ed* was even moderately successful. Her other three—*The Red Mill*, *Tillie the Toiler*, and *Quality Street*—were among MGM's biggest flops of the year.

Not that Marion Davies had ever been a big box-office star. And not that it mattered much whether her films turned a profit. Her production company, Cosmopolitan Pictures, was subsidized by her lover, newspaper magnate William Randolph Hearst. His tabloids were instructed to build her up big as a star, no matter how much (or how little) her pictures made.

She was a natural to hit it off with Billy. Born Marion Douras, she was a Ziegfeld showgirl and a teenager when Hearst, respectably married and the father of four sons, took her as his mistress. For nearly a decade now, Hearst had been financing her pictures, and his money was greatly appreciated by Metro-Goldwyn-Mayer, which distributed Cosmopolitan films and supplemented its production facilities. Marion was a terrific light comedienne, but Hearst preferred her in creaky, lacy melodramas. For her part, Marion just wanted to have a little fun; like Billy, for her making movies was merely the means to an end.

Billy was struck by both her down-to-earth personality and her taste for high living. "She was the first woman I had ever seen who wore a diamond necklace on a sweater," he said. They became fast friends, and he was soon a regular at San Simeon, Hearst's castle retreat up the coast near San Luis Obispo. This was the period when the great San Simeon extravaganzas were just beginning: You knew you had arrived in Hollywood when you were invited for a weekend at San Simeon. If Pickford and Fairbanks were the King and Queen of the colony—entertaining at Pickfair authentic royalty, presidents, heads of state, and ambassadors—Davies and Hearst were the Crown Princess and Knave of Hearts.

Although Hearst was in his mid-sixties, San Simeon was the place where Hollywood's younger crowd established their own court. In fact, Davies called her set of friends the "younger degeneration," and it consisted of Billy, Louise Brooks, Sally O'Neil, Buster Collier (who'd appeared with Billy in *Wine of Youth* and whose wife Stevie would become a special friend), Charlie and Pepi Lederer (Marion's nephew and niece), and others. Louise Brooks's biographer Barry Paris has written of the "adventurous hedonism" of this group — "the 'younger degeneration's' zest for Life, Liberty, and the Pursuit of Pleasure." Bisexuality was the norm. Billy had his share of flings with girls; essentially heterosexual women like Louise Brooks did, too. Brooks allied herself often with gay men, part of the giddy ambiguity they all prized.

For Marion, restrained in her own behavior by the ever-watchful eye of Hearst, these friends provided endless amusement. Billy was a particular pet: He could make her laugh like no one else. Certain friends Marion designated her "court jesters" — as Billy said, "all the loose ones, you know." They included Buster Collier, the actor Harry Crocker, the director Eddie Cline, and Billy himself, with Charlie Chaplin the "head jester." Billy recalled, "There was a great deal of jealousy among the lesser ones. Mr. Chaplin would get on and never get off."

Billy was equally outrageous. One of Marion's favorite stories was the time Billy came to a very exclusive party at San Simeon wearing an antique suit of armor, a recent acquisition for his collection of antiques. He claimed his dog had ripped his dress trousers to ribbons.

In the 1920s, before Hearst installed his private train, guests invited for the weekend assembled at the Ambassador Hotel. Everyone was assigned a special limousine, and the cars began the long trek up the coast — all in a line, never passing each other. "At times it reminded me of a funeral procession," cracked Hedda Hopper.

The ambience was hardly that. In the limousines the champagne flowed freely, but guests knew to arrive inebriated would be a major social faux pas. No one really got drunk at San Simeon parties — except, later, Marion Davies herself. Hearst kept his guests much too busy, with formal dinners, elegant costume parties, picnics, and games of tennis.

The castle was always bathed in floodlights when the guests arrived; the twin towers could be seen from miles away on the highway. The estate (Hearst called it his "ranch") contained more than 260,000 acres of land, as well as an oceanfront that ran for fifty miles. Guests would pass the San Simeon zoo and game preserve as they were taken up the long winding drive. Headlights would reveal Tibetan yak, Peruvian llamas, African giraffes, and the sacred deer of India. Marble steps led finally to the castle doors where, inside, guests were welcomed in the great Assembly Hall, surrounded by fine antique furniture and priceless paintings on the walls. Billy drew a good deal of inspiration for his house from San Simeon.

The Chief—as Hearst was known—was always there to greet each guest, a bear of a man with a high-pitched voice. Billy liked him, and the feeling was mutual: Billy was one of the few who could penetrate the old man's reserve.

"He was a man of enormous generosity . . . once you broke the shell and got inside," Billy would recall. "He hated to be thanked for anything he gave. But he loved to get small gifts, like candy, and he would open the packages with all the delight of a child."

In the company of their friends, Hearst and Davies did not have to pretend that they were merely business partners. With Marion at his side, the old man felt a sense of renewed vigor. Billy would remember Hearst playing the banjo and singing for them, even dancing. "He used to love to do his favorite Charleston dance. He was a towering six-footer—a *mountainous* man—and he did the Charleston like a performing elephant. He had as little grace as an elephant, but he had the *dignity* of one."

The legends are many: Marion's flasks of vodka hidden in the toilets, the outrageous costume parties, the ketchup bottles on the long dining table in the magnificent Refectory. A photograph from the period records one weekend of guests in the late 1920s: Billy, Jimmie, King Vidor, Beatrice Lillie, Richard Barthelmess, John Gilbert, Eleanor Boardman, Edmund Goulding, Charlie Chaplin, Nicholas

Schenck, Alice Terry, Harry Rapf, Aileen Pringle, Norma Shearer, Hal Roach, Natalie Talmadge, Buster Keaton, Constance Talmadge, Paul Bern, and Irving Thalberg.

For Marion, San Simeon was both paradise and prison. Her biographer, Fred Lawrence Guiles, wrote that as time went on she barely noticed the splendid candelabra, gold-framed diptychs, antique tables, and Oriental rugs. "What she did feel more than anything was the chill. It gave her ample excuse for a couple of toddies before turning in and she told a friend, 'It must be all that stone.' "

Billy alleviated some of her loneliness while she was there. It was during 1927—perhaps while work was being completed on his house—that Billy settled into San Simeon for an extended period. The story goes that Billy had been exploring the attics and unpacked boxes of antiques and fine china. He told Hearst he really should display these possessions, or at least catalog them. "Go ahead," the Chief offered. Although Billy was expected back on the lot Monday morning, that was no obstacle for Hearst. He picked up the phone, called Mayer, and requested he delay Billy's next picture. Mayer obliged. (A long interval between Billy's 1927 pictures—*Slide Kelly Slide* released in March and *Spring Fever* in October—suggests the story might have some truth.) "It was one of my little stays of three months," Billy would remember. "The days just seemed to run together."

For Billy, his sojourns at San Simeon were inspirations. "I'd pick up a particular piece of furniture, not knowing a damn thing about it," he said. "And I'd ask Mr. Hearst questions. He was very knowledgeable. We had a rapport, and he was very patient with me. I learned a great deal from him."

Although most everyone in Hollywood was invited up to San Simeon at one point or another, there was a certain exclusivity. Only a rarefied few—Billy and Jimmie among them—could be considered regulars. One who was definitely not a regular was Joan Crawford. There existed between Joan and Marion a superficial friendship masking a very deep antipathy. In public, Billy Haines's two "best girlfriends" always said very nice things about each other.

In private, however, Marion performed a near-perfect imitation of Joan, all "owl eyes and slash of lipstick." Joan sniffed that Marion knew nothing of professionalism. Who's to say there wasn't just a tiny bit of rivalry between them—not for roles, certainly, but for the affections of a certain best friend?

There was one woman who didn't share Joan's and Marion's high opinion of Billy. That was Elinor Glyn.

Whether she knew of Billy's distaste for her is unknown, but in March 1927, the grand doyenne issued a pronouncement that she knew would have direct impact on his career: She said that Billy didn't have It.

It's important to remember the influence this woman wielded over Hollywood. Reporters and studio publicists had been hounding her for months to come up with a list of film stars with It, that elusive quality she had concocted in her novel of the same name: an indefinable magnetism, part sex appeal, part glamour, part naturalism, part exoticism. Clara Bow was being promoted as the It Girl to great success, and Gary Cooper, a beautiful new face in films and Bow's lover, was being called the It Boy. Who else? Hollywood wanted to know. Who else had It? And, just as important, who didn't?

Glyn made her picks in the March 1927 issue of *Photoplay*. That she chose Clara Bow, John Gilbert, Greta Garbo, Pola Negri, Douglas Fairbanks, and Gary Cooper as possessors of It was hardly surprising, but the names of Emil Jannings and Wallace Beery caused a few raised eyebrows. Glyn went on to declare that Gloria Swanson and Tom Mix once had had It, but no longer. That she would dismiss Mary Pickford and Lillian Gish as being without It surprised few: Pickford's image was badly in need of revamping (within a year she'd snip off those famous curls) and Gish was widely presumed to have no sex drive at all. The men she singled out as lacking It caused considerable comment, however. Ronald Colman. Ramon Novarro. William Haines.

That two of the three were homosexual is likely not coincidental. The estimable Glyn did not take kindly to men who loved other men. If a man showed no interest in her, she blamed not her age or hideous appearance but his presumed queerness. Similarly, Ronald Colman had a reputation as being cultured and refined. "It" was the antithesis of culture, as was Glyn. It was the difference between Wallace Beery and Ronald Colman, Pola Negri and Lillian Gish.

Interestingly, while Glyn dismissed the likes of Billy, Novarro, and Colman, she pronounced that the rather wispy Prince of Wales, later Edward VIII, possessed It, as did Italy's dictator, Benito Mussolini. Napoleon, she wrote, was once "a glorious example of It." Such pomposity annoyed Billy to no end.

Immediately reporters began buzzing around him, asking him what he thought of Madame Glyn's decision. "It followed me around like a curse," he said later. "Elinor Glyn went a bit further and said I was a big ham. I replied that the best hams in the world came from Virginia."

Mayer, concerned over the impact this might have on his star's appeal, called Billy into his office. Something had to be done. A marriage, at best. A girlfriend, at least. Billy refused. Mayer, unaccustomed to such belligerence, alternately stormed around the office and blubbered tears, trying the old "my son, my son" routine. Billy was implacable.

"But she said you have no sex appeal!" Mayer demanded.

"You're quite wrong," Billy told him calmly. "Before I came out here, I was kept by the best men and women of New York City. I appeal to *both* sexes!"

Mayer was galled that Billy could sit in his presence with such self-assurance and refer to his homosexuality. There had been gay stars in his employ ever since he'd made the trek across the country from Haverhill, Massachusetts, but they knew better than to *acknowledge* it in front of him. Now Billy sat there, meeting his gaze, telling him that part of his drawing power was with *men.* Mayer just glared back at him. Billy would remember, "He never quite forgave me for that."

Mayer's personal moralizing affected his relationships with a number of his actors. His hatred of John Gilbert had nothing to do with Gilbert's style or talent; it had everything to do with Gilbert's extramarital affairs. Mayer's distaste for homosexuals was only one of his prejudices, and it predated Billy Haines. He was hostile to director Mauritz Stiller and his lover, Einar Hanson, when he brought them over from Sweden in 1924. He had never liked Ramon Novarro, and Nils Asther, recently acquired from United Artists, was already irritating him.

He had no problem with those homosexuals who acquiesced and played the game: Cedric Gibbons, for instance, MGM's chief art director, who, at the very moment Mayer was bawling out Billy Haines, was overseeing the redesign of Mayer's home. Gibbons's sexuality wasn't as threatening, of course: He was behind the camera, not as frequent a subject for the gossip columnists. "The public wasn't too concerned with executives or personnel," said publicist Hal Elias, "but movie stars are something else again." Just to be safe, Gibbons also married the beautiful Mexican star Dolores Del Rio, who had reason to agree to the marriage herself.

Mayer expected that his employees obey him like a father—or more like a coach of a baseball team. As Mayer biographer Charles Higham observed, "He had his minor league and major league, raising junior players to the top through careful grooming, not letting them go too far too fast. They treated him as a confessor, pouring their hearts out to him in a way they never did to the more cool and detached Irving Thalberg. He responded with intense emotionalism, crying with them or laughing with them; he had a deep understanding of the peculiarly egomaniacal, insecure, childlike, hypertensive and slightly daffy characters of actors and actresses."

That was the experience of Mayer for someone like Joan Crawford. Yet to a man, Mayer's gay stars (quite understandably) did not pour out their hearts to him, did not seek his direction. If they had, they would have been given the advice Mayer tried repeatedly to give Billy: Get married. Later, when the political winds had shifted in Hollywood, deeply closeted gay stars like Robert Taylor would be grateful for Mayer's guiding hand. In the 1920s, however, they found him petty, unfeeling, and manipulative.

Instead, they took support from Thalberg. Story editor Samuel Marx would later reflect on the differences between Mayer and Thalberg: "Thalberg was naïve, Mayer was sharp. Thalberg was frail, Mayer was robust. Thalberg was retiring, Mayer was pugnacious. Thalberg was searching for new meanings in life, Mayer was satisfied with the old."

Thalberg's close circle had always included homosexuals or men of ambiguous sexuality: Gibbons was a longtime buddy, as were Paul Bern and the playwright John Colton. There were some who suggested Thalberg himself had repressed his own gay identity, but that remains mere speculation. What is clearly evident is Thalberg's tolerance, not only in his choice of friends but in the material he allowed to reach the screen. He was committed to quality, and many times he was able to push pictures of intelligence and sensitivity past Mayer's moralistic objections. Possibly because he felt his life would be short, he had no time for routine Hollywood silliness. It's likely that Thalberg helped defuse the "It" crisis for Billy Haines, pointing out to Mayer that no matter what the old painted broad said, William Haines was a top moneymaker for the studio.

Billy got his comeuppance with Glyn not long after that. She was at San Simeon, holding court among the would-be stars who sat at her knee, all hoping to receive a benediction of It. When she smiled pitifully over at Billy, repeating in front of her entourage her claim that he lacked the necessary qualities, he paused and approached her. "Madame Glyn," he said, with a little bow, "you, of course, certainly *do* have It. But, madam," he added, "You left the 'sh' off of it."

Glyn's response, perhaps mercifully, has gone unrecorded.

Spring Fever was released on October 22, 1927, and, despite Glyn's damning assessment, proved to be Billy's biggest hit yet outside of *Tell It to the Marines*.

The formula, by now, was securely in place. Once again, Billy's a cocky wisecracker, this time a shipping clerk who breaks into a game of golf at an exclusive country club only to become a major golf star. Of course, along the way, he realizes the true meaning of sportsmanship and wins his leading lady's love. The picture was directed by Edward Sedgwick, who'd also helmed *Slide Kelly Slide*.

Joan Crawford played opposite Billy. They made an engaging team, helped certainly by their offscreen friendship. *Moving Picture*

World said of the effort: "[Haines] follows through with one of his usual smart aleck characterizations, with a winsomeness that has the audience pulling for him to win despite his wise-cracking."

So popular was *Spring Fever* that in June of the following year, Billy made a personal appearance at a professional golfers' tournament at Van Courtlandt Park, practicing his swing with golf pros Alex Smith and Augie Nordone. He was mobbed by fans. He hated every minute of it: the girls reaching out for him, thrusting autograph books in his face. He hated even more pretending to enjoy golf, which he "loathed."

Billy and Joan immediately went into production on their next picture, *West Point*, which would be released in December. The director was again Edward Sedgwick, and again the formula didn't deviate much. Billy plays an arrogant and irreverent West Point cadet who gets dropped from the football team for lack of team and school spirit. It's *Brown of Harvard* meets *Slide Kelly Slide*: Billy learns the error of his ways through the support of a noble fellow cadet (William Bakewell) and a true-hearted girl (Crawford), then gets restored to the team and wins the decisive goal in the big game against Navy.

Cast and crew spent about five weeks that summer in New York for location shooting at the military academy. William Bakewell, a teenager at the time, would recall that his agent arranged for his mother to accompany them so she could keep an eye on Billy. "Mr. Haines is rumored to be a homosexual," the agent told Mrs. Bakewell. There was a silence, then she asked, wide-eyed with puzzlement: "A homowhatsual?" Bakewell later laughed, saying, "The voice of innocence in jaded Hollywood."

"As for Bill Haines," he added, "however unorthodox his libido might have been, he was perfectly straight with the rest of us and a pleasure to work with. He had a sharp wit, with a flair for saying the most outrageous things, much to the amusement of the troupe."

It was Crawford who stirred up a bit of trouble, Bakewell recalled. His mother was shocked by her refusal to wear stockings, and one cadet was reported to have been expelled from the academy for skipping classes for a date with Joan.

The movie company stayed at the Thayer Hotel in Highland Falls. Billy and Joan were loaned a car in which they toured the surrounding countryside. On August 30, they were involved in an automobile accident near the military reservation. The car in which they were riding was sideswiped by a truck. Billy was uninjured, but Joan received slight bruises on her forehead and her right knee. Both refused to be taken to the hospital and instead returned to their hotel.

After filming was completed, Billy spent a few days in New York City, staying at the Biltmore and looking up old friends from the Village. He ran into reporter Constance Blake, telling her what a thrill it was to stay at the Biltmore. "You should see me strutting about those rooms," he said. "The big kick, you see, is that when I was a glorified office boy here for Straus and Company, I used to walk by the Biltmore on my lunch hour and think how swell it would be if I could ever eat there. And now I'm living there!"

While in New York, he couldn't have escaped the hype that was building for the release of Warner Brothers' *The Jazz Singer*. Billy was likely back on the West Coast when *The Jazz Singer* premiered in New York in October, but with sound film production centered in the East, New York newspapers were filled with developments of the emerging technology. Most folks in Hollywood paid scant attention at this point: Warner's Vitaphone and Fox's Movietone shorts were simply curious novelties. As Alexander Walker has written, "The possibilities of talking pictures were barely glimpsed by the industry they were about to turn upside down."

West Point was a colossal hit; each of Billy's next few films would build on the previous one's success, surpassing the grosses of the last. He told his brother Henry, "It's Lon Chaney and me who are keeping the MGM lion roaring."

The Smart Set premiered in March 1928, the story of yet another cocky athlete (this time a polo player) thrown off the team for lack of spirit. The film reunited Billy with *Brown of Harvard* director Jack Conway, who this time was eager to work with him. Alice Day took on the Mary Brian–Joan Crawford–Sally O'Neil role.

Telling the World was a little change of pace, released in June. Billy plays not an athlete but a reporter, who is (surprise, surprise) brash and conceited. The plot, thankfully, doesn't hinge on his eating humble pie for a change: The film changes gears and becomes much more of an adventure than a comedy, with Billy falling for a chorus girl (Anita Page) and following her to China. When she's falsely charged with the murder of the governor, Billy uses the telegraph to "tell the world" that an American girl is being threatened, and the U.S. Navy arrives in the nick of time.

Billy was delighted with the opportunity to do something a little bit different on the screen. His director was Sam Wood, with whom Billy enjoyed a close working relationship. Conservative and small-minded, Wood was also a practical joker, and it was that trait of Billy's that bonded the two of them.

Telling the World was Anita Page's first film since coming west (she'd made a few films in New York, including a small part in the classic *A Kiss for Cinderella*). She was a shy, sweet girl of eighteen, sheltered, not yet wise to the ways of Hollywood. When she made a test for *Telling the World*, she remembers her knees buckling when Billy came through the door.

"I'd had a crush on him since I was fifteen," she says, which would have been about the time *Brown of Harvard* first made him a big star. "I thought he had the most gorgeous teeth I had ever seen. He came in wearing riding clothes and we took the test. I was facing the camera and had my arms around his neck. It was the easiest test I have ever made."

Nearly seventy years later, Page still grows dewy-eyed remembering Billy Haines. "He was so good to me," she says. "Because, after all, I'd never been in a big movie before. He could have taken advantage of me in many ways." She and her mother were both grateful for Billy's mentorship, especially after Louis B. Mayer had made a very unsubtle pass at Anita in his office. Billy took them around the studio, introduced them to other stars and technicians, invited them to his house for dinner. He helped Anita with her makeup for the picture, experimenting with different shades for her eyelids.

One of the stars Billy introduced her to was Joan Crawford,

who—reportedly struck by Page's beauty—asked her out on several dates. Crawford's crush on Page became well known around the lot. "It may have been true in the beginning, that she wanted to know me for that reason," Page says today. Later, when they made *Our Dancing Daughters* together, their relationship would turn to rivalry, but in the first months of Anita's MGM contract, they took dancing lessons together and visited each other's homes.

Production began on Billy's next film, *Excess Baggage*, on April 19 and finished shooting on May 11. It was not released until September, however. The delay was due to the fact that the film ran into some problems with the Hays office. Set up in response to the scandals of Fatty Arbuckle and William Desmond Taylor, the Hays office—lorded over by Postmaster General Will S. Hays—allowed Hollywood studios to monitor their output without government censorship. The studio moguls agreed that Hays could be their arbiter of taste, but in reality, the Hays office—in the 1920s, at least—had no real power. Hays or his lieutenant, Jason Joy, director of the Studio Relations Department, might object to a film, but there was no way to enforce a change. Still, to keep up the public relations ploy, most producers tried to accommodate somewhat, giving a little to save a lot.

In the case of *Excess Baggage*, directed by the pioneering James Cruze and written by Billy's good friend Frances Marion, some compromises were made. The story of a vaudevillian and his wife trying to break into movies, it's a rollicking farce with considerable innuendo. The scene where Billy tells costar Josephine Dunn that if it weren't for him, she'd "still be playing comfort stations," was changed to "playing the sticks." Several spanking scenes between Billy and Josephine, especially one in which he deliberately lifts her skirts first, were trimmed back or excised completely.

It was also the first of Billy's films to be released with a synchronized musical score and sound effects, courtesy of Fox Movietone equipment. The sound revolution was under way, and it had taken many in the industry by complete surprise. Even with the premiere of *The Jazz Singer* the previous October, few in Hollywood sensed anything more than a fad. In fact, the picture's influence wasn't really felt until early 1928, when its phenomenal success all over the country became apparent. In April most people in Hollywood got their first look (and sound) of a talking picture with the premiere of Warners' *Glorious Betsy*, and suddenly the industry woke up. Conrad Nagel would recall, "The night it opened [at Warners' new Hollywood theater] — my God, all Hollywood was there to see it."

Then, in July, came the release of Warners' *The Lights of New York*, in which for the first time, dialogue instead of subtitles carried the narrative. In August, James Quirk, editor of *Photoplay*, wrote that the "talkers" (as sound films were initially called) "will change the map of the entire motion picture within two years." He was uncannily accurate. Paramount promptly announced that all of its 1929 releases would be sound films. Warner Brothers issued a statement saying that because of the great success of their talking features, they would discontinue all silent film production.

Billy was hard at work on his latest film, King Vidor's *Show People*, but the coming of sound was the buzz of the industry. He couldn't have escaped it. Actors were suddenly confronted with the prospect of having to speak as well as act in front of a camera, and few felt entirely confident of their ability to do so. Billy wasn't overly worried; his voice was strong and deep, and he'd managed to soften his Virginia accent while transforming himself into a stately host of an English manor. Still, he must have wondered what his voice would sound like on a recording. He had never acted on the stage; he knew nothing of diction or projection.

Of course, *Show People* would have a synchronized score and sound effects; that was now de rigueur. Vidor, like many serious directors, was highly anxious that the new technology threatened the art form they had created. Alexander Walker writes, "The love-at-first-sound affair between the public and the early talkies was a great shock to many professional filmmakers who knew, better than the public did, just how crude and retrograde the new device was rendering their established art."

Show People is a good example. A superb film, it succeeds as delightful pantomime, turning on the hilarious performance of Marion

Davies as ambitious actress Peggy Pepper. The scene where she cajoles the casting clerk into giving her an audition could never have worked so well in a talkie. Marching up to the casting office hatch, Marion insists on giving the clerk a display of "emotions" — meditation, anger, passion, sorrow, joy. Of course, she's horrible, but the bit's inventive enough — Marion's father unfurls a handkerchief to cut between her "scenes" — that the clerk lets her in.

The film is set on the MGM lot. Its most celebrated scene is a delightful moving camera shot around the studio commissary table: There's William S. Hart, Douglas Fairbanks, Norma Talmadge, John Gilbert, Mae Murray, Rod La Rocque, Renée Adorée, Leatrice Joy, George K. Arthur, Karl Dane, Aileen Pringle, Claire Windsor, Estelle Taylor, Louella Parsons, Dorothy Sebastian, and Polly Moran. In a creative, surreal scene, Peggy Pepper spots Marion Davies in an expertly cross-cut montage. Peggy makes a face, saying, "I don't care for her."

Show People is Marion's film all the way. Having suffered through a number of box-office failures, she had been encouraged by good reviews and decent box office for *The Patsy*, and Hearst agreed that she should give another comedy role a shot. Thalberg tapped Billy to play opposite her, reasoning that his box-office clout could only help the effort. "It was an act of pushing Marion along," Billy would remember. "I didn't need the picture, but she needed me. In fact, those were Thalberg's exact words." To give his friend and frequent hostess a boost, then, Billy willingly accepted a less-than-central role. "Marion had an enormous talent," Billy said, and she certainly proved it with *Show People*.

Despite his secondary role, Billy performs admirably. There are a couple of typical, in-joke wisecracks: When Marion says her acting is the talk of Savannah, Billy quips his is the "scandal of Hollywood." When Peggy spots Elinor Glyn, he dismisses her with, "She writes a lot of those It stories." Mostly he plays it straight, very convincing as the good-natured, humble boyfriend. Unlike his other parts, in which viewers only start liking him toward the end, he's incredibly likable throughout, and believable. The *New York Times* opined, "Mr. Vidor, who more than once has proved himself a wizard in handling players, has accomplished here the seemingly impossible, by eliciting a restrained performance from William Haines, who has knocked over the traces in a number of films. In *Show People*, he actually compels sympathy for the character."

His next film was *Alias Jimmy Valentine*, directed by Jack Conway. It offered Billy the chance to move even further away from formula, playing a safecracker who reforms. Comedy was secondary in this crime melodrama, and Billy was eager to see the public's reaction to his performance. *Alias Jimmy Valentine* was fated to play a different role in his career, indeed in the career of Metro-Goldwyn-Mayer: Instead of being seen as Billy's first dramatic film, it would be seen as his—and MGM's—first talking picture.

Once Conway had finished shooting, Thalberg ordered the film back into production. Certain scenes would be reshot with dialogue. Billy got the call unexpectedly. Without any preparation, he was told he would be the first MGM star to face the microphone.

5

EXCESS BAGGAGE

1928-1931

The coming of sound revealed what silence had obscured, the baggage many top stars and directors carried around with them: Norma Talmadge's Brooklyn twang, Pola Negri's outlandishness, D. W. Griffith's drippy sentimentality. Certainly William Haines had some baggage of his own, but cavorting with sailors in Pershing Square was still—as yet—not as damaging as a high-pitched voice. In 1928, at the dawn of talking pictures, Billy was still riding high, and there was no reason to think his fall was imminent.

Thalberg and Mayer were confident that Billy's voice—deep and resonant, his Southern accent not overpowering—was the vehicle to lead them into the revolution. Still, they took no chances. Along with everyone else, they had Billy report for voice lessons. A Broadway vocal coach, Oliver Hinsdale, had been hired to train the MGM players in elocution. Billy found his lessons boring and Hinsdale pompous. After Billy flubbed his recitations several times in a row, Hinsdale sniffed, "The trouble with you, Mr. Haines, is that you're lip-lazy." To which, or so the legend goes, Billy wisecracked: "I've never had any complaints before."

The coming of sound intruded into the carefully constructed artificiality of the silent film industry. Panic gripped many producers by the throat. Billy would remember, "It was like the discovery of clap in a nunnery."

Nowhere was such panic more potent than at Metro-Goldwyn-Mayer. While Paramount announced all of its pictures for the upcoming season would be "talkers," MGM still had no soundstages ready. "It was the night of the *Titanic* all over again," Billy recalled, "with women grabbing the wrong children and Louis B. singing 'Nearer My God to Thee.'"

Mayer was adamantly opposed to sound, fearing the loss of lucrative foreign markets. "It was certainly the opinion of Mayer that this was all a fad," Billy said. "A foolish, foolish man." Yet canny: Mayer knew that many in his stable of stars—so well groomed, so thoroughly trained—would not be able to meet the microphone. In October, *Variety* predicted that more than thirty percent of the current crop of "strictly picture" actors would not make the transition. "The clearance," the trade paper said, "will be filled by players drawn mainly from Broadway."

Already Hollywood was importing stage stars from the East: Jeanne Eagles, Fredric March, Fanny Brice, Eddie Cantor, and, of course, Al Jolson. Established film stars like Billy, Joan Crawford, Eleanor Boardman, John Gilbert, Norma Shearer, and even Garbo, all of whom had little or no stage training, understood the threat to their positions. Only Chaplin remained determined to ignore the revolution, vowing never to make a talking picture. Al Jolson just laughed at him: "If Charlie Chaplin doesn't make talkies, he won't make anything."

Alias Jimmy Valentine was MGM's first partial talking picture. It was a smart business move on the studio's part: Billy was bankable. "It was the height of my career," he would remember. "Anything I made they came to see. If they'd put me in *Fanny Hill* backwards, I would have brought 'em in."

The picture was also a well-crafted crime drama, the kind that would become commonplace in the coming decade. Billy plays the crafty Jimmy Valentine, a wisecracking safecracker. Lionel Barrymore takes the part of the detective out to get him. Both were forced to trek over to the Paramount soundstages to repeat their final scene with dialogue since the MGM equipment wasn't ready. With microphones concealed in flower arrangements and under furniture, the two actors sparred back and forth effortlessly. Barrymore, of course, had many years of stage work in addition to his long movie career. Billy—the former bond salesman and floor walker—comported himself just as competently.

"William Haines makes his debut in talking pictures with flying colors," said *Film Daily*. "His voice is rich and dramatic, without being at all theatrical." Another review commented: "Too much cannot be said in praise of Mr. Haines' thoroughly expert and engaging performance. Even though his natural voice has not been caught by the recording process, it is pleasant and distinct."

Half a century later, some historians would claim William Haines was a victim of sound; however, his voice was fine, roundly applauded by critics and public alike. Those who knew him still recall his voice as one of his chief attributes: He could roar like a bear and imitate a whole cast of characters. He was the absolute right choice to lead MGM into the sound era.

Alias Jimmy Valentine was a box-office bonanza, Billy's biggest hit since *Tell It to the Marines*. It brought in $478,000 in profits, one of the best showings of any film that season. Certainly the dialogue was a draw, but so was the story, giving Billy the opportunity to play more than just Tom Brown in yet another guise. *Film Daily* opined, "William Haines . . . scores in a straight part with just enough of his smart aleck stuff to get the snickers."

Once again, however, a Haines picture ran afoul of the Hays office. As sound became a fixture and not merely a passing novelty, this would happen more and more, not just to Billy's films, but to pictures across the board. "One of the toughest jobs that I have had since I've been here has been in connection with a series of conferences with MGM concerning their picture *Alias Jimmy Valentine*," wrote Hays lieutenant Jason Joy to Carl E. Milliken, secretary of the Motion Picture Producers and Distributors of America (MPPDA), the administration body for preproduction censorship. "When you see it, you will understand how difficult the task was."

Specifically, Joy objected to a scene set in a church. Upon

entering, Karl Dane, playing Billy's cohort in crime, cracks: "This one's on me. I'll get the tickets." Looking around, he adds: "Packed house. Doin' a great business, ain't they? Hope we haven't missed the opening chorus." Billy then has to keep him from picking the pocketbooks left on the pews.

Joy had suggested the scene be cut, but Bernard Hyman, the film's producer, held firm, arguing it symbolized Billy's conversion from a life of crime to the straight-and-narrow path. "There will probably be protests from those strict religionists to whom a hearty laugh seems completely irreligious," Hyman wrote to Joy. "This is the only class of people who could possibly be offended by this sequence which has been carefully, forcefully, and splendidly handled."

In just a few years, "those strict religionists" would be harder to dismiss so easily. They were gathering momentum even as that letter was being drafted, planning for the showdown that would ultimately change Hollywood far more decisively than even the coming of sound.

What sound had done was add yet another realistic element to movies that had already become sexier, grittier, and more violent. It's important to understand the reformers' reaction to the perceived excesses in Hollywood films; the dynamics set into motion at this juncture would have reverberations that impacted Billy's career—and indeed, the very notion of gay identity in Hollywood.

The late silent period was a flowering of artistic freedom, a renaissance for filmmakers who had mastered their craft. In those days, Will Hays and Jason Joy could only scold and warn. And everything was subjective: What one MPPDA critic might find offensive, another might consider harmless. The results were films like *Seventh Heaven*, where Janet Gaynor and Charles Farrell lived in unwedded bliss and the world longed to emulate them; *Sadie Thompson*, where Gloria Swanson as a tramp was preferable to Gloria Swanson as a saint; and *Alias Jimmy Valentine*, where a laugh at the expense of pious churchgoers was defended as integral to the plot.

The talkie revolution heralded a new call for censorship. Joan Crawford's moans as she made love to Robert Montgomery in her first talking picture, *Untamed*, took away any illusion of make-believe: That was *sex* up there on the screen.

"Silent smut had been bad," wrote Father Daniel Lord, a Jesuit priest who led the charge of protest against the movies. "Vocal smut cried to the censors for vengeance." It had been the Baptists and Presbyterians who'd shouted the loudest when the Fatty Arbuckle and William Desmond Taylor scandals erupted nearly a decade before. Now it was the Catholics' turn, with pastors around the country suddenly beating their pulpits on Sunday mornings condemning the excesses of the movies.

Will Hays, fearful that this growing chorus of criticism might translate into government-imposed censorship, called a meeting with Martin Quigley, an ardent lay Catholic who was publisher of *Exhibitors' Herald-World*, a film-industry trade paper. Quigley was also the originator of the Quigley Poll, which determined the most popular actor and actress every year based on exhibitors' reports. Despite his livelihood, Quigley agreed with his church's condemnation of the industry. Hays appealed to him to help prevent outside censorship, claiming—accurately—that it could wreck the movies as both industry and art form. Quigley agreed to intervene.

After meeting with top Catholic leaders, Quigley made a momentous proposal to Hays. The film industry could continue to regulate itself, outside of government influence, *if* they based their self-censorship on Catholic principles. He suggested that Father Daniel Lord, who had served as religious adviser to Cecil B. DeMille on *King of Kings*, draft a production code by which directors and studios would make movies. "What emerged," wrote historian Gregory Black, "was a fascinating combination of Catholic theology, conservative politics, and pop psychology—an amalgam that would control the content of Hollywood films for three decades."

The Code, drafted late in 1929, expanded on Hays's own list of "Don'ts and Be Carefuls," adhering to a philosophy that movies were morality plays for the masses. Church, government, and family were the foundations of society in the view of the Code. Deviance—whether it be sexual, criminal, or heretical—destroyed those foundations. Violators could not go unpunished; everything in a film must be geared toward maintaining (and ultimately venerating) the cultural, social, and religious status quo.

Hays encountered some resistance with the studios in trying to impose the Code. Irving Thalberg, notably, insisted that movies should not be any more restricted in their presentations than literature or stage plays. Along with Jack Warner and B. P. Schulberg of Paramount, Thalberg offered a counterproposal, saying, in effect, that the only guidelines needed were those set by audiences: If the public disapproved of a particular picture, they wouldn't pay to see it. In February 1930, faced with mounting Catholic threats for boycotts in the wake of the great crash on Wall Street, producers gave in and accepted Lord's proposal. The Production Code was born.

That was hardly the final word. Even as they attached their names to the agreement, motion picture producers knew it contained no teeth. Even as they shook hands with Lord and Quigley and Hays, who for the moment basked in the glow of self-congratulation, they were planning their next productions: *Madam Satan*, in which Kay Johnson would sashay half naked to seduce her husband away from his mistress; *Morocco*, in which German import Marlene Dietrich would kiss another woman full upon the lips; and *Little Caesar*, in which Edward G. Robinson as the cop-killing gangster would emerge as the unqualified hero, and every young impressionable boy in the audience would wish to be just like him.

What remained, however, as real as it had been in 1922, was a subject as yet unchallenged by Lord and his Catholic colleagues: the offscreen lives of the stars the public was emulating. While the content of a William Haines picture could be addressed under the Code, the star himself was still free to carouse and live his life the way most in Hollywood were living theirs.

The excesses of the Roaring Twenties were already drawing criticism. Already many clerics had denounced Clara Bow, the It Girl, from their pulpits. Her wild life away from the studio was much more colorful than any of her onscreen roles. Since the scandals of the 1920s, most performers had morals clauses written into their contracts. Should they engage in behavior scandalous to the studio, the morals clause would terminate the agreement between producer and performer. Some of the biggest stars were able to scratch out the clause and refuse to be bound by it. Warner Baxter, in his 1928 contract with Fox, apparently suffered no studio backlash for crossing out his morals clause. It's initialed by both Baxter and studio chief Winfield Sheehan. Clara Bow tried to do the same thing, but Paramount, unnerved by the potential of a freewheeling It Girl, made her annual bonus contingent upon her behavior.

Billy Haines's contracts remain locked in the vaults of Turner Broadcasting in Atlanta, which bought Metro-Goldwyn-Mayer and sealed off the studio's archives to scholars and film historians. Repeated attempts to gain access were rebuffed by the Turner legal department. However, in extensive unpublished notes left by MGM screenwriter Frances Marion, there are some tantalizing clues. Marion, who knew Billy quite well (she was often escorted by him to premieres and parties before her marriage to top cowboy star Fred Thomson), indicated that Billy, like Baxter, had enough clout by 1929 to cross out the morals clause in his new contract. He'd have had good reason to do so. Although the exact wording is obviously unknown, the clauses were similar from studio to studio. Baxter's scratched-out clause read: "If the artist shall conduct himself . . . in his private life in such a manner as to commit an offense involving moral turpitude under federal, state or local laws or ordinances, or shall conduct himself in such a manner that shall offend against decency, morality, or social proprieties, or in a manner that shall cause him to be held in public ridicule, scorn, or contempt, or in a manner that shall cause public scandal, then . . . the producer may at its option and upon one week's notice to the artist terminate this contract."

Marion wrote that Billy, being MGM's leading male draw at the time, was powerful enough to withhold his signature until the offending clause was removed. Like Bow, however, he remained a ticking time bomb without that safeguard for the studio. Mayer could not have been happy by this power play. Marion wrote that in response, the studio kept Billy on a short leash; his two-year contracts were unusual, in that most stars were signed on for five or more years. This was Mayer's out: If in fact Billy was able to cross out his morals clause, the studio made sure it wouldn't be stuck with him too long if his misbehavior became public.

Along with the increasing calls for censorship came a new and more difficult relationship with the press. With clergymen enflaming public opinion, there was a ready-made readership for stories critical of Hollywood. While no columnist or fan magazine writer was quite ready to bite the hand of the studios that fed them, many were getting a real taste of the increasing power they could wield. Alexander Walker has written of "the latent sadism" that suddenly revealed itself in the fan magazines with the coming of sound, magazines that just months before "had sucked up to [the studios] for interviewing and access privileges."

The *Hollywood Reporter*, which debuted in 1930, was representative of the new kind of trade paper. Billy Wilkerson, its publisher, angered a number of the studio chieftans by refusing to print verbatim their publicity releases. It was hardy investigative journalism, but more and more publications ran unflattering reports about the stars — or at least reports that deviated from the studio line. Louella Parsons, who'd recently expanded her duties from columnist to editor of the entire entertainment section of the Hearst newspaper chain, dared to criticize even the biggest. If Garbo hated making movies so much, Lolly wrote, send her back to Sweden: Jeanne Eagels would be just as good in *Anna Karenina*.

Parsons had been pampered by the studios ever since Hearst brought her out to Hollywood in 1926. Now, tired of her increasingly independent tone and frequent inconsistency with facts, a number of studio chiefs, including Mayer, stopped giving her forty-eight hours' preferential treatment. All reporters would get studio press releases simultaneously. That move prompted a greater rivalry among columnists, with each elbowing his or her way to the front, breaking news and scooping each other. Parsons responded by setting up special deals with actors' agents, who slipped her material ahead of the studios. Slowly, the meticulously balanced partnership among studio, press, performer, and public was being broken down.

There is the famous story of Billy Haines being caught in a raid at a gay bar in Hollywood. Constance Talmadge was said to be with him, along with Jimmie and a handful of other friends, probably Mitt and Larry. Some reports say they were arrested; others say they managed to slip out the back door when the cops burst in.

Anita Loos, yet again, tells the story: Louella Parsons, having been tipped off about the raid, called Talmadge's formidable mother, Peg, the next morning. "Peg assured Louella that her child would never dream of setting foot in such a low dive," Loos wrote. Louella snapped, "Don't give me that, Peg! This is *Louella*!" The irate columnist then slammed down the receiver. "Peg broke into a cold sweat and waited for the dread item to appear that would end Dutch's salary forever," Loos recalled.

Louella, however, apparently "had smellier fish to fry, and she dropped the matter." Still, Loos wrote that "vague hints of misdemeanor" regarding Billy began showing up in Lolly's column: "It was Louella's reportage that later helped to do him in."

There are several problems with this story, the most obvious being the implication of a vendetta waged against Billy by Louella Parsons. The columnist certainly knew Billy was gay. As Hearst's frontline warrior, she was a frequent visitor to San Simeon, where she regularly encountered Billy and Jimmie. Hearst liked Billy; it would not have made sense for Parsons to wage a campaign against a friend of the Chief. And Billy liked Louella, even if he (like so many others) thought her something of a hypocrite. While she railed against immorality in movies, she supported the extramarital affair of Hearst and Marion Davies, and was herself involved with a married man back east before her marriage to Dr. Harry Martin. Parsons had many gay friends; what mattered to her was the public perception a star could project. Garbo's antipathy toward making movies was much less forgivable than Billy Haines and Dutch Talmadge patronizing a gay bar.

The other problem with the story is its timing: The first establishments that might accurately be called "gay" did not appear in Hollywood until 1930. That was one year after Constance Talmadge had retired from films, unwilling to invest the energy needed for a transition to sound. ("Get out while you can," Constance cabled her sister Norma, after seeing Norma's disastrous talkie debut. "And be thankful for the trust funds Mama set up.") A raid on a "gay bar" would, then, have had to occur *after* Talmadge had ceased caring about her future in pictures.

Still, it's clear that *something* happened. Dutch Talmadge probably *was* there, as Loos's memory for these things was sharp, and likely Billy *did*—yet again—incur Mayer's wrath. Of course, this was during Prohibition, so if the establishment served alcohol it would have been forbidden (at least officially) by studio rules. The incident may have occurred while Talmadge was still in pictures, that is, 1928 or 1929. Although strictly "gay" clubs didn't appear until 1930, there were enough speakeasies serving sexually ambiguous clienteles that a raid may have been likely.

Billy was an avid nightclub patron in those early years. Harry Hay, then a young actor, recalls the opening of Jimmy's Backyard on Ivar Street on New Year's Eve, 1929, the first establishment to serve "an exclusively gay clientele." Hay says the place was spoken of "in whispers even that first night as the first of its kind in Hollywood." The walls were neatly whitewashed, the floor carpeted, and the scattered tables looked like what might have been expected at a backyard social. "It was furnished sufficiently to be comfortable for a light supper with drinks," Hay says. "It was my first 'Temperamental' event—my Cinderella's ball."

"Temperamental" was the term Hay and many homosexuals of the period used to describe themselves, to define who they were as part of a community outside the larger culture. The opening of Jimmy's Backyard, then, was a watershed event: It helped crystallize the identity of a large segment of the Hollywood population. In attendance, Hay recalls, were nearly three hundred men in ties and tails. "No drag, as I remember, although some, including the young friend who'd invited me, wore handsome fur wraps as overcoats." This was clearly a formal occasion: Even the scattering of women present were similarly tuxed and tailed. Hay doesn't remember if there was dancing; if police found same-sex couples dancing, it would be an excuse for a raid—but there *was* some hanky-panky: "I only remember going from table to table and lap to lap," Hay says. "I was a tall, slimly muscled eighteen, going on nineteen, still a freshman at Stanford."

Billy Haines arrived with an entourage, making no effort to disguise his identity, Hay recalls. "I remember him being pointed out to me along with other members of his party," which Hay believes included the "very dapper" Lowell Sherman. Sherman had been a handsome silent film villain since 1920's *Way Down East* with Lillian Gish. More recently he'd starred with Garbo in *The Divine Woman*, and was now directing as well as acting. Jimmie was likely there as well, and Edmund Lowe and Lilyan Tashman may also have been in attendance, as they were frequent companions of Billy's in the gay nightclub scene. Lowe, like Billy, was then at the top of his career, having scored a huge success in *What Price Glory?* for Fox. Tashman, too, a former Ziegfeld girl, was in her prime, having just finished *Bulldog Drummond* with Ronald Colman. That "Hollywood's smartest couple" would patronize such clubs as Jimmy's Backyard with relative impunity shows the degree of freedom Hollywood still allowed its players.

Jimmy's Backyard signaled a trend. Within the next year and a half, a number of other such clubs opened in Hollywood. Hay remembers Freddy's and Allen's, both "temperamental" speakeasies set up in apartments with bathtub gin and bare-floor bedrooms where patrons danced and occasionally put on shows. It was rare for such a place to go unraided for more than three weeks; after a raid, it would be closed down, only to be succeeded by another. "You kept an ear cocked to hear about whoever's new place about every six weeks," Hay says.

The "pansy clubs" soon became open secrets among the "in crowd." Hollywood was still a tolerant enough place that its top stars could play along the fringe of society, and even get photographed doing so. Gossip columns in the *Hollywood Reporter* were filled with stories of top stars patronizing the suddenly trendy female impersonator clubs. Most of these stars did, in fact, engage (at least occasionally) in gay affairs. One story told of Billy sitting around a table with Howard Hughes, Tallulah Bankhead, and Ethel Barrymore at B.B.B.'s Cellar, a cramped dark club where a line of ten boys performed as girls. The patrons were all given tiny wooden mallets and instructed to pound their tables whenever a new guest arrived, evoking a cacophony of noise and laughter.

The "pansy craze" swept most of the large cities in the country in the early 1930s. *Variety* took note of the trend as it hit Hollywood: "Several oo-la-la entertainers are figuring on opening spots here, believing the craze will build." In 1932, toward the end of the craze, the *Hollywood Reporter* spotted Billy and Joan Crawford at La Boheme over on Sunset Boulevard, where owner Karyl Norman entertained his patrons by dressing up in yards of feathers and lace. Norman had been a big hit in New York, but hit his stride in Hollywood. He ended his show with a scathingly accurate impersonation of Crawford as Sadie Thompson. Billy and Joan were delighted.

For a brief glorious moment, drag queens ruled Hollywood's nightlife. Jimmy's Backyard hosted Rae Bourbon's "Boys Will Be Girls" show and Francis Renault performed at Clarke's. The leading light, however, was Billy's old Village acquaintance Jean Malin, who, like Norman, had moved his act out to Hollywood. Billy arranged for Polly Moran to serve as Malin's "dinner date" to various Hollywood functions. In fact, Malin was very popular with the Hollywood set. He brought the camp and culture of Greenwich Village to a largely mixed gay-straight audience.

Officially, the pansy clubs served no alcohol, but they were still watched by the police for such "sins" as same-sex dancing and nudity. It might appear odd that Billy Haines would so publicly take part in a nightlife that could damage his reputation, should the police suddenly decide to clamp down (as apparently happened the night he was out with Constance Talmadge). He was hardly the only star to patronize the clubs: Jean Harlow, Ethel Barrymore, Cary Grant, Howard Hughes, Joan Crawford, Edmund Lowe, and Lilyan Tashman were all spotted at one time or another. None of them had any reason—not in 1929 or 1930, at least—to believe that their nightly romps were incompatible with box-office clout. Billy had come of age in Hollywood during a period of tolerance for difference. And besides, how could anyone criticize him for attending Karyl Norman's show with *Ethel Barrymore* sitting next to him?

Times were changing. Columnists now sniped at stars; innuendo crept into supposedly fluff magazine pieces. Gay stars took the most hits. One wag quipped that Billy would rather step out with Polly Moran than with a whole season of Wampas Baby Stars. (By now, the "romance" with Polly was tiring and more than a little embarrassing for Mayer.) Even the little items about Polly Moran and Jean Malin carried a certain edge: OH MY DEAH! one was headlined, referring to Malin as a "thing" and implying there was something odd about Polly for cavorting around town with such a creature.

The opening of gay clubs was a logical extension of the free living Hollywood had enjoyed throughout the twenties. Their flowering, however, was brief: Los Angeles police launched an all-out war against "the Nance and Lesbian amusement places in town" in 1932, although it would take another year or so before they were effectively shut down. An ordinance was passed prohibiting one gender from wearing the clothing of the other, sending Karyl Norman and Rae Bourbon's boys packing their boas.

George Chauncey has written, "The revulsion against gay life in the early 1930's was part of a larger reaction to the perceived 'excesses' of the Prohibition years and the blurring of the boundaries between acceptable and unacceptable public sociability."

In addition, as the Depression deepened, gender conflict escalated. With many men out of work, their sense of mastery over their lives and those of their families was threatened. In this context, homosexuals took on a greater menace. By their very natures, their very existence, they called into question fundamental cornerstones of society: male supremacy, gender and social arrangements, the sanctity of the church and family. The pansy craze led to a series of ordinances outlawing female impersonation. It is no coincidence that during this same period the Production Code also strove to eliminate any depiction of or reference to homosexuality in films.

It was in such an atmosphere of mounting intolerance that Mayer would have confronted Billy after the raid incident. If Billy *was* arrested, Mayer most certainly bailed him out and made sure none of the less-trusted members of the press got wind of it. Today, no arrest records remain, as is the case for several actors known or suspected to have been arrested. In general, the studios enjoyed a "working relationship" with District Attorney Buron Fitts, who could usually (although not always) be counted on to keep a star's record clean. Homosexuality was becoming more of a consequential issue, with the Catholics rallying their congregations around immoral pictures and the police raiding the pansy clubs. Billy Haines, on top of the world in 1930, having just made a successful transition to sound, could scarcely have predicted the impact this would have on his career.

Of course, the Depression itself was another factor in the changing social attitudes. At its peak, there were sixteen million Americans out of work, about a third of the available labor force. The widespread poverty and malaise that gripped the country for nearly a decade changed the psyche of the public: There was little tolerance for excess, for nonconformity, for frivolity.

Hollywood, in general, escaped the deadly grip that strangled many other industries into near ruin. Movies remained an important route of escape for a ravaged and weary population. In the first years of the Great Depression, movie attendance grew steadily: By 1930 it stood at 110 million weekly, double the figures from three years before. Metro-Goldwyn-Mayer saw its profits rise from $12 million in 1929 to $15 million in 1930. Other studios weren't quite as prosperous: Paramount was in economic ruin and Universal, despite the talkie craze, saw no bounce in its profits. Mayer wasn't about to take any chances, and toed a conservative economic line.

As well as a grandiloquent one. The studio chief rationalized Hollywood's profits and freewheeling spending as somehow patriotic. Even if the average citizen struggled along with hardly enough food on the table, Mayer insisted movie stars needed to continue living lives of opulence. "[The stars] have to keep living that way," Mayer believed, "so that the unemployed can plunk down their 25 cent admission charge and have renewed faith in the future."

Certainly Billy sailed through the Depression with little trouble. His father, an investment banker, had wisely advised him to invest much of his earnings in U.S. government bonds. Unlike many

Billy, age four, with his
preferred childhood playmate,
sister Lillion.
(UPI/Corbis-Bettmann)

. . .

The young William Haines of
Greenwich Village, circa 1920,
in his one spiffy suit.
(Collection of Sergei Troubetzkoy)

. . .

Jimmie Shields, as he appeared when Billy first met him in 1926.
(Courtesy of Charles Conrad)

• • •

Billy's breakout performance in *The Midnight Express* (1924), with Elaine Hammerstein, brought him to the attention of moviegoers—as well as Peggy Hopkins Joyce.
(Museum of Modern Art/Film Stills Archive)

• • •

Billy returned home to Virginia in 1926 expecting a marching band—but all he got was this family portrait. *Back, left to right:* Lillion; Billy; Ann; and father, George, Sr. *Front, left to right:* Henry; mother, Laura; and George, Jr.

•　•　•

The film that made Billy a star, *Brown of Harvard* (1926), was really a love story between two college roommates. Billy, as the title character, Tom, poses with Jack Pickford, in the role of the "sensitive" Jim. *(Michael Peter Yakaitis Collection)*

•　•　•

The "Haines castle," as Tallulah Bankhead called it, began being remodeled in 1926 from a small house on North Stanley Drive into a splendid palace showplace. Billy replaced the original Spanish Colonial exterior with a blend of colonial New Orleans and eighteenth-century England. *(Museum of Modern Art/Film Stills Archive)*

· · ·

The dining room featured a parquet floor, Sheraton table, Directoire chairs, and Billy's trademark hand-painted pictorial wallpaper. *(Museum of Modern Art/Film Stills Archive)*

· · ·

Billy and Jimmie lived like two "country squires." Note the sculpture here with Jimmie. *(Courtesy of Charles Conrad)*

• • •

Billy poses before a seventeenth-century portrait in his renovated home. Irving Thalberg, overwhelmed with the renovation as he was escorted around the house, asked Billy, "Who did this?" "I did," Billy replied simply. *(Museum of Modern Art/Film Stills Archive)*

• • •

A beefcake shot from *Tell It to the Marines* (1926). The movie later proved that Billy's success in *Brown of Harvard* had been no fluke. *(Michael Peter Yakaitis Collection)*

· · ·

Billy thought Lon Chaney, here with him in *Tell It to the Marines*, was one of many "actors who should have been hanging in the smokehouse." Still, he told his brother that it was Chaney and he who kept MGM afloat. *(Michael Peter Yakaitis Collection)*

· · ·

In 1928 Billy was a far bigger star than leading lady Joan Crawford, who here receives no billing on the poster for *West Point*. *(Collection of Sergei Troubetzkoy)*

Billy with two of his best girlfriends, Marion Davies and Constance Bennett, in 1929. *(UPI/Corbis-Bettmann)*

Billy could portray athletes from football, baseball, golf, and (as here, in 1929) polo, yet he despised athletics, especially the competitive kind. *(Museum of Modern Art/Film Stills Archive)*

• • •   • • •

Anita Page was one of Billy's most frequent costars—and the only woman he ever asked to marry him. Here they are in *Telling the World* (1928). *(Michael Peter Yakaitis Collection)*

Alias Jimmy Valentine (1929) showcased *many* of Billy's talents—not least of which was a great voice for talkies. *(Michael Peter Yakaitis Collection)*

• • •

Way Out West (1930) strikes modern audiences as very gay: Billy, swishing around for approval, is the prize catch for a group of cowboys. *(Collection of Sergei Troubetzkoy)*

• • •

Remaking Billy's image in *Just a Gigolo* (1931). The Hays office went berserk over the film's raciness, including this unzipping scene with Maria Alba. *(Michael Peter Yakaitis Collection)*

• • •

Billy had no better friend than Joan Crawford, here at the premiere of *Rain* in 1932 with her hubby Douglas Fairbanks, Jr. Billy and Bob Young arrived arm in arm. *(UPI/Corbis-Bettmann)*

• • •

Camping for New York
photographers, circa 1931.
(Collection of Sergei Troubetzkoy)

• • •

Despite the smile, Billy loathed his
in-person publicity show for *The New
Adventures of Get-Rich-Quick Wallingford*
(1931) at New York's Capitol Theater.
(UPI/Corbis-Bettmann)

• • •

Billy was in fine shape for the making of his last MGM film, *Fast Life* (1932), but the picture was barely released.
(Collection of Sergei Troubetzkoy)

. . .

A newly mustachioed Billy looked fit, trim, and ready to take on a new life when he returned from Europe in 1934. *(UPI/Corbis-Bettmann)*

. . .

Billy and Cary Grant
escorted Ina Claire,
Genevieve Tobin, and
Peggy Wood to the theater
in November 1935.
(UPI/Corbis-Bettmann)

· · ·

Birds of a feather flock
together. *Left to right:*
Alice Glasser, Lilyan
Tashman, Edmund
Lowe, Billy, and
George Cukor at a
party at Vendome,
May 1933. *(Museum
of Modern Art/Film
Stills Archive)*

· · ·

Out on the town in
1935: Billy, Kay
Francis, Harpo Marx,
Andy Lawler, and
costume designer
Charles LeMaire.
(UPI/Corbis-Bettmann)

· · ·

Billy's new career as decorator to the stars began with the grand palace of Phil Berg and Leila Hyams (circa 1935). *(UPI/Corbis-Bettmann)*

•   •   •

Then came the headlines of El Porto in June 1936. Little Jimmy Walker was brought to court by his mother and a sheriff. *(UPI/Corbis-Bettmann)*

•   •   •

The house Billy moved in to on Lorna Lane in the 1940s may have been modest compared to the North Stanley residence, but visitors marveled at the lush garden around the pool.
(Courtesy of Charles Conrad)

•   •   •

The friendship with Crawford withstood the test of time. In 1955 Billy and Jimmie hosted a posthoneymoon reception for Joan and husband number four, Alfred Steele, at the Haines-Shields home on Lorna Lane. *(Courtesy of Charles Conrad)*

• • •

Billy clowns with Lauren Bacall and Clifton Webb at Chasen's in the mid-1950s. *(Courtesy of Charles Conrad)*

• • •

The Beverly Hills studio of William Haines, Inc., showcased the talents of Billy and Ted Graber. This was their showroom in the early 1960s, a blend of Graber's more modern influences and Billy's signature chinoiserie.

· · ·

Even with the notorious toupee, Billy cut a striking figure, posing in his living room in the mid-1960s. Note the famous "Les Incas" wallpaper, which Jack Warner borrowed for a film and Billy had pasted back on the wall, an inch at a time.

· · ·

The redecoration of Winfield House for Walter Annenberg, named Ambassador to Britain by President Nixon in 1968, was the pinnacle of Billy's design career. Billy beams as he poses with Annenberg and his wife, Lee, the day the new envoy presented his credentials to Queen Elizabeth II.

· · ·

Despite tensions, Billy, Jimmie, Ted Graber, and Lee Annenberg were all smiles after nine months "to the hour" of work.

· · ·

The elegant, distinguished gentleman of seventy was a far cry from the boy who ran away from home at fourteen. *(Courtesy of Charles Conrad)*

· · ·

stars—notably Greta Garbo—he lost no money in the stock market crash. Indeed, when a reporter asked him how he and his Hollywood pals were surviving the Depression, he looked "rather vague" to the questioner, as if he hadn't given it much thought. "Why—a—I don't think we feel it much," he admitted. Everyone he knew was still working, still collecting a salary—and to top it off, living expenses had been reduced. "I am speaking of the contract players, of course," Billy added as an afterthought. "As for the others I can't say. I believe it hit some of them pretty hard."

It was a careful balance that had to be walked: The public still wanted its stars to live like gods, but did not want them to appear frivolous or to take their fortune for granted. Stories appeared in the fan magazines about Joan Crawford's charity drives, about Marion Davies serving dinner to the unemployed at Hollywood soup kitchens. It was all publicity, and it's quite possible that the public understood that. What mattered, in the end, was the maintenance of the myth.

It could be argued that Mayer was right, that the stars did indeed perform a public service by living as large as they did, providing glamour and intrigue to a world suddenly bereft of it. Billy Haines certainly did his part, spending the first years of the Great Depression buying up exquisite antiques and expensive fabrics to continue the transformation of his home into a Hollywood showplace. Several fan magazines ran photo spreads of the house Tallulah Bankhead would dub the "Haines castle."

Remembering that period, Billy would later downplay his affluence. "It's such a fallacy that we all made so much money. Everybody says, 'Oh, before heavy taxes, you all made so much.' Now, look. You come into pictures empty-handed. You don't have a goddamned cent. You have to buy clothes. Then you have to have your teeth fixed. Then your family comes out by horseback and covered wagon, and you have to take care of them. And if you're a respectable actor with any kind of background at all, you've got to buy them a silver tea service so they won't look like they came from the other side of the tracks."

By 1928 the rest of his family *had* come out (although by automobile and not by covered wagon). Laura had returned to Virginia earlier that year to gather up the rest of the clan. She and George and their two sons drove across country; Ann Haines Langhorne, recently divorced from her husband, took the train with her two sons, James and William, and their nurse-cook Buffy Braxton. Billy took care of them all, buying them not only the requisite silver tea sets but a whole lot more. He found them a small but comfortable house at 7084 Hawthorne Avenue. George Haines found work as an investment banker, while George, Jr., became Billy's personal secretary (Larry Sullivan was now running Billy's fan club). Ann took a job in a Hollywood millinery shop.

They also made a stab at the movies. In October 1930, Ann, who shared not only a physical resemblance with Billy but also his quick wit and irreverence, started doing extra work on the Metro lot. "She was a beauty," remembers Arch Case. "Fred MacMurray was chasing her all over Hollywood for a long time. But he never got her. Ann was a tough old broad, just marvelous."

Handsome and poised, brother George was considered perfect for the movies. "He had the looks of the family," says his younger brother Henry. Billy encouraged the idea of an acting career, securing George some walk-ons and offering to talk to Thalberg about a contract. Henry Haines recalls George was offered a major part in a film, but turned it down. "He was just too shy," his brother says. George, a sweet-tempered, friendly man, had none of Billy's bon vivant humor, none of his ease with people. He preferred the background role of secretary, always mingling uneasily at Billy's Hollywood galas.

For young Henry Haines, then just eleven years old, to be plucked from the hills of Virginia and resettled among the royalty of Hollywood was a fascinating experience. Cliff Edwards, also known as Ukulele Ike, was a frequent costar of Billy's and came by the family house often. "He had this very low-slung Italian car," Henry recalls. "If he drove into the driveway too fast, he'd hit the bottom of it." He also remembers meeting Joan Crawford for the first time: "My impression of her was that she wore too much makeup," he says. Billy rented a beach house in Santa Monica where Henry recalls seeing Ramon Novarro and Polly Moran. "But you know how children are. I wasn't really impressed. They were just like members of the family."

Still, Henry was very fond of his big brother. "He was very good to me," he recalls. "He was always slipping me ten bucks, and in those days that was a lot of money."

Louis B. Mayer was pleased with Billy's treatment of his family. The studio chief made a big show around the lot about family loyalty. One of the mitigating influences on his generally harsh opinion of Ramon Novarro had been Novarro's devotion as a son and brother. He felt similarly toward Billy, too, encouraging him to bring his family to the lot, agreeing to secure Ann and George some small parts. The only family member he resented, of course, remained Jimmie. Mayer would fume all day when he spotted Jimmie on the set of one of Billy's films, having brought lunch for cast and crew.

Billy's blood family shared none of Mayer's intolerances. They quickly accepted Jimmie as part of the family. As recipients of Billy's generosity, of course, they had little choice in the matter. But they were genuine, sincere people, with little use for those who sat in judgment of others.

In fact, Jimmie's mother, "Aunt" Ida Haselden, came for an extended visit around 1930 and must have met Billy's family as well. A notice on the society page of the *Daytona Beach New Journal* says Mrs. J. S. Haselden would leave for Hollywood, "where she will be the guest of her son, Jimmie Shields, and William Haines, at the Haines home, 1712 North Stanley Drive." Quite a public declaration of her son's relationship with Billy. Ida is pictured in the newspaper as a smiling, white-haired matron in a sleeveless black dress and long strand of pearls. It's obvious where Jimmie got his air of regality. Ida was also known to have fun: She had recently been elected vice president of the Daytona Beach Women's Golf Association. Some years later she won a local epitaph contest with this entry: "Here I am, gals, now old and sad/All because of this golfing fad/My raven locks have turned snow white/And I still can't hit that darned ball right!"

It must have made quite the party: Jimmie, Billy, Jimmie's mother,

Billy's parents, his divorced sister, her children, Polly Moran, Mitt, Larry, Cranberry Crawford. It was a very modern definition of family, one old Charles Haines back in Staunton could scarcely have predicted for his kin.

The Duke Steps Out was released in March 1929. It was not a talkie but was nonetheless a gigantic hit. MGM was slow at moving into talking pictures while it completed its soundstages. The success of *Duke* proved that the best silent films could still outgross mediocre talkies, no matter how much the public demanded sound. Despite the rewarding precedent of *Alias Jimmy Valentine*, this was a return to formula, Billy playing yet another smart aleck, this one dropping out of college to become a boxer. *Variety* summed up Billy's standing at the time: "For Haines, it's his usual routine and there's not much doubt he's the screen's top disciple of juvenile egotism."

So it was with particular confidence that the "screen's top disciple" decided the time was right to ask for a raise. He was particularly galled that John Gilbert, whose *Redemption* had actually *lost* money for the studio, was still receiving a higher salary than he was. Billy paid a call on Thalberg, but instead of being direct, he wisecracked about his box-office clout and his profitability for the studio. When Thalberg refused to take the hint, Billy grew pouty.

"Okay, take the nipple out of your mouth and tell me what's wrong," Thalberg said.

Thalberg could talk to him that way; Billy took no offense. He straightened up and asked point-blank for the raise. Given the studio's conservative Depression-era financial policies, Thalberg refused. Instead, he gave Billy a $10,000 bonus and told him to put it in an annuity. "Don't spend it," he urged. "This is a time to save."

He was right, of course, and Billy would later be grateful for Thalberg's advice. "He was a great, great fellow," Billy would say. "I was blind when it came to him. It was just the opposite with Mayer. I remember everything good about the one, everything nasty about the other."

Given their temperaments, it's no surprise that Billy and Mayer clashed. Mayer was orderly, controlling, and not inclined to frivolity.

Billy, on the other hand, was the antithesis to order, and it's a wonder his antics didn't ostracize more people than the studio chief. His behavior was sometimes so outlandish during this period that it's difficult to reconcile the two images of William Haines: irreverent wisecracker and cultured gentleman.

For instance, there was the time a writer from one of the movie magazines asked Billy for help in meeting Marion Davies. The writer was very nervous, and she very much wanted to make an impression on Marion. Billy thought her a bit too highfalutin, and figured he'd teach her a lesson. Just as Marion appeared in the doorway, Billy grasped the writer with his big paws and turned her over on her head, causing her skirts to flutter down, revealing her slip and garter.

Then there was the swank dinner party given by a notoriously frugal hostess, where Billy showed up with a large paper bag and solemnly distributed greasy doughnuts to each of the appreciative guests around the table. The hostess was shocked, but the next day forgave him. After all, that was what Billy Haines *did*.

At a costume party at San Simeon, Irving Thalberg arrived with wife Norma Shearer in identical West Point cadet outfits. Haines goosed him — actually walked up to the vice president in charge of production at Metro-Goldwyn-Mayer and *goosed* him. "Sorry, Irving." Billy winked. "I thought you were Norma!"

Once he learned that the other actors on a film were planning to quit at four o'clock. Determined that, as the star, he should have the same privilege, he stopped at the specified hour smack in the middle of a scene, cameras rolling, and announced: "It's four o'clock and I'm going home!" The director, exasperated, refused to let him leave, occasioning one of the famous Haines mood swings. He sulked the rest of the day.

This dual nature of Billy Haines keeps cropping up in the accounts of his life, from his childhood to old age. He had created a persona, both on the screen and off, that required a great deal of effort to keep up. Not only did he have to appear eternally witty, he had to constantly deflect questions that might pry too deep. His alternating bouts of manic energy and periods of quiet reserve, possibly even depression, may have been less a medical condition than inspired by his continual sense of performance. At home with Jimmie, he was often quiet and reflective. There was some publicity that he became a serious reader of Joseph Conrad—a publicist's invention, perhaps, but maybe he did indeed seek his own escape, the kind of refuge the public found in movies. Sometimes he'd go to the beach—not to swim, but just to sit there in the sun by himself.

When the sun set, he became animated, the wisecracker emerging. He'd call Polly or Mitt and they'd all pile into his car and crash a party at Cranberry Crawford's or Norma Shearer's. The hosts rarely got angry with Billy, or if they did, they chose not to show it. They knew what Billy could do with someone who got puffed up with air.

There was considerable drinking among his set; Mitchell Foster was a notorious imbiber. Drugs don't seem to have played a large part; some in his crowd used cocaine, but Billy preferred alcohol. He told one friend that he'd once gotten so drunk at Marion Davies's beach house, mixing his liquor until he couldn't even stand straight, that he ended up under the piano with Clara Bow. "She wanted to do it, right then and there," he said. "I was so drunk I said, 'Sure. Why not?'"

Billy's occasional forays into heterosexuality were less about trying to play the game than about living the free and independent life the 1920s had taught him. In 1929 he took off with one of his leading ladies for an impromptu trip to Mexico. There they had a few days of passion before coming back home to face the music. "Jimmie was hootin' mad," Arch Case says. He recalls Billy telling the story of the affair, and Jimmie still furious at the mention of it decades later.

The leading lady in question might have been Josephine Dunn, with whom he made *A Man's Man* in late 1928. Friends can only remember the incident being talked about, not the particular woman. Dunn has been dead for several years, and since there was no report of the affair in the press, it's impossible to confirm the woman's identity at this late date. A consideration of Billy's leading ladies from 1928 and 1929 leaves Dunn the most likely possibility. Anita Page says it wasn't her, and it certainly wasn't Crawford or Davies. Leila Hyams, from *Alias Jimmy Valentine*, was married to Billy's agent, Phil

Berg. And *The Smart Set*, with costar Alice Day, was probably a bit too early.

Billy and Dunn had made *Excess Baggage* together, so they already knew one another when *A Man's Man* started filming. During the earlier film, Dunn had been married, but now she was recently divorced and riding high after appearing with Al Jolson in the talkie hit *The Singing Fool*. Twenty-three, pretty, and full of spunk, she would have caught many a man's fancy—even one so otherwise committed as Billy Haines. It's to his credit that he never attempted to use the affair in the press. He could have, which would have made him no different than Edmund Lowe or Cedric Gibbons. Billy kept his infrequent liaisons with women as secret as many male stars kept theirs with men.

A Man's Man, released in May 1929, turned out to be yet another tremendous hit for the studio. Like *The Duke Steps Out* before it, this was a silent film with synchronized sound effects and musical score.

The talkie revolution now demanded full allegiance. Billy's next film appearance was as part of the all-star extravaganza *The Hollywood Revue of 1929*, released in June. It was MGM's attempt to introduce its stars' voices to the public, although many had already made their talkie debuts. Billy was billed fourth, under John Gilbert, Marion Davies, and Norma Shearer, but above Joan Crawford, Buster Keaton, Bessie Love, and Marie Dressler. In his vignette, he pretends to be in a sparring match with Jack Benny, his old friend from New York who'd made it big on Broadway and had recently been imported west. As Billy systematically tears Benny's tux to shreds, he says leeringly, "You're just too *sensitive*." Given the stories of Benny's deeply closeted homosexuality, one can only wonder about the double entendres of the sketch.

Next up was *Speedway*, released in September, another silent with synchronized sound effects. The plot was again formula: Billy's a race-car driver who gets wise and comes around by the last reel. *Navy Blues*, released in December, was more of the same, except for one important distinction: It was Billy's first all-talkie. Billy's a sailor in this one, and Anita Page is his leading lady for the third time.

Once again Karl Dane provided comic support (even playing another character named Swede, as he had in *Slide Kelly Slide* and *Alias Jimmy Valentine*). It was director Clarence Brown's first go-around with a Haines picture, but by then they hardly needed direction: They just spun out by rote—and made a bundle for MGM.

What makes *Navy Blues* significant is its crisp, fast-paced dialogue, the first time Billy's wisecracking was actually heard on the screen. It had been an exhausting process: One of the chief differences between sound and silent filmmaking were the number of rehearsals. Everything had to be on the mark, timed exactly right. Over and over Billy would say the same lines, as if rehearsing for a stage play. Yet his performance in the final product was fresh. *Variety* gave Billy's first all-talkie a mediocre review but bestowed upon Billy its seal of approval: "Haines can audibly kid his way through this type of fare. No worry there."

Billy had been very successful in flattening his Southern accent (although traces of it could still be heard in his speech even decades later). One reporter commented that audiences might "think he hailed from the home town of brown bread and baked beans," so complete was the eradication of his drawl. Possibly Mitt and Larry, Boston boys both, were giving him elocution lessons at home.

Despite his success, Billy simply didn't enjoy making talkies as much as he had silents. "When you make silent pictures you leave the studio and go out to play," he told a reporter. "When you make talkies, you leave the studio and go home to study your lines for the next day."

More significant, the differing techniques between silent and sound filmmaking left him frustrated. "In my three years on the screen I have been allowed the greatest freedom in so far as adlibbing is concerned," he said. "A situation would be written, of course, but if I desired to clown a bit here or there I had perfect liberty to do so." A silent film script was much more of an outline than the precise screenplays required by sound. "If I wanted to make a face or indulge in other pantomimic tricks, it was perfectly agreeable to everyone, providing that it was good for laughs."

Talking pictures were different. "Dialogue cannot be adlibbed," he complained. "There are too many machines and appliances of all kinds that must be turned on and off and the time element is very essential. Things must be timed exactly."

He admitted to being concerned whether or not he'd be able to ride the wave. So far, he'd been successful, but he said the talkies had made all of them stop and think. "One bad portrayal, voice or action, is liable to set a man back from the highest spot to the lowest. No screen player is definitely sure of his or her position now."

Billy was perceptive to be worried, but as 1929 turned over into 1930, there was still no indication of the storm that lay just ahead. Early in the year he got word that he'd been voted the number-one male box-office attraction in the Quigley Poll. Joan Crawford placed first in the female category. Billy was, in a real sense, the "King of Hollywood," although it would be some years before that particular appellation was bestowed upon the Quigley winners.

A number of William Haines fan clubs had sprung up. The official William Haines Club published *Haines Gem*, a bimonthly newsletter devoted to Billy's roles and career. One member wrote, "Here's to Billy Haines, the greatest actor on the screen, typical of the finest in American manhood. We're for you, Billy, now and always."

So popular was Billy that a gaggle of imitators had emerged. Chief among them was Robert Montgomery, whom Mayer had taken to calling the "new William Haines," as if the old one weren't still around. It was clearly an attempt to intimidate Billy, to keep him in place and well behaved. "No one is irreplaceable" was the unspoken message, and Montgomery's success in the Haines-formula *So This Is College* and *Love in the Rough*, a remake of Billy's *Spring Fever*, proved him an able contender for Billy's light-comedy crown.

Offscreen, they couldn't have been more different. Montgomery was a conservative man, both politically and socially. Billy eschewed any type of politics, and he considered Montgomery boring in social settings. He was actually more than boring: He was often downright nasty to people. Four years younger than Billy, Montgomery had become a star very quickly. His voice recorded well and the studio was eager to promote new male actors. His rush of success went right to his head: He demanded a raise after just six months. He was one of the most unpopular men at MGM; even Mayer, who shared his right-wing politics, despised him.

A reporter noted that Billy "high-hatted" (ignored) Montgomery on the lot, an indication that he was troubled by the younger star's rapid rise to the top. Certainly Montgomery did not go out of his way to make friends with Billy, either: he hated "fairies," as he'd tell anyone within earshot. Montgomery was a good example of the new kind of actor emerging after the coming of sound, a "manly" man despite his boyish looks. The studio widely publicized the birth of Montgomery's daughter in October 1930, promoting him as father and family man. (Elizabeth Montgomery would go on to become a star herself, and was much more liberal and gay-friendly than her father.) Such masculine posturing positioned Robert Montgomery well for the new decade.

While audiences once again loved Billy's next film, *The Girl Said No*, critics had had about enough.

Released in March 1930, *The Girl Said No* is the *Brown of Harvard* formula pushed to the nth degree: Tom Ward is a returning college hero—and one of the most dislikable of all Billy's characters. He forces himself on Leila Hyams: Many in contemporary audiences complain the scene is too suggestive of rape to feel funny, and surely many in 1930 must have felt the same way. He is generally loud, uncouth, and obnoxious. Even a surefire scene—Tom arranges to have soup spilled on Leila's date—falls flat because we dislike Tom so much. "One is perhaps justified in hoping that the fair Mary Howe, portrayed by Leila Hyams, may discover a more rational suitor before the close of the film," wrote the *New York Times*.

That same *Times* reviewer also noted the "loud and prolonged laughter" of the audience. Most moviegoers were still enthralled by Billy's antics: *The Girl Said No* was a gigantic moneymaker for MGM.

The picture is memorable less for Billy's role than for the supporting cast. Finally he got a chance to do a comedy bit with Polly Moran, who played his family's maid. She delivers an in-joke: "I want you to know I've got a good man I'm going to marry and get out of this mad house."

Also in the cast was Marie Dressler. She and Billy were never friends. "Everyone in Hollywood found her to be so great and so wonderful," he would recall. "I had my reservations about her greatness and wonderfulness." Dressler was aloof, quite taken by the rich and beautiful; it was as if she could never quite believe she'd been accepted into their circle. Such self-consciousness always irritated Billy.

Still, he expressed gratitude that Dressler had been so successful in *The Girl Said No*. "Nuts to these stars who are afraid to have another good actor in the cast for fear of having the picture stolen," he told the press. "If anyone can steal my picture, more power to 'em. I still get credit for it as long as I'm starred. If Marie can make a hilariously funny scene in my picture and get herself some good notices—let her. People will still say 'Bill Haines' picture is a knock out'—even though it is Marie who made it one."

Billy did become friends with his other costar, Leila Hyams, a perky twenty-five-year-old married to Phil Berg, a high-powered agent. It is perhaps from this period that Berg's service as Billy's agent dates, although contract players had less need of an agent than did the independents.

Billy next appeared, along with Lionel Barrymore, Buster Collier, Dorothy Sebastian, and Cecil B. DeMille, in a cameo walk-on in Buster Keaton's *Free and Easy*. Billy liked Keaton, preferring him to Chaplin.

Before beginning work on his next picture, *Way Out West*, Billy told reporters there was a new angle to this film. "I've always done the smart-cracking in my pictures and got by with it, but in this one the tables are turned and I get the razzberries."

Did he ever. After being totally unlikable in *The Girl Said No*, Billy's character in this one, Windy, a sideshow barker, has all our sympathies. *Way Out West* is notable today for its homoerotic overtones and gay in-jokes. The film opens in a carnival, with a half-man/half-woman dancing seductively. "She's got that thing they call

It," observes one fascinated cowpoke. Later, after Billy has fleeced a team of cowboys, they decide to lynch him. (Billy would later tell reporters that the scene almost ended in tragedy. The horse bolted and he really *was* hanging there by his neck for several seconds.) After the cowboys untie him, he recoils like a sissy: "I don't want to play with you kids. You're too rough."

Later, he meets Polly Moran, the cowboys' cook. Again an in-joke: Her name is Pansy, and she falls in love with him. When the owner of the farm (Leila Hyams) mistakes him for the cook, she says, "Good morning, Pansy." Billy cracks: "I'm the wildest pansy *you* ever picked." (This was at the time the pansy craze was just hitting Hollywood.)

Billy becomes the cowboys' prize boy. They try to outdo each other in how hard they can get him to work, becoming jealous when he seems to perform better for someone else. "Come here, good-looking," they take to calling him, leading him about by the hand. Any subversive message is repudiated by the ending, which upholds the fundamentals of civilization as seen by director Fred Niblo. The whole picture is about macho men getting the best of the dandified city slicker—that is, until the city slicker finally stops prancing around and slugs one of them; in effect, *becomes* one of them. Until that moment, *Way Out West* is Billy's gayest film. In one scene, he dresses up in his finery: "Not only do I have the clothes but I have the figure to wear them!" And he actually *swishes his hips* in front of the line of cowboys.

In truth, his figure had grown a little paunchy by this film: Douglas Fairbanks, Jr., who had recently married Joan Crawford, remembers that Billy's gourmet cooking had led him to put on weight around this time. When Billy first appears in the carnival scene, he's almost unrecognizable: In his tight, glittery vest, he looks plump and older than ever before. It's the "curse of thirty" that many men before and since have faced: an expanding waistline and a receding hairline. No wonder the thin, boyish Robert Montgomery caused him consternation.

In the spring of 1930, upon completion of the film, Mayer was apparently sufficiently satisfied with Billy's transition to talkies to sign him to a new long-term contract. Even by August, when *Way Out West* opened and *Variety* predicted it would do "the typical Haines business," there was no sign of the impending storm.

Variety was wrong: *Way Out West* proved to be the least profitable of any Haines film since he'd become a star. It was too different, too outrageous, perhaps. Or maybe Billy had just gotten too paunchy. Whatever the reason, there were more than a few stunned faces in the front office. While the picture didn't actually *lose* money—it made a decent profit of $84,000—the studio was accustomed to Billy's pictures bringing in $150,000 or more. *The Girl Said No* had racked up a stunning profit of $245,000. What made it worse was the expense laid out to make *Way Out West*: $413,000, one of Billy's most costly pictures.

In the summer of 1930, Billy agreed to a partnership in an intriguing business venture: an antique shop on LaBrea Avenue.

"It never occurred to me to start an antique shop until after I was besieged by friends who saw my home after my first few house-warming parties," he told reporters at the time. "They wanted me to get this, that, and the other thing. To help them buy antique furnishings. Some sent interior decorators to me. It interested me, naturally, but I was selfish enough to see that I could turn this hobby into an asset. It seemed a good investment. But even if I don't make a nickel I will be richer by experience and pleasure."

There's no indication, as some have alleged, that Billy knew his movie days were numbered so he set himself up in another business. He himself perpetuated the myth in his later years, saying he'd seen "the handwriting on the wall." It's true he may have sensed there was a change in the air, and certainly the Depression encouraged many actors to diversify their incomes. Eddie Nugent, who'd played a small part in *The Duke Steps Out*, had opened a curiosity shop in Hollywood. The following year, Cary Grant would open a men's clothing store. With declining film profits, stars were wise to have additional sources of revenue. In the summer of 1930, however, Billy was still the number-one box-office star in the country. The disappointing returns from *Way Out West* weren't even clear yet. The antique shop and the resulting decorating business were labors of love. He could not, at that juncture, have predicted it would turn into his life's work. "It was a transition that took place naturally, gradually," he admitted much later.

Yet Billy was not a businessman. "He didn't know anything about running a business," says Michael Pearman. "But he was smart enough when he opened the shop to have people with him who were first-rate, people like Mitt Foster."

The shop had, in fact, been Mitt's idea. He'd been involved with antiques ever since he'd come to Hollywood. When he wasn't working as Billy's stand-in, he was out buying and selling exquisite old pieces, many of which ended up in Billy's home. He had superb taste and style, but more important, he had a keen business acumen as well. He'd lost some money in the stock-market crash, and he approached Billy about investing in an antique shop. Billy saw it as a way to help a friend, but also as a way to indulge his own interests.

They rented a spacious old frame house at 1522 LaBrea Avenue just a short distance from the Chaplin studios. A notice in the *New York Morning Telegraph* on September 29, 1930, announced the gala grand-opening party, with most of Billy's Hollywood friends in attendance. It was a tasteful, subdued affair, prompting one wag to comment it was the first premiere in Hollywood that didn't require the services of Otto K. Oleson—the man hired by the studios to run the giant spotlights for movie premieres.

The only evidence that the quaint old house on the quiet residential street was a commercial enterprise was the small shingle that hung from an early-American lamppost in the front yard, with the word ANTIQUES neatly lettered in old script. Nowhere was the name William Haines apparent. There were no big show windows hawking merchandise, no attempt to lure the passing trade. Inside, soft candlelight illuminated the rooms, giving the house the feel of centuries past. From the start, Billy and Mitt had envisioned this as a place where the serious collector might find what he or she had been searching for, where the like-minded could come and share their interests. Indeed, rooms would be specifically furnished for a customer who called ahead with a particular interest.

Two *Photoplay* reporters visited the shop shortly after it opened. There's much disbelief, even mockery, in the reporters' description of the Haines enterprise. It was apparently difficult to see Billy in any other role than a wisecracker. The reporters admitted that they expected the welcome mat on the doorstep would be jerked out from under them, or that a bucket of cold water would fall on their heads when the front door opened. But instead, Billy greeted them impeccably groomed and tailored in a soft gray suit. "He showed us a lot of things we can't imagine the use for," the writers observed. "This brash Haines person not only seems to know what he's talking about when it comes to antiques but apparently knows just a little more about it than most so-called period authorities."

In the end, the reporters were impressed. "There is nothing about the shop suggesting in any way the William Haines we know of from the screen. It is proud, dignified, in perfect taste." Which, of course, reflected the dual nature—clown and gentleman—of Billy Haines.

"In a way, I really hope nobody buys anything," Billy would say, fondling the arm of a Sheraton chair. Of course, people did. His Hollywood friends were his first customers—Joan Crawford and husband Douglas Fairbanks, Jr., dropped a fortune furnishing their portable dressing rooms with Billy's antiques. Very soon nonmovie folk ventured into the shop as well, giving Billy his first real contact with the world of Los Angeles high society outside the studio gates.

Larry Sullivan served as the shop's secretary; Mitt was the firm's buyer. "Mitt Foster was a fascinating guy," remembers Michael Morrison, later a friend and an employee of Billy's in the design business. "A real gentleman, snow white hair, moved very sedately. He used to do all the buying for Bill. Everybody in England was crazy about Mitt. He's the one who bought all the great Regency furniture in the 1930s, brought it over here when no one in England had any money."

It wasn't just Mitt's and Larry's show. Despite his movie duties, Billy took an increasingly active role in the shop, arranging the rooms, mixing and matching objects. Within a year, the enterprise was a success. They incorporated as Haines-Foster, Inc., with Billy as president, Larry as vice president, and Mitt as secretary-treasurer.

Haines-Foster could be commissioned to design entire rooms or houses. Despite his lack of fondness for her, Billy put together a series of rooms for Marie Dressler's house on Alpine Drive. He did the same for Wallace Beery. Mr. and Mrs. John Barrymore commissioned him to furnish and decorate their parlor, and Douglas Fairbanks, Sr. — encouraged perhaps by his son's friendship with Haines — even placed an order for Pickfair.

Hollywood was quickly overrun with stories of Billy's salesmanship. One tale, probably apocryphal, had both Constance Bennett and Joan Crawford browsing through the store, unsure of whether or not to make a purchase that particular day. Taking both aside, Billy whispered that each had bought the other a Christmas gift at the shop. With neither woman wanting to be one-upped by the other, they both picked out suitable gifts, and Billy made a nice little profit that day.

Crawford also hired him to redecorate her house on Bristol Avenue in Brentwood. When Doug Fairbanks moved in, the house was christened El Jodo in droll homage to Pickfair. Fairbanks, a cultured, sophisticated man, was struck by the kitsch of Joan's house, and welcomed his wife's idea for Billy to redecorate. For years, Billy had been after Joan to get rid of her prominently placed doll collection, numbering two thousand and including a life-size hen that clucked and laid eggs. There were also portraits of dancing girls done in black velvet with real blond hair and rhinestones hanging on the walls. "I thought them beautiful," Joan would remember. It was an uneven hodgepodge of silent-film gaudiness and Kansas City kitsch.

Now that she had to compete with Pickfair, Joan reluctantly admitted Billy had been right. "Turn the place into a house of distinction," she implored. The first thing Billy did was toss out the dolls and black-velvet dancing girls. Then he painted the entire living room white and furnished it with white sofas and carpeting. Antique tables and chairs from the shop were distributed throughout the house, with Wedgwood blue used as simple but effective color accent to offset the white. Joan's gilded piano was replaced with a white Steinway grand. Billy even oversaw the construction of a new dining room and kitchen.

"Billy still loves to tell the story of those black velvet girls," Crawford remembered years later. "He very tactfully began steering me in a new direction. Not that it was all tact and harmony. We'd fight like cats and dogs over some of his ideas. He always won because of his excellent taste and knowledge and my lack of both."

Douglas Fairbanks, Jr., claims that Billy took a hint from Syrie Maugham, the wife of Somerset Maugham, in the creation of the all-white rooms. It's possible, as Billy no doubt by this time had met Maugham on one of his visits to Hollywood. Whatever the inspiration, Crawford adopted the white as her signature style. Fairbanks says she was so "enamored of this style and so fanatic about cleanliness that when the house was finished, she insisted that everyone, even her closest friends, take their shoes off when they entered."

Fairbanks liked Billy. "He was a frequent dinner guest and I knew him to be very amusing," he recalls. "Billy Haines was, in most ways, [Joan's] most intimate confidant, but since he wasn't interested in girls I welcomed his good, earthy advice to her."

In 1930, Noël Coward visited Hollywood. It was during a break in the run of his play *Private Lives* in which he was performing with Gertrude Lawrence on Broadway. Coward made a point to meet Joan and Doug; there were whispers that Coward had a crush on Fairbanks, and that his later song, "Mad About the Boy," was inspired by his meeting with the star. During this visit Coward also became acquainted with Billy. They would remain friends, although not intimates, for many years.

Fairbanks's friendships with gay men led to some rumors that he might be homosexual himself. Mayer was relieved when he made the match with Crawford: "I was beginning to worry about him," he said. The fact that—in contrast to his bullish, braggart father—Doug, Jr., was a refined, well-read, cultured man led many to question his sexuality. Fairbanks was not gay, but such impetuous gossip had become common in Hollywood, and it was about to get even more reckless.

Billy was nearly thirty-one years old, and he'd never been seriously linked in the press with any woman. Gossip columnist Rose Pelswick observed coyly in her column that Billy "has never been engaged to anyone but Polly Moran and a lot of people still think it's on the level."

After so many years of the same stories, the public was beginning to see through Billy's wisecracks. A revealing "hometown of the stars" article written by a reporter from Staunton appeared in *Photoplay* about this time. The young Billy Haines—who would make his career playing star athletes—was revealed never to have engaged in athletics, preferring instead to sew doll clothes for his sister and make candy with his mother. It could not have enhanced his reputation.

As usual, Billy didn't help matters, at least not from the studio's point of view. He despised lying, so he kept up the wisecracking. "The marrying age for a man is from twenty to twenty-five," he said in a remarkable "as told to Marquis Busby" piece in *Photoplay* in late 1929. "After that he becomes a little more 'picky,' less inclined to compromise between sheets and blankets and take sheets."

That was just it: Did Billy prefer sheets or blankets? "There is bound to be a certain amount of gossip in Hollywood," Billy said, facing reality. "You have to talk about something, so why not about each other?"

Another *Photoplay* article not long after contained a series of "insider" quotes about Billy. "Moody as a prima donna," one wag snipped. "He's kind of nuts on fancy furniture and antiques," said another. "He's not like other bachelors," the article concluded. "Bill runs his house himself, and he is amazingly good at it . . . just like a housewife."

Photoplay told its readers that Billy's dearest possession—"among all the lace pillows and pretty pictures that he likes to sit and look at by the hour"—was, in fact, a miniature of his mother. A photograph of Billy and Laura graced the article, identifying his mother as "the one great love of his life." The caption read, "Haines swears he'll remain a happy bachelor."

In another interview, Samuel Richard Mook of *Picture Play* visited Billy at home on a Saturday night. Jimmie was not mentioned. Billy was depicted as alone and "dateless" until Polly Moran called. He perked right up, saying: "You gotta come up for dinner tonight. You haven't been here in a coon's age. Roger'll be here and no one else. We'll have a swell time."

Roger was Roger Davis, as obvious a homosexual as there was in the film colony. Publicity like this must have concerned the studio. Mayer no doubt cringed reading Mook's report in *Picture Play*, portraying his star hero as brooding alone in his mansion, entertaining other single men and gap-toothed comediennes. Where were the starlets? Where was the romance? The public, too, was beginning to wonder.

Roger Davis was just one of the new circle of friends with whom Billy had surrounded himself by 1930. Davis had been a "stooge" for Fanny Brice; when she came to Hollywood, he tagged along. Brice was close with Polly Moran, and through her became a frequent guest at Billy's home.

Davis, then in his mid-forties, was quite taken with the handsome, younger Billy Haines. They took a road trip up to San Francisco together, stopping to spend the night at a hotel halfway up the coast. They turned in for an uncharacteristically early night at ten o'clock because Billy was determined to make it to San Francisco early the next day. He insisted that they leave no later than seven-thirty the next morning.

Billy arose at seven, washed, and dressed. Roger grunted whenever Billy would try to rouse him. "What time is it?" Roger finally asked groggily.

"Seven-twenty," Billy told him.

"Well, my contract calls for seven-thirty," Davis said, rolling over to catch ten more minutes of shut-eye.

Billy roared with laughter. "When a fellow can waken out of a ten-hour sleep with a crack like that," he'd later say, "that's my idea of humor."

Roger quickly became a Hollywood staple. By 1930 he and Billy were part of a dynamic circle of gay friends that included Anderson

Lawler, a young contract player at Paramount; Louis Mason, an actor known for his rustic roles (he'd play the sheriff in *Stagecoach*); and the director George Cukor. Cukor had arrived in Hollywood in 1929 as an assistant director at Paramount. He had directed Andy Lawler in summer stock and remained friendly with him; perhaps he met Billy through him. Or perhaps the two had known each other in New York, as some claim. In any event, almost from the time of his arrival, Cukor was seen in the company of Billy Haines. They formed a fast and solid friendship. Cukor delighted in Billy's outrageousness, his sense of himself. Like Davis, he may have been somewhat smitten by his handsome friend at first: Cukor was fat and homely, and always admired tall, masculine, self-assured men.

They shared many friends in common. Not just gay friends like Lawler and Davis, but also the famous ladies who seemed drawn to gay men: Ina Claire and Fanny Brice, for example. (Brice's husband, Billy Rose, quipped: "She's up to her arse in nances.") Brice often was the only woman at gatherings that included Billy, Cukor, Roger Davis, Andy Lawler, and others.

By 1929 there was another young man in that circle as well, a star of some stature: Gary Cooper, the It Boy. As beautiful a young man as ever came to Hollywood, Cooper had recently emerged from an affair with Clara Bow and was now dating both Lupe Velez, the fiery Mexican actress, and Andy Lawler. Lawler's cousin, William Kizer, says emphatically that Andy and Gary were lovers, and fairly open ones at that. Just as Billy lived openly with Jimmie, so Gary Cooper freely carried on his relationship with Lawler. They used pet nicknames for each other and were photographed all over town together, from Hollywood Bowl concerts to film premieres. A robust, athletic man, Lawler was nonetheless cultured and articulate. He could move with Billy's gay clique as well as with the "he-man" crowd of Richard Arlen and Jack Oakie, a trait that no doubt appealed to Cooper. While the fan magazines concentrated on the affair with Velez, several scribes began making caustic note of Cooper's relationship with Lawler, who actually moved in with the star for a time during 1929.

It was, again, part of the era of free love. The "new morality" of the 1920s had yet to be subdued by the Depression-era reformers. In the space of a year, new attitudes began to surface. The Cooper-Lawler friendship may have had something to do with Lawler's option being dropped by Paramount. After 1930 their joint photographs disappear from the newspapers. Lawler was out of a job, something he'd remain bitter about for many years. Despite their loss of intimacy, however, Cooper and Lawler stayed friends for life.

Billy must have been aware of the shifting winds that separated Gary Cooper and Andy Lawler, the forces that caused the It Boy to disappear from his and Cukor's gatherings. Yet he remained living openly with Jimmie. Theirs was not a relationship so easily split apart.

Their most frequent "double dates" these days were Mitt Foster and Larry Sullivan, especially with the success of the antique business. The four of them—Billy and Jimmie, Mitt and Larry—made a harmonious quartet. Their relationships were quite similar: one partner masculine and "in charge"; the other more passive and effeminate. "Mitt was a big, handsome guy," Michael Pearman remembers. "Both he and Larry were beautifully dressed always, getting all their clothes made in London. Larry was rather a sissy, a little boy. Sometimes Larry would get mad at Mitt, shake his fist, and say, 'See this? I'll *smash* you!' Of course, everyone just laughed. But they were together an awfully long time."

As with Billy and Jimmie, the relationship worked. Jimmie and Larry made homes for their lovers, created spaces where their more dynamic partners could relax, find comfort, and be themselves. When Jimmie was away—which wasn't often—Billy missed him a great deal. Without ever mentioning Jimmie, reporter Samuel Richard Mook described a quiet night with Billy at home in 1930 during a time when Jimmie was obviously away. Billy commented that he'd been alone in the house for three days. He was uncharacteristically quiet, contemplative, even lonely. "I can't wait for things to get back to normal," he said.

Billy's devotion to Jimmie was well-known. "What Jimmie wanted, Jimmie would nag and nag until he got," Arch Case recalls.

"But it was Billy's pleasure," adds Ted Graber. "That's very important to remember."

Indeed it is. The commitment between the two transcended the mere acquisition of material goods. Billy *needed* to provide: It gave him a sense of fulfillment. He acted similarly with his biological family. There was never a thought that the relationship was unbalanced: Billy played his part and Jimmie played his. Billy might have been benefactor, but it was a role he relished.

For his own part, Billy grew less ostentatious while Jimmie's pretensions intensified. Billy still drove the same car he'd been driving since 1926, a Franklin convertible he'd purchased after *Brown of Harvard* allowed him to start living like a movie star. Recognizing the practical realities of the Depression, he told a reporter in early 1931 that he suspected he'd still be driving it five years from then. He never drove the car himself, however: He was always chauffeured, and he insisted that the top always be down. He wanted the air, he said, hating the feeling of being closed in. He was rarely seen without a beret as he sported around Hollywood in his car. It was a matter of style, he told his friends. In reality, he despaired of the way the wind whipped his hair, no matter how much he plastered it down. As he slid into his thirties, his hairline was receding and the hair on the top of his head began thinning out. He was hardly bald, but he nonetheless became "easy prey for any and all hair-growing systems," according to Douglas Fairbanks, Jr. Then as now, of course, none of them did the trick.

Billy's first film after signing his new contract was *Remote Control*, a pleasant comedy released in November 1930. The picture went through four directors, with Malcolm St. Clair and Nick Grinde ending up with screen credit. Billy's a radio announcer who foils a plot by a rival broadcaster to send out a code to gangland members over the airwaves. Again, a break from formula, and it worked somewhat better at the box office than had *Way Out West*. But again, returns were less than half of what a William Haines picture brought in just a year before.

It's important to remember that Billy's films *were still profitable*. Critics judged his voice fine for talkies. He was still given the star treatment at the studio and in the fan magazines. Yet he had fallen rather quickly from the top spot at the box office: Usually a performer lasts on the top of the list for at least a couple of seasons. Already he'd been replaced as the number one male star by Charles Farrell. Crawford, too, had taken a tumble, being succeeded by Farrell's onscreen love-interest Janet Gaynor.

The reasons for his fall are numerous. A risky change of formula with *Way Out West*; an earnest but hardly vital follow-up with *Remote Control*. There may have been something else coalescing as well. After so many stories about antiques and bachelorhood and the romance with Polly Moran, might the public have begun to suspect something queer about their all-American hero?

It was at this point that Thalberg concluded Billy needed an image change. His next few films were designed to edge him away from the image of the wisecracking college boy and establish him as an urbane playboy. Wrote one reporter: "Maybe it's time Willie Haines showed us why the girls should stay interested."

A Tailor-Made Man was designed to do just that. "Bill's a ladykiller in this one," said one publicity line. The wisecracker image was downplayed; instead, he's the handsome matinee idol in advertisements for the film.

Billy told the press: "Ever since I've been in pictures, people have looked for something funny to happen when I appear. No matter how serious the situation I'm in, the audience always looks first for a laugh." This film was meant to give him an opportunity to do something different. Directed by Sam Wood, the film, released in early 1931, is an engaging story of a witty pants-presser (Billy) who dreams of hobnobbing with the owners of the expensive clothes he presses. There's a good deal of comedy, but enough romance to rightly call it a melodrama.

Also in the cast was Billy's friend Hedda Hopper. Even then one of the town's most notorious gossips, Hopper never uttered a bad word about Billy Haines. "Hedda Hopper once told me that I would be the last person she would wish as an enemy," Billy remarked. Even the woman all of Hollywood feared knew how easily Billy Haines could puncture a windbag of hot air.

The critics, on the whole, liked *A Tailor-Made Man*. "This is a blues-chaser," *Photoplay* said, "and superior to the recent Billy Haines laugh operas. Although Haines has his usual jaunty self-confidence, he plays it with restraint, thereby proving he's a good actor."

For all its merits, *A Tailor-Made Man* saw returns dramatically lower than even *Way Out West*. It still turned a profit, but this time, just barely. Clearly there was concern. Though Billy appeared with Joan Crawford in the all-star fundraising short *The Stolen Jools*, Mayer was beginning to have doubts about his star's appeal. Supervisor Bernie Fineman, effectively acting as producer, was assigned to Billy's next outing, an adaptation of the Broadway hit *Dancing Partner*. In late February, Billy was called into Fineman's office and told in no uncertain terms to leave the trademark William Haines wisecracks and mannerisms out of his performance. He was to play it straight—in all the meanings of that term. He was instructed to imitate Ronald Colman for the picture.

Stunned, Billy refused to see any film with Colman in it, terrified he'd unconsciously mimic him and come out looking like a ham. Then Fineman informed him he would be coached by Leslie Howard, the English actor newly arrived on the lot.

Billy, humiliated, dragged himself over to Howard's house. He didn't blame Howard. "He was a gentleman," Billy would remember, "and must have been just as embarrassed about the situation as I was." Howard read through the script for Billy, emphasizing mannerisms and inflections. "It was the most awful few hours I have ever experienced," Billy said.

There's little that resembles Howard in the final product; the part is Billy's own. The picture, retitled *Just a Gigolo*, is among Billy's best. The script attempts to boost Billy's heterosexual appeal, but he retains the sly, campy humor that set him apart. He is cocksure but likable as the confirmed bachelor whose rich uncle desperately wants him to marry. Since he's having too much fun sleeping around, he tries to prove all available women immoral in a bet with his uncle. If he cannot get Irene Purcell to sleep with him within thirty days, he'll find a good woman and settle down. If he *does* get her into bed, his uncle agrees to stop pestering him and leave him to his playboy ways.

As might be expected, the Production Code censors went berserk. "The picture contains numerous lines and situations which are not in conformance with the ethics of the Code," intoned Jason Joy of the Hays office in a letter to the studio. Several cuts were suggested: Billy's line, "I've seen too many husbands fooled to give some other fellow a whack at me," as well as the uncle's quip, "He won't marry her if he can—he'll only marry her if he *can't.*"

In the end, as was the case with most films, the entire script was left intact. Thalberg knew such tampering would destroy any sense of plot, and the film went into general release as it stood. Joy just shrugged. "There is nothing more to be done about it because there remains no scene, lines or situations the changing of which would clear the picture," he wrote to Thalberg in May.

State censors, however, many of whom were in the pockets of local Catholic bishops, had the last word. The film was hacked up by censorship boards in Massachusetts, Virginia, Ohio, and elsewhere. Several Canadian provinces rejected it outright, as did a number of European countries.

More important than any script concerns for Billy, however, was the fact that he also served as art director on the film. He's not credited—Cedric Gibbons's contract decreed that his name would go out on every MGM picture—but *Variety* reported the assignment on March 25. Perhaps it was a perk granted to him, given the humiliation he'd had to endure. It bears his style: antique furnishings set against round modern mirrors and plush white carpeting. There's lots of statuary, a favorite flourish in many Haines decors. A white statue of Venus stands starkly atop a black column; a Roman bust looks out over the room from a wall pedestal. There's a touch of the garish as well, a necessary concession to the film's racy plot and the MGM style: zebra-print upholstering and leopard-print curtains.

Just a Gigolo followed the same pattern as the previous two Haines pictures. It made money, but only a tiny fraction of what Billy used to pull in. It was the least profitable of any of his films, ever.

Billy had no way of knowing this as he and Jimmie boarded an eastbound train shortly after the completion of *Just a Gigolo*. They were embarking on a trip to Europe—Billy's first—and the first vacation he'd taken since his trip back to Virginia in 1926.

They sailed on the *Ile de France* for London. The trip would also take them through France, Belgium, and the Netherlands. Much of the trip was spent acquiring statuary and antique furniture. Billy was inspired by the great European manors and villas he visited, influences that would appear frequently in his designs over the next few decades.

His standing as a movie star was fully intact on the tour. He was given the royal treatment everywhere he went, dining with Noël Coward and Bea Lillie in London and with friends of the Countess di Frasso, Hollywood's premier party-giver, on the Continent. He met an authentic royal as well: Charles, Prince of the Belgians and Count of Flanders. The son of King Albert and Queen Elisabeth, Charles was a serious, scholarly young man just a few years younger than Billy. He was also obsessed with the movies. Meeting Billy was as much a thrill for him as it was for Billy to meet genuine European royalty. Charles had been indulged by his cultured mother, who raised him in the company of intellectuals and artists. His fascination with American movie stars was something of a youthful rebellion.

Billy enjoyed the trip tremendously. He was certainly concerned about the recent box-office record of his pictures, but he wasn't overly worried. He knew that once you had made it as a star, you were taken care of. Looking back, Ramon Novarro observed, "When you had arrived, you had *arrived*—and weren't frantic if a picture turned out not quite so good as its predecessor." Stars weren't put out to pasture because of a few disappointing pictures. Thalberg and his assistants would get together and create a new Haines formula if the old one quit working. Already Joan Crawford was moving from her wild flapper parts to the determined shop girl out to make good.

Billy had only to point to John Gilbert, whose early talkies had been abysmal failures, losing a ton of money—and he was still employed by the studio. Billy laughed off *Way Out West, Remote Control,* and *A Tailor-Made Man* as "big juicy lemons." He was still confident that *Just a Gigolo* would make good and that future films would restore his clout.

Upon his return to Hollywood, he had to acknowledge that things were different. There were so many new faces stirring up excitement: Robert Montgomery, Clark Gable, Edward G. Robinson, James Cagney. He later admitted feeling some at the studio had turned their backs on him. "Not Joan, or Eleanor, or Polly," he said. "Not that swell girl, Marion Davies, but the rest of the gang."

Whom did he mean? Mayer? But Mayer had never looked upon him kindly. Possibly some of the other players, but their opinions wouldn't have mattered. He was likely referring to the producers— people like Hunt Stromberg, Bernie Hyman, Harry Rapf, and even Thalberg, whose efforts were geared toward making stars out of Gable and Montgomery, with little concern about reviving Billy's stalled career.

One has to ask why. His pictures were still moneymakers, albeit in reduced numbers. He had been a loyal player, always cooperative on the set. Producers and directors generally liked him. There had to be a sense that he was increasingly *not worth salvaging*—that Billy's situation outside the studio threatened his appeal.

What was clear from the numbers was that Billy's audience was steadily deserting him. There are many theories about the reasons behind this, all of them containing some truth. Billy was getting older, and looked it. The public seemed to accept him only as the wisecracking Tom Brown character. Yet more important, the public may also have grown a little wise to Billy Haines. They may have begun to see through his artfully designed shell, the facade that allowed him to get away with things without really lying. He'd predicted such an outcome in the interview with Marquis Busby in 1929, when he said he didn't go for personal appearances or premieres. "It destroys an illusion. The public may find out you have liver spots and halitosis."

The public seems to have discovered *something*. In June, "The Lowdown" column, a series of facts and opinions compiled as "star portraits" in the *Hollywood Reporter*, reported that MGM seemed to be neglecting Billy because the public had appeared to turn its back. Any notion that his looks were failing him is disputed by the column: "He is very good-looking. Face and physique." It goes on: "He is a perfect host. His exquisite taste is reflected by the home he built, furnished and lives in. He has capitalized his hobby with a successful antique shop. He is a bachelor for many reasons."

A letter to the editor of one fan magazine just about this time summed it up. "What's the matter with William Haines? He can't be serious about Polly Moran. I simply do not trust what he says anymore. He is always kidding. And why has he never gotten married, anyhow?"

Billy met it all with typical aplomb. "Last year I was pointed out as one of the best drawing cards on the screen," he told a reporter. "Now they say, there goes that big lug."

The career of William Haines in this changing, increasingly conservative period must be seen in context with the careers of other stars—both those who refused to play the game and those who went along with it. Billy's story informs theirs; theirs shed light on his.

Gary Cooper and, later, Cary Grant both began their careers with an attitude toward their personal lives very similar to Billy's. They lived lives of quiet freedom, choosing to associate with male lovers quite openly, believing in the old distinction between private lives and public images.

It is Greta Garbo—one of the few female stars Billy couldn't abide—with whom the comparison most aptly fits. "She ran her own train," her niece would recall for Garbo biographer Barry Paris. "She didn't feel she had to get married; she wore her hair and makeup the way she wanted to; she furnished her home the way she wanted to—she did *everything* the way she wanted to."

After the final break with Gilbert in 1928, Garbo surrounded herself almost exclusively with women, many of whom were very open about their lesbianism. What men remained in her life were invariably gay: Cecil Beaton, Noël Coward, George Cukor. Mayer was not happy about this, but as with Billy, there was little he could do to force Garbo into playing the game. Fan magazines noted her shopping trips and special closeness with clothes-horse Lilyan Tashman. When Tashman's bold streak and penchant for publicity became too much for the privacy-obsessed star, Garbo started being seen with Fifi D'Orsay, the new "French" sensation of musicals (she was, in reality, from Montreal). One article dated February 1930 says, "Greta Garbo and Fifi D'Orsay have become inseparable friends. Everywhere that Greta goes, Fifi is sure to tag along and vice versa. Greta stays in her shell and is so reserved that Hollywood has been greatly amused and interested in this dalliance. Fifi is Greta's first pal since Lilyan Tashman and Greta parted company."

It was with Mercedes de Acosta that Garbo really formed a substantial partnership, however. The eccentric Spanish writer had come to the United States to write a script for Pola Negri, but it was Garbo with whom she fell in love. A woman of distinctly modern sensibilities, de Acosta blithely refused to disguise her lesbianism. It was just one of her exotic traits: There was also a belief in the occult and a fierce advocacy of equal rights for women. In 1931 she and Garbo struck up an intense intimacy that lasted, on and off, for more than a decade. Garbo bought a house next door to Mercedes, who lived with the gay writer John Colton. The two women became inseparable: Around town they were known as "the Garbos." They liked to shock partygoers by both arriving in pants, as obvious a code for lesbianism in the 1930s as existed.

The press was now beginning to titter, just as it was with Billy. "What strange reason exists which keeps the most excitingly beautiful Garbo from committing matrimony?" asked *Screen Book* in 1931. Garbo, like Billy, never lied to the press. When she was pushed about her affair with Gilbert, she merely shrugged. "I shall never marry," she said. "My friendship with Mr. Gilbert? It was only a friendship, nothing more."

By telling the truth, Garbo forced the fan magazines to interpret her life to fit the prevailing norms. "She shall never marry," editorialized one writer, "because she has set impossibly high standards in the search for true love." This while she was passionately involved with de Acosta.

When de Acosta assumed management of Garbo's career, Mayer and Thalberg were forced to deal with her. Thalberg seems to have liked her, but he would not agree to her ideas that Garbo play Hamlet, St. Francis of Assisi, or Dorian Gray. "Do you want to put all America and all the women's clubs against her?" he asked. "You must be out of your mind."

Yet Garbo survived as a top star; her allure lay in the very fact that she was different, an enigma. No such magic protected Billy or the other gay stars. Ramon Novarro was still a friend. His intensely modern house must have intrigued (but ultimately repelled) Billy: Built high in the Hollywood Hills and designed by Lloyd Wright, it was called "expressionistically sensational." Novarro had become increasingly reclusive behind the high tiled walls of his house. He neither played the game nor flouted the rules. He simply retreated. A devout Roman Catholic, he enjoyed his sexual romps yet increasingly came to feel guilty about them. "Poor Ramon," said George Cukor. "He was a very unhappy and sensitive fellow, and a rather lost one."

A 1929 *Photoplay* article said: "Novarro's life is peculiarly innocent. He has kept away, more or less, from Hollywood atmosphere, preferring the residential section of Los Angeles to the gaudier Beverly Hills."

In 1931 he was still riding high at the studio. He'd had a string of talking successes, such as *The Pagan*, *The Flying Fleet*, and *Devil May Care*. Nonetheless, assistant publicity director Howard Strickling was urging a romance. The gossip columnists were snickering: "Ramon *still* has never been linked to any actress, and it's been ten *years*."

While similar comments were being made about Billy, the differences between the two are obvious. Billy was involved in a committed, fairly public relationship with another man. Novarro rarely went out. More significant, Novarro's films were still among the top moneymakers at the studio. Unlike their attitude toward Billy, the front office still cared passionately about preserving and maintaining Novarro's star status. They were also increasingly wary of him.

Finally, however, it is Nils Asther who best illustrates the situation Billy and others found themselves in by the early 1930s. Asther was even more of a problem than Billy or Novarro. "I don't care for this love-making so much," he had admitted to the *New York World* in 1928, making a wry face as he thought about it. "I wish I could have a role in which I wore a beard and ragged clothes. You can't make love in a beard."

He made other disparaging comments about Hollywood's ideas of lovemaking. His belligerence irritated Mayer to no end, but his extracurricular activities in Pershing Square were even more troublesome. When he kissed Garbo too hard in *The Single Standard*, she pushed him away, saying, "I'm not one of your sailors."

Then, in January 1930, trade papers announced the studio would not be renewing Asther's contract, despite his extraordinary success in *Laugh Clown Laugh* and *The Single Standard*. One report said, "The first big upset of the year is the news that Metro-Goldwyn-Mayer is not renewing Nils Asther's contract." The article cited Asther's accent as the reason, and said the actor was considering vaudeville.

The accent seems a dubious reason. He was quite popular; not even giving him a shot at talkies seems absurd. There was Oliver Hinsdale and the voice school Mayer had set up. Besides, actors were in demand for exotic foreign roles. Perhaps it was nothing more than a scare tactic, a phony statement released to the press by a front office annoyed at Asther's refusal to play the game.

Interestingly, the next mention of Asther in the trade papers is not about his dismissal from the studio, but his very sudden marriage to Vivian Duncan, of the singing-dancing Duncan Sisters. (He also reportedly proposed to Garbo, who turned him down. Asther, in his memoirs, would later insist he'd been in love with his fellow Swede.) Nothing more is heard about his supposed firing. It's known that Asther was having immigration troubles; surely marriage to an American woman solved those. It may have solved something else, too: The studio had one less "moody bachelor" on its hands for the press to wink about. And by pairing him with Vivian, whom he'd known since they made *Topsy and Eva* together at United Artists, the studio was killing two birds with one stone. Vivian herself was a bit too wild for MGM's tastes. Dating actor Rex Lease, she was frequently getting into scuffles, receiving a black eye from Lease in one highly publicized incident. Marriage to Asther quieted her down; her husband then dutifully reported for work on *The Sea Bat*, any talk of his dismissal or problems with his accent now past.

The two were miserable, however. Within months, Asther had moved into the Grand Hotel in Santa Monica, refusing to take his wife's calls unless she wanted to talk about something "important." Mayer was outraged. By mid-1931, once again there were reports in the trade press that Asther would be let go.

One last effort was made to polish up his image. He and Vivian took off on a European trip, where their daughter was born in Paris. MGM publicists bombarded the press with stories of the happy couple. Every newspaper and magazine ran pictures of the beaming parents. *Motion Picture Classic* announced in August that Asther, "the romantic lover, was back." That same month, a trade paper reported that "contrary to all rumors," MGM had indeed taken up Asther's option; in fact, he had been given a brand-new contract at a higher salary. "It was considered that his popularity was too great and his talents too ample to be allowed to rust." The same article noted how much he was looking forward to the return of his wife and daughter from Paris.

It was a last chance for Asther. Whether or not he'd take it was unclear. The point was, he played the game—snarling, griping, kicking his feet, but he played the game, something Billy Haines simply refused to do.

Billy was being more than uncooperative; he was being reckless. Just what happened in the late winter or spring of 1931 will never be known, but *something* happened, and most likely Billy was arrested. Legend has it that during a police raid at the YMCA, Billy was caught with a sailor. "There were quite a few scandals with the police while he was at Metro," says Michael Pearman. "He would never talk about them later on. But oh, yes. They were very real, all right."

In some published interviews, Billy himself alluded to an arrest. He was never very specific, except in his bitterness toward Louis B. Mayer. By 1931 Mayer had grown extremely uncomfortable with his star. The latest incident, whatever it was, seems to have been the final straw. If Billy was arrested, the studio bailed him out, got the charges dropped and his record erased. Nothing exists in the criminal files in the Los Angeles County Superior Court. Whatever the nature of the incident, it convinced Mayer of one thing: With the changing political climate, keeping Billy Haines on the payroll was trouble waiting to happen. He hadn't retreated inside the gates of his mansion the way Novarro had; he hadn't consented to a marriage the way Nils Asther had; he didn't have some mysterious allure with the public to protect him the way Garbo did.

This, too, while all of Hollywood was smack-dab in the middle of the Clara Bow brouhaha. She was the most gossiped-about of all stars. She'd had well-publicized affairs with Gary Cooper, Victor Fleming, and even Bela Lugosi. A scandal that year with a married man whose wife sued Bow for alienation of affections prompted none other than Will Hays to order her to marry her fiancé "and settle down." It was an early example of the new censorial attitude extending from the screen to offscreen lives.

At first, Bow's studio, Paramount, rode the publicity wave, releasing her pictures with racy campaigns: "Clara Bow invites you to *Her Wedding Night*." But in early 1931, when Bow's trusted secretary, Daisy DeVoe, tried to blackmail her, there was no stopping the torrent of scandal. Clara took DeVoe to court, but what ensued wasn't a blackmail trial: it was the trial of the It Girl, charged with excess and immorality, reflecting the new moral and economic shift in America. Every producer feared one of its stars might be next. The precarious balance of power between studio, star, press, and public was shattered when the scandal sheets on the It Girl were blanketed across town.

In the end, DeVoe was convicted of only three of the thirty-four charges against her. It was *Bow* who was found guilty in the court of public opinion as details of her lurid affairs were released to the press.

Convention was broken down. There was no partnership except that between the insatiable curiosity of the public, spurred on by the newly discovered umbrage of the clerics, and the greedy new purveyors of trash. Frederic Girnau was part of a new breed of Hollywood reporters. His *Coast Reporter* exposed the secrets studio publicists had so long kept under wraps, as well as making up a few juicy lies along the way. The *Coast Reporter* claimed Bow was the mistress of several men at one time and that she enjoyed an assortment of lesbian affairs. But her preference, the scandal sheet said, was for her Great Dane.

Such copy would have been unthinkable just a few years before. Although the *Coast Reporter* was underground trash—and Girnau eventually served a jail term for distributing obscene material—the precedent for a long line of half-truth exposé sheets had been set, stretching from the *Coast Reporter* to *Confidential* magazine in the 1950s to the myriad supermarket tabloids of today.

Reformers called for Paramount to fire Bow. Although her pictures had been big moneymakers, her latest, *Kick In*, had been a disappointment. As with Billy Haines, one has to ask why that was the case. Did Bow's box-office appeal plummet because of bad press? Gossip, as Adela Rogers St. Johns so astutely observed, can only *help* a career. When it turns into scandal, and if a studio cannot—or isn't willing to—fix it, then careers are destroyed. In May 1931, Paramount released the beleaguered Bow from her contract.

It was just a month later that Billy learned his own contract would not be renewed. At precisely the same time, however, Nils Asther agreed to give his marriage another try and was set for a new picture. It was all a matter of who played the game—and who didn't.

6

THE DUKE STEPS OUT

1931-1933

Probably the worst insult wasn't that *The New Adventures of Get-Rich-Quick Wallingford* was slated to be Billy's last film at MGM. No doubt he loathed even more the absurd publicity of playing baseball with costar Jimmy Durante. The film crew had put together a team, and publicity chief Howard Strickling loved the idea, calling in the photographers. Durante, new to Hollywood, dubbed the team the "Get-a-Run-Quick Niners." Despite his boredom with sports, Billy was forced to suit up and bat a few balls; it wouldn't do for Slide Kelly Slide to hide out in his dressing room.

The trade papers had reported that Metro had decided to drop William Haines because he was asking for a pay raise. That was hogwash. As Billy would later admit: "I would have stayed on any terms and the studio knew it. I wanted to be with them on any basis whatsoever."

As might be expected, he was not in a good frame of mind during the making of *Wallingford*. Cast and crew, many of whom had been with him during his glory days, were sympathetic. Director Sam Wood, with whom he had made several hits, went easy on him, shooting shortened scenes so Billy only had to learn a few pages of dialogue at a time. Bernie Hyman was supervisor, a position he'd also held on *Brown of Harvard*. He privately told Billy that he'd do everything he could to make the film a success, and thus salvage his career. Hyman arranged for screenwriter Charlie MacArthur to write the dialogue for *Wallingford* in the evenings, as he was already working on another picture during the day. Billy sat up half the night learning lines for the next morning. Wood worked patiently with Billy to bring out a classic 1930's-style tough-guy part.

Although he liked Jimmy Durante, cast in a flashy supporting role, Billy must have bit his tongue to keep from making a wisecrack when he saw the red carpet Mayer rolled out for him. Mayer was thrilled to have the wildly popular stage star join the studio, and insured Durante's prodigious nose with Lloyd's of London for $1 million. He saw to it that Durante was feted all over town, even at Pickfair. To Mayer, *Wallingford* was a Jimmy Durante picture.

Not to Hyman or Wood, however. It's evidence of just how much Billy was liked by his peers that the film's supervisor and director worked so hard for him. Their efforts—and Billy's—paid off, for *Wallingford* turned out to be a hit. Not a gigantic one, not the kind of blockbuster Billy used to pull in, but still a certifiable moneymaker, considerably more profitable than his last three pictures had been.

Certainly Durante's popularity helped. As the sidekick to Wallingford the con man, he brings much of his vaudeville schtick to the film. Billy is surprisingly good as well. *Wallingford* was based on the stories of George Randolph Chester that ran in Hearst's *International Cosmopolitan*, featuring professional con artist J. Rufus Wallingford and his schemes to get rich. Billy captured the essence of the con man delightfully. It was the logical evolution of his 1920s wisecracker: what Tom Brown would do for a living when he grew up. He's shrewd, manipulative, and charming—a little boastful but never off-putting, as he had been in *The Girl Said No*.

While Durante snatched the lion's share of publicity, Billy impressed the critics. *Variety* said, "Too bad with Haines in for such a good showing Durante should steal the picture." The *New York Times* assessed his portrayal as "emphatically satisfactory."

Billy would later say that it was only at a screening of the completed film that Mayer agreed to give him a new contract. It made for a great story: Billy lurking in the wings, thinking his MGM career was all over, when he suddenly overhears a couple of studio executives saying, "We've got to get to Haines. Mayer wants him back." Maybe it did happen that way. Whatever the circumstances, Billy understood clearly that the studio was giving him a second chance—at about the same time Nils Asther was *also* being given the nod to try one more time.

It's quite possible that—just as it was with Asther—the announcement that Billy was being dropped was merely a ruse, an excuse to cut his salary and scare him into line. It's possible the studio *never* planned to let him go, as he was still a draw, diminished or not.

In any event, the new contract was signed in September, just prior to *Wallingford*'s general release. The contract was not a starring one, a demotion Billy accepted with public equanimity. The *Los Angeles Times* reported, "Rather wisely, he has chosen to let stardom pass for a while. Haines is a clever comedian, but too much wisecracking hasn't helped his advancement." The *Times*, trying to find a silver lining, said being a featured player would offer Billy more opportunities as an actor.

There's some truth to the idea that Billy was looking forward to greater acting challenges under his new contract. With *Wallingford*, MGM had hit upon a new formula for Haines pictures: the fast-talking con guy, which Billy could parlay into a variety of characters, just as he had with the wisecracking, cocky college kid. "I want good stories," Billy told the press. "I don't want to be typed. What matter if I am the star or simply play the leading male role—so long as I get a good picture?" (Of course, just a year before, being *the star* had mattered a great deal. What did it matter, he had asked then, if Marie Dressler stole the picture or not? People would still know Billy Haines was *the star*.)

The demotion also meant a dramatic cut in pay. *Variety* reported Billy's salary was sliced from $1,750 a week to $1,500 a week. That may have only suggested the severity of it. At his height, Billy was making $3,000 a week. Unless there had been an earlier cut, the *Variety* report may have been based only on what the studio *admitted*

paying its stars. According to Henry Haines, Billy bought a dachs-
hund about this time and named him "Fifty," a wry comment on his
salary cut. Fifty percent of $3,000 is $1,500.

He had to face the realities such a cut in pay imposed. He and
Jimmie moved out of their house and into a smaller apartment in
Hollywood. Always pennywise, Billy knew he could pocket a good
chunk of cash from the rental of his fabulous home. He couldn't
have found a more suitable client: the flamboyant Tallulah Bankhead, who had just descended upon Hollywood to make several pictures for Paramount and wanted to live like a big Hollywood star.
She adored the place, hosting elegant but always slightly outrageous
soirees there for several months. It's not known if Billy attended—it
would have been difficult to be a guest in his own home—but several
news clips do reveal Jimmie escorted Tallulah around the town.

Hollywood was abuzz with the Haines demotion. *Film Weekly*, in a
supposed behind-the-scenes story in November, said that Billy "had
put his foot down," demanding he no longer be typecast as the wisecracker. With his antique shop doing well, the publication reported,
he could afford such a drastic move. Given the rental of his home,
this seems inaccurate. And while Billy was indeed tired of playing
the juvenile, the story ignores the very real ego bruising the demotion must have had on someone who, just a year ago, had been
named the number-one box-office draw in America. A demotion
from star to featured player was not usual—at least not such a *public*
demotion, nor one that occurred so swiftly. From number one at the
box office to featured player in the course of one year—the slide was
awfully precipitous.

Certainly Billy hoped that the success of *Wallingford* would herald
a new starring career, and it should have. One movie magazine, after
seeing the picture, predicted Billy would become a "new dramatic
star in Hollywood's firmament." By all logic, he should have been
ushered into a new, more hardboiled picture to capitalize on the success: not as rough-hewn as Gable, perhaps, but certainly anything
along the lines of what Robert Montgomery or Lee Tracy were then
playing. In fact, Montgomery had scored a hit in *The Big House*, a
jailhouse picture, and Tracy's breezy con men were simply exten-

sions of the parts Billy had always played. Billy had every reason to expect that such roles would be given him: He'd proven he could play them, he had a great voice, and—it has to be stated over and over—although diminished, he could still pull an audience into a theater.

Mayer's demotion of Billy left a bitter residue that lingered for the rest of his life. Even more than the final break with the studio in 1933, this demotion was the blow that rankled. Few other stars had ever had to endure such a public punishment—and what else could it be called? Coming so soon after the Bow affair and Billy's own troubles, it's obvious Mayer was using the public humiliation as a way of showing Billy he meant business: stay in line, play the game, or else.

Despite the reinstatement, Mayer for the first time pointedly declined to invite Billy to the annual New Year's Day party at the Mayer home—a snub that was also extended to John Gilbert, whom Mayer had always detested, and Ramon Novarro. Billy was willing to ride out the storm. He had willingly humbled himself before the powers that be; he fully expected such a gesture to pay off for him in the end. He was possibly grateful to the studio for getting him out of a scrape with the police, but he was also hopeful he'd be rewarded for submitting to their new demands so cooperatively.

Of course, the one demand he hadn't submitted to was marriage. Therefore, the studio needed yet a new William Haines. Howard Strickling and the Metro publicity department set out to create him.

Screen Secrets at the time had a regular feature in which fan letters were supposedly answered by the stars. The letters are obviously phony, little more than bon mots to the studio publicity departments. Clearly there was an attempt to boost Billy Haines in the period after his reinstatement. An "Evelyn K" wrote in the September issue that Bill Haines "sure is a regular feller." In fact, Evelyn gushes, he's her "ideal kind of man."

The studio-generated "response" sounds nothing like Billy. "That was a mighty nice letter you wrote about me," he supposedly replied, adding that he was a graduate of the Staunton Military Academy—

although he had gone to pains to dismiss that old chestnut as publicity nonsense just a year before—and that he was currently busy
learning football, baseball, boxing, polo, and golf.

The publicity surrounding his rehire all turned on Billy. According
to the "logic" disseminated by the studio, it had been *Billy's* fault that
his career had slowed, blaming it entirely on his playing one role for
too long. (Even if this *were* the case and not some oversimplification,
it wasn't Billy who chose the roles he played.) "Billy Gets Wise" ran
the header in the February 1932 issue of *Picture Play*. "William Haines
was about to get the gate," the article read, "but snapped out of it
in time." Just what it was that he snapped out of isn't really made
clear—but whatever it was, it was Billy's fault.

There had been much gossip about the private visit by Prince
Charles of Belgium to Billy the previous September (just before he
rented his house to Bankhead). Just as the announcement of Billy's
new contract was released to the press, a scattering of notices about
his houseguest—clearly identified as the prince—had appeared in
several columns. Many asked why the bachelor prince was visiting
MGM's demoted bachelor star. Hollywood gossiped about it for
weeks.

Seeking to spare any embarrassment to MGM *or* the Belgian
royal family, the studio decided to take action. An elaborate story
was woven about Charles visiting California incognito because he
wanted to meet a local girl he'd met on the trip across the Atlantic.
In January the magazine section of the *Los Angeles Times* ran a large
story about the prince having fallen in love with an Oakland laundry-
man's daughter. In true fairy-tale fashion, he'd hidden his identity
from her, and after the ship had docked in New York, had set off
across the country to find her. When he did, another idea struck
him. "Hollywood isn't far from here," he supposedly said. Maybe if
he went there, he could meet his idol, Mary Pickford. "I thought
maybe I might get her to autograph a photo."

Of course, while he was staying at the Hotel Biltmore in Santa
Monica, he somehow made the acquaintance of Billy Haines, there
"to join a party of yachtmen who were going to spend the holiday on
the blue." The magazine report says Billy literally tripped over

Charles's sprawled legs on the esplanade. "Haines' quick eye took in the exterior attributes of a rather gawky plebe in an ill-fitting hand-me-down," the article reported. Introductions were made: The prince called himself Charles Dawson. Very quickly, "Dawson" was staying as a guest at Haines's home, and it wasn't until Billy's butler discovered underwear with the royal insignia on them that the prince was exposed.

Billy may well have introduced Charles around town as "Charles Dawson" (also reported as "Frank Dawson") or at least used that alias to keep the press at bay, but it seems absurd to think that he didn't know the identity of his houseguest. Ted Graber says Billy had met Charles in Belgium during his trip to Europe the year before, and the fact that the prince was known throughout the Continent to be gay further makes the story ludicrous.

Even with the studio's attempt at obfuscation, the press played the story with enough homoerotic suggestion that savvy readers could easily pick it up. Billy's "chance meeting" of Charles at the Biltmore reads like a gay cruising scene. Even the headline, "Why the Royal Undies of the Belgian Prince Charles Betrayed His Incognito," with the subhead, "Even after the discovery of the distinguished guest's Paris-made 'shorts,' Bill Haines didn't know he was Prince Charles," is suggestive. What's so amusing about the whole affair is that it was simply the visit of one friend to another. It just so happened that one was a royal prince and the other a prince of the silver screen, and both of their images were suddenly up for scrutiny.

Most reporters could see right through this new attempt to micromanage Billy's public image. Still, some had their own prejudices. While most of them liked Billy a great deal, many saw homosexuality as a sickness or a form of degeneracy. Many assumed that gay people led tortured lives, no matter how happy they appeared in public, secretly wishing to find a way out of their hellish existence. Certainly Nils Asther's sour reflections on life and Ramon Novarro's reclusive existence must have lent credence to such beliefs. Billy would have laughed out loud at such a suggestion. His life—exuberant, passionate, and authentic—proved the lie to that theory. Yet faced with this sudden barrage of publicity about the "new William Haines," many reporters assumed that Billy's happy-go-lucky, wisecracking persona had been a shell to cover his true misery.

Modern Screen wrote an article entitled "The Real William Haines," saying: "The reason for the creation of the familiar clown which we all know as William Haines is a revealing and ironic commentary on human nature. It is at times a sad, bitter story . . . for is it not an un-happy thing to see a youngster twist and bend his whole personality into an unnatural form—simply because he was too sensitive to let the world see himself? Fear was the reason for Bill Haines becoming a comedian. . . . And yet, with the mask on, so cleverly and success-fully has he worn it, I doubt if there are many . . . who realize behind that grinning face is a serious young man, torn and perplexed by life."

If anything, Billy was much more torn about his place in the film industry now than he had ever been before. The message had been made clear to him: The time had come to start playing the game—or else he was out.

"What will the decision of the public be?" *Modern Screen* asked. "Will his former great body of fans become as devoted to the new William Haines as it was to the clown, Bill? Or will they resent see-ing the funmaker in the new—his real—guise?"

As part of his "reinvention," Billy was forced to undergo what he despised most: a personal appearance tour.

Thalberg convinced him it was for the best. It was, as the gossip columns noted, an attempt to let the public see who William Haines really was. The irony, of course, was that the tour was designed to do the very opposite.

Billy admitted at the outset that he hated the idea of a publicity tour. "But if Irving wants me to do it, that's that. He's been my friend through all this." Billy would tour with *Wallingford*, starting in Balti-more, then up to New York, settling in for several weeks at the Capi-tol Theater beginning on October 9. Jimmie accompanied him for at least part of the trip (Tallulah Bankhead was still living it up in their home), but several friends recall that Jimmie kept out of sight for a while, abruptly ending his lunchtime visits to the studio. The tour would move on from New York to several of the leading theaters in the Loew's chain.

In New York, Billy appeared on the Capitol stage before the film in a playlet written expressly for him by William Allan Woolf. It was the first time Billy had ever performed live on stage, and he deplored the experience. He had to perform the same act five times a day, before each showing of the film. He was used to his elegant, antique-furnished bungalow on the Metro lot; now he had a dressing room through which stagehands climbed as they made their way from one end of the stage to the other. He told anyone who'd listen that if he was ever offered a role on the legitimate stage, he'd turn it down flat.

Appearing with him in the revue was up-and-coming entertainer Milton Berle, who with his Great Guns Show got most of the laughs. Billy's sister Lillion Stone, then living on Long Island, acted as his personal assistant. A reporter commented on Lillion coming backstage at the Capitol, calling her a "beauty" and questioning why she had never gone into movies herself. At that point, Billy may well have wondered why he *had*.

For all his unhappiness, however, Billy did prove something by his tour: He was still very, very popular. A crowd of fans and photographers was there to meet his train at Grand Central Station. Even if this had been arranged by the studio for publicity purposes, the subsequent throngs could not have been manufactured by even the best publicist. Everywhere Billy went, he drew crowds. The manager of the Capitol told the press he'd never before had such business; the closest he got was for a Garbo picture. The *New York Daily News* reported in October that "the Haines popularity still endures," with long lines of women waiting to get a glimpse of him at the Capitol. So successful was *Wallingford* and Billy's promotion of it that the tour was extended, much to his dismay, through the end of the year. He appeared in New York through December, "packing them in" every night, according to the *New York American*.

One eager fan, an eight-year-old boy named Willy Woods, snuck into Billy's dressing room on October 11. Holding up a chocolate soda to the guard, Willy said smoothly, "Mr. Haines sent me out for this." He was waiting for the star when he returned to his dressing room. Billy, recognizing a photo opportunity, called in the photographers. The picture that was splashed all over the newspapers the next day shows Billy, in satin smoking jacket, holding the soda while the boy sips it through a straw. The studio was thrilled with the publicity: The new William Haines could be a hero to young boys, much the way Gable or Montgomery was.

In November he took the revue out to a Loew's theater in Yonkers, then up to Syracuse on December 11. Again he was met with big crowds. Certainly the studio must have been gratified by this surge in support for their beleaguered star. Crowds crushed into the theater, pushed and clawed toward the stage for autographs. Of course, it just made Billy despise personal appearances all the more. "This business of living in a trunk and on sandwiches and having to stay in a dressing room all these hours is very depressing," he admitted to a reporter. "It's the four or five shows a day that makes it so confining."

A few days later, *Variety* reported that he was "throwing fits" about the extended tour. He snapped he'd "walk back to Hollywood" if he had to. Eventually he quieted down and finished the tour. He'd made a bargain, and he would stick with it.

Back in Hollywood in late January, he was given his first script under the new "featured player" contract. Tellingly, it was originally slated as a Robert Montgomery picture. It was a measure of how far he had fallen that Billy was now being handed the rejects of the "new William Haines."

Whereas Montgomery's name would have gone above the title, Billy was now billed below. The picture was *Are You Listening?*, based on the novel by J. P. McEvoy. Madge Evans, who had just finished playing with Montgomery in *Lovers Courageous*, was cast as his leading lady. Actually, he had three: Karen Morley, quickly becoming a hot property at Metro, plays the shrewish wife he hopes to divorce, and Anita Page essays the smaller part of Evans's sister. Page, too, had fallen from favor: In a dispute with Mayer, she'd thrown a chair at him.

Released in March 1932, *Are You Listening?* was a straight melodrama, with little room for comedy. Billy plays a radio gag writer
who gets falsely accused of murdering his wife and then is the subject of a manhunt coordinated by radio broadcasters. The only
laughs come with the bad gags he writes; a little more humor could
have leavened the whole production and made it much more enjoyable. In the attempt to revamp Billy's character, it was a mistake to
throw out all semblance of the wisecracker.

Still, the picture turned a small profit, although not as impressive
as *Wallingford* and nowhere near the Haines grosses of old. More
devastating was the critical reaction. The *New York Times* didn't even
bother to review the picture. *Variety* trashed it, calling it "one of
those disagreeable messes." The review ended with an interesting,
albeit enigmatic, aside: "The picture presents William Haines at a
great disadvantage in more than one respect. In an endeavor to take
him out of the wise-cracking category, he brodies as a dramatic
actor, and further hurts himself by his actions and delivery to the
insiders."

This grammatically challenged sentence carries some ambiguity:
Who are these "insiders" with whom Billy has hurt himself? Insiders
in the radio industry, possibly, who would have disapproved of
Billy's unconvincing performance. The passage could also be read as
the "insiders" being the studio brass, the ones who had endeavored
to take Billy out of the "wise-cracking category." The *Variety* reviewer, who would certainly have been following Billy's troubles
over the past year, and could well have heard the rumors of scandal,
might have reasoned that with Billy's failure to cut it as a dramatic
actor, he had thereby further "hurt himself" with his bosses.

The question of why Billy had been given this particular script
needs to be asked. Although in remaking his image it was clear that
the old "Haines formula" wouldn't do, by stripping him of *all* vestiges of his former personality the studio had to know it would jolt
his still-loyal army of fans (who had been evident during the personal appearance tour). *Wallingford* had succeeded because it had allowed Billy to play an adult with the same kind of light touch he'd
brought to his juvenile roles. Why stick him with a Bob Mont-

gomery reject? Why wasn't a property carefully chosen expressly for him to inaugurate his new contract and kick off his new image?

One answer, of course, was that he just wasn't worth it, that there were more important considerations now at the studio: Gable, Robert Young, Charles Starrett, Montgomery himself. Still, MGM was a big place, with hundreds of employees. Certainly *some* care could have been given to a player who just signed a new two-year contract. The studio protected its investments. Billy had just proven himself with *Wallingford* and with the very successful tour. Why wasn't more care taken in choosing his new vehicles?

The answer is complicated. It's too easy to say that Mayer simply wanted him out because he was gay and had caused them headaches in the past, yet that cannot be dismissed as part of it, as perhaps the part that infused everything else. By 1932 Billy's heyday as a top star had faded from the minds of most of the studio executives. It was a fast-paced, quickly changing world. Although he'd been a top talking picture star—indeed the studio's first—Billy was lumped into the old silent school, and silent stars, so went the conventional wisdom, were yesterday's news. (Garbo, Shearer, and Crawford—almost alone in the industry—remained the exceptions.) Billy had a more damaging label stuck to his back as well: troublemaker. And in an industry still smarting over the Clara Bow debacle, that didn't go away quickly.

Play the game. That remained the unspoken message. Or perhaps it *was* spoken, clearly and forcefully. "They were after him all the time at the end," says Arch Case. "They wanted him to get hitched to some broad." During the filming of *Are You Listening?* Anita Page says Billy asked her to marry him. Previously, he had been like a big brother to her. He was ten years her senior, and although she still claims ignorance about his sexuality, she knew Jimmie Shields quite well. When Billy had kissed her in earlier pictures, she recalls, he had invariably "held back." Now that changed.

"We were standing outside," she recalls, "when all of a sudden he grabbed me and gave me a big kiss—I mean, he *really* kissed me. I thought, *wow!* I was in a daze."

He popped the question, and she told him she'd have to think about it. She went to Mayer for advice. "Don't you know what he is?" Mayer asked her.

"All I know is he's my friend," she replied.

"Haven't you seen that man, Jimmie Shields, hanging around the set?" Mayer boomed.

Page bristled. "If you'll notice, Mr. Mayer, he's not there anymore."

According to Page, Billy would come onto the set singing, "Nothing could be sweeter than to see my Anita in the mo-o-orning." She'd blush, dazzled by his attention. "I'd say, 'Billy, I'm not *your* Anita.' "

Eventually she turned him down. "He was very nice about it. We stayed friends. He never let it bother him."

It's quite possible, perhaps even likely at this point in his career, that Billy contemplated finally playing the marriage game. He wanted desperately to hang on to the studio. He wanted very much to be a star again. His demotion had left him in a small apartment while Tallulah Bankhead whooped it up at his house. The standard of living to which he had become accustomed was suddenly threatened. In a weak moment, he could well have considered marrying Anita Page. She was a sweet, good-natured, pretty girl. And also a rather innocent one; just as Cary Grant would wed Virginia Cherrill a couple years later, Billy Haines could have married Anita Page and counted on her naïveté to preserve his independence. Jimmie would have had to move out of the house, of course, and Billy's life would have taken on a murky duplicity that would have stood in stark contrast to the forthright way in which he had lived before.

Lucky for Billy Haines that Anita Page turned him down. Lucky, too, of course, for her.

In the midst of all this, his mother died. Since coming to Hollywood five years before, Laura Haines had continued to suffer from hypertension and arteriosclerosis. Her health steadily declined, and, as a convert to Christian Science, she refused to be treated. Chronic nephritis plagued her for the last year; her kidneys failed and she was confined to her bed.

Christian Science had won many followers in the Hollywood community, including Joan Crawford. Its tenets fit with the idealism of many sunny Californians: Purity of thought cures disease. Up until the end, Laura Haines believed she could cure herself. A copy of *Science and Health with the Key to the Scriptures* was near her bed. No amount of cajoling from the family could sway her, and it took a cerebral hemorrhage on July 10 to finally get her to a hospital. She was admitted to Good Samaritan Hospital in Los Angeles and died a week later, at 1:35 on Sunday afternoon, July 17, 1932, with her family around her. She was only fifty-four.

"My father was distraught," Henry Haines remembers. Billy, too, was devastated. To him, his beloved mother did not have to die. Had she accepted treatment, he argued, she might have been cured. She might at least have lived longer. She died as she believed: pure in thought according to her spiritual practice. She was buried on July 19 following a service at the Wee Kirk o' the Heather in Forest Lawn Memorial Park. A Christian Science reader officiated.

Everyone who remembers Billy eventually comments on his extraordinary devotion to his mother. She had, after all, been the first to believe in his talents, the first to champion his unique and special gifts. She had allowed him independence in his formative years and had taken pride in his success. Despite the teachers who had once despaired of him, Laura Haines always had faith that Billy would triumph. He had been proud of her, too, these past few years in Hollywood, as she played the elegant hostess at his soirees. "I'd like to introduce you to the goose who laid the golden egg," he'd say, laughing, to his friends. Her death, while a terrible blow, left him not so much depressed as determined — determined to find a new position from which to continue making his mother proud.

Let anyone try to say Billy Haines was over the hill. Just let them try.

During the spring and summer of 1932 Billy underwent a massive exercise and dieting routine, committed to proving any critics wrong who thought he looked too old to play snappy leading men. "It was driven into our minds that old meant thirty," Billy would remember. "Somebody who was thirty could never stay in motion pictures."

To combat this mentality, he tried to reverse some of the aging trends. There was little he could do about his thinning hair (those hair-growing potions had all been busts), but he *could* attack the softness around his waist. He stopped snitching in the middle of preparing his elegant five-course gourmet meals. He began swimming, running, even going so far as to lift some weights. The results pleased both himself and the studio. A flurry of press releases went out showing him in tip-top shape, which refutes the simplistic notion held by some historians that he had merely gotten too old and out of shape for MGM to keep him. In 1932 he weighed in at a lean 185 pounds, compatible weight for a six-foot frame. Several scenes in his next picture, *Fast Life*, were arranged to show him off in bathing trunks, and he cuts a surprisingly fine figure, tighter and more defined than in similar scenes in his silent films.

Fast Life, originally called *Let's Go*, was released just before Christmas in 1932. It was directed by Harry Pollard, whose recent credits included Robert Montgomery's *Shipmates*, a typical "Haines formula" film that bears similarities to *Fast Life*. Production began on September 26; it was completed by early November. The studio seemed to have learned a lesson from *Are You Listening?* William Haines without humor just didn't work. Like *Wallingford*, *Fast Life* blends its comedy with a fast-paced action adventure. Like *Wallingford*, too, *Fast Life* gives Billy a wisecracking sidekick, this time played by his friend Cliff Edwards.

While Edwards gets most of the laughs, Billy is back in smart-aleck form. When Madge Evans, again cast as his leading lady, remarks, "I like your nerve," he quips: "That's a good start. Gradually you'll like all of me." She does, of course, especially after the next scene. Wise to his playboy ways, she orders him off her property. "And that's *my* bathing suit," she says. So he takes it off—beyond the camera range, naturally, but Madge and her friends watch in wide-eyed amazement. Pretty risqué stuff, and even more unusual that it's the man who's being ogled.

The plot gets a bit convoluted, with Billy uncovering and foiling a plot by Conrad Nagel. That Nagel, who just a few years ago was the boy wonder of the talkies, should be so quickly reduced to a supporting part in a Billy Haines programmer speaks volumes about the expendability of players. Karl Dane, too, a major character actor in the silents—and a regular in Haines pictures—is here in an unbilled bit. (Dane would find himself selling hot dogs outside the studio gate before he took his own life in 1934.) Billy's fall cannot be seen outside of the context of what was happening to other actors. Nagel would rebound—something that Billy, after this film, was never able to do.

Fast Life is not a bad film. Billy is in fine form, and Nagel and Cliff Edwards provide great support. There are some exciting boat-race scenes and the ending is a climactic boat chase, all well photographed. The reviews were not universally bad, either, as some later historians have assumed. The *New York Times* liked Billy's performance "exceptionally well" and thought the picture "a thoroughly suitable diversion for this season, for the fun of it is of the variety that will appeal to both adults and children."

Variety, however, seemed to sum up the studio's attitude. Recognizing Haines's fall from star status to feature player, the trade paper opined that it was Cliff Edwards who saved the picture from being a total bust. "It's cut to order for Haines, who's still playing smart alecks and here, as mostly in the past, overdoing it," the review noted. "Or it's getting stale stuff for most audiences and tearing down Haines' box office value. Perhaps Metro figures there's nothing else for Haines but this type of amusement."

Fast Life was the first William Haines picture to actually lose money for MGM. It was also his last film for the studio. Most stars could weather one all-out flop, the first one of their careers—but Billy Haines was not most stars.

Despite their attempts to remake William Haines, the studio hadn't been able to completely control the publicity.

By 1932 the number of Hollywood reporters had swelled dramatically. Nearly every newspaper in the country had entertainment pages with writers assigned to cover the movies. A huge article in the *Philadelphia Ledger* on February 21 profiled Hollywood's bachelors: William Haines, Ramon Novarro, Phillips Holmes, James Dunn, and George O'Brien. The headline read: "Step Lively Girls—

Only a Few Romeos Left." Writer Alice Tildesley says coyly about Billy: "[He] just won't be serious on the question of matrimony. He says his hair turned blonde once following a nitroglycerine explosion and would turn white if he got in sight of a marriage altar." That's just the kind of answer of which Mayer had grown very weary.

Then in April, Douglas Fairbanks, Jr., wrote a short, remarkable profile of Billy for *Vanity Fair*. It's a curiosity, especially given their friendship and the growing suspicion of Billy's lifestyle. Fairbanks paints Billy as an aging, effeminate prima donna. "He is muscular without being athletic," Fairbanks wrote of the star of numerous sporting films, "yet when he walks there is a certain grace that suggests delicacy. There is masculinity in his actions, yet a definite tendency toward femininity in his thoughts." Fairbanks went on to observe there was "a great deal of the woman" in Billy, best expressed in his discriminating taste in decor, style, and art. Billy and the studio must have dove for cover when the issue hit the stands.

Vanity Fair wasn't the typical fan magazine; it was able to flex a much more independent muscle. The publication was "in the know," and it liked to remind its readers of that fact. A photograph of Marlene Dietrich and Garbo in pants had recently run under the heading: "Members of the Same Club." Fairbanks's piece was part of a similar mentality. The question remains: Why had Fairbanks written it? Today Fairbanks cannot recall the circumstances of the piece. It could be that he never intended his remarks to appear as they did. It was most likely "as told to" an unnamed *Vanity Fair* writer, who then slapped the piece with Fairbanks's byline. It's interesting to note that, at the time, Fairbanks had recently left MGM. His marriage to Joan Crawford was unraveling because of her affair with Clark Gable. There were no ties of loyalty left to Billy. One imagines that their friendship may have been a little strained after the publication of the article. The result, of course, was further suspicion among the public.

In November, Valmond Maurice Guest wrote in *Film Weekly* that Billy was called the "Funny Bachelor" in Hollywood. Guest, who was friendly with Haines, attempted a bit of obfuscation, saying Billy had seen too many marriages go wrong in Hollywood to say "I will" very quickly. "Girls have come and girls have gone," Guest assured his readers, but added that only Polly Moran had any endurance.

The innuendoes continued. In January, *Picture Play* ran a cartoon showing Billy in a tux prancing effeminately through a department store with the legend: "William Haines used to be a *floor walker* [emphasis theirs] in a Richmond, Virginia, department store before he became the screen scream." The word "walker" was commonly used to designate a woman's homosexual escort; "screen scream" also has obvious sissy connotations. Another newspaper ran a photo of the star with the caption: "William Haines has his own ideas on how to run a home and he doesn't want a wife around who'd interfere with him." Mayer grumbled; no real man cared which side of the plate you stuck the fork. They were snickering out there in Peoria, and Louis B. could hear them all the way in his Culver City office.

True to form, Billy didn't help matters and continued to quip. He told one reporter that he once snitched Garbo's new slippers from her dressing room and broke them in for her. "We both wear a size 11," he said, winking. It wasn't the first time he'd linked himself in print with other gay stars. Like his earlier crack that he and Ramon Novarro sang in the same choir, he was using the same code as the *Vanity Fair* heading: They were all members of the same club.

When the numbers came dwindling in for *Fast Life*, Billy had to suspect that his days were numbered.

He must have been angry: *Fast Life* was treated as a B film, distributed poorly. There was little ad campaign for it; it doesn't appear prominently in any MGM press book. The odds were stacked against it from the start. He couldn't expect a rational argument with the studio; the whole dynamic of the place had changed, and that fall of 1932 was perhaps the most chaotic period since Metro-Goldwyn-Mayer had first coalesced back in 1924.

By late spring, business at New York's biggest movie houses was at the lowest level ever. Film profits had fallen yet again, the effects of the Depression finally making their way up to the top levels of the movie industry. From $6.2 million in 1931, MGM profits dropped to

$5.2 million in 1932. They would fall again in 1933 before rebounding in 1934. A major cost-cutting program was enacted in December. Even if studio publicists had *wanted* to push *Fast Life*, ad campaigns were selective and cautious. The financial worries didn't end there. In March 1933, stagehands at most of the major studios went on strike. Once that was resolved, Mayer ordered a fifty-percent salary cut for directors, actors, and writers. (All were restored to their former levels after six weeks, however.)

Even more troubling was the rapid-fire explosion of bad publicity that fall. On September 3, 1932, the shy, soft-spoken producer Paul Bern—the same who a decade before had pined after Barbara La Marr—stuck a pistol to his head and pulled the trigger. It was nearly two months to the day that he had married MGM's latest sex sensation, Jean Harlow. She had been known to hang on his arm, point to burly football players, and say, "Daddy, buy me that." It was the biggest scandal to hit Hollywood since the Clara Bow trial the year before. Was Harlow involved? And what did Bern's cryptic suicide note mean? "Dearest dear," he'd scrawled. "Unfortunately this is the only way to make good the frightful wrong I have done you and to wipe out my abject humiliation." In a postscript, he added: "You understand that last night was only a comedy." The press, as might be expected, went nuts.

This was just what Mayer had been fearing. Like the Bow scandal, the Bern suicide involved a red-hot sexy female star and hinted at tawdry details of Hollywood sex lives. (Nearly every report mentioned the suicide note, the fact that Bern was found nude, and soon it was learned that he'd had a common-law wife in San Francisco.) What made this even more sensational than the Bow headlines was that a death was involved. A criminal investigation had to take place to officially declare Bern a suicide. Of course, the Catholic reformers began shouting even louder. No matter that a Production Code was in place, Hollywood was still Sodom. Meanwhile, Harlow's latest film, *Red-Headed Woman*, was about as raunchy as raunch could get, and reports were that her next picture, *Red Dust*, would be even steamier.

Mayer called an emergency conference. Present were Thalberg,

Rapf, story editor Samuel Marx, and producers Benjamin Thau, Albert Lewin, and Hunt Stromberg. Word had leaked to the press that Bern suffered from impotency, that his genitals were malformed. What would this do to Jean Harlow's image? "You understand that last night was only a comedy" rang in all of their ears. But worse: Mayer charged at the meeting that Bern was a homosexual. What if some *Coast Reporter*–type of rag got wind of *that*?

Thalberg, reportedly, denied that Bern was gay. Certainly Bern had been in love with women, although the Harlow marriage *does* seem to have been a partnership of convenience. Everyone was aware of Bern's devastation when his close friend Joseph Jackson drowned at Malibu that previous May while both were swimming. Mayer was desperate to keep the press from hinting about Bern's sexuality. Impotence was bad enough, but Mayer would not abide queer rumors. He bullied Thalberg until he broke down and admitted that yes, Bern was at least sexually ambiguous. Hunt Stromberg admitted he knew "for a fact" that Bern was a "fairy."

A week later, there was more trouble. One of Edmund Goulding's bisexual orgies had gotten out of hand. The details are unclear, but several women threatened to press charges. They would have revealed the details: men with men, women with women—and who knew which MGM stars were present. Thalberg sent Goulding to Europe until the threat of public scandal blew over. Meanwhile, the necessary arrangements were made with District Attorney Buron Fitts to get the women to back down.

Still more bad news: Greta Garbo was on a European vacation, and reports of her embarrassing behavior there had reached the States. The less reserved European press commented on Garbo's frequent companionship with the Swedish Countess Ingrid Wachtmeister. The Countess, like Garbo, preferred boots and trousers, and was known in Sweden as a lesbian. On a trip to Paris, they were spotted at a lesbian bar. One account called it "one of the most lurid nightclubs in Montmartre, frequented by hard-boiled women of the Paris demimonde, who go there attired in mannish costumes to give lady tourists the shock they are looking for by asking them to dance." It was reported that the countess danced the night away with "female gigolos," while Garbo, in black wig and glasses, watched from the bar.

Then Tallulah Bankhead arrived on the lot, fresh from her recent successes at Paramount and her stay at Billy Haines's house. (Billy had likely moved back in by this point.) Mayer offered her a contract, and her first assignment would be to take over Jean Harlow's part in *Red Dust*. Bankhead refused, saying she didn't want to take advantage of Harlow's recent tragedy. Mayer explained that the studio needed to put Harlow on ice for a while, alluding to the details of Bern's life and death. Bankhead was incensed. There were several other homosexuals on Mayer's staff, she said. Should she name them? Mayer narrowed his eyes and asked her if it was true she liked girls. "Like girls?" Bankhead asked. She pointed to a photo of Garbo. "You mean the way *she* likes girls?" (Of course, Bankhead did, and made no pretense of it.) Mayer promptly withdrew his offer.

The story is likely apocryphal, yet whatever its underlying truth, it reveals Mayer's attitude toward his gay employees by the end of 1932. When George Cukor was hired as an MGM director that following February, some reports say Mayer asked him point-blank if he was homosexual. Mayer biographer Charles Higham says that by 1933, the studio chief "had had enough of that breed." In October, Mayer had launched an ambitious publicity campaign to prove that at MGM, "men were men." Arthur Loew was sent on a daredevil flying expedition two-thirds of the way around the world. When Loew's plane crashed, Mayer tried to keep it out of the papers, but to no avail.

That fall, the *Hollywood Reporter* was filled with stories of Billy, Bankhead, Jean Harlow, and others patronizing B.B.B.'s Cellar, the speakeasy with female impersonators. The reports enraged Mayer, who felt he was losing control over his stable of stars. Several times Howard Hughes is mentioned as being at the club in the company of Billy and others. The club, although patronized by rich and famous straight folk, was nonetheless a gay bar. Hughes was just coming off production of *Scarface*, one of the biggest hits of the year. He was known around town to be lovers with Paramount contract player Randolph Scott, although his affairs with women were given huge publicity.

The worst blow to the studio came in December. On Christmas Eve, having weathered years of conflict with Mayer now compounded by the scandals of the fall, Irving Thalberg suffered a heart attack. He was the patron to many at the studio—including Billy—and his illness put them all on guard. He was out of commission for nearly a year—he and Norma Shearer went off to Europe so he could recover in peace—and many who had looked to him for advice and protection were now left on their own to face Mayer.

To make matters the worst they could be, the Catholic Church had stepped up its attacks. The Production Code had proven weak and ineffectual; a letter from the bishops to Will Hays urged new, stricter regulations. The specter of censorship once again threatened the sunny California skies.

Such was the atmosphere at MGM as 1932 turned the corner into 1933. Attitudes were changing—among studio executives but also among the public, weary and angry from the deepening Depression. As happens whenever such conditions converge, heads were going to roll.

Sometime in early 1933, Billy Haines parted company with Metro-Goldwyn-Mayer. It had been eleven years, and what a ride it had been.

Was he fired? Did he quit? Billy's departure from MGM is the stuff of Hollywood legend. Even those unfamiliar with the details of his career often know about his break with the studio. The legend goes something like this:

After finding Billy with another sailor, or bailing him out of jail yet again, Mayer hauled the star into his office and issued an ultimatum. "You're either to give up that boyfriend of yours," Mayer said, "or I'll cancel your contract."

"Without even a hesitation," wrote Anita Loos, "Bill opted for love and told L.B. to tear up his contract."

A very pretty story. And what makes this particular Hollywood legend so fascinating is that, unlike so many of the others, it's probably true. Even if not entirely accurate, it's true in spirit. Most likely, Mayer *did* call Billy into his office and tell him he had better start playing the game. Billy refused, point-blank, and so his career was ended.

It's hardly likely, however, that Mayer's ultimatum came in response to another scandal-in-the-making on Billy's part. Given the atmosphere in Hollywood after Bern's suicide and the media embarrassments of the fall, it would have been lunacy for Billy to tempt fate in that way. He had just been given a reprieve after *Wallingford*'s success, and he wanted desperately to stay within the safe confines of the Metro lot. It's hard to imagine him one day considering marriage to Anita Page and the next putting himself at risk for a scandal.

Of course, it might have been that *Jimmie* ran afoul of the law, as some longtime friends believe, and that Billy was either there or came to bail him out of jail. No arrest records for either Billy or Jimmie exist, but that doesn't eliminate the possibility that they had been detained. "I think, at the end, Billy may have paid for something Jimmie did," says Michael Pearman. Bob Wheaton concurs: "I liked Jimmie, he was a friend of mine, but he was the kind of boyfriend who messed things up."

Jimmie *did* frequently solicit young men on the street or at the park to bring home for sex; often Billy would join in. "I guess it kept their marriage fresh," Wheaton says. Indeed, one of the few things that was constant and stable in Billy's life at this point was his relationship with Jimmie. It will never be known if Jimmie was the catalyst for Billy's break with MGM. It's unfair to Jimmie to assume it to be true; it nevertheless remains a possibility.

Billy, on the other hand, most likely behaved like an angel during this period, but Mayer, unencumbered for once by Thalberg, decided he was too much trouble anyway.

Given the stressful situation at the studio in the first months of 1933, it's not a difficult scenario to imagine. Louis B. Mayer was in just the right frame of mind to issue ultimatums. Anita Loos, while sometimes a bit melodramatic, was usually on the money in her recollections. In 1932 she'd just arrived on the lot to script *Red-Headed*

Woman for Jean Harlow. She and Billy quickly became acquainted. They shared the same high spirits, the same irreverence, and many of the same friends. They had partied together at San Simeon and at Marion Davies' Santa Monica beach house. Loos would surely have known the details of Billy's last days at MGM.

The ultimatum that came from Mayer was probably not about dropping Jimmie, except indirectly. Jimmie was almost irrelevant to Mayer; what the studio chief wanted to see was Billy married, Billy beyond the wink-wink of the gossip columnists. Ted Graber and Arch Case confirm that Billy often told them the reason Mayer had it in for him was because he refused to get married. That's likely what the last confrontation with Mayer was all about: Billy was told he'd better finally begin playing the game—as even Ramon Novarro had now consented to do—or else he was out.

According to all reports, Billy's answer was a resounding no. He may have dallied with the idea a year before, but by early 1933 he wouldn't consider it, not even to save his career. Arch Case remembers, "Billy always told me that he said to them, 'I'm already married,' and so that was that. End of discussion."

Except not quite the end. Billy still had another year on his new contract. There was no tearing up that document, as Loos grandiosely suggests. Throughout 1933 Billy is still referred to in the press as an MGM player. The notices of his official departure do not appear in the trades until September.

Case says that Billy told him he sat out the remainder of his contract. "What I was always told was he took sick for that last year," he explains. "Because the studio had to live up to its side of the contract, they had to keep paying him."

Given the scarcity of evidence, that scenario seems to make sense. Until such time as the MGM archives are again open to the public, there can be no definite confirmation as to the exact nature of Billy's split with the studio. Still, the basics can be deduced. Although Billy would, many years later, refer to "being kicked out the door" by Mayer, it was an indirect kick. It wasn't exactly a firing: Mayer was bound by the contract, and so had to continue paying his former star. It wasn't exactly quitting on Billy's part, either: Had Mayer not pushed him against the wall, he'd likely have continued to play in programmers like *Fast Life*.

Even then, Billy was hopeful for another eleventh-hour reprieve. It's very likely that had Thalberg been at the studio in early 1933, Mayer never would have issued an ultimatum to Billy. Billy said as much in interviews later on. Still technically an MGM employee, Billy surely had hopes that upon Thalberg's return, he'd be reinstated. From every indication, Billy was eager to stay (providing he didn't have to get married, of course). He'd have been willing to move into supporting or character roles — as a character player, Billy's love life would have been less important to the ever-hungry media.

For now he simply sat home. If any films were offered by the studio, which they probably weren't, he refused them. He was waiting for Thalberg to return. Thalberg, as usual, remained his last best hope.

It's probably safe to say that had *Fast Life* been an enormous hit, MGM would have kept Billy, married or not. It's also probably safe to say that had Billy played the Hollywood game all along, he never would have ended up in a programmer like *Fast Life* in the first place, a picture that was practically designed to fail.

Billy should have been able to survive his first and only flop. As Novarro said, that was the beauty of the studio system: There was security. Wallace Beery's *A Lady's Morals* took a huge loss in 1930, but Beery went on to his best years of stardom after that. Gilbert Roland saw his *Men of the North* crash and burn that same year, but he wasn't booted out the door. Walter Huston watched in despair as his *The Wet Parade* bombed in 1931, but he would go on to be nominated for an Academy Award for *Dodsworth* in 1936 and win one in 1948 for *Treasure of the Sierra Madre*. The argument, as some have made, that Billy's dismissal was entirely about economics is as simplistic as theories that he was fired solely for being gay.

Mayer, given the growing pressure from reformers and the recent scandals, was fed up with taking chances. Billy was risky, and unlike other risky players like Garbo or even Novarro, his recent box-office returns didn't justify continuing the gamble. Had he been less of a risk, of course—had he gotten married and played the game like Edmund Lowe—he could have moved into the kinds of character parts that Lowe, once a box-office champ like Billy, was now playing. While Billy was being shown the door, Lowe was essaying a suave supporting part in George Cukor's prestigious, all-star *Dinner at Eight*.

Some argue that Billy's dismissal was part of a larger general trend, in which all of the major male silent stars—gay *and* straight—were shunted aside. John Gilbert went into alcoholic exile; Norman Kerry retired into oblivion; Rod La Rocque went into real estate. For every failure there are stories of success, however. Edmund Lowe has already been cited. Consider also Adolphe Menjou, who moved from leading roles to debonair support, becoming one of Hollywood's busiest and most versatile character actors. Menjou had, perhaps, greater talent than Billy Haines, but what of Neil Hamilton? He carried on into the sound era, moving from the handsome male lead to the handsome *second* male lead. Conrad Nagel, who had been a star for even longer than Billy and had fallen even lower (as a supporting player in *Fast Life*) was soon back in leads (*Ann Vickers*) and important supporting roles (*All That Heaven Allows*) through the 1950s.

Nagel is a good example for several reasons. His public following may have dipped, but his career revived for one important reason: He was the ultimate game-player. Chummy with Mayer, a studio-appointed president of the Academy of Motion Picture Arts and Sciences, Nagel was protected by the old-boy network that ruled Hollywood, even if he wasn't generally liked all that much (certainly not as much as Billy was liked).

Charles Farrell, a gay actor who succeeded Billy as number one at the box office, also knew the rules. Although, like Billy, he fell from the top post rather quickly, Farrell continued to play leading roles until the end of the decade, then started a second career as a character actor both in films and television. Farrell—like his popular costar Janet Gaynor—took solace in a happy marriage of convenience with Virginia Valli. Anita Page recalls dating Farrell around 1930,

but giving him the heave-ho when she tired of the fact that he wore
more makeup offscreen than she did.

The studio was willing to tolerate stars who kept up appearances,
who didn't cause trouble, whose boyfriends didn't bring them
lunches every day on the set. Louise Brooks's later contention that
"they put Billy Haines out when they found out he was a homosexual" is far too simplistic—there were many other conditions that
ended his career at MGM. Yet Hal Elias, who was working in the
publicity department at the time of Billy's ouster, said he was "inclined to go along with" the theory that ultimately Billy was "pushed
out" for being too open about his homosexuality. The bottom line is,
by 1933, the only way anyone even had a *chance* to survive the upheaval was to play the Hollywood game.

Part of that upheaval was a changing attitude toward masculinity,
brought on by the Depression's direct challenge to gender roles and
the increasingly conservative tone of the times.

In one published interview, Billy is reported to have said his
screen image, like others', went out of style because it was considered "soft and pampered." Certainly a new kind of male hero was
emerging from the ashes of the Roaring Twenties. The sweep that
washed away Kerry and La Rocque and Billy Haines left in its wake
Cagney and Tracy (Lee *and* Spencer) and Clark Gable.

Just three years before, Irving Thalberg had told an audience at
the University of Southern California that William Haines, with his
"go and get it attitude," was the quintessential hero of the times.
How those times had changed. The Depression called for a hero
who, instead of "going out and getting it," made *it* come to *him*. Billy
could kid a girl, lead her along, and flirt up a storm. Gable slapped
her across the face and carried her up the stairs. The rugged heroes
of the 1930s hid their vulnerability; there would be no hecklers in
the audience laughing at Gable's tears as they did at Billy's in *Brown
of Harvard*.

In addition—in the face of the mounting calls for decency and
old-fashioned morality—movie heroes could no longer be ambigu-

ous. They had to be straightforward and direct. Onscreen, they shot guns and scowled a lot. Offscreen, they were men of few words: Gable's "aw shucks" and Cooper's "yep" were about as much as they dared to say. Billy's wisecracks, his clever parrying with the press, were styles of a more frivolous time.

Billy knew Gable. In fact, they had a rather special bond between them. At some point, they'd had a sexual encounter. The details are murky, but Billy told a number of friends about it and he was not known to lie about such things. In fact, Joan Crawford confirmed the stories late in her life, and she was in a position to know. Gable was most definitely heterosexual, and Billy was likely the only man he ever had sex with. But the incident just wouldn't go away; it became part of Hollywood folklore, much to Gable's chagrin.

Just when the encounter took place is unclear. The author Jane Ellen Wayne claims it occurred during the filming of *The Pacemakers*, a series of short subjects produced by FBO in 1925. She wrote that Billy was the star, and Gable, an aspiring stage actor and former roustabout, was doing some extra work. According to Wayne, Gable consented to the sex (presumed to be oral, with Billy doing the servicing) because he wanted Billy to help him in his acting career.

Gable was indeed in several films as an extra in 1925, and may have worked in *The Pacemakers*—but Billy definitely was not in it. Exhaustive research at the Academy of Motion Picture Arts and Sciences has turned up no evidence of Billy being a part of the series. This would have been pre–*Brown of Harvard*, so there's little likelihood of a cameo star shot, either. And besides, in his pre-*Brown* days, Billy was still struggling with his *own* career. He'd have had little to offer Gable.

The encounter more likely took place at MGM. Gable may well have been an extra in one of Billy's pictures, or just hanging out on the lot, when he caught Billy's eye. This was before Gable had turned rough and surly, two definite turn-offs for Billy. Gable in 1925 was not yet the King of Hollywood; he was still soft and very beautiful. The implication that he only had sex with Billy because he was trying to curry favor seems a latter-day invention, designed to explain away a defiantly heterosexual man's transgressions. In the more relaxed days of the 1920s, explanations weren't needed. Both were lusty, attractive, virile young men; Billy was twenty-five, Gable twenty-four. One friend insists the encounter took place during a party at the Beverly Wilshire Hotel. "It wasn't a blow job," this friend insisted. "Billy *fucked* him in the men's room. Billy was a fuck*er*, never a fuck*ee*."

Whatever the exact details of the encounter, it's clear *something* happened between the two men. The irony that the era's quintessential new hero—Clark Gable—had, in fact, once tricked with Billy Haines certainly could not have been lost on either of them. Gable's torrid affair with Joan Crawford—on and off for two decades—must have made for some interesting chat between Billy and his best friend. In later years, Joan would admit to Billy's encounter with Gable, as well as her own affair with the King, but she never revealed if they ever compared notes.

While he waited out his contract—and for Thalberg to return—Billy busied himself at the shop. His contract would not allow him to appear in any other pictures outside Metro, but it couldn't stop him from decorating.

"In all that mess," he told writer Constance Blake, "in all the tinsel shifting of Hollywood, I wanted something that was permanent and beautiful. I'd go down to my shop and look at a perfect piece of old furniture and the world wouldn't seem so lousy after that."

In March he revamped Crawford's Brentwood home to mark her divorce from Fairbanks. She insisted that Billy replace all of the toilet seats. She'd call him in to do it again when she divorced Franchot Tone in 1939 and again in 1946 when she divorced Philip Terry.

One of Billy's major projects that summer was the home of Leila Hyams and Phil Berg. They had just built a mansion in Beverly Hills designed by architect Paul Williams and wanted Billy to decorate it. He composed the living room in a sea of blues, finishing it off with hand-painted Chinese wallpaper, which would become a trademark touch. He was determined to obliterate, as he had with his own house, any traces of the pseudo-Spanish architecture of the place.

Paramount star Carole Lombard also became a friend around this time, probably through Andy Lawler. She had many gay friends; in fact, she delighted in gay male company much more than that of female companions. After her divorce from William Powell in the summer of 1933, she bought a home of her own in Brentwood and asked Billy to design the place. "Any male who ventures to set foot inside Carole Lombard's new house, decorated for her by William Haines, will feel as shaggy as Tarzan," opined *Motion Picture* magazine. "Its femininity is so unmistakable that your first glance tells you that it is occupied by a single woman—a woman, moreover, who has no intention of marrying." (At the time, Lombard was seen everywhere with her constant companion-secretary, Madalyn "Fieldsie" Fields. The two women took up residence together in the Brentwood house.)

Billy modeled the decor after Lombard's personality: quirky but feminine, using splashes of brilliant color in place of the all-white rooms he had popularized at Crawford's residence (which had been emulated to the point of tedium). Lombard's bedroom was covered in plum satin, with a mirror screen on either side of her bed (another touch quickly copied around town), and her drawing room was hung in blue velvet. *Motion Picture* said the house was "no place for tweeds or slacks but a perfect setting for trailing tea gowns and evening dresses."

Billy refused to accept payment for his work on Lombard's house. "I offered to do her house without charging a fee," he said, "knowing that if people liked what I did, I'd have a business foundation."

He was clearly thinking wisely, for he would need the Hollywood community's support if he were to make it outside of Metro's pearly gates. Certainly he remained as popular as ever in the film colony— perhaps even more so now that he was helping so many of them decorate their homes.

That spring he was one of the stars at the gala launch of the Vendome nightclub on Sunset Boulevard. Owned by Billy Wilkerson of the *Hollywood Reporter*, the club attracted Hollywood's brightest. The Countess di Frasso christened the place with an Old English Costume Ball in June. At Billy's table were Eddie Goulding, dressed in drag as an English nursemaid; Lilyan Tashman as the Duchess of Devonshire; Joan Bennett as the fair maid Elaine; and George Cukor in monk's robes. Billy came dressed as an Eton schoolboy. All the stars were chatted up amiably in the gossip column written by Wilkerson's wife, Edith Gwynne.

Billy was still on the A list to meet important visitors to the screen colony. Goulding introduced him to the noted British photographer Cecil Beaton, who'd come to Hollywood with the hope of meeting his idol, Greta Garbo. (He did; they became fast friends.) In April Billy was at the famous San Simeon gala feting George Bernard Shaw. It was a very exclusive party, with invitations among the most coveted prizes in Hollywood—but Billy was left unimpressed by the esteemed dramatist. "I thought he was a horrible-looking old man," he said. "He needed a shave."

The San Simeon affairs of the 1930s had less of the spontaneity of the 1920s. They had taken on an air of genteel elegance, despite Marion's rapid downward descent into alcoholism. Hearst installed a private train that ran from Glendale station to San Luis Obispo, departing promptly at 7:35 P.M. on Friday night and arriving close to midnight. Among the regular attendees at the weekend galas on Enchanted Hill were Gary Cooper and his new paramour, the Countess di Frasso, Charles Farrell and Virginia Valli, Cary Grant and Randolph Scott, Thalberg and Norma Shearer. Special guests at various times included New York Mayor Jimmy Walker, Charles and Anne Lindbergh, and Winston Churchill.

At San Simeon, Billy socialized with the stars who had replaced him: Clark Gable was a guest a number of times; so was Robert Montgomery. At the Hearst castle, however, it was Billy Haines who was still top dog. Jimmie nearly always accompanied him; all of Hollywood knew him as Billy's spouse. In an ironic (and hypocritical) twist, the unmarried Hearst and Davies insisted that only married couples could spend the night together at San Simeon—the exceptions being, of course, the gay couples. Often Billy's sister Ann accompanied them for the weekend as well. A delightful series of pictures survives of Billy at San Simeon from this period. In one he sits in a marble birdbath with his hand in the mouth of a gargoyle, imitating the creature's face. In another, the six-foot Billy hoists Charlie Chaplin and socialite Winnie Law up under each arm.

Polly Moran wasn't a part of the San Simeon weekends, but she was still a frequent presence at Billy's home, where she would regale visitors with fantastic stories based on the illustrations in his Chinese wallpaper. During the portentous summer of 1933, Billy was photographed with Polly attending the premiere of Lilyan Tashman's *Grounds for Divorce*. The caption under the photo in *Photoplay* read: "Ah, William Haines, up to your old tricks again! We thought everything was off between you and Polly, but you both come up, smiling as in the days of yore. Well, Miss Moran, you make a very charming couple. Nothing to it? Never was? You both say." The picture surely must have irritated Mayer, and made any case Thalberg might make for reinstatement more difficult. Billy's image seemed implacably fixed in the media's perception.

This was the period during which the Production Code battles were coming to a head, and once again the career of Billy Haines cannot be seen outside of this context.

The period of 1930 to 1934 saw a number of films produced that defied Production Code regulations, pushing the limits of what had been previously acceptable onscreen. Mae West ignited a firestorm of criticism with the bawdy *She Done Him Wrong* and the even more outrageous *I'm No Angel*. Ernst Lubitsch's *Design for Living* presented Noël Coward's bisexual ménage à trois cheerfully and unapologetically. The Warner Brothers musicals were known for their raunchiness: *Golddiggers of 1933* featured Ginger Rogers singing "We're in the Money" covered in nothing but strategically placed gold pieces.

Even at the MGM of self-professed "family man" Louis B. Mayer, films had become sexier and riskier. It's a glaring example of Mayer's hypocrisy that he could rail against his directors for not making pictures his daughters could see—and against his stars for living lives he considered sinful or immoral—while at the same time approving a campaign "to go all out for sex" in 1932. Jean Harlow completed *Red Dust* after Bern's suicide; that tale of sex and adultery in steamy, sticky Indochina outraged women's groups across the country. There were dozens of others like it, too. In *Possessed*, Gable and Crawford live together in highly charged unwedded bliss. In *The Mask of Fu Manchu*, Charles Starrett is stripped and whipped while Myrna Loy writhes in orgasmic pleasure. Even Billy's *Just a Gigolo* had pushed the envelope, inviting local censorship boards to clamp down on the film.

Most of these projects had been pushed through by Thalberg, who despised the Code and the limitations it set. He actively (if clandestinely) encouraged his directors to defy it. This infuriated Mayer, who bore the brunt of the heat from Will Hays. As a strategic move against Thalberg, Mayer had named his son-in-law, David O. Selznick, as a rival producer. Thalberg's heart attack just months later has been attributed by some historians to the stress Mayer put on him during that fall of 1932.

Thalberg reported back to work in the summer of 1933. By then, David O. Selznick had made quite a name for himself at the studio. With his position not quite as secure as it once was, Thalberg could only take the most calculated moves. He would need to weigh the risks of every action he took—and the situation in the late summer of 1933 was as precarious as it had been the previous fall.

That spring, the federal government had announced that the National Recovery Administration—the program for cooperation between government and business to spur economic recovery—would consider regulating the motion-picture industry. Hollywood wasn't being singled out: All American industries, from steel to coal to automobile manufacture, would be given their own codes for economic stabilization and fairness. Yet there *was* one exception by which the movies were being treated differently: Alone among American industries, motion pictures were to be handed a moral as well as economic code.

In response to the growing complaints by Catholic leaders, Washington was prepared to put into federal law many of the tenets of the Production Code of 1930. In the past few years, the Code's author, Father Daniel Lord, had broken with the Hays office and had gone on the road to condemn the film industry. A meeting was scheduled for August in Washington between government and industry officials. Will Hays, in his memoirs, remembered the event as "a momentous meeting that brought home . . . how badly the guilty minority had besmirched the standing of the screen."

Before heading to Washington, however, Hays had stopped off in Hollywood, making the rounds of the studios. He urged producers to adopt a self-enforcement policy to avoid government censorship. Hays met with both Mayer and Thalberg, arguing the only way to stave off economic disaster *and* government regulation was to give the Hays office veto power over finished films. Otherwise, the Catholic boycotts would be enforced. Already, Bishop John J. Cantwell, later Archbishop of Los Angeles, was proposing a "legion of decency" that would monitor the film industry. (Indeed, by year's end, an official Legion of Decency was formed by Catholic bishops, a grassroots movement of outraged religionists who could mobilize their forces at a moment's notice.)

Mayer and Thalberg had reason to fear Hays's words. Catholics accounted for twenty percent of the U.S. population and were mainly centered in urban areas where movies made most of their revenue. In Europe, the percentage was even higher. It's notable that an industry run primarily by Jewish immigrants, with most of its stars of Protestant background, succumbed finally under pressure from the Roman Catholic Church.

In such an atmosphere was Billy Haines's final fate decided. One week after Hays's visit, Billy learned that Thalberg had taken no action to forestall his release. On September 7, Mayer and Hays left Hollywood for the Washington conference on the Code. On September 12, *Variety* carried a notice that William Haines was now at large.

The story of Billy Haines's departure from MGM has never before been seen in context with what else was happening that summer. His exit only fully makes sense when the pressures of the time are realized. The Code was indeed enforced later that year; Will Hays did get veto power; and overnight Hollywood movies were sterilized. It was a far cry from the freewheeling, free-loving place Billy had discovered a decade before.

"I was kicked out of the front gate," Billy would say years later. For all intents and purposes, he was right—although, it could be argued, it was all for the best. Billy once said, "Louis B. Mayer kicked me out and it was the kindest thing he ever did for me." Free of the studio, Billy no longer had the despised studio chief hovering about, badgering him to get married, to play the game. His dismissal from MGM would also allow him to discover his life's true calling: design and decoration.

Bitterness lingered, however. Billy never blamed Thalberg for his inaction; he reserved all of his animosity for Mayer. "A dyed-in-the-wool son of a bitch," he would call his former boss. "A liar, a cheat, despicable."

Shortly before his death, Billy was still vilifying Mayer. "He was a ridiculous man, a *ridiculous* figure," he said. "The tears that would run down his face, how he'd get down on his knees—he was a bad Bertha Kalich, that's what he was." (Bertha Kalich was the highly strung Jewish tragedienne of the 1920s whose melodramatics, according to Billy, "ate up more furniture than the summer stock companies in the country.")

It's as apt a description of Louis B. Mayer as ever was. That ridiculous figure, that bad Bertha Kalich, had just cut short the career of an actor who a mere three years before had been the most popular star in America.

The experiences of a number of other stars were similar, in comparable time frames, and an overview of their situations and ultimate fates casts important light on the life and career of Billy Haines. And again, their stories have never been seen fully in context with their times and one another.

Shortly after Billy may have considered marriage to Anita Page, Nils Asther divorced Vivian Duncan. It was the precipitant to the end of his MGM career. Certainly Billy must have been aware of his colleague's troubles.

The separation was announced in September 1932, shortly after the suicide of Paul Bern. It was no time for Mayer to look with sympathy upon Asther. The nasty publicity that resulted from the

Asther-Duncan divorce must have discouraged Mayer even further. He had given Asther a second chance, but the actor remained moody and uncooperative, no longer willing to play by the rules.

After the divorce was announced, *Screenland* magazine ran a large article exploring "The Strange Case of Nils Asther," revealing how he would often disappear on his wife for places unknown. Never was there a mention of another woman or an adulterous affair; as Adela Rogers St. Johns wrote, that kind of gossip would only have made him more intriguing. As it was, America could only think of Asther as a "strange case," and so, therefore, could Mayer.

Asther's next picture, *Storm at Daybreak*, released early in 1933, turned out to be a dud at the box office. Mayer washed his hands of the star then and there. Desperate, Asther turned for advice to Marion Davies, who cajoled Hearst into intervening with Mayer, suggesting maybe Asther could do some work with Cosmopolitan Pictures. Mayer was in no mood to talk. Asther had been in the headlines once too often to make any efforts to salvage his career worthwhile—and Mayer had other ammunition besides the divorce. Like Billy Haines, enough innuendo in the press had made the public suspicious. When Wallace Pahk, a twenty-two-year-old Korean dental student who had been living with Asther, was arrested in 1933 for forging several checks with the actor's name, Mayer had had enough. He failed to renew Asther's contract and, with little fanfare, the once-great screen lover found himself outside the studio gates.

Ramon Novarro lasted a bit longer. By mid-1933, *Variety* estimated that MGM had only six "bankable" stars left: Marie Dressler, Wallace Beery, Joan Crawford, Clark Gable, Norma Shearer, and Ramon Novarro. "The rest of the contract list . . . mean little at the box office," the trade paper noted.

The fact that Novarro was still making money for the studio is significant. He'd had an easy transition to sound: His opera training paid off nicely, giving his voice a well-modulated, lilting quality. In 1931 *Ben-Hur* was reissued with sound effects, a tremendous success, making more money for the studio than it had upon its original release. Novarro was still a hot property, despite his films of the early 1930s being a mixed bag for MGM: *Devil May Care* and *The Barbarian* were big hits, but *Daybreak* and *The Son-Daughter* were flops.

Like Billy, Novarro had never allowed his name to be linked to an actress for publicity purposes. To make up for that, MGM sent valentines in his name to every female who'd ever written the studio. The innuendos in the press, just as they had with Billy, grew more damaging as the tenor of the times changed. *Picture Play* asked in 1930, "Is Novarro a failure?," citing the actor's "loveless" life. Novarro defended himself in one article, saying, "People have such different ideas of love." The *Philadelphia Ledger* wrote about him in 1932: "Romance still stays far away from the handsome Ramon. . . . [His] name is never linked with that of a woman."

Accordingly, a major publicity campaign was launched in early 1933 to change Novarro's image (much as had been done the year before with Billy). The Novarro campaign commenced just as Mayer and Billy had their final confrontation, prompting Billy to sit out his contract. Novarro was apparently more compliant, however. After years of resistance, he went along with plans to link him romantically with women. He allowed his name used for an article entitled "What Women Want to Know," in which he talks about supposed sweethearts back home in Mexico. Then, coinciding with the release of his latest film, *The Barbarian*, he was linked romantically with his costar, Myrna Loy.

The Novarro-Loy publicity is proof that the studios actively tried to distract the public from a star's perceived or rumored homosexuality. In later years, Myrna Loy debunked the publicity. "It was preposterous," she said. "Ramon wasn't even interested in the ladies." She protested to Mayer, but, as her own career was on the fast track, she didn't push the issue.

The studio went all out to hype the story. In an article in *Modern Screen* notable primarily for its disingenuousness, Katherine Albert (who knew *everybody's* real story in Hollywood) wrote that it was impossible to sort out which star romances were real and which were creations of publicity departments. She then proceeded to pronounce that the affair between Vivienne Gay and Randolph Scott (who was living quite openly with his lover Cary Grant at the time) was "one to keep an eye on." And the Novarro-Loy affair was "one of the loveliest romances in Hollywood at the present time."

What happened seems obvious. Albert had gotten a call from Howard Strickling, her former colleague at the MGM publicity department, who asked her to play up the Novarro-Loy story. She willingly complied.

"Those who saw the meeting said it was love at first sight," Albert wrote. "So far it has thrived. It is in its early stages and is very genuine. Ramon has never been the 'ladies' man' type. There have been very few romance rumors about him because he has led a rather cloistered life, but now these two seem to be in love."

Instead of marrying Myrna Loy, however, Novarro went to Europe and South America for a series of operatic concerts. In early 1934, his contract was allowed to lapse. The rest of his life was a sad descent into alcoholism. Throughout the 1940s and 1950s, there were scattered reports of drunken driving arrests, and poor Ramon—his beauty bloated by alcohol—was reduced to paying teenage hustlers for sex.

By the end of 1934, with the agreement by all the studios that no film would be released without a seal of approval from the Hays office, Hollywood had become a place many no longer recognized.

Within the year, Hollywood's output was sanitized. Gone were the racy situations, the suggestive dialogue, the passionate love affairs. Marriage and family became sacrosanct. The Code was strictly adhered to; when a cut was now ordered by the censors, it was rigorously obeyed.

The stars, too, reformed themselves, polishing up their images until they shone like the apples Mom used in her pies. Myrna Loy, the seductive siren, became the perfect housewife. Ginger Rogers, the fun-loving whore, became the cheeky, all-American girl. A Clara Bow could not have existed in the latter half of the 1930s; neither could a William Haines. Male stars became upstanding, rugged defenders of home and hearth. Gable might start out the picture as a loner or a lout, but by the end, Loy or Crawford or Lana Turner had tamed him, convincing him that marriage is the only route to true happiness.

The Hollywood press corps changed, too. Gone was the precise balance that defined the relationship between star, studio, press, and public in the 1920s and early 1930s. By the end of the decade, Hedda Hopper rivaled Louella Parsons as a gossip queen, and the level of acrimony in the columns increased a hundredfold. That's when gossip columnists and fan-magazine writers realized their full power. Instead of playing the publicity department's artfully crafted game, they could now play their own. Now they could say to the studios, "You do things our way or you'll see some stories you don't like."

Homosexuality remained theoretically unmentionable, yet it is surprising how often the gay card was played. One had to be married to be acceptable by the late 1930s. *Motion Picture* ran an exhaustive series in 1937 called "Who's Whose," itemizing hundreds of stars' marriages and romances. It was embarrassing for the very few who had nothing but a quip listed after their name. It was, in effect, an announcement of who was playing the game and who was not. Nelson Eddy, for example, had only this terse comment: "MGM is still looking for a romance for him."

Louella Parsons, emboldened by the change in political climate, was more direct in her attack, "The big laugh in Hollywood these days," she wrote in 1936, "is Nelson Eddy's feminine pursuers. Who next will cause the unhappy Mr. Eddy to shrink into his shell and cry for help? Strange that Clark Gable, Gary Cooper, Dick Powell, William Powell, or other of our handsome male heroes have never suffered the embarrassment of having so many girls ready to die at their feet. Come on, Mr. Eddy, think up a new one. Even the hinterlands are wise to you."

In 1939 *Modern Screen* ran a remarkable article entitled "Vincent's Priceless Hat—Being the Revelations of a Very Gay Fedora on His Even Gayer Boss." Although not as widespread as it is today, "gay" had already entered the lexicon as euphemism for homosexual. Price was an up-and-coming leading man who'd begun his career by being rather open about his sexuality. After 1933, of course, that began to change. The article was purported to be written by Price's hat, which waxed nostalgic for the days when it and Vincent were inseparable, when the urbane actor treated it with tenderness. Then one day, Vincent up and married his wife, leaving his hat in Vienna. "Somebody must have planted a suggestion that I be retired," the hat sighed.

The hinterlands, as Parsons called them, may or may not have understood the innuendo of the piece. No doubt the studios did. This early form of "outing" would never have happened in Billy Haines's day. What had happened in the interim was dramatic: With the change in political and social attitudes, the mythology of the Hollywood stars needed to be adapted. The cooperation that had created the mythology in the first place—the partnership between star, studio, press, and public—had broken down. Now the only cooperation existed between star and studio, the least secure of the links in the past. The press took each press release as it came from the publicity department and, given its particular whim, either ran it as it was or slashed it to ribbons.

The public no longer willingly swallowed the stories, either. Instead, it demanded the "truth"—except that it didn't really want the *real* truth. The public just wanted to be *told* something was true. This way, they could go on believing a whole new set of myths based on a whole new set of values. Gone was the allure of difference, of excess, of deviance. Instead, Joan Crawford was the ideal mother; racy Jean Harlow was really a sweet kid; Spencer Tracy and Katharine Hepburn were star-crossed lovers; and Marlene Dietrich, underneath it all, was just a regular girl.

And homosexuality did not exist in Tinseltown.

Film historian and gay activist Vito Russo wrote in *The Celluloid Closet* that by the time of the enforcement of the Production Code in 1934, "homosexuality was denied as assiduously offscreen as it was on, a literally unspeakable part of the culture." For those gay stars who struggled to hang on, that meant adapting their lives to the new conventional wisdom.

Gary Cooper, who'd jumped from Clara Bow's bed to Andy

Lawler's and was now the very public gigolo of the much older Countess di Frasso, married the actress Sandra Shaw—also known as "Rocky" Balfe—in December 1933. He'd been chafing under the countess' controlling hand, and as an escape had taken to spending evenings with Cedric Gibbons and Dolores Del Rio. There, at their glamorous Art Deco home with bedrooms discreetly placed on separate floors, Cooper had met Rocky, a teenager Del Rio had taken under her protective wing. When Cooper met her, Rocky had just completed the film *Blood Money*, in which she played a very obvious lesbian. Within a matter of months, Gary and Rocky were married; Gibbons and Del Rio served as godparents for their daughter.

Even more telling is the story of Cary Grant. In February 1934, Grant married Virginia Cherrill. They had begun dating in September 1933, the same month Billy Haines was let go by MGM and the Production Code hearings were concluded in Washington. Grant hadn't started out playing the game; in the beginning, he was as open as Billy Haines about his sexuality. When the former Archie Leach came west in January 1932 (along with his former lover, Jack Orry-Kelly), it had been the final sunset of Hollywood's days of freedom. Grant met and fell in love with Randolph Scott, the six-foot, handsome former boyfriend of Howard Hughes. Grant and Scott were instantly drawn to each other; they decided on the spot to live together. Neither was a big star yet, so their arrangement made for little comment in the press. They often dined out together as well, being photographed around town with Billy Haines and Jimmie Shields. But as they became better known, their happy domicile began to be whispered about.

Much like Billy, Cary Grant was accustomed to the freedom he'd known in Greenwich Village, and found Hollywood society—at first—to be as open and tolerant. But that was 1932. By the very next year, there had been enough of a change in climate for reporters to smell blood in the water when they learned of Cary and Randy's living arrangements. Paramount was forced to issue releases that their two upcoming stars were merely sharing expenses in the face of the worsening Depression. As Charles Higham has pointed out, at a $400-a-week salary, each man could have easily afforded a

$75-a-month rent. Surely there were enough bright readers out there in fan-magazine land to figure that out.

It seems absurd that some writers still dispute the fact that Cary Grant was gay. They suggest that historians who see his cohabitation with Scott as a homosexual relationship are merely looking through a prism of contemporary consciousness. Such a theory, however, denies the context of so much other evidence: Scott's well-known reputation as being homosexual, the reminiscences of such friends as George Burns and George Cukor, the testimony of such lovers as Orry-Kelly and the photographer Jerome Zerbe, the friendship with Billy and Mitt Foster in New York. It also fails to take into account the prevailing political forces that rocked Hollywood in the 1930s. To argue that Cary Grant would not dare live in an open homosexual relationship in the early thirties is to be unaware of how different the movie capital was during that period than later on.

Cary Grant and Randolph Scott had assumed they could live their lives as openly and as authentically as had Billy Haines and Jimmie Shields. There were several connections between the couples. Mitt Foster was part owner of the house where Cary and Randy lived, 2177 West Live Oak Drive, in the Los Feliz district. And Cary's secretary, Frank Horn, a delightful, campy fellow, became a regular visitor to Billy's house. Following their friends' example, during 1932 and the first part of 1933 neither Cary Grant nor Randolph Scott was seen dating any woman; instead, they turned up at film premieres together. Press reports called them "Hollywood's twosome" and the "happy couple."

Paramount must have applied some pressure, for Cary and Randy agreed to be photographed "on the town" with a couple of women. Suddenly Cary Grant's career shifted into high gear, with substantial roles in Marlene Dietrich's *Blonde Venus* and the Tallulah Bankhead–Charles Laughton picture *The Devil and the Deep*. Just as suddenly, Cary called Virginia Cherrill, a sheltered, shy, sweet actress who'd appeared with Chaplin as the blind girl in *City Lights*. According to Charles Higham, Orry-Kelly came to see her and said she should be very careful, that Cary was the lover of Randolph

Scott and he (Kelly) was "in a position to know it." As young and innocent as she was, Virginia dismissed the warning.

Virginia moved with Cary's gay set, choosing to ignore what was going on all around her. When Grant and Scott costarred in *Hot Saturday*, Ben Maddox of *Modern Screen* visited their house. Maddox knew the score. It was old-time fan-magazine reporting, with the truth being told between the lines. "Cary and Randy are really opposite types," Maddox wrote. "That's why they get along so well. Cary is the gay, impetuous one. Randy is serious, cautious. Cary is temperamental in the sense of being very intense. Randy is calm and quiet. Cary tears around in a new Packard Roadster, and Randy flashes by in a new Cadillac. Oh-oh-oh how the girls want to take a ride!" ("Gay" and "temperamental" were both code words used by homosexuals of the period.)

Old-time fan-magazine reporting, however, was no longer swallowed whole by a more suspicious, savvy public. When a series of remarkable photos of the two at their home were published, gossip escalated. There were Cary and Randy, sitting down for dinner together. There they were posing together on the diving board of their pool, Randy's fingers touching Cary's bare back. There they were again, harmonizing at their piano. Columnist Jimmie Fidler sniped that the two men were "carrying the buddy business a bit too far." Even Carole Lombard was reported in the *Los Angeles Times* to ask: "I wonder which one of those two guys pays the bills?"

Suddenly Cary became obsessed with the idea of Virginia. He'd just been given his big break opposite Mae West in *She Done Him Wrong*; if he were to make the most of it, he needed Virginia. That was now obvious. The publicity about him and Randy was damaging; yet a story about him and Virginia at a party given by the Countess di Frasso was glowing, calling them beautiful together.

From all accounts, Cary Grant's whole demeanor changed. Light and carefree in his first year in Hollywood, now he was driven and moody. After a vicious argument, Virginia fled to London. Cary followed; they reconciled and were married in February 1934. Back in Hollywood, Randy Scott wasn't completely out of the picture. He moved into the unit next to the Grants' new home in the La Ronda apartments in Havenhurst. Edith Gwynn in the *Hollywood Reporter* wrote: "The Grants and Randolph Scott have moved, all three, but not apart."

The marriage was miserable. Cary began drinking heavily, even on the set, hiding booze in coffee cups. Virginia walked out on him after only a few months. In October, after Virginia had told Louella Parsons she was filing for divorce, a drunken Cary called her, begging her to come back. When she refused, he said, "This will ruin me!" and hung up. Concerned, she called later and asked the houseboy to check on him. Cary was stretched out on the bed, dressed only in his underwear, a large bottle of sleeping pills nearly empty beside him. An ambulance was called, and at the hospital, Cary had his stomach pumped.

After he came home from the hospital, Cary went back to living with Randy. He said he'd never get married again, no matter what the pressure. The gossip resumed. Edith Gwynn concocted a party game in her column in which stars would come dressed as famous movie titles. She knew whom to single out. Among her innovative suggestions: Dietrich as *Male and Female*, Garbo as *The Son-Daughter*, and Cary as *One-Way Passage*.

The studio pushed him back into the arms of women, and he obliged. After all, this was 1935. Betty Furness was his constant date, although he went off on a romantic holiday with Howard Hughes on his yacht in mid-1935. Although Randolph Scott married Marion duPont in 1936, they never lived together. In fact, he and Cary continued sharing quarters off and on until 1942. By now, however, Cary had begun his pattern of frequent marriages. He'd continue to have affairs with men, but these became secretive, clandestine, tortured encounters.

Although Randy would remain a lifelong friend of Billy's and Jimmie's, Cary was never a part of their social set after the mid-1930s. Billy, in fact, had nothing but contempt for him, telling friends he was a "phony." Cary married three more times, continuing to drink and descend further into surliness and abusive behavior in his private life. The once carefree and gay young man who first came to Hollywood in 1932 was nowhere to be found. Late in life he said,

"I pretended to be somebody I wanted to be, and finally I became that person." In the 1970s he sued the comedian Chevy Chase for calling him a "homo" on national television.

If Cary Grant was forced by circumstances to become the polar opposite of Billy Haines, there was one figure who resembled Billy a great deal in terms of integrity, honesty, and authenticity.

Most everyone in Hollywood knew director Dorothy Arzner was a lesbian. In the beginning, despite the whispering, producers paid little heed to her sexual orientation. Like Billy Haines, Arzner shared her home with her lover, Marion Morgan, a dancer and choreographer with whom Ramon Novarro had worked when he first came to Hollywood.

Several accounts have tried to paint Arzner as "one of the boys"— even going so far as to say she had an easier time with studio executives than a gay male director like George Cukor. However, as Judith Mayne has pointed out in her groundbreaking study of the director's career, Arzner's films were often patronized by reviewers, who never failed to mention that "Hollywood's lady director" had been at the helm. Mayne writes, "Any eagerness to define Dorothy as 'one of the boys,' for whatever reasons, can offer only a completely distorted view of the obstacles she encountered as a peripheral member of the boys' club." Arzner understood full well that she could not afford failures the way a male director might. The "boys' club" would have been only too eager to bounce her out the door the moment it was perceived her pictures no longer made money. Like Billy Haines, Dorothy Arzner was tolerated only as long as the boys in charge wanted to tolerate her.

In March 1931, after refusing Paramount's request that she accept a pay cut, Arzner decided to take a chance on a freelance career. Her first picture was for RKO, *Christopher Strong*, featuring a daringly butch Katharine Hepburn and a transgressive, feminist subtext about love between women. It did not exactly endear her to the old boys' network. In fact, for several years, fan magazines and newspaper accounts had never failed to mention Arzner's "boyish bob," "mannish clothes," heavy eyebrows, or unmarried status somewhere in the course of the article. Such innuendo was as damaging to Arzner in the eyes of the studio bosses as were stories of Billy Haines's antiques and good housekeeping—perhaps even more so.

Like Billy Haines—like Clara Bow—Dorothy Arzner did not fit the picture Hollywood was trying to create by the mid-1930s. Her pictures were too subversive, her lifestyle too undisguised. In 1937 she directed *The Bride Wore Red* at MGM starring Joan Crawford. The experience made it plain to Arzner that her Hollywood career was over. Following this film, Mayer sent her several scripts, which she rejected as inferior. The truth was, just as in the case of Billy Haines, Mayer had no desire to continue working with Arzner, and so he suspended her after she'd turned down the scripts.

Arzner would recall years later that the experience with Mayer convinced her to retire from pictures. "Mayer put out the word that I was difficult," she said, "and you know how producers talk to each other. I think that was the reason I left." In fact, she used the word "blackballed" to describe Mayer's reaction to her, suggesting an orchestrated effort on Mayer's behalf to kick Arzner out of the boys' club for good.

The story of William Haines, then, is not just the story of one man, one movie star. It is the story of the institutionalization of the Hollywood closet, a tradition that has persisted for more than fifty years. It is the story of how an industry changed, how a community of artists and free thinkers and individualists turned its back on its own in the face of organized, traditionalist pressure. Those who played the game were rewarded with stardom, endurance, and protection: Cary Grant, Robert Taylor, Barbara Stanwyck, Rock Hudson. Those who refused—people like Dorothy Arzner and Billy Haines—were ushered out.

7

A FOOL AND HIS MONEY

1934-1936

In the first months of 1934, Billy honestly believed his film career was not over. He had the desire to continue and the faith that it could happen. MGM might be the grandest studio in Hollywood, but it wasn't the *only* studio. On one level, Billy's ambition was fueled by practical necessity: He was not yet confident that a decorating career could maintain the standard of living to which he'd become accustomed. On another level, of course, it was purely ego: *He'd* show Mayer he could still get parts.

Michael Morrison, who later worked with Billy in the design business, says Billy thought he could make it on his own, that he left MGM with the conviction he would be hired elsewhere. "He thought he was going to make a killing by going on his own," Morrison recalls. "That's why he walked out on Louis B. Mayer. He really thought he'd be better off on his own."

Billy left it up to his agent, Phil Berg, to find him new employment. Berg was one of the most prominent agents in town, credited with being the first to offer package deals. His other clients included Joan Crawford and Dolores Del Rio, as well as the writers F. Scott Fitzgerald, Anita Loos, and Zoë Akins. Interestingly, his roster also boasted the names of Clark Gable and Robert Montgomery, but he was particularly loyal to Billy. Still, even as a package deal, Billy would prove a hard sell.

It's not known what studios Berg approached on Billy's behalf, but evidently he tried them all. He'd been optimistic at first, pointing to the example of Clara Bow, who after being let go in disgrace from Paramount, had returned in triumph in *Call Her Savage* for Fox. Apparently Billy's "sins" were worse than Clara's. La Bow could cash in on her notoriety (at least for a time, before she, too, fell by the wayside), but Billy's reputation as a homosexual wasn't the kind of currency studios were looking to trade on.

For the rest of his life Billy was convinced that Mayer blacklisted him. It's not inconceivable. Dorothy Arzner also believed that Mayer blacklisted her. It's known that the studio chief threatened to blacklist Gable and Harlow when they misbehaved in 1931. Such a move would certainly not have been out of character.

Whether the result of a Mayer blacklist or not, no other studio seemed willing to touch Billy. His history of minor legal skirmishes, his publicity chock-full of innuendo—these were enough to warn producers away. The argument that he couldn't get a job outside of Metro because his last pictures had done only lackluster box office just doesn't hold up. Billy would have accepted supporting or character parts; even these were not offered. Many former top silent stars were now playing secondary leads in talkies. Billy should have been one of them.

He felt depressed and foolish. He told Joan Crawford, "When you start to lose your career in the picture business, it's like walking on nothing."

Such are not the words of a man who had made peace with his exit from filmmaking. No matter how much his later colleagues and friends might insist, Billy Haines did not walk away from movies gladly. Certainly, it turned out for the best, as often life's greatest disappointments do. In 1933–1934, however, Billy did not want to go. During his hated personal appearance tour through New York, he had told a reporter, "We are creatures of habit after all, aren't we? I used to think I'd love to get away from studio life for a while, but now I see how much it is a part of me."

He admitted to the writer Constance Blake: "When I read the box office reports on my pictures and saw them falling steadily, I was sick. For I loved my work, you see, and I loved being a success."

In 1929, at the top of the world, he'd asked rhetorically: "What will I do when I leave pictures? I'll be too old to learn anything else."

As the saying goes, you're never too old to learn something new. Just a few months after the final break with MGM, while Phil Berg was out hustling for him, Billy took off on a three-month trip to Europe and the Near East. He left Los Angeles by train the first week in February. There was a short stopover in New York, where he and Jimmie stayed at the Waldorf-Astoria. Part of the trip, he told the New York press corps, was to bring back inspiration and artifacts with which to decorate William Powell's new home. Powell was a recent commission, probably referred by ex-wife (and still good friend) Carole Lombard.

"Don't tell a soul," Billy stage-whispered to a reporter from the *New York Telegraph*, "but the real reason for our expedition is to bring back home a pyramid."

"That is, if we can find them cheap enough," Jimmie added.

The trip was more than just a business expedition. It was also a much-needed respite after the long fight with MGM. Billy and Jimmie were accompanied by Mitt Foster and Larry Sullivan, with the intent to relax and explore as much as anything else. Billy had adored his first European visit in 1931. Now trips to Europe became regular and rejuvenating jaunts every few years.

The foursome sailed on February 10 aboard the S.S. *Champlain*. They spent a month in London, where they were entertained by Noël Coward. From London they crossed the Channel to Brussels, where they all enjoyed a reunion with Prince Charles. There was some rumbling from neighboring Germany that troubled the Belgians: Adolf Hitler had become chancellor the year before and opposition to his dictatorship was being quashed. Billy decided to bypass Germany and headed by train through France to Italy, then on to Greece and Egypt, taking a spectacular cruise up the Nile. All along the way, he and Mitt purchased antique furniture and relics for their business. Tons of marble statuary were shipped back home from Athens; exotic Egyptian tiles were carefully chosen for Bill Powell's home.

Upon the travelers' return aboard the S.S. *Ile de France* on May 22, the New York photographers barely recognized Billy. There was no attempt now to hide his receding hairline, and he had grown a mustache while overseas—no doubt a little act to celebrate his freedom from studio dictates. Photographs of Billy posing aboard ship show him rested and very much at ease with himself. The wind whips his hair and the flaps of his coat. He appears mature, confident, and ready—a new man. The Hollywood he was returning to had changed even more than he had.

The best Phil Berg had been able to obtain for him was a two-picture deal at Mascot Pictures, one of the lowest of the poverty row studios. Founded in 1927 by Nat Levine, gambler and film distributor, Mascot was primarily a producer of serials, and its stars were usually on their way up or their way down. John Wayne and Victor McLaglen starred in serials for Mascot before hitting their stride elsewhere. Harry Carey, Billy's costar from *Slide Kelly Slide* as well as one of Hollywood's busiest character actors, also top-lined at Mascot. But it was also home to Tom Santschi and Henry B. Walthall, stars from the teens who were happy taking whatever jobs they could get.

Billy had a number of connections with Mascot. In 1934 two other old costars, Ben Lyon and William Bakewell, were also starring in a Mascot picture, *Crimson Romance*. There was also Edward Hearn, who appeared in a number of Mascot serials, including its most famous, *The Vanishing Legion*. Hearn was a gay actor with whom Billy surely was familiar: he'd appeared in Mae West's *The Drag* and with Crawford in *Winners of the Wilderness*.

Hearn appeared with Billy in the first of his two Mascot pictures, *Young and Beautiful*, directed by Joseph Santley. Production took place in the summer and the film was released in September, one year after Billy's official departure from MGM. It had been a full two years since he'd last faced the camera—"the one-eyed monster," as he called it—and the taut, youthful William Haines of *Fast Life* was nowhere in sight. In *Young and Beautiful*, he was anything but: Balding and a little chubby, he was surrounded by that season's Wampas Baby Stars, and the whole exercise seemed a little tawdry. What gives the film a modicum of interest is seeing Billy play a publicist, dreaming up an "image" for his actress girlfriend. Billy knew a thing or two about publicists' tricks, and he seemed to enjoy making the film.

Franklin Pangborn—famed for his "sissy" portrayals in scores of films in the 1930s and 1940s—is on hand as a radio announcer. Whether Billy knew Pangborn socially at this point is unknown; he would certainly become acquainted with him in a few years, when Pangborn was one of the regulars at Cole Porter's soirees. Perhaps the most ironic name associated with Billy Haines's first film comeback after being dismissed by MGM is Dore Schary, who wrote the screenplay for *Young and Beautiful*. Schary would replace Louis B. Mayer at MGM in 1951.

The reviews for *Young and Beautiful* weren't terrible. The *New York Times* said: "Mr. Haines continues to play the brash and arrogant juvenile in the amusing style which he popularized a decade ago." *Variety* reported: "There are some laughs and [the film] should fare fairly well. In most spots, they'll have to be told about it, but it's a good production to come from an indie source."

In August, Billy began production on his second Mascot feature, *The Marines Are Coming*. Its title harked back to better days, when *Tell It to the Marines* was MGM's number-one picture of the year. It was directed by David Howard, with Esther Ralston, another former silent screen star, as leading lady. The picture was released in December, although most theaters didn't get it until early 1935. Problem was, very few theaters got it at all. Billy's second go-around as a U.S. Marine was a dismal melodrama, with none of the snappy pacing that made his 1926 hit so memorable. The *New York Herald Tribune* wrote: "According to rumors from Hollywood, William Haines has been devoting the days of his cinema exile to the profession of interior decoration. After watching the onetime screen prankster endeavor to register a histrionic comeback, one is more kindly than cruel in suggesting that he may have made a mistake in leaving the job of glorifying the salons."

Concurred *Variety*: "Same smart aleck role which Haines used to play. Picture will need support."

So would Billy.

Even with the disastrous experience of *The Marines Are Coming*, however, Billy didn't give up all hope of finding a niche in movies. Although the fan magazines now referred to him as a decorator and not an actor, he made the point in every article that he was still willing to take another screen role if it came his way.

He sensed the truth, however. The *Herald Tribune* could rest assured: He *hadn't* left the job of glorifying the salons. With each new commission, Billy moved further away from the world of soundstages and arc lamps. It was, in truth, a world that he barely recognized anymore. Even socially, things had begun to change, in large part because of the Depression, but also reflecting the new rigidity of the times. "There aren't nearly as many parties as there used to be," Billy told reporter Helen Ludlam, "and those that are given usually break up early."

Curiously, the parties quieted down in Hollywood just as Prohibition came to an official end. Billy did attend a belated New Year's Eve party at the Vendome in November 1933—"belated" because the revelers were making up for the lack of legal bubbly the previous December 31. He also attended the opening of Billy Wilkerson's second nightclub on the Sunset Strip, Cafe Trocadero, in 1934. Despite these festivities, the industry just wasn't in the mood for much revelry these days.

Gone were the days of Billy arriving in armor or passing out greasy doughnuts at parties. He was older now—mid-thirties—and most of his friends were also that age or older. Billy tended to host more subdued, more elegant soirees these days, such as the one he gave in honor of Mrs. Patrick Campbell in the summer of 1934. The sixty-nine-year-old theatrical legend was making a rare appearance in Hollywood and was feted by Billy and Jimmie. It's a measure of the esteem in which he was still held that Billy was the one to host the party. The elite of Hollywood turned out. Eleanor Boardman recalled Norma Shearer and Irving Thalberg arriving at Billy's house "very late, very dressed up," with Norma "going straight across the room to sit at Mrs. Pat's feet." The appearance of the Thalbergs was another indication that despite Billy's fall from MGM, he still enjoyed social clout and prestige. In fact, Thalberg was making a very public declaration of his friendship with Billy, probably to Mayer's chagrin.

It was left to Carole Lombard to preserve some of the madcap days of the old Hollywood. The fan magazines dubbed her the "foremost social hostess in Hollywood's social whirl." After Billy had finished decorating her house, she threw a huge party. Everyone was eager to see what Billy had done. When the guests arrived, Carole had removed all the furniture; they had to be invited back to see Billy's handiwork. Her crazy theme parties kept Hollywood guessing what was next: a hospital party with dinner wheeled in on an operating table; Roman banquets with everyone eating on pillows; various costume parties that would find the likes of Billy, Noël Coward, and the director Mitchell Leisen all done up as storybook characters.

Lombard surrounded herself with gay men. Only George Cukor wasn't taken by her charms: He considered her foul-mouthed and vulgar. That she could certainly be. Billy found the anomaly of a glamorous lady acting and talking like a reckless hoyden bewitching. He recalled a conversation with her in which she nonchalantly disrobed and changed her clothes. "I was startled when she stripped completely," he said. "She never wore a bra, you know. That was no secret, but oftentimes she didn't wear panties either, and this was one of those times. . . . I remember her saying the cutest thing: 'I wouldn't do this, Billy, if I thought it could arouse you.' "

Billy's strategy worked: Lombard's house was indeed the talk of the town, and by the time he'd finished *The Marines Are Coming*, the jobs were lined up waiting for him. Crawford helped, too, sending her pal Claudette Colbert his way.

A November 1934 notice in the *Los Angeles Times* said Billy was busy building a "sumptuous" new shop at 8720 Sunset Boulevard. This would become his famous studio, no longer merely an antique shop but an office from which Billy and Mitt Foster could coordinate their burgeoning interior-decorating business. Opened in early 1935, the studio's rooms each showcased Billy's work: One room featured English antiques against leather-laced suede curtains, rapidly becoming a Haines trademark, and another featured Greek and Egyptian statuary and relics.

By this time, Mitt functioned primarily as a buyer. He was not a designer and had no ambitions to be such. Billy hadn't been schooled in the art of interior decoration, either, of course. "Most of the big decorators didn't have any formal training," says Michael Morrison. "They just had their own innate sense of taste and style. That was certainly the case with Bill Haines."

His taste and style perfectly fit the times. Billy helped impart a classier, more enduring style to Hollywood than it had been accustomed to. "He gave Hollywood its sense of style," says Mary Anita Loos, niece of Anita and a screenwriter herself. "He did away with so much that was tacky. We're all grateful for that."

In later years, William Haines, Hollywood designer, became inaccurately associated with Art Deco, the sleek, streamlined "moderne" look first popularized at the landmark Exposition des Arts Décoratifs in Paris in 1925. Art Deco became the look of so much of Hollywood in the 1920s and early 1930s, but it's not accurate to say that it was Billy's style. "Bill certainly was influenced by Art Deco," says Michael Morrison. "Looking back at some of the houses he did in that period—with suede walls and rounded edges—there are certainly Art Deco touches."

Billy had nothing but disdain for the ultramodernistic look that came to popularize MGM pictures. Once, visiting Joan Crawford on the set of *Our Dancing Daughters*, he recoiled visibly at the film sets with their highly modernistic style. "It looks like someone had a nightmare while designing a church and tried to combine it with a Grauman's theater," Billy said.

He considered many of Art Deco's flourishes—fluted arches, polished black floors, and jagged wall reliefs—ridiculous. In particular, he had little patience for the pomposity of MGM art director Cedric Gibbons, who had attended the 1925 Paris exposition and brought the Art Deco style to American movies. Billy considered Mayer's home—designed by Gibbons—to be a monument of bad taste, with its thirteen onyx-and-marble baths.

Modernism, however, was not long a trend ("Trends?" Billy once sniffed. "There are all sorts of epidemics") before a classical revival swept Hollywood, much to Billy's relief. The leading architects of southern California during this period were all masters of period style: Wallace Neff, Paul Williams, Roland Coate, John Byers, John Woolf, and James Dolena. Billy became a master of period styles— Regency, Monterey, and English Tudor among them. Design historian Tim Street-Porter says Billy was likely influenced by the part Regency, part Classical work of the New York–based English designer Robsjohn Gibbings, who had just decorated a series of houses for architect James Dolena (also an early collaborator of Billy's).

Even calling Billy's style Regency or Classical is not enough, however, since he added his own, often whimsical, innovations. Chinoiserie was a favorite touch, adding an exotic flavor to the French and English antiques. This mix of elements became a Haines trademark, long before "eclecticism" became popular.

Billy's work is most closely identified with a style that grew out of the film colony itself: Hollywood Regency. Design historian John Chase calls Hollywood Regency "theatrical," saying it "resembled a stage set. . . . This architecture of glamor required the seemingly effortless balancing between the formal and the casual, as well as for well-placed exaggeration and well-chosen omission."

Billy was part of a general shift in the world of interior design during the 1930s, when, according to architect and design historian Aaron Betsky, most of the emerging decorators of note were men. During the previous decade, the field had been heavily influenced by several women, notably Elsie de Wolfe and Julia Morgan. Billy knew both of them and was familiar with their work. Morgan had been the architect at San Simeon; de Wolfe, whom Billy would later encounter at the Hollywood soirees of Jimmy Pendleton and Cole Porter, had been designing homes in both the United States and

Europe since the 1890s. Billy seems to have been influenced by her work. While she was a "modernist" in that she rejected the extravagant clutter of the Victorian period, she replaced the velvet draperies and "Turkish bazaar" trappings with classic eighteenth-century antiques. Both she and Billy had reputations for open spaces and carefully harmonized patterns and colors. De Wolfe became famous for white rooms—a motif Billy carried to its extreme a decade or so later in Hollywood. He shared de Wolfe's vision about how a house should function: "a synthesis of comfort, practicality, and tradition."

While it was the architect who provided the foundation from which to work, it was the decorator who placed the final stamp on the look of the house. For all things to come together as a unified whole, architect and decorator needed to share similar visions. "I contend there's no decorator in the world who can make a house good if the architecture is bad," Billy would say. "The interior decorator, the landscape gardener, and the architect should all be consulted in the beginning. The three should be hired as a unit and work together. Each one should know what the other is doing. Also, the architect should respect the decorator as much as the decorator respects the architect."

This was a new and radical idea. Within a matter of years, Billy Haines would bring a new sense of respect to the job—to the *art*—of interior design. The days when Cedric Gibbons—a set and costume designer—could be given the job to design a house were over. "I'm tired of this word, 'interior designer,' " Billy later said. "Any woman who has a pair of white gloves and last year's hat calls herself a designer. They are *decorators*. They fetch and carry."

Billy won the respect of the architects he worked with, notably Paul Williams, Roland Coate, and James Dolena. Williams, self-taught, African-American, and fanatically attuned to details, was the architect on the Berg-Hyams house. Billy admired him greatly; both men had risen to the top of their professions without benefit of prestigious schooling. It was Dolena, however, with whom he forged his first real working relationship. The Russian-born architect had gotten his training in pre-Revolution St. Petersburg; many of his Neo-classical houses in Los Angeles reflect that experience. Dolena was, in many ways, a mentor: a decade older than Billy, he was a fire-brand and a stickler for only the finest craftsmanship. From Dolena, Billy learned quickly that only the very best would do.

Dolena was the architect on William Powell's home, a Beverly Hills bungalow that was transformed into a classical pavilion with a colonnaded entrance. Billy's decor needed to fit the grandeur of the architecture. In reporting on his European trip, the *Los Angeles Times* remarked: "He is going to supply Powell with parts of the Parthenon, or duplications thereof. He may bring home some of the Acropolis with him. Anyway, Powell's new place is destined to smack them in the eye if Bill can do anything about it." He could—and Powell was eminently pleased with the results.

"A home is the most personal thing in the world," Billy would say. "The designer has to know the clients better than they know each other if it is to be a successful partnership. Do they eat chocolate at 3:00 in the morning? One must know these things."

Billy's clients in the beginning were all people he *did* know; he knew their tastes, their habits, their quirks. "Joan loves blue," he told the press during one of his frequent retouchings of Crawford's home. "Blue is a spiritual color. Joan is also a meticulous house-keeper. If somebody else can't do it, she knows how—and does."

Joan also loved the telephone—Billy became known for the prodigious use of phones throughout his houses. A phone became de rigueur in bathrooms; Crawford would conduct business while sit-ting in the tub. Billy's other innovation for stars' bathrooms was un-flattering light. Crawford fixed her hair and makeup beneath the most glaring light possible. "I told her if she can make herself look good in that light, she'll look good anywhere," Billy said.

Actors, Billy said, were far more vain than actresses. "When do-ing an actor's home," he told columnist Ezra Goodman, "if I can give him plenty of mirrors quietly and never mention it, it is a happy solution."

It was with actresses, however, that he formed his closest collabo-rations. With Connie Bennett, he got into some pretty heated ex-changes regarding the design of her elaborate dressing rooms on the

RKO and Twentieth Century lots. He also came to know Claudette Colbert when he began work at her recently acquired home in Brentwood. Colbert was at the time very close with Marlene Dietrich, spending more time with her (so the press noted) than with her husband, Norman Foster. Billy may have been suspicious when Colbert told him she and Foster had separate residences, but he said nothing.

The house had previously belonged to Garbo. "It was pretty cobwebby, of course," Billy told reporter Harriet Parsons, "because Garbo had only used the sleeping porch and two coffee cups."

Colbert wanted the bedroom done over; she found it too depressing. "Claudette's only instruction to decorator Haines was that the room should be gay," Parsons wrote in *Movie Mirror*. "But Bill, recognizing Claudette's good breeding and intelligence, realized it would have to be a restrained gaiety—gaiety tempered by good taste."

The Colbert bedroom was done with a risky color—milk-chocolate brown—but it paid off handsomely. It was a prime example of what was coming to be known as the Haines style. The classic form of directoire chairs perfectly complemented the modernistic lamps of arrows and mirrors. The soft brown contrasted splendidly against vivid reds. Off the bedroom, Billy decorated Colbert's dressing room more frivolously, with white carpeting, white organdy drapes, and a red-velvet dressing table. "It's a swell room for Claudette to sing 'Pagliacci' in," Billy quipped.

At the time, he was also redecorating Lionel Barrymore's drawing room. He told his *Jimmy Valentine* costar that his beloved old sofa had to go: It was far too large and bulky. He gave it to the Salvation Army and told Parsons he'd done a great favor for the city's homeless and unemployed, "since a goodly number of them can be housed in the ex-Barrymore sofa."

In most of the fan magazine articles of this period, Billy indulged the writers by continuing to wisecrack. It was part of his nature by now, and readers had come to expect it. When Billy told Parsons that Barrymore's drawing room had an "air of Chinoiserie" about it, she couldn't help but smile. "Every time he uses a phrase like that he watches me out of the corner of his eye, like a small boy who is telling a fib and wondering whether he'll get away with it. As a matter of fact, I know Bill's sense of humor includes himself, and when he uses the decorator's esoteric jargon it is with his tongue in his cheek. Which in no wise alters the fact that he is an artist, a man of taste, and a darned good decorator."

It was true that Billy could laugh at the pretentiousness of some in the design field, yet it was no act he was playing when he assessed the Barrymore room's "air of Chinoiserie." By 1934 and 1935, Billy was deeply committed to his new profession, finding not only that it was beginning to pay off handsomely, but that it could give him the same kind of thrill he'd felt in his glory days of making pictures. And while he'd never lose the wisecracker label — or the ability to wisecrack — there was a new image of Billy Haines emerging: a man of discriminating, even exclusive, taste.

"I loathe cozy cottages," Billy would sniff. "They were made for farmers and peasants, not ladies and gentlemen."

While not denying the inherent humor in such statements, Billy nonetheless meant exactly what he said. Certainly he could have been talking about his pal George Cukor's house, which was little more than a hillside cottage overlooking the Sunset Strip when Billy took it on as a major redesign project in 1935. Following his own preferred working relationship, he worked closely with architect James Dolena and the landscape designer Florence Yoch in fashioning a showplace that Cukor prized the rest of his life.

The house was designed in the style of an Italian villa, with seven living rooms. It lent itself to the easy flow of people. Billy had a ball decorating the house, both encouraging and marveling at Cukor's whims. Queen Anne blackamoors and a Dresden chandelier covered with shellfish graced the downstairs hall. "Sounds mad," Billy admitted to *Vogue*, "but Mr. Cukor likes it." The mix of furniture represented Billy's love of unexpected combinations: Sheraton chairs alongside Greek statuary and Empire bronzes. Turquoise velvet curtains offset the dark brown walls of the dining room, perfectly balanced against Victorian chairs covered in hunter-red leather.

Just as Billy had his upstairs parlor, so Cukor had a special room reserved for intimate friends. This was the oval lounge, the centerpiece of his house. Its walls were covered in leather—another Haines trademark—and French doors swung open across an elaborately designed parquetry. Displaying his knack with color, Billy painted the ceiling sky blue, and generously distributed copper throughout the room as a complement. A large, curved sofa was set against a floor-to-ceiling window that looked out over the gardens.

"Cukor's house is like nothing I have ever seen," wrote screenwriter Sidney Howard. "Never has anything been so done by decorators. It is, I think, as beautiful as any interior I have ever seen, but each room is, in the most nance sense, a perfect show window rather than a room."

It's perhaps not surprising that a heterosexual visitor like Howard would pick up on the "nanciness" of a gay man's house, as designed by another gay man. Cukor's home was a shrine to his independent status in Hollywood. One journalist called Cukor's secluded palace a "bachelor pleasure dome." There was no lady's dressing room, no husband's quarters, no nursery, no "romp room" where the children might play. Everything was precise and elegant, but with an air of "camp" as well. Dozens of shiny objects picked up at flea markets sparkled throughout the house: carvings done from coral, paintings on glass, Han dancing figures. A bronze bust of Tallulah Bankhead greeted visitors not far from the front entrance. On the walls of the hallway leading to Cukor's office hung the framed and autographed pictures of his fabulous friends: Noël Coward, Gladys Cooper, Ina Claire, Kate Hepburn, Lillian and Dorothy Gish.

Cukor biographer Emanuel Levy says that the house "became the center of Cukor's universe." He'd certainly paid enough for it. "I'm afraid I shall have to work the rest of my life to pay it off completely," Cukor said in 1934. Indeed, Billy Haines didn't come cheap, not even for friends. In letters to Cukor, Billy urged him to remember that only the best materials would do, that money was well spent when a job was done right. Cukor usually agreed, albeit somewhat reluctantly. "You certainly know how to get me to spend my hard-earned pay," he wrote to Billy, who would work on and off at Cukor's for several years.

———

Cukor's house became famous for more than its unique decor. It also became one of the most frequent gathering places for a new, still-coalescing circle of Hollywood gay men.

During the 1930s, an interesting phenomenon occurred among the Hollywood gay set. Whereas in the Roaring Twenties there was a good deal of social integration, by the early 1930s there was a greater tendency to gather with one's own kind. That doesn't mean that exclusively gay parties didn't exist in the 1920s — or that gay actors and directors didn't socialize with their heterosexual counterparts in the 1930s. Far from it. There *was* a dividing line, however, even if it was rarely acknowledged and sometimes difficult to see. Such a division becomes evident after going through hundreds of back issues of trade papers and fan magazines, after sorting through an even greater number of photographs of Hollywood stars out on the town or gathered together at movie premieres.

The *Hollywood Reporter*, for example, was quite precise at naming who sat with whom at the Vendome or the Trocadero. Time and time again it's names like Edmund Lowe and George Cukor and Billy Haines and Cary Grant that are linked. One remarkable photograph by the New York photographer Jerome Zerbe (who writer Brendan Gill reports was a lover of Cary Grant's), was apparently taken at a party thrown by the Countess di Frasso. Billy, Grant, Clifton Webb, Marlene Dietrich, and Claudette Colbert are all lined up together. In another, Billy, Cukor, Lowe, Lilyan Tashman, and Kay Francis are seen around a table at one of Hollywood's nightspots. There are dozens of examples — stars and directors who on the surface had nothing to link them: no films together, no studio in common. There was a bond, however, that went far deeper.

Of course, pictures of Billy with Joan Crawford and Connie Bennett are also found, and photos can be unearthed of Clifton Webb standing next to almost anyone. Still, the evidence — including Billy's and Cukor's dinner party guest lists — suggests that there were at least two factions in Hollywood. If not divided by sexuality, they were certainly divided by temperament and politics: the Bogarts and Bennetts and Hepburns versus the Robert Montgomerys and Loretta Youngs and Clark Gables. Gatherings might occasionally include both George Cukor and Robert Benchley, but never Cukor and John Wayne. As a more conservative attitude settled over the film colony in the 1930s, the entire community became a little more guarded. For the gay set—at least the gay set that was relatively open (that is, *not* the Tyrone Powers and Robert Taylors)—it was just more comfortable to gather at Cukor's and not have to worry about watching your tongue. It was just easier to step out with Eddie Lowe and Lil Tashman, because you knew their story and they knew yours.

In many ways, the gay circles were seen as more fascinating and glamorous. "Homosexuality in that period had two levels," said the writer Leonard Spigelglass. "One, it was held in major contempt, and the other, it was the most exclusive club. That's terribly important to realize—that it was a club into which [heterosexual Hollywood] couldn't get. I mean, no ordinary certified public accountant could get into the Cole Porter–Larry Hart–George Cukor world. That was their world. That was Somerset Maugham. That was Noël Coward. . . . On the one hand, if you said, 'They're homosexual,' 'Oh, my, isn't that terrible,' was the reaction. On the other hand, if you said, 'My God, the other night I was at dinner with Cole Porter,' the immediate reaction was, 'What did he have on? What did he say? Were you at the party? Were you at one of those Sunday brunches?' So you had this awful ambivalence."

The gay circles of the 1930s formed around just a handful of top names: Billy, Cukor, the composer Cole Porter, and, to a lesser degree, the director Mitchell Leisen. Dozens of other names—some well-known and others known only to those in the industry—were part of a revolving set who gathered at private parties and at restaurants and nightclubs. Of the gay silent stars, only Billy and Edmund Lowe remained in the social whirl. Ramon Novarro was a guest at Billy's house a few times in the early part of the decade, where he met Cukor, but after leaving MGM he became pretty much a recluse. Lowell Sherman died in 1934, and Nils Asther remained bitter about being fired from MGM.

Some initially moved with the gay set but dropped out as their careers demanded a new image to accommodate the changing times.

Cary Grant disappeared from Billy's and Cukor's table after about 1935. "Cary stopped coming around," says Michael Pearman. "I don't remember seeing him at any of the [later] parties." His friend and secretary, Frank Horn, a plump, jolly, ex-vaudevillian Cary first met in New York, was a frequent participant in the gay gatherings, however, whether at Cukor's, Billy's, or Cole Porter's. Billy found him very amusing.

Horn was also discreet. "Frank Horn covered up for Cary until the end of his life," says Bob Wheaton. Horn remained Cary's secretary until he was quite old, and then was put on a monthly annuity by his former employer. Wheaton once asked Cukor why Grant didn't simply find an insurance company to take care of Horn the rest of his life. Cukor told him, "Sending someone a check every month is a much better guarantee of keeping them quiet." Wheaton laughs. "It might not have made the best business sense, but it worked."

While Cukor and Grant remained friendly—Grant did, after all, star in some of the director's most memorable pictures of the 1930s—the actor would never have come to any of the parties. Randolph Scott, on the other hand, did continue to occasionally socialize with Billy and Jimmie. Jimmie Shields's nephew Charles Conrad recalls his uncle arranging a golf game for him with Scott during a visit to California in the 1950s.

If some were distancing themselves from the gay circles, there were others who, despite the less tolerant tenor of the times, embraced them. Clifton Webb had been brought out to Hollywood in 1935 by MGM but the studio didn't know quite what to do with him. He was acerbically funny, a brilliant performer, the hit of several Cole Porter shows. In the end, MGM did nothing with him, and he went back to New York to star in another Porter musical, but he did manage to become a regular in the gay social scene before he left. He and his constant companion, his mother Maybelle Webb, were the toast of several parties.

Then there was Cesar Romero, who took a cue from Billy Haines and refused to play the marriage game. He walked a dangerous line: He started at MGM the same year Billy was let go, and became known in the gossip columns as a "confirmed bachelor." He survived because, although he never took a wife, he encouraged the tongue-wagging that inevitably occurred each time he was seen out on the town with another woman. Which was quite frequently—Romero was the number one choice to escort Hollywood's leading ladies to parties and premieres whenever they found themselves without a husband or a date. He was perfectly happy to act as a "beard," dancing the night away with a lesbian actress who wanted to keep up appearances. Barbara Stanwyck often dreaded going out in public, but when she absolutely couldn't avoid it, she told a reporter, "I call good old Butch Romero, and he says, rather reluctantly, 'Well, if you *have* to go, I'll take you.'"

Orry-Kelly had an easier time of it because he toiled behind the screen as Warner's costume designer. He was a frequent guest at Billy's and an occasional visitor to Cukor's. "Orry-Kelly was outrageous," says Bob Wheaton. "Everyone loved him." Despite—or perhaps because of—problems with alcohol, Billy's old friend from New York was known as the life of the party.

Billy and Orry became even closer as the years went on. They tried to one-up each other with practical jokes. Once, arriving early for a party at Orry's house, Billy waited downstairs while Orry was still upstairs dressing. Billy took a sponge and made a large wet mark on the living room ceiling. When Orry came downstairs, he had a fit, thinking there was a leak and his party would be ruined. Billy laughed uproariously.

At Cukor's a regular group of friends gathered for Sunday parties around the director's Olympian swimming pool. Usually there were some well-known Hollywood names for brunch. Most often these were Cukor's actress friends: Katharine Hepburn, Dorothy Gish, Ina Claire, Alla Nazimova. Billy knew them casually through Cukor. He'd socialized with the great Nazimova through Fanny Brice, but Hepburn says that although she was often in Billy's company, she really only knew him well enough to say, "Hello, hello." After the famous females left, the party would continue with Cukor's "regulars." Said the Baroness d'Erlanger wryly: "Mr. Cukor has all these wonderful parties for ladies in the afternoon. Then in the evening naughty men come around to eat the crumbs!"

Chief among those "naughty men" were, of course, Billy and Jimmie. The rest of the regulars were sometimes referred to as "the cronies," and included Andy Lawler, Frank Horn, Roger Davis, and Louis Mason, as well as a revolving group of others. Lawler, split from Cooper but still friendly with him, was at this time one of screenland's most frequent "beards." Photographers snapped him with Cooper's ex, the Countess di Frasso, as well as with Tallulah Bankhead and Ilka Chase, and the gossip columns speculated all sorts of marriage plans. "Andy Lawler was the one always chosen by the studio executives to escort their wives to some event or to play bridge with them," says Bob Wheaton, who was not yet on the scene but came to know all of the cronies intimately and heard their stories. "Andy was what was known as a 'safe date.' "

Jean Howard, a well-known Hollywood hostess and then the wife of high-powered agent Charles Feldman, confirms that Cukor and his friends would often dance the night away with the ladies at parties after their husbands had retired to the other room to talk shop. Billy was happy to whisk Jean Howard and Ann Warner around the dance floor, but Howard says he drew the line at the kind of public appearances for which Lawler was known. No gossip columnist would ever believe it anyway, he told her.

The other members of the gay set were a varied lot. Grady Sutton was a frequent guest at both Billy's and Cukor's. He was a popular character who specialized in Southern-accented "sissy" roles — jumping up on top of a table at the sight of a mouse in *Movie Crazy* (1932). Sutton continued playing similar parts through the 1950s, then turned up on television (*The Odd Couple*). Until his death, he maintained a stony silence about the gay subculture of Hollywood.

Other cronies included costume designer Charles LeMaire; screenwriter Rowland Leigh, whose credits included *The Charge of the Light Brigade* and *Tarzan the Ape Man*; dialogue director James Vincent, who'd worked as Katharine Cornell's stage manager; actor John Darrow, whose career by the mid-1930s had gone nowhere, with just small parts to his credit (he later worked as a talent scout); and Tom Douglas, a British stage actor.

Michael Pearman, who worked as Cukor's personal assistant on a number of films and also performed in Cole Porter productions, was a strikingly handsome young man and a good friend of Billy's. "It was a constantly changing scene," he says of the gay circle. "There were parties at George's, and parties at Billy's. We all knew each other eventually. We all got around to meeting each other sooner or later."

They certainly did "get around." In the 1930s, one of the perks of being a part of the circle was the sharing of tricks. Someone might bring a young man to Cukor's or Billy's house one weekend; at the next gathering, the young man was with someone else. There was no hitting on a date at the particular event, but a handsome young man was often passed along from one friend to another. Billy and Jimmie brought a sailor to one dinner at Cukor's; he'd later become intimate with a number of their friends, including Cukor and Andy Lawler. Bob Seiter, the handsome brother of the director William Seiter, first entered the group in this way. Later, he was accepted more as a friend than as a trick.

Often, a band of "cronies" went out on the town together, hopping from one club to the next. Dozens of photographs exist showing Billy and Cukor at nightclubs together. There were also group excursions to the beach to pick up men.

The center of Hollywood gay life was found at Cukor's Sunday gatherings. His house was almost a required stopover for the famous personalities who passed through town. To Cukor's regularly came Somerset Maugham, Noël Coward, Tennessee Williams, Cecil Beaton, and George Hoyningen-Huene, whenever they were in Hollywood. "They [the gay elite] all flocked to George," said the producer Joseph L. Mankiewicz, "because George was their access to the creme of Hollywood. George was really queen of the roost."

Billy's house was also the scene of many important gatherings. Cukor's fame eclipsed Billy's on the world stage by the late 1930s, and so it is his house that is remembered and gossiped about; but in Hollywood, Billy was at least the equal of Cukor in hosting parties. His house was more sumptuous, more grand, and his parties tended to be far more elegant than his friend's.

A photo from Edith Gwynn's column shows a party at Billy's

house in 1935. He might no longer have been a motion-picture star, but he could still draw the photographers to his house. Billy's cutting a ham, grinning up into the camera. Cesar Romero jauntily holds aloft a pineapple, George Murphy (MGM hoofer and later a U.S. senator) dangles grapes in the air, and Sonny Chalif (a Hollywood exec married to Mary Pickford's cousin) stands behind amused.

It's interesting to note that Billy hosted a party in which two recent MGM hirees—Romero and Murphy—were among the guests of honor. Might he have been doing Thalberg a favor? Clearly, despite the dismissal, being seen with Billy Haines was still a good publicity move in 1935.

"At Billy's parties there were always more girls," says Michael Pearman. He remembers Crawford, of course, but also Colbert, Dietrich, Kay Francis, and Lil Tashman.

Hollywood's lesbian crowd was more connected to the gay male world than has been generally realized. While certainly distinct, there was an unacknowledged alliance and the occasional social overlap. Much of that in the 1930s had to do with Billy Haines. Having decorated Colbert's house, he became a frequent guest at her parties and she at his. At the Countess di Frasso's, Billy and Jimmie spent a good deal of time with Colbert and Dietrich, who were engaged in a brief but passionate affair in 1935.

Billy was acquainted with many of the women who made up the "all-girl" poolside parties at Alla Nazimova's house on Sunset Boulevard, among them Pola Negri. Later, when Nazimova had sold her house and had it converted into the swanky Garden of Allah Hotel, Billy often attended parties there as a guest of Constance Talmadge or Lil Tashman.

Tashman was a ringleader: Her fame in the lesbian community was unparalleled. Never a great beauty, she was nonetheless the most sexually aggressive woman in Hollywood, a trait Billy probably found amusing. Her reputed affair with Garbo made her quite popular—after all, who wouldn't want to slip between the sheets with an ex-lover of Garbo's? Even the daughter of Louis B. Mayer wasn't safe from Tashman's advances. Irene Mayer Selznick told Barry Paris: "When Lilyan had some drinks, it was best not to go in the powder room with her. I did once and was never so startled in my life. I'd known Lil from way back, but nothing like that had ever happened to me in my life. So overt. I'd never seen anything like it—couldn't believe it was happening. Didn't know it *ever* happened."

When Tashman died in 1934 following an emergency brain-tumor operation, she was only thirty-three years old. Her funeral was mobbed by thousands of fans. The *New York Sun* reported that ten thousand mourners—"mostly women"—thronged around her casket as it was being carried to the grave site. The newspaper reported: "Hysterical women rushed past the police, jumped over hedges, bumped into and in some cases knocked over grave markers in their eagerness to get a close up of the scene." Pallbearers had to rescue several women from falling into the grave.

Kay Francis was another friend. A close chum of Andy Lawler's, she'd sometimes show up with him at Billy's or Cukor's. Like Tashman, she was known as a clothes horse on the screen, starring in a series of fluffy pictures for Warners. Also like Tashman, she was married to an actor, Kenneth MacKenna—but he was hardly the companion Edmund Lowe was for Lil. When Francis divorced MacKenna in 1934, she said he had "continually nagged and harassed" her—possibly because she had been rarely home, preferring the city's night spots with lesbian pals. When Orry-Kelly took over as costume designer at Warners, he'd sometimes bring Kay along to parties at Billy's as well.

Billy's closest friend among the lesbian set was Claudette Colbert. Friends insist that Claudette never explicitly told Billy she had a preference for women, that she and Dietrich would socialize with Billy and Jimmie with nothing being said. Many years later, when her second husband, Dr. Joel Pressman, died, Colbert announced that henceforth her friends should consider her longtime female companion her spouse, and treat her accordingly. "Billy was simply astonished," remembers Bob Shaw. "He said, 'I've known Claudette all these years and I never knew she was a dyke.' He went on and on like that. 'I can't believe she didn't tell *me*,' he said. Finally, I just said to him, 'You know, Billy, you don't own a *patent* on it!' "

The truth is, Colbert didn't try to hide her relationship with Dietrich until (like Cary Grant) she was forced to "straighten out" her image. With her first husband she had maintained separate residences; they were divorced in 1935, just about the time her relationship with Dietrich began. That same year, at a party at the Venice Amusement Park thrown by Carole Lombard, the two women came wearing pants. (Garbo and Mercedes de Acosta had made wearing pants a code for lesbianism, or at least sexual rebellion.) A photo of Colbert and Dietrich careening down a slide together was syndicated widely, causing considerable gossip and embarrassment for Paramount, home studio to both women. By the end of the year, Colbert had married Pressman, and Dietrich was suddenly romantically linked to John Gilbert.

Dietrich, who enjoyed sexual relations with both men and women, seems to have been genuinely interested in Gilbert. She was also involved with Mercedes de Acosta, Garbo's companion, ever since Garbo had gone off on her extended trip to Europe in 1933. Their affair was carried on quite openly. It wasn't exclusive; de Acosta continued her relationship with Garbo, although it eventually became a passionate platonic friendship. Dietrich, too, was emboldened by de Acosta's example to act more aggressively, making a play for Carole Lombard by leaving notes and flowers in her dressing room. The no-nonsense Lombard replied: "If you want something, you come on down while I'm there."

By the beginning of 1936, less than three years after his departure from MGM and only a year since the release of his last film, Billy Haines's fortunes were looking up. If he once had been unable to visualize life beyond the movies, he was now finding a livelihood and a social life that in many ways were far more satisfying than those during his tenure on the Metro lot. Let Mayer and the Production Code be damned: They held no power over William Haines, Decorator to the Stars.

Then came El Porto.

Much has already been written about the night of May 31, 1936, the infamous Decoration Day weekend when the scandal Louis B. Mayer had always feared finally came to pass. Much of what has been written, however, has been notoriously off the mark. In his *Hollywood Babylon II*, Kenneth Anger paints a portrait of a white-hooded mob descending on Billy and his friends, threatening to burn down their beach house. Even people who know nothing else about Billy Haines—not about his days as America's top box-office star, not about his flourishing career as an interior designer, not even the circumstances of how he left pictures—seem to know that in 1936, he was beaten and chased by a mob who claimed he and his friends had molested a little boy on the beach.

The truth, as usual, is far more complicated. And fascinating.

For several years, Billy and Jimmie had rented a summer beach house in Santa Monica, not far from Marion Davies's seaside mansion. In the spring of 1936, however, they decided to rent elsewhere, in the popular seaside community of El Porto, a part of the town of Manhattan Beach, a conservative, middle-class community some thirty minutes south of Hollywood. They took a house at 221 Moonstone Street.

"Billy rented that place from my father, who was in real estate," says Anita Page. "It was a charming house, facing the water, very near the beach."

It's a lovely area, and was even more so sixty years ago. Now an asphalt parking area lines the Strand, the road that runs parallel with the coast. Then, a Pacific Electric rail line ran along the strip, regularly bringing visitors from Los Angeles and San Diego. The beach would have been far more accessible in those days, with summer residents stepping from their hillside homes onto the dramatic sweep of sand and surf. It's a long open stretch of exposed coast; the Pacific beats fiercely against the fine sandy beach. When the sun sets over the ocean, the brilliant spill of color reflects off the glass panes of the facing homes.

An embankment rises sharply from the beach; most of the houses here belonged to the summerfolk. The streets on the embankment are narrow and steep, twisting between clusters of two- and three-story homes. The native population tended to live farther back, where the real estate wasn't as pricey. Hollywood realtors

(like Anita Page's father) made bundles from summer r[
out-of-towners.

Manhattan Beach attracted many of Hollywood's glitterati. Every summer the movie people would make the trek down to escape the clutter and commotion of Los Angeles. Like most tourist towns, there was always a slightly edgy relationship between the "townies" and the summerfolk. The natives were hardworking people, most involved in manufacturing: electrical supplies and pottery. It was the tourist trade that helped keep the town's economy solvent.

Beginning in March, the population swelled; the streets were jammed with automobiles; loud music was played from the terraces of beach houses; and the rowdy movie folk were often drunk and lascivious on the street late at night. The former child actor Jackie Coogan was one of those arrested for speeding through town.

Still, it was, in most respects, a quiet community. "The two police cars and two motorcycle officers would cruise around looking for some means of revenue," one longtime resident remembered. "The town boasted of one accident in the whole year, and dirt collected daily in the two cells of the jail."

Local historian Jan Norris says the area also had its darker side. Nearby Hermosa Beach was a seat of Ku Klux Klan activity. In the entire Manhattan Beach area, there were very few nonwhite residents. And there were some—who slept with guns under their pillows—who wanted to keep it that way.

The annual influx of movie people was an irritant to many in Manhattan Beach; for others, it was much more than that. Hollywood was Sodom in their minds, and the values of Tinseltown did not translate well half an hour south. Charlie Chaplin's ex-wife Lita Grey got remarried in Manhattan Beach; a judge later ruled that she had committed bigamy. The El Porto Beach Club, patronized by many vacationing movie people, was raided for "making book"; its owner was also charged in a shooting in Redondo Beach. And in 1936, screen star Lila Lee was involved in a murder investigation at the home of well-known novelist Gouverneur Morris—a mystery her son, the actor and playwright James Kirkwood (*A Chorus Line*) would dramatize in his book *There Must Be a Pony*. (Kirkwood's father, James Kirkwood, Sr., had starred in Billy's early film *Circe the Enchantress*.)

Into this mix came Billy Haines and Jimmie Shields. Mitt Foster and Larry Sullivan rented the house next to them on Moonstone, and beginning in March, the four friends spent nearly every weekend there. As the weather got even warmer, Jimmie would spend longer chunks of time in El Porto, shopping in town and sunning on the beach, while Billy and Mitt went back to Los Angeles. They invited the "cronies" for several parties. George Cukor was there a number of times. So was, possibly, Cole Porter, who'd become friendly with Billy after arriving in Hollywood in 1935. Andy Lawler was a near-constant visitor, several friends recall.

This gathering of friends on holiday was generally well behaved, but understandably may have become a little boisterous at times. However, these were men of a certain age, taste, and style; they weren't college kids out to trash the place.

Still, they may have attracted some attention from the locals. Certainly word got around that 221 Moonstone was occupied by movie star William Haines—and much of the public by now had figured out what all that innuendo in the fan magazines had been about. That, coupled with the steady stream of nattily attired male visitors (girlfriends like Cranberry Crawford and Eleanor Boardman don't seem to have been a part of the El Porto crowd), could well have produced scuttlebutt in the town's cafés and barbershops.

The week before Decoration Day Jimmie was at the beach house; Billy was in Hollywood. On the afternoon of Thursday, May 28, Jimmie encountered a local boy on the beach: six-year-old Jimmy Walker, the son of Manhattan Beach businessman V. O. Walker. By all accounts, it was a chance meeting, casual and friendly.

Kenneth Anger tells the story of Billy's and Jimmie's poodle, Lord Peter Whimsy, who had been dyed purple by his owners that previous Easter. It was the poodle, Anger asserts, that initially attracted little Jimmy Walker. The boy hung around all afternoon, and finally (so Anger writes) Jimmie gave him some pennies and shooed him on home. Although there is no report of a poodle in any of the contemporary accounts, nearly every report concurs that Jimmie gave the child some money, ranging from 6 to 15 cents.

Billy arrived in El Porto late Friday night, apparently with Mitt and Larry. They had planned a Decoration Day party weekend, with friends arriving from Hollywood. Contemporary accounts report there were seventeen others besides Billy, Jimmie, Mitt, and Larry on the night of May 31. Three were staying with Billy and Jimmie, and another three were houseguests of Mitt and Larry. Eleven others had come down for the day. Today no one is left from among those guests; the only friend in that age group still living, Michael Pearman, says he wasn't there. Some of the younger cronies, for whom Decoration Day 1936 became something of a legend, believe strongly that George Cukor was present, one of the three staying at Billy's house. "George absolutely refused to discuss that weekend," says Bob Wheaton, "would just never, ever talk about it." Although we can never be certain, sometimes silence tells more than words.

Andy Lawler *did* speak of the weekend, however, and often. "He was certainly down there," Wheaton says, "he'd tell the whole story to anyone." Lawler and Louis Mason were likely the other two guests at Billy's house, as one press report identified one of them as "Mason." Of the other fifteen, it's speculation, but educated guesses can be made. Grady Sutton, Frank Horn, Jimmy Vincent, Tom Douglas, Roger Davis, John Darrow, Rowland Leigh—any and all might have been there for the day, some of them perhaps staying with Mitt. It's also a good possibility that Billy's chum Orry-Kelly was present, and maybe even Cesar Romero and Clifton Webb (sans mother). In any event, the twenty-one men partied throughout the day on May 31, oblivious to any mounting sentiment against them.

That evening, Billy, Jimmie, and their three houseguests walked up the steep hill from Moonstone Street to Highland Avenue, the main thoroughfare that runs from El Porto into the town of Manhattan Beach. There, at an Italian café, they enjoyed a spaghetti dinner. Billy was planning to return to Hollywood that night. As they wound their way back down the hill toward the house, several men approached them. According to press reports, one of the men said:

"We don't want you to live here. We'll give you just an hour to get out of town."

Billy later told police: "I didn't know what it was all about." He attempted to joke with the men, but one of them suddenly struck Jimmie, who fell to the ground. Billy instinctively leaped at the man, but he was hit from behind. He, too, fell to the pavement. When he attempted to get up, he was struck in the face. "I realized the men were drunk," Billy would say later, "and to fight them might result in fatalities. So when I was struck, I decided to remain in a prone position."

By this time, more people had gathered on the street. They began shouting curses at Billy and Jimmie. "We've been waiting for a chance to get you," one man told them. At some point, Billy helped Jimmie to his feet—his forehead was bleeding quite severely—and they managed to enter the house. They applied a temporary bandage to Jimmie's head, but he was now hopping mad. He wanted to go back outside and confront his attackers, who still stood in the street catcalling. Billy calmed him, and they quickly packed to leave.

Once back outside, they attempted to make their way to the car. The mob—now numbering about fifteen, including several women—pushed and shoved at the departing five men. Billy's car had been smeared with tomatoes. He pleaded with the crowd to just let them go; eventually, they made it into the car and sped out of town.

All of this happened in a very short period of time: ten, fifteen minutes at the most. The group, after jeering Billy's car as it left, then turned and headed over to Mitt's house. According to the *Los Angeles Times*, they chanted, "Let's clean up the town." It's likely the remainder of the weekend party guests had seen at least some of what happened. Several of them were outside, anxiously packing Mitt's car to leave, when they were approached by the mob and told they were "undesirable residents" and "had thirty minutes to get out."

Mitt told reporters: "A mob gathered around [the car] and ordered us out of town because we were Haines's friends. I told them we didn't need thirty minutes, we were getting out now."

One of the women in the group then took a tomato and smashed it in the face of one of the departing houseguests. As the cars all kicked into gear and screeched down the street, a torrent of tomatoes followed them, along with jeers and curses. Afterward, the mob hooted and cheered; the police, having been alerted that a riot was taking place, finally arrived, but only after it was all over.

The mob attack guaranteed headlines would ensue. Even as they sped back up the highway toward Hollywood, Billy and Jimmie—and whoever their famous houseguests were—must have known that.

At some point they must have questioned the motive for the attack. Although it's not reported in the press accounts, it's hard to believe the attackers didn't taunt Jimmie with the accusation of molestation. No formal complaint had yet been made to the police by the child's parents; all the mob had to go on was the gossip that had spread like wildfire through the town's coffeeshops and taverns over the weekend. Surely Billy and Jimmie knew by the time they were speeding out of town what the melee had been about, and how lurid the headlines might be. And worse: There was no Howard Strickling and the MGM publicity department to protect them now.

They stopped at the Vermont police substation and reported the brawl to Deputy Sheriff S. W. Kirkahofe, who promised an investigation would take place. Until such time as more information was gathered, however, no charges were pressed.

Given that the incident happened on a Sunday night, there was nothing in the papers on Monday. On Tuesday, June 2, The *Long Beach Press-Telegram*, the first to report on the incident, ran a front-page article. The paper reported both of Billy's eyes had been blackened, but nothing was speculated about the motive for the attack. That's because it was only June 2—two days after the attack and five days after Jimmie met the boy on the beach—that Mrs. V. O. Walker, little Jimmy's mother, and two other local women officially sought a morals complaint against William Haines and "James Doe." They appeared before Justice of the Peace A. F. Monroe in Inglewood, who advised them the evidence on which to base such a complaint was "flimsy" and that a proper investigation should be made first.

The next day, June 3, papers all over the country ran the story on their front pages. The *Los Angeles Times* headlined "Mob Beats Ex-Actor," with photos of Billy from his MGM days. The *Los Angeles Examiner* read, "Haines Beaten by Band of 50; Ousted from Home." The accompanying story featured photos of Jimmie with bandages on his forehead. The *New York Daily News* splashed: "Mob Chases Bill Haines from Home." Even back home in Virginia, The *Staunton Leader* proclaimed, "Haines and His Companion Are Beaten by Mob." No mention was made that Billy was a local boy; he was simply called a "handsome ex-film star."

Worst of all, of course, were the allegations below the headlines: "Six-year-old boy allegedly abused at Haines' home." The women's attempt to file a morals complaint against Billy was noted in all of the reports, as was the portentous statement: "An investigation will be made of the charges."

What made the accounts so frightful, of course, was that the "charges" were so vague. In an era when child abuse and sexual molestation were not the subjects of the intense media discussion they are today, any allegation of "abuse" was mysterious and unspecified. All Billy could do was tell reporters, "Some wild, untrue rumor must have stirred them up."

That "wild, untrue rumor" was in fact the story told to V. O. Walker and his wife by their son after he trudged back up to their home on Highland Avenue on the evening of Thursday, May 28. In his hand he carried some coins. When asked where he got the money, he told them about the man—also named "Jimmy," he recalled—who lived down on Moonstone Street.

Mr. Walker left later that day for a business trip to Chicago. His wife, however, apparently told a few of her acquaintances what little Jimmy had told her, and word of it quickly got around. Neighbors called to tell her they'd seen her son in the company of a man at the Haines house; they added a few details of the "unsavory" parties that had gone on there for weeks.

Although some accounts claim that Mrs. Walker took part in the attack on Sunday night, that appears highly unlikely. She was extremely distressed by the furor and the resulting publicity, perhaps as much as Billy and Jimmy. "I am very sorry that my boy's story, told in confidence to my husband and myself in the presence of a deputy sheriff, should cause the trouble which it has," she told the press after filing the morals charge. "The sheriff's officers said this would be taken care of quietly, but after Sunday's affair, I suppose it is impossible to keep the child out of it."

On June 3, reporters descended on Manhattan Beach and discovered that many townsfolk were openly bragging about the attack. The perpetrators were being hailed as "heroes." Some envious citizens were even claiming they'd participated when, in fact, they were probably home sleeping or listening to the radio. Initial accounts report between fifteen and twenty people took part in the attack; a day later, that number was upped to fifty. By the end of the week, the riot was being estimated at a hundred people.

"We didn't touch 'em while they were on the ground," one man, described as a "businessman of the community," told the *Los Angeles Examiner*. "But when they got to their feet we sort of pushed 'em around. You know, we bounced 'em from one to the other like you bounce a volley ball."

Photographers in Los Angeles, meanwhile, snapped a smiling, cherub-faced Jimmy Walker as his mother led him by the hand into the Hall of Justice to be questioned by District Deputy Attorney Dave Coleman. The boy told Coleman that he had met Jimmie Shields on the beach and that Jimmie had bought him a hamburger. The *Los Angeles Times* report concluded ominously, "He then related other details of their meeting."

Also summoned to the Hall of Justice was Mrs. Larry E. Kimball of 216 Moonstone Street. Mrs. Kimball told Coleman she witnessed Jimmie and the young boy entering the beach house at 221 Moonstone. Investigators found her an unreliable witness: She said Jimmie had bought the child a hot dog, instead of a hamburger, and insisted a second boy accompanied them into the house. No evidence—including from little Jimmy himself—could be found to corroborate her story.

It's possible that Mrs. Kimball was eventually disregarded by investigators because they came to believe she'd been hostile toward her neighbors for some time. She admitted to Coleman that her husband had told Mr. Walker about seeing his son with Jimmie, and that she knew of others who told Mrs. Walker "not to worry, for Shields and his friends are going to be ordered to leave town."

Was it some kind of Klan action? Although there are no reports of any white hoods or sheets—as Anger insinuates—the term "White Legion" *was* used by some of the boasters around town following the assault. Certainly with Hermosa Beach being a center of white supremicist activity, it's possible there was a connection. Billy himself eagerly told the press on June 3, "I have since learned that the place used to be a hotbed of clannish activities—and someone has said that a 'White Legion,' whatever that is, exists in that community."

The *Long Beach Press-Telegram*, in its front-page story on June 2, had made the charge "White Legion Mobs Beach Town Party." But by the next day, such allegations were being referred to as speculation. The *Los Angeles Times* said only that there were reports of a "mysterious White Legion which assertedly drove Haines and the others out of town." Whether the Sunday night attack was an orchestrated attempt by local white supremacists to maintain its order, or whether some of the attackers simply had sympathies in that direction, it's clear that part of what motivated the incident was not just outrage over what little Jimmy Walker had reported, but also a hatred against homosexuals. Today, such an assault might be classified as a hate crime.

Billy and Jimmie were finally ordered to appear before Deputy District Attorney Coleman on June 4. By all accounts both of them were sick over the incident, with Jimmie absolutely devastated. Still, they were photographed as they arrived with their lawyer at the Hall of Justice dressed in spiffy suits and smiling. Billy confidently told the reporters gathered at the scene that their lawyer accompanied them only as a formality, that they had no need for legal advice.

Meanwhile, Coleman was telling the press that Billy was not under investigation, that he was merely being interviewed. Jimmie, however, had been identified as the "James Doe" who allegedly brought the child into the beach house. They met for several hours, then emerged to pose for photographs with William J. Bright, the sheriff's chief criminal deputy. Coleman told the gathered reporters: "Mr. Shields told a straightforward story. He said he merely romped with the boy on the beach the afternoon of May 28. He said he is fond of children and declared that Jimmy Walker is a particularly likable chap." Any action, Coleman said, would be held in abeyance until the boy's father had returned from Chicago.

Billy, meanwhile, was being urged to file charges against his attackers, something he—as well as most of his friends—was apparently loath to do. "I couldn't identify them in the first place, and wouldn't in the second place," Billy explained in announcing he'd press no charges. "The whole affair was caused by irresponsible hoodlums. I am disgusted and humiliated with it all. I would be more than glad to let the entire matter drop."

That was the last of it in the press, as Billy no doubt hoped. Unlike the contemporary obsession with court cases, there was no pack of reporters hanging around the Hall of Justice, waiting for the next word from the district attorney. The matter reached its unexpected conclusion away from the glare of photographers' bulbs with which it had begun. Until now, the full story of that conclusion has never been told.

Jimmy Walker is today a genial, gregarious man of sixty-seven. He still lives in the Manhattan Beach area, having devoted much of his life to public service. He had a long, respected career on the City Council, serving a term as mayor in the mid-1980s. He's retired now, with grown children, and his memories of six decades ago, he admits, are a bit hazy. Even when the names William Haines and Jimmie Shields were first mentioned to him in connection with this book, it took several minutes for him to remember who they were.

He does recall that afternoon of May 28. "We were on the beach," he says of himself and Jimmie. "He took me up to his apartment, which I believe was on Moonstone. We took a shower or something, and we got in bed, and he gave me a blow job."

When this prompts an expression of outrage and shock—he was, after all, just *six years old*—he takes it in stride. "I don't recall it being an enjoyable experience," he says, "but I don't recall it being horrible, either. I don't know that it screwed my life up."

He's familiar with the infamous *Hollywood Babylon* account of the incident. "I don't know about any poodle," he says. "I don't know where they got that from. The implication I got out of *[Hollywood Babylon]* was they [Billy and Jimmie] were discriminated against, and my experience with them was all a sham. That simply isn't true. Sixty years goes by and I still remember."

Yet the investigation failed to indict Jimmie. According to Walker, whose parents are now deceased, there was a closed hearing at the Hall of Justice sometime after his father returned from Chicago. Billy and Jimmie were both present. Walker says: "One of the attorneys asked me, 'In the courtroom, can you see the person who took you into the shower and stuck his mouth over your pee-pee?' So, little six-year-old that I am, I start looking out in the courtroom. I go all over the courtroom and I don't see him sitting out there. Nobody asked me, 'Is he sitting at the table?' They said *the courtroom*. And I said, 'I don't see him in the courtroom.' I was just getting ready to say, 'But he's sitting right there next to you,' when [the attorney] said, 'Your Honor, we ask for a dismissal,' and the judge said, 'Granted.' "

Still, Walker says he holds no grudge against Jimmie, and neither, he says, did his parents. "They were never really all that hard-nosed about any of that," he says. "They knew I had not been harmed." He adds that they were incensed over the Sunday night brawl. "My Dad would've been really upset about that. They were kind of liberal people. As a matter of fact, I think my old man went to [one of the alleged perpetrators] and told him to go fuck himself."

There are no records of a hearing taking place on the incident; that doesn't mean Walker's recollection is wrong. In fact, it's likely some kind of hearing did occur to resolve the issues Coleman left dangling on June 4. Nonetheless, the memories of a six-year-old boy more than sixty years later—especially in light of the furor that accompanied the case and the power of suggestion—must be considered for what they are.

Psychologists say it's possible that "false memories" can often be as compelling as actual recollections. One study involved kindergarten children, who were asked several times whether they'd ever seen anyone steal anything from their classroom. During the first few go-arounds, the children all said no. Gradually after the question was repeated several times, some of the children seemed to recall seeing a thief, when none had ever really existed. Their memories of the "robbery"—down to precise details—were very exact. False memories, psychologists say, can occur as distortion of real events on the child's part, especially when there is stress or adult influence present.

Jimmie Shields is no longer alive to defend himself. It's important to note that there was never any suggestion, before or after this event, that Jimmie might be a pedophile.

"Absolutely not," says Michael Morrison.

"Jimmie liked them young," says Arch Case, "but not *that* young."

Everyone who knew Jimmie, even those who found him an insufferable snob at times, insists he never would have harmed a child. "What happened was Jimmie chased a little boy down the beach," says Ted Graber. "It was harmless."

Not one person interviewed believed Jimmie had any sexual desire for children. He was known for his sexual dalliances, but this was the only instance in which there was a charge of pedophilia. Jim Walker, former mayor of Manhattan Beach, on the other hand, believes Jimmie Shields got away with a crime. "There was no injury or physical abuse or harm, but who forgets their first blow job?" he asks. The absolute truth will never be known.

There are a few additional facts to consider. The irony is, of course, that the whole brouhaha would not have made it to the front pages had Billy still been an MGM star in 1936, protected by the studio. Then District Attorney Buron Fitts would have been called and a deal would have been made—as perhaps was done earlier in the decade to cover Billy's (or Jimmie's) transgressions.

Yet the affair does have a kind of unfinished quality to it, supported by Walker's memory of a hurried hearing that never made the papers. What if George Cukor, as many believe, was indeed one of the three houseguests returning with Billy from dinner just before the assault? Cukor was then among MGM's top directors; he was about to begin filming *Camille*. The studio would have stepped in to pressure the district attorney's office, fearful that Cukor's name might be linked to the scandal. Already, Louis Mason's name had been printed (albeit just his surname) as one of those at the beach house. Someone might easily tell the reporters nosing around El Porto that they'd seen George Cukor with the rest of them. Cukor's biographer Patrick McGilligan was told stories of Cukor being arrested at about this time. Details were murky, but many suggested Billy Haines had been with him. Might this be the circumstance that was being recalled for McGilligan?

There were other big names possibly there that weekend as well: Orry-Kelly, Clifton Webb, Cesar Romero. The likeliest possibility remains Cukor. Louella Parsons noted in her column on June 3 that Mayer and Strickling had just arrived back in Hollywood from a visit to New York. They would have returned just in time to see the headlines and hear the rush of gossip that swept through Hollywood. It's at least conceivable (and, if true, terribly ironic) that Mayer stepped in to keep Cukor—and by extension, Jimmie and Billy—out of trouble.

It is interesting to note that while the Los Angeles newspapers focused on the attack, the *Manhattan Beach News*, perhaps understandably, devoted its attention to the alleged molestation of one of its younger citizens. On June 5 the weekly newspaper printed a commitment from local authorities to uncover the truth. "We will go to the bottom of the matter," the sheriff's office promised. "If the facts warrant we will seek complaints or ask District Attorney Buron Fitts to refer the entire matter to the county grand jury."

The matter never went that far. It's perhaps notable that Buron Fitts was up for reelection that summer; he counted on support from the movie colony. In any event, nothing further on the Walker case was reported in the *Manhattan Beach News*.

Other cases were. The very next week, Dr. Frederick Klaus, the highly respected principal of Pier Avenue School in neighboring

Hermosa Beach, was arrested on a morals charge. G. R. Smith, a Hollywood banker and the father of a fourteen-year-old boy, claimed Klaus had improperly touched his son. Then, in July, A. W. Shade, a music teacher at Union High School, was accused by parents of conducting classes in an "improper manner" and was put "under advisement." Suddenly Manhattan Beach seemed in the midst of an epidemic of child molesters. Could Jimmie have been just one of the victims of local fundamentalist paranoia?

Whether Jimmie was innocent or guilty, the effect on Billy was tremendous. For his part, Jimmie seems to have bounced back quite well from the ordeal; Billy sent him on an extended trip to Europe to escape the Hollywood gossip and he returned home as chipper (and as randy) as ever. Billy, however, after so many years of fearing a public scandal, remained press shy for the rest of his life. Only in his last decades did he begin to trust the media again, and then he nearly always insisted the conversation be limited to decoration, not movies or anything else about his past.

"Billy took all the blame for what happened, and he wasn't even there," says Ted Graber. While not quite accurate—Billy was never accused of anything—Graber has a point: The public didn't know or care about Jimmie Shields. The only reason the whole affair received such sensational publicity was Billy's fame, and consequently it was *his* name that was linked to the case.

The Haines family was just as disappointed by the lack of public conclusion as the Walker family. They waited for notice of the exoneration to appear in the papers; it never did. Billy was grateful that at least his mother had been spared the ugly publicity, but for his father and siblings, it was excruciating. Henry Haines was then just eighteen years old; he'd always idolized his older brother. "I remember writing Bill a note in regard to it," he says today, the pain of the experience still evident. "I was trying to be supportive."

The family blamed not Billy or even Jimmie, but William Randolph Hearst—Billy's friend and mentor—for allowing the story such play in his newspapers, especially the *Los Angeles Examiner*. Henry Haines even believes Hearst may have had a hand in cooking up the scandal because he was envious of Billy's friendship with Marion Davies. "This was an example of the yellow press at its worst," says Henry.

There's no basis for such a theory. In fact, at least one of Billy's friends heard the exact opposite story. "The newspapers were all covering the business at the beach, but for two days the *Examiner* did not touch it," says Bob Wheaton. "At the end of the second day Hearst called Billy and said, 'You're a dear friend of mine and I hate to do it, but I've got to cover that story. The other papers have had it for two days.' Billy said he understood and Hearst promised to give it the best treatment possible."

The truth is neither the *Times* nor the *Examiner* ran the story until June 3, a day after it had appeared in the *Long Beach Press-Telegram*. It's possible that Hearst *did* sit on the story on June 2, but was forced to print it once he heard it would appear on the front page of the *Times* the next day. After that, he didn't try to stop the story, but he may have tempered it a bit. Unlike the *Times*, which featured large photos of Billy on the front page, the *Examiner* ran its pictures on page 2. But as the days went on, the *Examiner*—true to form— ran the story as splashily as it did every other Hollywood scandal.

"It was horrible," Billy told the *Los Angeles Times*, his only comment about the affair's impact. "I've never imagined such a ghastly experience. How such things can happen in a civilized country is beyond me."

Billy rarely discussed the incident with his family or friends. "I'd heard about the scandal down at the beach, of course," says Bob Shaw, who became part of Billy's circle in the 1950s. "But he certainly never mentioned it. I always thought it would be interesting to go the *L.A. Times* and read about it. But I knew better than to bring it up."

"Jimmie talked to me about it," says Geoffrey Toone, a British actor with whom Billy and Jimmie became friendly in the 1940s. "But without bitterness. He was enormously concerned at the time on Bill's account, not his own." Despite what others might say, Toone believes Jimmie "had no personal vanity. He was devoted first to Bill. He was a very dear man."

There had never been a scandal quite like this one in Hollywood. It combined the two most unspeakable taboos—sex with children and homosexuality. Charlie Chaplin had married the sixteen-year-old Lita Grey in 1924, and Errol Flynn would be charged with the statutory rape of two teenage girls in 1942, but this was far, far more shocking.

In the days immediately following the headlines, Billy spent a good deal of time with George Cukor. The director, reticent about discussing his own involvement with the case, nonetheless enjoyed telling one particular story to friends. "Oh, he *loved* to tell it," says Bob Wheaton. "I heard it many times." The same week of the lurid publicity, Cukor hosted a small dinner party. Billy was there, very depressed. Robert Benchley, known for his wit and open mind, was also invited, as was Lili Damita, then married to Errol Flynn but also a likely lover of Dolores Del Rio. Damita "got into her beers," Wheaton says, going on about how life was terrible. She was upset about a review of one of her latest pictures, which had called her more of a circus tightrope walker than an actress.

There was an awkward silence. Damita looked around the table for sympathy but got none. Finally Billy, who'd also had a few drinks, shot her a glance. "Honey, that's nothing," he said, "How would you like to wake up to find the *L.A. Times* had called you a cocksucker on the front page?"

Robert Benchley was finally roused to life. "Oh," he said, looking up, "I'd much rather be called a cocksucker than a tightrope walker."

Billy's laugh caught in his throat. Because while the scandal might have been more damaging had he still had a career in pictures, in some ways it wounded him far more deeply than anything that had happened at MGM. He had thought he was safe, thought he had carved out a niche beyond the glare of publicity. Instead, what he faced that summer of 1936 was another round of uncertainty: Would he be able to sustain the life to which he'd become accustomed— indeed, the lifestyle he'd left Staunton all those years ago to find and worked so hard to maintain?

If there had been any lingering thoughts of finding work again in pictures, they were forever banished that summer. The Code ruled Hollywood now with an ironclad grip. Everyone was married; everyone was apple pie and God-fearing. In the beginning of July, Will Hays even ordered a chimp's bare ass covered with Max Factor hair in *Girl of the Jungle*. There could be no going back to the movies now for Billy Haines.

8

A TAILOR-MADE MAN

1936-1945

Billy had been one of the best-liked men in Hollywood, but after the headlines about El Porto beach he found himself off the invitation lists. His former costar Junior Coghlan, then a teenage actor at RKO, says he remembers feeling very sorry for Billy, "because people were saying some pretty rough things about him." Billy would have to re-create himself—yet again—if he were to find any sense of personal fulfillment or financial success.

It didn't matter that he wasn't the one accused of anything; there's guilt by association in many people's minds. For some, he had it coming; how many scandals had been hushed up at MGM? "They finally got him for something," one friend says. "Some people said he got what he deserved."

Even some of the gay set felt similarly. Miles White was then a young man in his twenties, just embarking on a glorious career of costume design that would eventually earn him a Tony for *Bless You All*. He was not yet in the Cukor–Haines–Cole Porter circle, but like most aspiring young men in show business, he'd heard about the scandal. It left an impression on how a gay man needed to comport himself to be successful. "I was horribly disappointed by the scandal," White says. "It was as if he'd let us down—especially those of us just coming into our own [in show business]. He didn't seem to care about advancing homosexual safety. In fact, he pushed it back a ways for the rest of us."

Billy's fall was primarily a local one: Louella Parsons, for example, chose not to mention it in her column. It didn't really matter (except perhaps to Billy's ego) what the folks out in Peoria might think. He was no longer a movie star; box-office grosses were not his concern. Where the scandal hurt him was in Brentwood and Beverly Hills—where his decorating business had been beginning to thrive. Perhaps even more important, the affair hurt him among people with whom he valued a sense of community.

Whether the scandal had the effect of driving away clients from his decorating business is debatable. Looking back over his list of jobs more than sixty years later, there doesn't appear to be a dry period. How many months went by between finishing Cukor's home and starting the Jack Warner residence? It's impossible to know now whether Billy's expectations for larger commissions were met. There must have been some fallout: While he probably wasn't shunned, he wasn't likely to be embraced, either, at least not in the way he had been. Sadly, it makes sense: El Porto beach was the dirtiest kind of scandal, and just the excuse for homophobic Hollywood husbands to forbid their wives from seeing or employing Billy Haines. Longtime Hollywood reporter Bob Thomas, who knew Billy, wrote that "most of Hollywood's homes were closed to Haines" after the scandal.

"But not Joan Crawford's," Thomas added. "At a time when William Haines was considered a pariah in Hollywood, Joan refused to abandon him. He and Jimmy [*sic*] were invited to every party and every Sunday gathering."

It is part of Billy Haines's legend that it was Joan Crawford who salvaged his career, repaying him for guiding her along the road to stardom years earlier. That might be overstating the fact a bit, but Joan's loyalty was real, and made a difference. She made sure that Billy and Jimmie were at her annual Christmas party in 1936. Her new husband, Franchot Tone, played Santa Claus, distributing elaborately wrapped gifts from under their tree. The guest list was curious, especially in light of the previous June. Absent was Irving

Thalberg: The boy wonder of MGM, Billy's friend and sometime protector, had died in September of pneumonia. Billy's onetime rival Robert Montgomery was there, however, and Joan had even asked Louis B. Mayer to stop by. It was perhaps the first time he'd seen Billy since 1933. One can only imagine the conversation between them, if any occurred at all—but clearly Joan was sending a message. If she wasn't ashamed to be seen with Billy, no one else should be, either.

Also present were Jack and Mary Benny. Jack had just completed *The Big Broadcast of 1937* for Mitch Leisen. Billy's old friend had come to Hollywood when sound arrived, when MGM had been desperate for stage-trained performers. Billy had connected with him again then, but it was only as the decade went on, as Benny's star as a radio performer grew, that the two began socializing frequently. Often on hand were George Burns and Gracie Allen, for whom Billy provided decorating tips. Despite the scandal, the Bennys and Burns and Allen remained friendly with Billy and Jimmie. Along with Joan, they helped "rehabilitate" him in the minds of many in Hollywood.

The friendship with Crawford was to prove one of Billy's most enduring relationships. Joan's daughter Christina Crawford says "Uncle Willie" was a constant presence at the house on Bristol Avenue. He was forever tinkering with something, changing the toilet seats or installing new carpet. Christina, who was adopted in 1939 soon after her mother's divorce from Tone, says, "It wasn't until I was an adult that I understood what a big movie star [Billy had been] at MGM, or what an enormous amount of courage it took for him to walk away, for both love and principle." Joan had reduced Billy's story to its simplest terms for her daughter: Billy had been an important star and he had given it all up for love. Her celebrated comment—"Uncle Willie and Uncle Jimmie have the happiest marriage in Hollywood"—was told to Christina at a young age, reflecting Joan's own wistful dreams for matrimonial bliss.

It reflected something else, too: Joan's easy acceptance of homosexuality. She may have had her own occasional affairs with women, but was essentially heterosexual, with a voracious sexual appetite for men. Her gay friends offered her companionship and intimacy; they were safe, entertaining, and nurturing. Besides Billy and Jimmie, Joan was close with Cesar Romero, George Cukor, and Clifton Webb.

"Homosexuality was almost taken for granted when I was little, in that so many of the adults were," Christina Crawford says. "However, I did know the difference between the norms in the house and those outside."

For Christina, Billy was "always a favorite visitor because of his humor and lack of reverence." She confirms that he continued to tease her mother with the name Cranberry and make light of her fastidiousness and obsessive need for control. "He was one of the very few that could have done so!"

After Christina, Joan adopted three other children, a boy and two more girls. Whereas the youngest daughters have defended their mother, Christina's book *Mommie Dearest*, published a year after Joan's death, revealed a rigid, often abusive childhood for the Crawford children. Billy must have been aware of the difficult lives the children endured. His friend Geoffrey Toone once asked him what Crawford did with her children when she went off on location for filming. "Probably puts them in Bekins," Billy cracked — Bekins being the warehouse where Hollywood stars stored their furniture.

"He used to get after Crawford about the children," says Jean Mathison, Billy's close friend and employee for twenty years. "She would parade the children around at parties. Billy tried to be helpful [to the children]."

Just what form that help took is unknown, but Christina remains very fond of Uncle Willie and Uncle Jimmie. "They treated me as a person," she says, "although they didn't have much time for children. [But] they often included me in invitations to dinner, which I enjoyed."

Like most of Crawford's friends, Billy didn't push the issue of the children with her. In those days, a parent's right to discipline a child was seen as inviolable; nothing was as important as that. And Billy, accustomed to Joan's easygoing lack of pretense around him, may have only glimpsed the other side of her, the side she showed only to her children after the guests went home and the front porch light was turned off. Already she was beginning to drink heavily, and by the time she adopted Christina, she had been labeled "box-office poison" by movie exhibitors. The fury and frustration she felt was not directed at her friends. They could only watch in awkward silence as she paraded the children past them at parties or kept them confined to their rooms when they'd done something to "offend" her.

Billy preferred not to see that side of his old friend; to him, she was Cranberry, the fun-loving, high-spirited flapper with whom he'd danced the night away in a very different Hollywood, not so long ago.

Not all of Billy's friends proved as loyal as Joan Crawford. In the wake of the El Porto scandal, Carole Lombard gradually distanced herself from Billy—as well as from most of her gay friends. She had become involved with Clark Gable in 1936, and by the following year their romance was the hottest thing in the tabloids. The still-married Gable was in the throes of a bitter estrangement from his wife, who wasn't letting him go without a fight. The movie public rooted for Clark and Carole; they were the "perfect couple," according to the fan magazines.

Not all the fan magazines were happy with Lombard's sudden preoccupation, however. In 1937 *Modern Screen* ran an article entitled "What's the Matter with Lombard?" It lamented the days when she was "free and easy," when she "always gave swell, honest copy, told the truth, and didn't blue pencil every word she spoke."

In the past, Gable had grudgingly endured gatherings with Carole's gay friends: Billy, Andy Lawler, and Mitch Leisen chief among them. The legend goes that he once snapped at her, "Don't you have any girlfriends?" To which Lombard replied, "Sure. Lots of 'em. Why, there's Billy Haines, Mitch Leisen . . ."

By 1937 she had turned her back on most of those "girlfriends." "There was a falling out there," Ted Graber says. "I'm not sure exactly what about, but there was something. The friendship ended." That year she was in a new home in Bel-Air; her decision to decorate it herself and not ask Billy was conspicuous. Certainly the El Porto scandal must have made Gable even more uncomfortable around

Billy. By 1937 Carole had pretty much abandoned her wacky parties and drunken carousing with the gay boys. Instead she went off fishing and duck hunting with Gable and his heterosexual friends: the macho-posturing Vic Fleming, Andy Devine, Eddie Mannix, John Ford, and Jack Conway (Billy's director from *Brown of Harvard*).

Yet one of the more interesting names to take an implicit stand in *support* of Billy during this time was Dorothy Arzner. The director understood well ostracism from the power structure of Hollywood. She may also have felt some brotherly connection with him: Both lived openly with their same-sex partner. Billy's friendship with many in the lesbian circle must have been known to Arzner. In any event, she hired Billy to redesign the sets on her new film for Columbia, *Craig's Wife*, starring Rosalind Russell.

What makes the job even more intriguing is its timing: The very week that the El Porto headlines dominated the front pages of the nation's newspapers, *Variety* reported that Arzner was set to direct *Craig's Wife*. She could not have been unaware of Billy's predicament. That she offered him a job just weeks after this was courageous; it was also a signal of support. There's no evidence that Arzner and Billy knew each other prior to *Craig's Wife*, no link beyond their sexual orientation. (Billy may have been aware of Arzner's decade-old affair with Nazimova; Cukor, friends with Nazimova, certainly was.) Had the hiring taken place at almost any other time than it did, it could be argued that Arzner only wanted Billy for his reputation as a decorator. She certainly wanted those skills, but coming on the heels of the El Porto scandal, Arzner's action carries more significance.

It's known that Columbia chief Harry Cohn (who'd once wanted to hire Billy away from Goldwyn) threatened to fire Arzner after the expense of Billy's redecoration was revealed. But Arzner felt him well worth the cost. She'd been disappointed with Stephen Goosson's set designs, despite Goosson's impressive reputation (he'd win an Oscar the next year for *Lost Horizon*). So she called in Billy. They spent weeks together, heading over to the studio after hours to transform the sets. Together they fashioned a very theatrical look for the Craigs' house. The story revolves around a cold, controlling woman

(Rosalind Russell) for whom being a wife means little more than acting out a role. The set, particularly the living room, has a very definite Haines touch to it: Greek statuary and antique furniture
assembled in a room with highly modern angles and curves. But it's
distant, cold, not the inviting decors one sees in photographs of
George Cukor's house, or Lombard's, or Billy's own. "As a result,"
writes Arzner biographer Judith Mayne, "the sense of the Craigs'
house as a stage on which to perform, rather than a home in which
to live, is accentuated."

Billy received no screen credit for his work; instead Stephen
Goosson receives sole billing as art director. The reason for this is
unclear: Perhaps Goosson's contract dictated it, or perhaps because
of the scandal, Columbia preferred that Billy's name not be attached
to the film.

Regardless, he acquitted himself admirably, and one has to again
ask the question why more movie work—in this case set design
assignments—did not follow. It was partly, of course, due to his own
preference for real houses over movie sets, and a certain loathing to
once again become embroiled in studio life, even behind the camera.
There may have also been a reluctance on the part of producers to
work with him in the aftermath of El Porto, and it's to Arzner's
credit that she hired him—and fought to keep him. *Craig's Wife* was
Billy's first job after the scandal, and also the last motion-picture
work he ever did.

By 1937 Billy had turned his full attention to Haines-Foster, Inc.,
determined that the business would not only survive, but flourish.

His next commission guaranteed his success: the Jack Warner estate in Beverly Hills. It was, by far, his biggest job yet. That the head
of Warner Brothers would turn to Billy Haines—he of the MGM
dismissal, he of El Porto beach—sent an unmistakable message to
the community. Henceforth, William Haines would be the designer
of choice for the movie elite.

Billy owed a great deal to two friends for helping him land the
Warner account: Orry-Kelly and Jack Warner's wife, Ann. Orry, as
chief costume designer at Warner Brothers, continually clashed with

his boss, but he shrewdly became best friends with his wife. In 1936 Warner had married the former Ann Page (also known as Ann Boyar, a sometime film actress) after divorcing his first wife. The ambitious Ann wasn't content to simply move into her predecessor's place. She convinced Jack that the whole estate needed to be revamped, turned into a Hollywood showplace. And she and Orry had just the man to design it.

Billy had known Ann Warner for some time, ever since she was a young and sultry starlet married to the Latin star Don Alvarado. She spent most of her time with Dolores Del Rio and Lili Damita, however, and the three ladies often turned up at Billy's house for parties. When Jack Warner made the moves on her, Ann decided he offered more than Alvarado — or Dolores or Lili — ever could. As wife of the chief of Warner Brothers, the incredibly ambitious and imperious Ann was determined to play queen — and she wanted Billy Haines to design her castle.

A castle it was indeed. A 13,600-square-foot Georgian-style mansion, it was set on nine acres of lush green lawn. Originally the house had been of the now-detested Spanish Colonial style, but Ann had different ideas. With Billy's cooperation, she called in architect Roland E. Coate, who redesigned the fifteen-room house in the Georgian style and added an imposing Greek Revival portico. The grounds were elaborately landscaped by Florence Yoch, who had also designed the outdoor estates of George Cukor and David O. Selznick.

Ann was very precise about what she wanted. "There was a road that went up to the house," says Arch Case. "It went past maybe half a dozen houses from the main road. After they decided to redo the place, Ann said she didn't like all the other houses so nearby. So they bought all the land and tore down the houses. The road became their driveway. That was Ann's way."

Billy was quite simply enthralled to be working on such a magnificent project, and tremendously grateful for the opportunity. Jean Mathison says he made a special trip to Europe to find suitable antiques with which to furnish the Warner house. In keeping with the house's grand facade, he decorated the rooms in a Georgian style and added his own signature touches: eighteenth-century Chinese hand-painted wallpaper panels, corner niches for displaying Wedgwood china, blackamoor pedestals flanking the fireplace.

The front door opened onto a two-story entranceway, with intricately patterned parquetry floors and a majestic cantilevered staircase. "Billy found a magnificent Viennese chandelier for the entry hall," says Jean Mathison. "And shortly after it was installed, the butler was cleaning it up on a ladder, turning it around as he did so. All at once it crashed to the floor, completely shattered. He'd been *unscrewing* it." Ann simply instructed Billy to replace it. No word on whether the butler was also.

"They spent over a million dollars simply on furnishings," says Mathison. "That's like ten million today!"

Jack Warner's favorite room was the library. There Billy scaled the furniture low, to accommodate the studio chief's diminutive stature. On the walls were the film scripts of every Warners picture ever produced, and hidden behind the drapes was a large movie screen. Projectors were installed behind panels that were operated by moving the head of a Buddha mounted onto the wall. Next to the library was a bar, presided over by a statue of the Buddhist deity Guanyin, of whom Ann Warner was a devotee. Above Guanyin hung an 1820 Mexican chandelier, and the bar itself was ornamented with Tang Dynasty pottery.

Ann often held intimate soirees with her girlfriends in the oval ladies' sitting room, centered around a cozy three-seat Louis XVI–style confidante. The main party place was the sunroom. Invitations to the Warner estate had surpassed those to Pickfair or San Simeon as the most coveted by the Hollywood set by the late 1930s. Billy and Jimmie, thanks to Ann, were present at nearly every party. They were there when the portrait of Ann by surrealist painter Salvador Dalí was unveiled in the early 1940s, before three hundred assembled guests. Later, Ann had Billy design a home for her and Jack in Palm Springs.

In 1938 both Bennett sisters, Joan and Constance, hired him to decorate their homes in Holmby Hills. James Dolena was the architect on both houses, designed in the French Provincial style. Joan involved herself intimately in the process, working closely with Dolena on the plans and then with Billy in choosing the furniture and wallpaper. Connie, on other the hand, was more free-spirited, entrusting Billy with all the decisions and then getting furious over his choices. Still, she was pleased with the result: a "Hollywood-French" castle, as she called it, complete with the Billy Haines trademarks of Chinese wallpaper and Louis XVI furniture. She threw a huge party (as she was wont to do) to celebrate the house's opening, feting Billy as if she had never had a cross word with him. Glenn Miller's band played into the wee hours of the morning; Billy danced with Dietrich and shared stories—and vodka—with Noël Coward.

He had conquered Hollywood with his decorating sense and skill: Now he wanted recognition from the larger design industry, which tended to look at him—and other Los Angeles decorators—as Hollywood froth.

"What really established him," recalls Henry Haines, "was the World's Fair up in San Francisco. Bill was one of the few decorators they invited to show. He really made his mark there."

The Golden Gate International Exposition (GGIE) opened on February 19, 1939. Like its sister (and more famous) exhibition the New York World's Fair, the GGIE was built like a small town, with permanent buildings and sculpture. The GGIE was erected on a specially constructed island in the middle of San Francisco Bay. Known today as Treasure Island, the site was begun in 1936 and finished just in time for the fair. An underwater area of four hundred acres was filled in to create the island; it was connected by causeway to the north end of Yerba Buena Island.

From the city, recalled one observer, the GGIE was "a place of lightness and brightness, filed with magic fountains and far-off music and flowers that smelled like perfume ads read." The purpose of the expo was to celebrate the close ties between San Francisco (indeed, the entire West Coast) and Asia and the Pacific islands. The fair's subtitle was "A Pageant of the Pacific," and a huge statue of Pacifica dominated the central courtyard. Visitors were bombarded by beauty and spectacle: Italy shipped art treasures for exhibit, Bell

Telephone demonstrated a machine that duplicated speech, Du Pont displayed nylon hosiery, and showman Billy Rose offered an Aquacade extravaganza.

In many ways, like its New York counterpart, the GGIE was the last celebration of a more innocent and optimistic time: The Depression was over and America had not yet become involved in World War II. When closing ceremonies were held on September 2, 1940, more than seventeen million people had visited the fair.

It's not known what connection brought Billy the GGIE assignment. Certainly his reputation with the Warner and Cukor houses spoke for itself, but such a request from the fair's organizers was extraordinarily prestigious. Already at the New York World's Fair a number of designers had made names for themselves with exhibits. Alvar Aalto, a Finnish designer and architect, was praised in the New York press for his office designs. So was Gilbert Rohde, a New York decorator with several exhibits of rooms and furniture at the fair. The exposure only served to advance their reputations; Billy must have been eager to make a splash at the GGIE.

He certainly did. The room he designed for the Yerba Buena Club building was a departure in style. There was nothing of the English or French manor here: It was an authentically American room, designed with a desert motif. The colors of the room reflected the American desert: cream, tan, deep brown, and black. Walls were made of Joshua-wood veneers, laid in blocks in their natural, unvarnished tones. The rest of the room was almost entirely made of different finishes of leather. The floor was layered in brown leather with natural rawhide crossbars; a backgammon trestle table was spanned with rawhide; and its two saddle chairs were done in deep burnished leather and laced with rawhide. The desk, too, was covered in very pale rawhide, with silver and turquoise hardware. On the wall behind the desk hung illuminated horns of Lucite, gaining their brilliance from a central silver receptacle. A fireplace with silver and turquoise insets complemented the desk; beside it sat a sofa upholstered in fawn felt. Two high windows were draped with curtains of sheer mohair.

One contemporary account calls the room the most popular of the

Yerba Buena exhibits. Another says it was "bold and unique," but despite the attention it brought Billy, reaction on the whole was mixed. "A room which is among the most popular in the whole series and yet which seems cold and lacking in integration," wrote one reviewer. "Individual elements are extremely beautiful, yet the composition seems somehow lacking in warmth or charm."

Still, Billy benefited tremendously from the exposure and publicity. He scored a major coup when he secured permission to use a painting from the artist Georgia O'Keeffe. The exact painting has not been identified; it was one of her series of Southwest desert images. Henry Haines believes it could have been her famous "Animal Skull with Flowers." That an artist of O'Keeffe's standing would consent to her work being used as part of a decorating exhibit is significant. Whether the agreement came about as a result of a personal meeting is not known, but it's possible. O'Keeffe was then the darling of the New York social set, although she was herself unimpressed by their airs. Billy would have had access to her through any number of people: Cole Porter, Elsa Maxwell, Anita Loos. In February 1939, the month the GGIE opened, O'Keeffe boarded a train to the West Coast as part of her journey to Hawaii. She could well have met with Billy then and struck the deal. In any event, her name added considerable luster to Billy's publicity. In 1940 she was named one of the twelve most accomplished American women by the World's Fair Commission.

At least in Hollywood, Billy, too, was — once again — being viewed as a man of accomplishment.

There are virtually no references or photographs of Billy Haines in the trade papers or movie magazines for almost two years after the El Porto scandal. Then, gradually, his face began reappearing on the society page, his name dropped here and there in the columns. Louella Parsons gushed over his work on the Warner house in 1938. He was photographed escorting Constance Bennett and Ann Warner to the premiere of *The Real Glory* in 1939. In October 1940 he was pictured with none other than Mary Pickford in *Movie Mirror*, at a Hollywood fund-raising dinner for the European relief effort. If the doyennes of Hollywood were willing to be photographed at his side, then surely Billy Haines was once again persona grata.

His major reentry into the social word had come at his old pal Marion Davies's Santa Monica beach house in 1938. Ironically, it was also the swan song of William Randolph Hearst: His gala seventy-fifth birthday party would turn out to be his last major public appearance at the fabulous beach house he'd built for Marion. Like San Simeon, the house had been an inspiration to Billy: Hearst imported entire rooms intact from European castles. "Beach house" is a stunning misnomer: The Georgian mansion actually had a total of 110 rooms and 55 baths. Hearst spent $7 million on its construction, deeding the place to Marion. (Mrs. Hearst could—and frequently did—lay claim to San Simeon.)

Ocean House, as the Santa Monica estate was called, boasted the same kind of stellar guest list that San Simeon enjoyed. The King of Siam spent several nights there. There was a 60-foot-long dining table, taken from an Irish estate and reassembled in California, and a ballroom lifted from a Venetian palazzo. The 110-foot-long swimming pool was lined with Italian marble, spanned by a Venetian-marble bridge. Extending across the back of the house facing the beach were eighteen Grecian columns: "more columns than the Supreme Court building," cracked Charlie Chaplin. Indeed, actress Colleen Moore called it "the largest house on the beach—and I mean the beach from San Diego to the Canadian border."

Billy's decors in the early 1930s have the same sense of Old World aristocracy. He was both influenced by and an influence on Ocean House. As Billy's decorating grew, Marion—who ruled Ocean House in a way she never did San Simeon, of which she grew less and less fond—would often call him and ask his advice. Billy never officially decorated Ocean House, but Mitt Foster often bought furniture for Marion on his buying trips to Europe.

Now that the Depression was winding to a close, the parties were cropping up again in Hollywood, and none more opulent than those at Ocean House. "At the slightest drop of a hat, any occasion at all, we would say, 'Let's make a costume party,' " Marion recalled.

The most famous of all was Hearst's seventy-fifth birthday party.

It was a spectacular circus extravaganza that went on for several days. The double tennis courts were covered in a huge tent, with a full-scale carousel trucked in to spin continuously throughout the weekend. The Chief played ringmaster. Several friends were snared into performing under the big top, and everyone came in costume. Henry Fonda arrived as a sad-faced clown; Bette Davis turned up as a bearded lady. Hedda Hopper prowled around the floor with a whip, slinky as an animal trainer. Bareback rider Dolores Del Rio rode in on the arm of her husband, Cedric Gibbons. Most notable of all, Cary Grant performed a daredevil acrobatic stunt with Randolph Scott. They called themselves the Flying San Simeons.

Among the other guests were Jack and Ann Warner (Marion was now working for Warner Brothers), Gable and Lombard, Loretta Young, Mary Astor, Adela Rogers St. Johns, Frances Marion, Joan Bennett, Leslie Howard, Robert Montgomery, William Powell, Irene Dunne, George Jessel, James Stewart, Van Johnson, Patsy Kelly, Sonja Henie, and, of course, Louella Parsons. Old friends from the silent days were there, too — Ramon Novarro, Aileen Pringle, Dutch Talmadge, Claire Windsor. Serenading them all was Tommy Dorsey and his orchestra.

Hearst had the time of his life playing ringmaster to the stars. The audience cheered the agile antics of Grant and Scott; they oohed over the stunning grace of Del Rio and Gibbons; they laughed uproariously at the tomfoolery of Ed Wynn. When Hearst announced the next act, there was sustained applause: Billy Haines, in tights and paste-on mustache, strode out onto the ring and took a bow.

"I am a magician," he declared, and he was right. Certainly the crowd loved his act — seeming to decapitate Marion Davies — but they were also applauding his ability to re-create himself, as if by magic, yet again. His position as one of the privileged princes had been reaffirmed by his appearance with Marion at his side. When the old man — William Randolph Hearst — dropped his big arm around Billy's shoulder, there could be no denying that William Haines was back on top.

———

Among those cheering in the audience was Jimmie. He, too, had been welcomed back by Hollywood society, all things forgiven and forgotten.

Not everyone felt so kindly toward the pair, however. Even among those gathered at Ocean House there were some who found Billy and Jimmie a bit too outrageous, a bit too different. Cary Grant had distanced himself from them, for obvious reasons. Bob Montgomery still grumbled under his breath about all the "fairies" in Hollywood. The very Catholic Loretta Young always thought Billy a bit too scandalous for her taste. Once, when she asked him to contribute something to an auction benefiting unwed mothers, he sent over an antique vase—filled with condoms.

Most striking of all, however, was the distance between Carole Lombard and her old friend and designer. Sitting with Gable in the bleachers during Billy's act, there must have been some tension, some words left unspoken. Did Gable ever admit to Carole the encounter with Billy? If not, he must have wondered if Billy ever had.

Gable and Lombard were finally married in 1939, during the filming of *Gone With the Wind*. Margaret Mitchell's best-seller was being triumphantly transferred to the screen by David O. Selznick, with George Cukor directing. Gable made no secret of his unhappiness with Cukor; he claimed he was "throwing the picture to the women," particularly his friend Vivien Leigh. It was true that Leigh and her lover Laurence Olivier were frequent Sunday guests at Cukor's house; such familiarity troubled Gable. He was even more disturbed by the director's habit of addressing his actors—male and female alike—as "darling" and "dear." Cukor's fussiness over hairdos and costumes irritated Gable to no end. Lombard egged him on with her own anti-Cukor tirades: She had never forgiven the director for once calling her uncouth and refusing to let her into his house. Gable told Selznick he would much prefer his buddy Victor Fleming to take over the helm.

"He and Victor Fleming were very macho people and they had great intolerances," Selznick's assistant Marcella Rabwin told Cukor biographer Patrick McGilligan. "One of the intolerances was for gays, and one was for Jews. They always referred to Mr. Selznick and Mr. Cukor in very unflattering terms. They always referred to David Selznick as 'that Jewboy up there' and Cukor as 'that fag.' "

Billy Haines was Cukor's occasional guest on the *Gone With the Wind* lot. The director borrowed one of Billy's eighteenth-century paintings to hang on the walls of Tara. His presence may have further unnerved Gable. The legend goes that Andy Lawler was at a Hollywood party and announced, quite loudly and quite likely high on cocaine, that "George is directing one of Billy's old tricks." The laugh at Gable's expense got back to him, and he was outraged. (One story has Gable going to Billy's house and threatening to beat him "within an inch of his life" if he ever heard the story repeated again. It could have happened, but probably didn't.)

Whether there is a direct link between Lawler's remark and Cukor's subsequent firing from the picture—an ouster demanded by Gable—will never conclusively be known. Reportedly, Gable snarled on the set, "I won't be directed by a fairy," and Cukor walked off. Gable then failed to report to work. Struck by such an impasse, Selznick made the only decision he could. The public would accept no one else as Rhett Butler; they really didn't care who directed the end result.

Kevin Thomas of the *Los Angeles Times*, a longtime, respected Hollywood reporter, emphatically believes the "Billy's trick" comment had nothing ultimately to do with Cukor's departure from *Gone With the Wind*. There were many other forces at work there, the creative clash between Cukor and Selznick topping the list. Cukor himself was always coy on the subject, claiming he couldn't remember why he was fired.

Bob Wheaton says the story of Gable's outrage over Lawler's remark—and his decision to force Cukor out because of it—was considered gospel among Cukor's intimates. Michael Pearman also stands by the accuracy of the story. Cukor did admit privately to friends that he'd known about Billy's encounter with Gable. Certainly that was information the macho star (and his Cukor-loathing girlfriend) would have preferred he didn't have. It would be too naïve to assume that gossip about Billy and Gable had nothing to do with the antagonism between star and director—just as it would be perhaps too simplistic to say it caused Cukor's ultimate dismissal. Lawler's wagging tongue, however, might just have been the proverbial straw that broke the back of an already strained, angry, and frustrated star.

Far away from such studio backstabbing, Billy spent the late 1930s and early 1940s enjoying the fruits of the bountiful harvest provided by the Warner commission. He bought the house next door to his on North Stanley; this became the home of his father and two brothers. Their old housekeeper, Buffy Braxton, came back from Virginia to cook and clean house. Billy also brought his beloved widowed aunt Mary Haines Fifer to Hollywood. With Laura gone, Aunt Mary became a surrogate mother to him. She had helped the family financially back in 1917; now Billy was glad to return the favor.

Eventually both his brothers married and left the house on North Stanley. George's wife Julia worked for Billy at the design studio. Henry and his wife Margaret had two daughters, Virginia and Amanda. When Billy's father George became too old to care for himself, he went to live with Henry and Margaret and their family.

Billy made sure his family never wanted for a thing. That was especially true for Jimmie. Unbroken by the El Porto headlines, Jimmie continued to live as high as Billy's income would allow. Until 1939 Billy had driven a Franklin, and was content to keep his cars for years at a stretch. Jimmie, however, then became enamored of the new Lincoln Continental, introduced to the market just that year. Designed by Edsel Ford, the car became an overnight status symbol. It was long and low, with classic, simple, sweeping lines, powered by a smooth twelve-cylinder engine. "Some people called these the most beautiful cars man has ever made," observed Charlie Barnard of *Time*. "Others, more interested in how automobiles performed than how they looked, called the sainted Continental a dog on wheels."

For Jimmie, appearance was always more important than performance. Only a handful of Continentals were built, creating an exclusive club of drivers. Jimmie desperately wanted to be one of them. Of course, Billy complied. Of the five thousand cars built between 1940 and 1948, more than half were still running when the third generation, the Mark III, debuted in 1968. No other American car has ever beat the Lincoln Continental's survival rate. Jimmie wasn't satisfied with just the original, however: He had to have each new model as it came out. Michael Pearman remembers him whining, "Oh, Billy, buy me another Continental." And each time, Billy did.

In his own home, Jimmie was the most precise host, insisting on the proper silverware and after-dinner liqueurs. At other people's parties, however, especially after he'd had a few drinks, Jimmie often stirred up trouble. "There was a sense that Jimmie should've learned his lesson from the beach incident," says one friend, "but he just continued to carry on." More than one embarrassed host or hostess had to apologize to a handsome young actor or soldier who'd been the recipient of an unwanted grope from Jimmie. Now thirty-five, Jimmie was watching his own youthful beauty slip away, and the handsome movie star he'd married was balding and not a little bit paunchy. "Jimmie, unlike Billy, was not going gracefully into middle age," the friend explains. "I guess you could say he was kind of acting out—as so many of us old queens do."

Not all the old queens, however. Among their crowd some had begun to weary of Jimmie's shenanigans. Many couldn't understand why Billy continued to put up with him.

George Cukor was one who thought this way. There has been an assumption that Cukor's celebrated friendship with Billy endured for decades, when, in fact, they grew steadily apart after the early 1940s.

The reasons remain hazy. "I think Jimmie broke that up," says Arch Case. "There was always talk that Jimmie caused some mischief at George's house," adds Bob Wheaton.

Wheaton became friends with Cukor in the mid-1940s. He doesn't remember Billy at any of Cukor's parties or Sunday brunches during the period. Billy is never listed among the names on Cukor's dinner-party guest lists after 1940, and only rarely is he mentioned in the director's voluminous correspondence after that date.

"George never talked directly about what the problem was," says Wheaton, "but he'd say, 'Jimmie is a mischief-maker. He stirs things up.' " Wheaton assumes Jimmie somehow violated Cukor's house rules. "George had a very strict rule that only he was allowed to break, and that was you never messed with anybody else's boy-friend. George would say, 'The fun of [the gatherings] is that we get all these new faces. If somebody starts stealing them, then people aren't going to bring new faces around anymore.' "

The "new faces" were aspiring actors, sailors on shore leave, the pretty young nephews of studio executives. Sharing tricks was one thing; horning in on somebody's date was another. "There was a pro-tocol to it all," Wheaton continues. "If George liked the boy you were with one weekend, he'd tell you, 'I think he's awfully attractive. Could I ask him for dinner sometime?' And you'd say yes or no. If you said yes, then he'd wait for an appropriate time and he'd ask the kid and take it from there. But Billy and Jimmie—especially Jimmie—broke that protocol."

What might they have done? Friends think it was probably as simple as Jimmie being overly flirtatious with someone else's date. Worse, he may have hit on a young man in whom Cukor was inter-ested. Some have suggested, on no real basis, that Cukor discovered Jimmie (or Billy, in a variant account) in the bushes with another guest. While that's possible (the suggestion would also be made a few years later at Cole Porter's), more likely their offense was merely a breach of Cukor's highly disciplined protocol.

Still, there had to be more than that to sever a decade-long friend-ship. It may well have been that Cukor had grown weary of the un-predictability of Billy and Jimmie—a delayed reaction to his scare at El Porto beach, perhaps. The flap over Gable and *Gone With the Wind* may have further strained the relations between the three friends.

Cukor put some distance between himself and Andy Lawler around this time, too. It was a "quieting down" period in Cukor's life, in that he rarely went out to nightclubs and often even declined

dinner invitations to private parties. His Sunday gatherings continued, and the steady stream of famous friends continued to pass
through his house. Now, however, there was less of a boisterous
spirit, less recklessness. By all accounts, by 1940 Cukor was no
longer interested in the kinds of sexual romps he and Billy had
searched out a decade before.

Such was not the case with Billy. He still enjoyed a party at the
Vendome or, later, at Chasen's or Mocambo. He was notorious for
being the center of a party. He enjoyed making people laugh and
sometimes drank too much. Cukor was not a big drinker; there was
never much alcohol stocked at his house. Sometimes Billy and Jimmie would bring their own bottles to Cukor's soirees. They both enjoyed their liquor, and drank more as they got older. Similarly, Andy
Lawler often brought a stash of cocaine, but knew never to make his
habit obvious to the more straitlaced Cukor. By the 1940s, Cukor
surrounded himself with more serious-minded people than Billy or
Lawler, people with whom he could sit in his oval room and engage
in witty, animated discussions of art, theater, and literature. For his
part, Billy found such conversation far too pretentious.

The tightly knit group of cronies from the 1930s gradually drifted
apart. As often happens, people change, interests diverge. Andy
Lawler, on the strength of his friendship with Virginia Zanuck, wife
of Twentieth Century-Fox chief Darryl Zanuck, was named producer of *Somewhere in the Night*, directed by Joseph Mankewicz. Suddenly, late in life, this washed-up actor and Hollywood "walker"
saw his career take off. He moved to New York, where he copro-
duced Jerome Chodorov's *Oh Men, Oh Women!* and later Tennessee
Williams's *Camino Real*, directed by Elia Kazan. Billy noted with
pleasure his old friend's "second chance" at life: Billy, too, had
proven the Hollywood skeptics wrong by reinventing himself.

It couldn't have helped Billy's standing with Cukor, either, that by
this time he was good pals with Cole Porter.

The composer had become Cukor's chief rival as Hollywood's gay
host. They knew better than to set themselves up in direct competition: Porter's Sunday gatherings were for lunch, Cukor's were for

dinner. Bob Wheaton says their rivalry was mostly an unspoken thing—they were extremely friendly in public—but friends who were invited to both houses knew to be diplomatic. "I had lunch at Cole's and dinner at George's," Wheaton says with a laugh, "but you never told one about the other."

In 1936 Porter—the toast of the Broadway musical stage—began spending half his year in Hollywood. Although he was married to the much older Linda Porter, Cole was quite open about his sexuality, at least among the Hollywood insiders. He took particular delight in the raunchiness of the Hollywood crowd. After one memorably risqué dinner, Linda Porter told one guest, "My dear, I've heard all those words before, I've even *done* most of them, but I'd prefer not to dine on them." Thereafter, for the remainder of their marriage, Linda was rarely in Hollywood, preferring to remain back east.

Porter offered Billy something that Cukor—for all his steady parade of fascinating guests—could not. Porter was an integral part of a dazzling international social set, skipping from party to party and city to city and continent to continent. He moved in a world that included royalty and industrial barons. He was part of a new and still coalescing phenomenon, a high society–show business hybrid dubbed Café Society. To a great degree, he and Linda had helped create this phenomenon during their years living in Europe. Linda was quite comfortable with the considerable gay component of Café Society. Her dearest friend was the decorator Elsie de Wolfe, who made no secret of being a lesbian, even after her marriage to Charles Lord Mendl. There was also Lucius Beebe, a Boston Brahmin who coined the phrase "Café Society"; Maury Paul, "Cholly Knickerbocker" of the Hearst press; and Elsa Maxwell, hostess extraordinaire.

To the Hollywood gay scene Porter brought an East Coast—even a European—sophistication. Now it wasn't just Dutch Talmadge or Cranberry Crawford partying with the boys. It was Dorothy Parker, Diana Vreeland, and Lady Diana Duff Cooper. There were some in Porter's circle with whom Billy was already friendly: Noël Coward, Michael Pearman, Jean Howard, Anita Loos, Fanny Brice, Tallulah Bankhead. Through Porter he now also met Scott Fitzgerald, Philip

Barry, Prince Michael Romanoff, Howard Sturges, and Moss Hart. He also became acquainted with the actor Monty Woolley, who had been Cole's friend since their days at Yale.

In Hollywood, their gathering spot of choice was the Vendome. Porter's Café Society friends—from the European royalty to the American capitalists—all added California to their annual travel itinerary. Billy was eager to find a place in this world, and he appears to have been welcomed.

Certainly their sensibilities gelled. In the mid-1930s, Lucius Beebe wrote in his syndicated column that perhaps no more than five hundred people in the world qualified for "membership" in the society. They were Renaissance men and women, Beebe wrote, "in that they did something well and never in their lives thought to consult anyone else as how to conduct their persons. They all possessed that one radiant qualification: the knowledge of excellence. . . . If anything is worth doing, it is worth doing in style, and on your own terms, and nobody goddamned else's!"

Billy's defiance in the face of studio manipulation served him well in the minds of these people. Even more, his re-creation of himself into Hollywood's premier designer—and one who challenged old notions of what was considered fashionable—endeared him to many. It's interesting to note that Billy—who never suffered snobs gladly—would be so eager to find acceptance within Porter's crowd. Beebe, of an old Massachusetts family like Mitt Foster, proudly called himself "one of the last few true snobs of America." He was also gay and quite campy; indeed, there is an element of irreverence in most Café Society members that Billy would have found appealing.

Still, there was also a sense that these people—more than the Louis B. Mayers, the Clark Gables, even the George Cukors—were the top echelon. There must have been something quite affirming for Billy to find acceptance among the most fashionable, most exclusive club in the world, an affirmation that not even William Randolph Hearst and Jack Warner had been able to give him.

Cole Porter was his means of entry into this world. As he had with Cukor, Billy introduced Porter to the gay circles of Hollywood. The composer was soon addicted to the place—the climate, the easy money (MGM paid him $75,000 for twenty weeks of work on *Born to Dance*), and the raucous social whirl. He rented the luxurious mansion of Richard Barthelmess, a great old movie-star house with tennis courts and a large swimming pool. "I like it here," he told the columnist Dorothy Kilgallen. "It's like living on the moon, isn't it?"

Part of what attracted him was the seamier side of the film colony. In the mid-1930s, he and Billy, along with Monty Woolley and Howard Sturges, often wandered along the beaches or picked up sailors in Pershing Square. Billy helped introduce Porter to the more notorious cruising spots in the area; their bond was fast and immediate. A love of sex was something they had in common.

There's a story that upon Porter's arrival in Hollywood, he and Billy Haines had a brief but tempestuous affair. It's an intriguing tale, but peculiar if true. Porter did look far younger than his forty-four years in 1935, and he had the handsome, soft features that attracted Billy. But none of their mutual friends believe the story to be true. Billy's sexual escapades tended toward anonymous tricks with younger, unknown names. Jimmie would not have tolerated an ongoing affair with someone as prominent as Porter. More likely Porter and Billy were simply whispered about: A new friendship between two known homosexuals was enough to set the town's tongues wagging.

Even after his riding accident in 1937, which left him with minimal usage of his legs, Porter didn't slow down the social whirl. Elsa Maxwell threw a "coming out" party for his legs in 1938 when the casts came off. Among the guests were Clifton Webb (a frequent performer in Porter musicals), Bea Lillie, Ethel Merman, and Moss Hart. Billy wasn't there—the party was held in New York—but he *was* at another party Maxwell chronicled in the 1940s. Arriving in Los Angeles from San Francisco, Maxwell wrote, usually required a week to acclimate—"but not when you step practically off the train into Cole Porter's lovely house and garden near Santa Monica." At this party, rival host Cukor deigned to visit; Maxwell wrote that he was "witty and brilliant." Cary Grant was also there, "handsomer than ever," as were Constance Collier, Jack and Ann Warner, the Basil Rathbones, and Somerset Maugham.

This party was held at Porter's new residence, a house he rented from Billy. It was a magnificent mansion at 416 North Rockingham Drive in Brentwood, next door to Joan Crawford's house. Billy bought the house from the director Henry Hathaway during this period; it's possible he saw himself living in it at some point. Most of his friends and associates now lived in Brentwood or Beverly Hills or elsewhere; very few continued to live in Hollywood itself, as Billy still did. He decorated the Rockingham house elegantly, and threw a huge bash to christen it. Cole came, fell in love with the house on the spot, and begged Billy to rent it to him. "He couldn't *buy* a house out here, you see," says Arch Case. "He couldn't live here because then he'd be taxed here. So he spent exactly one day less than six months every year in Hollywood."

Beginning in the spring of 1942, Billy began renting the house to Porter for $6,600 a year. He was thrilled to see so many from the international smart set enjoying themselves at a house he owned. Jean Howard remembers a typical guest list at Porter's house on Rockingham Drive included Noël Coward, Fanny Brice, Clifton Webb, Gertrude Lawrence, and Elsa Maxwell.

Bob Wheaton says he met Billy and Jimmie at Cole Porter's house in the early 1940s. "They were often there then," he says. "They were all quite good friends."

And it wasn't just the sexual adventures that bonded them. Cole (and Linda, for that matter) appreciated the same kind of elegant living Billy did. Cukor might host fabulous dinner parties, but they lacked the exquisite taste and formality—some might say pretension—so evident at Porter's. "The Porters had a great deal to do with brushing Hollywood up on its social graces," says Jean Howard. "For instance, most of us were accustomed to arriving at parties at 8 o'clock and never getting near the dinner table before ten. Naturally we'd be pretty well looped by then. Well, the Porters put an end to that. You were invited for 8:15, had time for two drinks, and were served dinner on the dot of 8:45. If you were late getting there, too bad."

Both Porter and Cukor were fascinating in their contradictions. Whereas Porter tended to be more elegant in his formal dinners, his

Sunday gatherings were casual and often giddy, with parlor games and loud music. Cukor forbade music, and he often proclaimed to be shocked by risqué stories. "He acted scandalized, like some maiden aunt," one friend said. Porter, on the other hand, delighted in ribald tales, and certainly Billy knew a few of them. When it came to serving guests, Cukor was famous for his double standard: French wine for Miss Gish, a California vintage for his buddies. Porter, whose guests included self-proclaimed snobs like Lucius Beebe, was far more egalitarian. "He would serve the same thing to everyone, sailors or royalty," one friend recalled.

Just as they had at Cukor's, however, both Billy and Jimmie enjoyed imbibing more than their host. Porter, much like his rival party-giver, had no tolerance for sloppy behavior. Orry-Kelly, who was fast becoming a famous lush, was known to never get an invitation to Cole's. As long as Billy and Jimmie confined their more raucous behavior to their jaunts with Cole to Pershing Square, they were welcomed as part of the posh soirees at Rockingham Drive.

The gatherings at Cukor's and Porter's might have been the best-known and most fabulous gay circles in Hollywood, but they weren't the only ones.

One of Billy's newest competitors on the decorating scene was James Pendleton, a New York decorator who moved out to Hollywood in 1940. His stunning house in Beverly Hills was built by architect John Woolf, modeled on drawings of pavilions at Versailles. Billy must have encountered Pendleton at Cole Porter's; Pendleton was close with Linda Porter's good friend Elsie de Wolfe, who had helped in the design of his house. Pendleton's parties were known to attract a number of famous names; even Garbo was known to seek refuge there, swimming naked in his pool. Frank Lysinger, then a handsome young serviceman, recalls seeing Billy and Jimmie at a number of Pendleton's galas. Despite his lovely house, Pendleton was not considered in the same league as Cukor or Porter.

"There *were* other circles," says Bob Wheaton, "but not of any eminence. There were other people who gave parties, but they didn't have the big houses or the big names."

One who did was the Paramount director Mitchell Leisen, but his preference was for less ostentatious gatherings. This despite the fact that his reputation for camp and carousal was famous throughout Hollywood. Leisen was rarely a guest at Porter's, and never a guest at Cukor's. "I suspect," says the artist Don Bachardy, whose lover, the writer Christopher Isherwood, had recently arrived in Hollywood, "Leisen may have been a bit too flamboyant for George. George had a very discreet wish to not draw attention to his queerness."

Bob Wheaton says, "You never saw Leisen at Cukor's. I suppose they wouldn't have liked sharing the spotlight. Parties, you see, were given by celebrities for a bunch of acolytes—there was only one person allowed center stage."

Two who loathed the spotlight were the director James Whale and his partner, the producer David Lewis. There's some debate over just how much the change in the political climate of Hollywood impacted their careers. Like Billy and Jimmie, Whale and Lewis lived openly together. Lewis was not yet at MGM when Billy departed in 1933, but he did produce Cukor's *Camille* in 1936; it's likely that Billy met him and Whale at least then. They tended toward reclusiveness, but Lewis was friendly with Norma Shearer, Frances Marion, and Kay Francis, so it's possible Billy encountered them socially. The careers of both Whale and Lewis were essentially over by the early 1940s, however; in at least one published interview, Lewis implied they were victims of the studios' intolerance. After that, they retreated far from the Hollywood social scene and seem to have played little part in the gay set.

Much different was Clifton Webb, who had returned to Hollywood in 1942, signed to a contract by Spyros Skouras, president of Twentieth Century-Fox. Webb became a close and lifelong friend of Billy's. They were, despite their obvious differences, two of a kind. Gossip columnists might still sometimes link Cukor romantically to an actress; MGM even went so far as to cast Cary Grant as a devotedly heterosexual Cole Porter in *Night and Day*. There was no such tomfoolery about William Haines or Clifton Webb. "Oh, yes, they were certainly a pair," says mutual friend Bob Shaw. "Good, good friends—a lot in common. Both very funny, very independent men."

Webb was to the 1940s and 1950s what Billy had been to the 1920s and 1930s: an actor who did not try to disguise who or what he was, and got away with it through a quirky relationship with Hollywood and with the press. Billy used his wisecracker persona to deflect probing questions. Webb, even in a more conservative era that saw the rise of such scandal sheets as *Confidential*, was able to weather any innuendos in the columns through a witty persona of his own. After his enormous success as a columnist with a viper's tongue in *Laura* (1944), he launched into his phenomenally popular *Mr. Belvedere* series of pictures. Mr. Belvedere—with his witty, bitchy banter that sounded as if it had been lifted from one of Cole Porter's parties—allowed Webb to adopt a cynical, untouchable persona that seemed impervious to gossip. His age, too—he was fifty in 1944—made the studios less concerned about his "old maid" image. He and his mother Maybelle became one of Tinseltown's most popular couples.

Webb was the anomaly. The new models for the new decade were Janet Gaynor and Adrian, who married in 1938, and Barbara Stanwyck and Robert Taylor, who wed in 1939. Gaynor, who'd have a long relationship with the actress Mary Martin, embarked on an almost-as-durable marriage with MGM's gay costume designer. This was just as her stalled career was revived with *A Star Is Born*. Stanwyck, who'd told Crawford she was through with men after her divorce from Frank Fay, agreed to pair off with (and eventually marry) Taylor when studio executives felt it would be good for both of them. Such alliances were given big promotions in fan magazines, depicting the happy couples to be gloriously in love. Hedda Hopper went all out to tell how mad Gaynor was for Adrian. The players involved even sometimes came to believe the myth.

Robert Taylor, before being selected as the latest MGM player to be groomed for top stardom, had been involved with Gilmor Brown, the director of the Pasadena Playhouse. Brown's homosexuality was well-known, and he was a frequent guest at many of the town's gay soirees. Harry Hay recalls Brown, with the very young and very beautiful Robert Taylor on his arm, attending a party at Mercedes de Acosta's. Taylor seems to have struggled personally with his sexual identity; his marriage to Stanwyck was not simply a "twilight tandem" but a genuine attempt to conform. Stanwyck, too, threw herself into the effort, despite the fact they never shared a bedroom. She would be incensed by Taylor's affairs with other women; there were no reliable reports of any affairs with men.

Given the nature of the times, it would have been *impossible* for a young gay actor to blossom both in his career and in the natural development of his sexuality. Unlike a decade previous, when the carefree Cary Grant first landed in Hollywood, there was no freedom, no differentiation between screen image and offscreen life. As new stars emerged, they did not have the example of Billy Haines to point to as Cary Grant did. Instead, they had Grant himself: trapped in a series of disastrous marriages.

By the late 1930s there was a new kind of gay star: deeply closeted, even to close friends. Tyrone Power, who catapulted to stardom in 1938 with *In Old Chicago* and *Marie Antoinette*, seems to have been primarily homosexual. He'd been lovers with John Barrymore's stepson Robin Thomas, and then replaced Robert Taylor in Gilmor Brown's affections. Later he reportedly was involved with the sexually freewheeling Errol Flynn. And yet even to himself he seems never to have identified as gay, not even to the degree Cary Grant admitted it to himself. If such a word had been in common usage then, Power and those like him might have toyed with "bisexual" as a personal description, but Power was no more bisexual than Billy was. He had affairs with women and married several times, but that didn't make him heterosexual—*or* bisexual. His biographer Hector Arce talked with a well-known Hollywood hustler with whom Power had had a longstanding relationship. In this man's opinion, Power "was basically a homosexual who 'found himself married with girls from time to time.' "

Power, linked to Janet Gaynor before his marriage to the actress Annabella, might have found a life similar to Billy's had Hollywood been the way it was a decade earlier. According to several sources, the handsome star had a lovely romance with Cesar Romero. They took a studio-sponsored tour of Latin America together and remained close friends. For any sense of an ongoing relationship with

a man, however, Power was forced to pay his hustler. Later, he became friendly with Rock Hudson, providing a closeted role model
for a yet another generation of gay actors.

Deeply closeted stars like Power would never have been seen at
one of Porter's or Cukor's parties. "Oh, no, never," says Bob
Wheaton. "Tyrone Power would have been too uptight, too worried
about his career." Power and his wife instead hosted their own Sunday afternoon galas in their Brentwood home, not far from Cole
Porter's. They'd bought their house from Grace Moore, a friend of
Porter's; they could have mixed with that set had they chosen.
Rather, their parties featured Keenan Wynn and his wife Evie
(who'd later divorce him and marry Van Johnson); James Aubrey
and his wife Phyllis Thaxter; Rex Harrison and Lilli Palmer; and
David Niven and his wife Primmie. The only guest who straddled
both worlds was Cesar Romero, who was notoriously tight-lipped
about Power at any gay soiree he attended.

Edie Mayer Goetz, the daughter of the despised Louis B., entered
Billy's life again around this time. She was often at Cole Porter's, and
she threw some fabulous parties herself. "Cole Porter loved me," she
said, "because he was a hedonist and he loved the way I entertained."

Her husband was William Goetz, studio chief at Twentieth
Century-Fox. Mayer had desperately wanted his son-in-law to work
for him (his other son-in-law, David O. Selznick, had tried that for a
time before going off on his own), but Goetz was an independent
man, quite the opposite of the belligerent Mayer. Billy liked both
Edie and her husband, and no doubt appreciated the irony of his
friendship with the daughter of the man who'd wrecked his career in
pictures.

An even bigger irony, of course, was his commission to redecorate
the Goetz home in Holmby Hills. By hiring Billy, Edie Goetz was
ensuring that his new career would prosper. Like the Warner estate,
the Goetz house was a plum: Edie and Bill were one of the most
popular couples in Hollywood, and getting an invitation to their
home was a major social accomplishment.

Billy's plan for their house was simple and elegant, designed to showcase their magnificent art collection. There were Cézannes, Renoirs, Manets, and Picassos; a Degas sculpture of a dancer stood on a table in the living room. Although Edie would later have a much-publicized quarrel with her father (they never reconciled), they were still friendly at this time. One can only imagine his comments about the house the first time he saw it after Billy had finished; he was said to be very impressed.

Another important commission with a Mayer connection was Jean Howard's house, completed in 1942. Howard, also part of the Cole Porter set, was then the wife of Hollywood agent Charles Feldman. In the early 1930s, she had been ardently wooed by Mayer, who'd been infatuated by the former Ziegfeld girl's beauty. She made a few films but wasn't really an actress; Mayer promised to divorce his wife and make all her dreams come true. Instead, she married Feldman—a severe blow to Mayer's ego.

Billy worked on Howard's house for a number of years. "Bill Haines has great taste," Linda Porter wrote from New York in 1938. "I am sure your rooms are lovely." They were indeed—she has never changed them since. The walls have never even been repainted. Writes design historian Tim Street-Porter, "It remains, more than fifty years later, a showcase of timeless design."

Although decorator Tony Duquette did some touch-up work in succeeding decades, Howard takes pride in having one of the few Haines decors still extant. She'd been impressed with the Warner estate, she says, and insisted only Billy could do her house. Her living room especially remains just as he decorated it, with his signature touches of chinoiserie in the lamps and chandelier. "He was absolutely marvelous," says Jean Howard, the last of Hollywood's great ladies. "And his work still stands the test of time."

On December 7, 1941, their carefully constructed world forever changed. After the Japanese attack on Pearl Harbor, President Franklin Delano Roosevelt declared war against Japan. Three days later, war was declared against Germany and Italy as well, and America was officially part of World War II.

Sentiment had been growing in Hollywood—and all across the

nation—that the United States had no choice but to get involved. Sympathies were clearly on the side of the Allies, especially after the fall of Paris in June 1940. In Belgium, Billy's old friend Prince Charles was a virtual prisoner of the Nazis, to whom his brother, King Leopold III, had surrendered unconditionally. When Leopold was forced into exile in 1944, Charles stepped in as regent. Unlike the king, who was called a traitor for his surrender, the prince was viewed as a hero by his countrymen. The United States later conferred upon Charles the Order of the Legion of Merit for his services to the Allied cause both before and after Belgium's liberation.

Billy must have been aware of his old friend's heroism. For Hollywood, with its large British community, the war really arrived much earlier than Pearl Harbor. It was part of the town's consciousness from the moment Britain declared war against Germany in 1939. Movie executives feared the loss of European markets; many British stars returned to their homeland; and some gung-ho Americans ran off to join the conflict even before the United States was officially at war. Billy probably found Robert Montgomery's dramatic departure to serve in the American Field Service in France a bit theatrical. Soon others had joined him: Douglas Fairbanks, Jr., secured a position in the Navy, and Jimmy Stewart enlisted in the Air Corps.

Billy found the whole idea of Fascism frightening; he believed the danger to the United States to be very real. On December 9, two days after Pearl Harbor, the *Los Angeles Times* ran the headline, "Enemy Planes Sighted over the California Coast." Whether true or not, it was enough to convince Marion Davies that she'd seen a Japanese plane shot down over the beach at Santa Monica. Billy encouraged her to leave Ocean House and take refuge at San Simeon.

War fever continued to build. The California Evacuation Corps was formed, with three of Billy's friends—Robert Young, Cesar Romero, and Buster Keaton—being recruited because they owned station wagons. They practiced drills for the best routes out of the city and to the hospitals. Jack Benny converted his badminton court into a victory garden, growing vegetables for the servicemen overseas. Claudette Colbert trouped around the country raising money for the families of those killed in action. Carole Lombard embarked on an ambitious tour selling U.S. defense bonds. When the interning of Japanese-American citizens began in California, few were surprised. Most, fired by fear, supported the idea.

Still, Billy's life proceeded quite as it had. He was completing work on the Goetz and Howard homes; the parties at Cole Porter's continued unabated. Except for the occasional European relief fundraiser, he didn't throw himself into war work the way some had. When in January 1942 Lombard's airplane, returning from her highly successful bond-selling tour, crashed into the side of a mountain and killed everyone on board, she was hailed as a war hero. Billy was stunned and deeply saddened by his old friend's death. Although he'd been hurt by her distance from him, he maintained the marriage with Gable couldn't have lasted. "She'll come back," he told friends. Now she never would. Touched by her death, Billy even sent a note of condolence to her widower.

Lombard's death moved Gable to enlist in the war. That was hardly Billy's reaction. "Can you imagine *me* as a soldier?" he asked friends. Apparently Uncle Sam *could*, because in the fall of 1942 Billy was drafted into the Army. He was both shocked and horrified at the prospect, although he had to have known it was possible. In December a new selective service law had been passed, making men between the ages of eighteen and forty-five liable for military service. The law also required all men age eighteen to sixty-five to register. Billy complied with the registration, but probably assumed that his age — forty-two — would keep him out, even in the chance he was called. Just as his youth had (barely) kept him out of World War I, now he hoped his maturity would do the same.

In 1918, however, the argument could have been made that he had a family to support; in 1942, that wasn't the case (at least not according to the government's definition of family). What's ironic is that the more macho Spencer Tracy, who was the same age as Billy, was never drafted; he was heckled around Hollywood for his lack of service. Fred Astaire did, in fact, have a low draft number and might have been called, but at age forty-three, married and with three children, he was passed over.

As it was, Billy's entry into the war afforded him greater respect in Hollywood. Those like Tracy who avoided service endured the community's scorn. John Garfield, despite his founding of the Hollywood Canteen with Bette Davis, was nearly blacklisted by the studios and fan magazines for his refusal to enlist. Lew Ayres's pacifism earned him stinging rebukes from columnists. Even the forty-six-year-old Charles MacArthur, husband of Helen Hayes, felt people looked down on him for his lack of service. He eventually caved in, secured himself a major's commission, and went off to war.

Billy certainly would have faced pressure from his peers, but nothing as public as those still actively working in the film business. George Cukor held out while older colleagues like Frank Capra and John Ford quickly enlisted. Finally Cukor joined up, around the same time Billy was drafted, serving as a private in the Signal Corps.

Often (as was the case with Cukor) studio officials tried to work out agreements with the Pentagon, finding appropriate work for their actors or directors—and preferably duties that would keep them out of harm's way. Billy had no guardians to look out for his interests, but he appears to have made a case that he could best serve the war effort stateside. At age forty-two (almost forty-three), a bit plump, and easily winded (all those years of smoking were having an effect), he wasn't a prime candidate to fight in the trenches anyway.

He was certainly not his grandfather, a hero of the Confederacy. Still, he faced the inevitable with determination and dignity. He left the business in the care of Mitt Foster; any decoration work, however, was put on hold. Jimmie was evidently excused from service on the basis of his 1925 medical discharge. Billy was officially inducted into the U.S. Army in San Francisco on October 6, 1942. He endured three weeks of basic training—a grueling experience for anyone, but especially for someone who detested brute physical labor the way Billy did. The days were long—up before dawn and training past sunset. He was forced to jog three miles a day. If nothing else, the experience put him in the best physical shape he'd been in in ten years.

At the end of basic training, he was transferred to Tucson, Arizona, where he was given a special assignment: camouflage. "What else did you expect for a curtain hanger?" he'd say later, laughing, to friends. Clearly, the military had listened to Billy's argument that his special skills should be accommodated. He was soon in charge of a unit that designed, among other things, special netting to cover cannons (Billy concocted an artistic mosaic of twigs, leaves, and soil) and elaborate covers for Army buildings. "The Axis will never see a thing," he promised his superiors. He also oversaw the production and painting of camouflaged jeeps and uniforms.

Recognizing his abilities, the Army promoted him to a staff sergeant. His brother says Billy took his duties seriously, lecturing the soldiers about the necessity of hygiene. "He couldn't stand the smell of dirty socks in the barracks," Henry Haines says.

Within a matter of months, however, he was honorably discharged, separated from the Army at Tucson on March 19, 1943. Reports in the Hollywood trades said he was being released because of his age, adding that he'd go into "defense work" at home. What kind of work that was is unclear: Likely he continued to contribute to the war effort in some way, donating materials, ordering furniture, or "hanging curtains" at military bases.

What Billy found upon his return to civilian life was a town overrun with handsome young servicemen. After the war ended in 1945, their numbers only increased, as many left their Midwest homes and settled in Shangri-la.

"Billy had an absolute thing for uniforms," says one friend. "Maybe that's why he was so good in those marine pictures. He just couldn't resist a handsome young man in uniform."

Frank Lysinger was one such man. "I met Billy at the old Club Gala on Sunset Boulevard," he recalls. They were both just out of the service; Club Gala was known to attract a large gay clientele, many of whom were servicemen. "There was a man named Johnny Walsh who played the piano there and sang. He was sponsored by the old Baroness d'Erlanger. She was kind of in her dotage then, poor old thing, with her hair dyed red and white roots. But a sweet old gal. She'd wander around and make all of us feel at home."

Lysinger was still in the Air Force, a young buck in his midtwenties with a flashing smile and spiffy uniform. "I guess Billy kind of fancied me at that point," Lysinger admits. "I went to the rest-room, and he followed me in. He patted me on the rear end and propositioned me." Lysinger is prudent in revealing what happened next. "I'd heard he was a top man, and I said, no—well—wrong thing."

There were plenty of other, more compatible young men. "Holly-wood was brimming with horny, available young soldiers," says one friend. "Absolutely brimming!"

Frank Lysinger was one of the few who moved on to become a friend. He says Billy's—and Jimmie's—exploits in the early 1940s became legendary. "Bill loved gang bangs," Lysinger says. "More than one at a time. I had a friend who used to be invited up to Bill Haines's very often. For daisy chains, you know."

Billy was squarely in middle age by this point; the beautiful college boy of *Brown of Harvard* was long gone. Besides the thinning hair and paunch around the waist, he'd developed vitiligo on his hands and scalp, causing discoloration and blotches on his skin. Many men, vain about their own fading looks, become increasingly sexually aggressive in their forties, hoping to prove themselves still vital and attractive. Billy had always enjoyed a healthy sexual appetite, however.

He wasn't alone in his pursuits. Jimmie, too, continued to put the moves on men he found appealing, and the "daisy chains" he arranged on North Stanley Street for himself and Billy were frequent and delightfully decadent. It certainly kept the erotic fire burning between the two of them after nearly twenty years of marriage.

If anything, Jimmie's libido was even stronger than Billy's. "Jimmie was a happy little whore," says their longtime friend and client Francie Brody.

"Jimmie had hot pants," says Ted Graber. "He'd get everybody all riled up."

One of those riled up was Cole Porter. As in the split with Cukor, the blame for the break with Porter is usually laid at Jimmie's feet. Unlike with Cukor—where the end of the friendship seems unspecific and vague, perhaps the result of a growing difference in person-ality—the estrangement from Porter came about suddenly after a messy incident at the house on Rockingham Drive. "Something happened where they were no longer friends," says Arch Case. "Just what that was, who knows anymore."

Several friends offer plausible scenarios. "It broke up, as I understand, because Billy—everybody—had had a few too many drinks," says Bob Wheaton. "Everybody would change clothes in the same dressing room, and it turned into a kind of bath house." Very often, Wheaton says, there were servicemen invited to Porter's parties, and apparently this particular Sunday afternoon Billy—or Jimmie—or both—found them too hard to resist.

Bob Raison, another friend of Porter's, often told the story that Cole happened to discover Jimmie in the act with a serviceman out in the bushes in the middle of a Sunday luncheon. As with Cukor, things had been building up for some time. "One Sunday afternoon, it just came to a head," Raison said.

"Cole was not the kind of man to tolerate that kind of behavior," says Wheaton. "Yes, he was gay, and he talked a lot, and made a lot of jokes, but you didn't come out and talk about blow jobs—or do it—in the middle of lunch."

Most likely, Porter said nothing upon discovering his guests. He just returned to the table. Frank Lysinger remembers, "Cole would say, 'I would never make a fuss with anyone who was behaving badly, but they would never be invited again.' "

Which is precisely what happened to Billy and Jimmie. They would have realized their expulsion from Café Society only gradually, when the invitations stopped and didn't resume. The break likely occurred sometime in 1944. Wheaton says he left for the Navy early that year; things were fine between Porter and Billy then. When he returned in 1946, things were different. "Something happened in this period," he says, "because Billy and Jimmie were never invited after I got back."

In 1944, too, there is other, dramatic evidence of their falling out: Billy tried to evict Porter from his house. Their agreement had stated that Cole had the option to renew his lease at the end of every year. Billy—possibly perturbed by the sudden hostility—asked him to vacate that spring. Porter dug in his shoes. He filed suit in federal court to force renewal of the lease, charging that Billy had rented him the property two years previously with the express understanding that the lease could be renewed at the end of each year. The one provision was that Porter had to give written notice of his intent to stay sixty days in advance. Porter claimed he'd met the terms of the agreement; Billy charged he'd never received notice.

The suit was resolved before making it to a judge: on what basis is unknown. Billy was soon adding a sunporch to Porter's house at the composer's request, and the residence remained Porter's Hollywood address for the rest of his life. Jimmie's nephew Charlie Conrad says Billy tried to get Porter out of the house for years, jacking the rent up at each renewal. The composer just kept paying the increasingly outrageous sums. Finally, the hostility was smoothed over, but Billy and Jimmie were never again part of Porter's circle.

Once again, they had proved just a trifle too outrageous for the gay social arbiters. Don Bachardy's observation that Mitchell Leisen may have been too flamboyant might also be applied to Billy. While not "flamboyant" in the general sense of the word — meaning, among gay men, flighty, campy, prissy, or queeny — Billy was, nonetheless, fond of acting out. "Billy could be very campy," says one friend. "Sometimes he'd get on stage and wouldn't get off. He could get a little flirtatious. He was an outrageous camp." Might that have been just too much for Porter to bear?

"No, that wouldn't have bothered Cole," insists Wheaton. He cites as an example one Mother's Day when Roger Davis showed up at the house dressed as Whistler's Mother. "All the white ruffles and everything," Wheaton says, "with a Marine on one side and a sailor on the other. It had all been worked out by Billy and Jimmie. They'd organized it. Cole loved it. So that kind of thing wouldn't have bothered him. he was just put off by raw sex. 'After all,' he'd say, 'we're gentlemen.' "

Still, Charles Williamson, a friend of Cukor's, recalls that Billy had a reputation for "exaggerated behavior." He was known for being unpredictable. That alone made both Porter and Cukor — control queens of the first order — uneasy.

The ostracism Billy and Jimmie faced by the mid-1940s was not from the community at large. They'd never have considered pulling such mischief at Edie Goetz's house, or the Warners'. There, they were indeed "gentlemen," perfectly—even elegantly—behaved. At the homes of their gay friends, however, they felt more comfortable dropping their reserve, their cultivated manners, becoming again the reckless boy who'd made his way through Greenwich Village and the young lusty sailor who'd picked him up on the street.

Of course, another factor was their increasing fondness for alcohol. Both Cukor and Porter had an aversion to sloppy drunks, and, sadly, there were times when such a label could be applied to Billy and Jimmie. "He was still going out to the gay clubs, you see, places like Club Gala," says one friend. "He was a middle-aged man who didn't know it was time to go home. He was like someone who'd stayed too long at the party."

Another friend, then a young man newly arrived in Hollywood and later a well-known clothes designer, recalls being at a gay party in the 1940s where Billy was present, one of the oldest guests there. "He was very, very drunk," the friend says. "At some point he went into a room and a line formed outside the door. He was servicing everyone who lined up. I know. I was third in line."

Such behavior was enough to exile him from the most exclusive gay circles. Billy Haines had always been known to push the envelope. Now he pushed himself too far. Or rather, gay Hollywood—restrained by its own discipline to not rock the boat or draw attention to itself—pushed *him* away. As far as it could.

9

THE SMART SET

1945-1968

After the war, after the split from Porter and the Hollywood gay social scene, the life of Billy Haines became his own. His fame now existed chiefly in retrospect. A new generation of gay players arrived; George Cukor and Cole Porter were left to play dowager queens, receiving homage and granting favors. To many of the new crowd — actors, reporters, studio chiefs — Billy Haines was a name from a far-distant past.

Curiously, it was only after the war that Billy settled into the life he'd always sought to find, became the person those close to him consider the "real" Billy Haines. "A cultured host," says one friend. "A man of superb taste," says another. "The preferred decorator of the privileged classes," one newspaper account opined. "Friend of the rich and famous," adds one associate, "and I don't mean just movie stars."

Indeed, the last twenty-eight years of his life were marked by affluence and privilege beyond what he'd known among the movie set. Billy had made enough friends through his decorating to sustain himself both financially and socially, and from these friends he ingratiated himself into a world of ever-increasing prestige. He didn't need Porter or Cukor to provide entrée to the elite anymore; he had Ann Warner and Edie Goetz. From them he gained Francie Brody and Anita May, and from them Lee Annenberg, Betsy Blooming-dale, and Nancy Reagan—among many others.

"Bill Haines was friends with all of the great society ladies" of southern California, says Jody Jacobs, former society editor at the *Los Angeles Times*. These were, most often, the wives of the area's "merchant princes," the largely self-made men who'd made their fortunes and reputations as retail or industrial giants. Others, like the Reagans, were ambitious politicians. All wanted to live like royalty, as befit their hard-fought-for status. And to whom did they turn to make that dream a reality? Their wives knew: Billy Haines. He was their darling, and in many cases, their mentor. They found him—as so many of his female friends had over the years—both charming and amusing, cultured and refreshing, a delicious respite from the stodgy male company they were used to.

They called themselves "the girls," says author Kitty Kelley, who spoke with hundreds of people in Los Angeles high society for her biography of Nancy Reagan. "They weren't to the manner born," Kelley writes. "Nor were they schooled in the niceties of old-family decorum. Most were former actresses and divorced models who acquired their taste from their interior decorators." Their husbands "had earned their money in the get-rich-quick areas—nursing homes, used cars, oil, and gas—not in the professions of law, medicine, and banking. Such wealth might not have been acceptable to the Cabots of Boston, but it made little difference in the social circles of Beverly Hills."

Billy did several houses, dating from the late 1940s, for Tom and Anita May of the department store family—so many houses that he jokingly said he should change his name to "William May Haines." Through the 1950s and early 1960s, he also did work for oilman Henry Salvatori and his wife Grace; publishing magnate Walter Annenberg and his wife Lee; Sears Roebuck heir and movie producer Armand Deutsch and his wife Harriet; and the Canadian prospector Duncan McMartin and his wife Hilda, including two houses in Bermuda. These were people who didn't flinch when Billy said he spent $50,000 per room in a thorough redecoration—and that didn't include the cost of the art and antiques. During this time, if Billy Haines, the boy from Staunton who'd once hustled himself along the streets of New York, *didn't* become a millionaire himself, he came very, very close.

It was in this world that Billy spent nearly the last three decades of his life. It was a world he'd aspired to and prepared for ever since his ambitions were first stirred by the upper-crust glamour of his Fifth Avenue paramour. This world, like those of Cukor and Porter, offered its own challenges and potential traps. Billy Haines's navigation among the aristocracy of Los Angeles ultimately proves as illustrative and insightful as his passage through gay Hollywood.

As if to symbolize their departure from the past, Billy and Jimmie moved from their elegant movie-star house in Hollywood to a more modest but infinitely better located address in Brentwood. Billy didn't sell the house on North Stanley right away; for a time he rented it out to the actor John Garfield. Henry Haines recalls that when Garfield vacated the house some years later, he left the formerly exquisite mansion in a sorry state of disrepair.

Billy's new house was at 601 Lorna Lane. "He took my father and me up there to see it," says Henry Haines. "To put it mildly, I was unimpressed. But Bill knew what could be done with it."

Especially after the grandeur of North Stanley, many of Billy's friends and associates were surprised by his choice. The new house was set in a modest neighborhood on a small lot, built by the previous owners with a loan from the Federal Housing Administration. (Billy would joke that he decorated castles, but *lived* in an FHA house.) The property was purchased for just $5,600 from Arthur James Zander on May 22, 1944. Notably, for the first time, Jimmie's name was included on the deed. Both he and Billy were granted an "undivided, one-half interest" in the property.

According to Henry, Billy called in an architect, made plans to raise the ceilings by four feet, then took off for Europe with Jimmie. By the time they'd returned, the house had begun its transformation. "I liked it better than the big house," says Henry Haines's wife

Margaret, "because the rooms were arranged more comfortably." Still, she admits, "it would take a certain amount of showmanship to use it to its advantage."

Billy's motivation for such showmanship was not only for himself. "This is where I bring clients and prospective clients," he said. "If we were selling automobiles, this would be our demonstration car. Not that we take pen and ink in hand and sign a client at the table. It's simply the best way to expose them to a certain quality of life as I live it. Showing is always more meaningful than telling over the barren top of a desk."

He filled his new home with the treasures of his old residence: the antique chairs, the magnificent chandeliers, the priceless paintings. In the living room, a nineteenth-century white marble fireplace rose from the center of the floor. He knocked down a few walls and installed large glass windows overlooking the pool. Outside, Greek and Roman statuary stood among the cypress trees. Jimmie's nephew Charlie Conrad recalls the lush setting around the pool, the sense of "peaceful splendor." Christina Crawford remembers her first visit to Uncle Willie's new home and being awed by his "fabulous" garden.

Most memorable, however, was the hand-painted wallpaper that formed an elaborate mural, "Les Incas," in the sunken living room and the bar area. "It was absolutely, fantastically beautiful," recalls Henry Haines. So beautiful, according to Billy's friend Bob Shaw, that Jack Warner insisted at one point he needed it for a film. "Billy agreed to have it all peeled off very carefully and sent over to the studio," says Shaw. "Warner kept it so long Billy finally had to say, 'I'm going to sue you, you bastard,' to get it back." When Warner at last complied, Billy had men on ladders, pasting it back onto the walls piece by piece. It took about six months to complete the task.

Billy planned to enlarge the house even further, according to Arch Case, but was thwarted by his own lack of foresight. "Billy was cheap a few times in his life," says Case, "and one of them was when he didn't buy the vacant lot next door when he should have." Consequently, the Haines home remained a small but resplendent jewel.

———

As time went on, Billy added more and more modern elements to the period decor of 601 Lorna Lane, as well as to his designs for others. Much of this was due to the influence of a young man who, after Jimmie, became the most important person in his life.

"Ted Graber was the son Billy never had," says Jean Mathison. That dynamic came to characterize their relationship, but it didn't start out that way. Ted Graber was a bright, charming, and extraordinarily handsome young man the day he first stepped into Billy's office in late 1945. He was fresh out of the war, twenty-six years old, and as ambitious as the young Billy Haines had been a generation before. He was the son of Edgar Graber, a highly regarded antiquarian and furniture maker in the Los Angeles area; Billy had purchased a number of pieces from him over the years, notably for the Warner house. Edgar Graber provided his son with an invaluable apprenticeship. "In those days," Ted would recall, "craftsmen . . . could do anything. Because I had a thorough grounding in *how* to do something, as well as in *what* to do, anything I dreamed up could be accomplished."

Such cocky determination appealed to Billy. Ted was a great deal like him: brash, resourceful, and unapologetically gay. (So well accepted was Ted's homosexuality that his mother actually fixed him up with his lover Arch Case some years later.) Ted was also some things Billy was not: well-educated (he'd studied at the Chouin and the Art Institute in Los Angeles) and attuned to the changing times. In the postwar era, Billy Haines needed someone like Ted Graber.

"It was one Saturday after I'd gotten back from the war," Ted Graber recalls today. "My mother and I stopped by Billy's studio, just to chat. He was an old friend of my father's, who had just died. Billy asked what I was going to do now that I was home. I said I thought I'd try the studios, maybe do sets. He said, in that great big voice of his, 'That's not for *you*. You don't want to get in that rat race. Why don't you come in and work for me?' "

Whether just such a scenario had been Graber's hope from the beginning he won't say. He admits he didn't have to consider Billy's offer very long. "I accepted right there and then," he says. "If I was going to be a decorator, I was starting at the top."

His lover Arch Case suggests there may have been a little sub-
terfuge on Billy's part as well. "Ted was young and very cute," he
says. "But wise. Wise enough to say no." Graber understood that to
have lasting impact, he had to be more than the trick of the week.

If Billy had envisioned a pretty young assistant around the office,
submissive and subservient, he was taken by surprise when Graber
reported for work the following Monday. "Billy was always scrubbing the floors and keeping everything clean," he says. "When I
came in, he was down on his hands and knees scrubbing the john. I
gave him a kick in the ass and said, 'Get up.' I said, 'You hire a cleaning lady. Don't you ever clean this shit house again while I'm with
you.'" Billy just looked at his new assistant a long while. Then he
said, "You tough little son of a bitch."

It was the start of a tempestuous but loving relationship that
lasted twenty-eight years. Ted did indeed become a surrogate son to
Billy, who always called the younger man "boy." For Graber, it was a
dream come true, both professionally and personally. "To have had
two fathers in one life has been an extraordinary gift," he says.

Billy learned a great deal from Ted as well. What started out as an
apprenticeship became, in all but name, a partnership, with Billy
recognizing Ted's craftsmanship and his uncanny sense of the changing times. Although he had (and still has) a deep respect for period
styles, Graber was determinedly modern in his approach to design. "I
lean to light, modern backgrounds," he later told an interviewer, "to
twentieth-century upholstery to fit the twentieth-century man. Have
you ever *sat* on a Sheraton love seat? You were happy to get off, I'm
sure."

Out went the uncomfortable antiques; in came new, modern,
more relaxed furniture. Out, too, went Mitchell Foster, who had actually withdrawn from active involvement in the business during the
war. Foster wasn't a designer; that had never been his interest. He
was approaching sixty, and with the move toward the modern, he
decided to retire. He and Billy remained good friends for the rest of
Foster's life, however.

"Billy sensed there was a change coming," says Graber. "He said,
'We have to leave things in the past. We have to go for the modern.'"

The new enterprise, William Haines, Inc., wasn't simply a decorating concern: Now, spurred by the talents of Ted Graber, they began designing and constructing furniture for their clients as well. One innovative design—a sleek, modern upholstered chair with a tight seat and back, all in one piece—was dubbed "The Seniah" ("Haines" spelled backward). Design critic Pilar Viladas has praised the Haines-designed furniture as "strictly no-nonsense," while retaining a sense of style. "His simple elegant sofas and armchairs are as comfortable as they look," she writes. Particularly innovative was the hostess chair, "an invention that was to Haines rooms what the slipper chair was to [New York designer] Billy Baldwin rooms." Billy had actually first come up with a rudimentary design for the hostess chair in the 1930s for George Cukor's house. Low to the floor, it was sometimes swiveled and always grouped with others around a low table, creating "an intimate scale even in a grand room."

As much as Billy's overall sense of style may have inspired such pieces, however, the credit for their design and construction must really go to Ted Graber and, a few years later, to Michael Morrison. "Billy was incredibly fortunate to work with such gifted employees," says one friend. "They allowed him to continue beyond the war years and be accepted as a modern designer of note."

To celebrate the new direction and image for the company, Billy moved from his studio on Sunset Boulevard to a spectacular new space at 446 South Canon Drive in Beverly Hills. Billy owned the building, but leased the front spaces to retail businesses. The studio was housed in back, a stunning display of modern architecture and design. It was even photographed and written up in the prestigious art journal *Interiors* in 1949. Designed with architect William F. Cody, it was built primarily of brick and spun glass on an irregular plan. This allowed for the incorporation of small garden courtyards within the property, providing daylight to each room. In the showroom, the fireplace was made of polished brass; around the cantilevered sofa the apostles of Buddha stood on nearly invisible blocks of Lucite. The walls of Billy's private office were painted pink; his desk was robin's-egg blue.

Such modern style would have been inconceivable a decade before. Billy's studio quickly became the talk of the town. *Interiors* called it "a design which combines working efficiency with a lush, almost regal air—the better to impress clients with." Once more, Billy Haines was setting the trend by which Hollywood designed their homes.

In 1950 he hired another young, talented decorator, Michael Morrison, who was also an architect. There was bound to be some rivalry between him and Ted. Both are circumspect about it today, saying only complimentary things about each other. Graber's lover Arch Case says, "It became very competitive between Ted and Michael [over] which one was going to be the right-hand man of the studio."

Morrison says Billy allowed him—and Ted—great leeway. "All the time I was working for him he was very busy. He just let me do all the stuff. I was his designer. We'd kind of stockpile things. He'd use this chair and that table for different jobs. It's really funny to see people extolling the Bill Haines designs that I made over the years. But even after I left him, Bill was very generous about giving credit. I ran into Lee Annenberg once, after Bill had done her house in Palm Springs. He'd told her that I'd designed every single thing in her house."

Billy's staff had grown considerably. In addition to Graber and Morrison, there was also his brother George, who ran odd jobs, and George's wife Julia, who acted as office manager. In 1955 Billy made another significant hire: Jean Hayden, who today goes by her married name of Mathison. "I'd come down from Oregon to Los Angeles on holiday," she recalls. She was then just out of college, looking for a career. "I took one look at the palm trees on Wilshire Boulevard and said, 'This is for me.'" She took a job in newspaper advertising, but after that company went under, she landed a two-week temp job at Billy's studio, filling in for Julia Haines. When the two weeks were up, Billy asked her to stay on as secretary. She was faced with a dilemma: She'd wanted a career in newspapers, and wasn't even sure how long she'd stay in Los Angeles. "So I told him,

'Yes, I'd like to join your family.' Really, in just those two weeks, that's how I felt about the office. But I wouldn't let them get me a desk. I sat on a kitchen chair for two years. Of course, thirty years later I was still there." And yes, she finally got her own desk.

They were, in fact, a functioning family: Billy as Dad, Ted and Mike the competitive brothers, Jean the supportive sister. And Jimmie the occasional Mom, bringing lunch over to the studio and taking them all out on shopping sprees.

"It really *was* a family, that's the only way I can describe it," says Mathison. "I admire Billy Haines more than anyone else I've ever known. His essential decency, his integrity, his generosity, his compassion. That's not to say he didn't get angry. With that booming voice of his, he could be like Thor when he wanted. But we were quite the team."

They were the pick of the elite, and their fame quickly spread. "Billy used to tell stories of women who'd come out from Iowa on the bus," says Bob Shaw. "They'd walk by and see his name out front. Billy was always very cordial when they came in. He'd let them talk and talk and gush all over him. They'd say, 'I have this blue sofa and my living room is pink and Mr. Haines, should I buy a pink pillow or a blue one?' And he'd tell them, 'I'd love to help you. I should tell you first, however, that my fee is a thousand dollars an hour.'

"With that, they were always out of there and back on the bus."

By 1950 Billy estimated he had decorated, in full or in part, four hundred homes. One of his new projects was for Sid and Francie Brody, and it became a landmark of modern design.

A sharp, funny, classy lady, Francie Brody is the daughter of the legendary Albert D. Lasker, called the "father of modern advertising" for bringing such products as Kotex and Kleenex, Sunkist and Studebaker, Pepsodent and Palmolive, to America's consciousness. By the time he left advertising to concentrate on philanthropic works with his wife Mary, he'd made $45 million—more than anyone else had ever made in advertising. Francie came from considerable wealth, and Sid Brody had made his fortune in the expanding market of shopping malls. Together they were one of the most affluent couples in Hollywood.

"When I was a little girl," Francie Brody recalls, "I thought William Haines was sensational up on the screen." She was just ten when Billy made *Brown of Harvard*, fourteen when he was the country's top box-office star. "I fell in love with him then, and fell in love with him again later on."

It almost didn't happen that way. She and Sid met Billy at a dinner party given by Joan Crawford. Billy, knowing they were looking to design a house, had arranged to sit at their table. Even the prospect of new clients didn't keep him on his best behavior. "Bill was absolutely stinking drunk," Brody says. "He was terribly insulting. He never stopped talking and taking digs. Perhaps he thought he was being funny, but he was terribly offensive. It was a horrible evening. Well, the next afternoon, I came home to my rented house in Beverly Hills and there, in the very small front hall, was a box the size of a coffin filled with cut flowers."

Ted Graber recalls the episode. "Billy said the next day, 'I've been baaad.' He decided to send her a roomful of flowers to make up for it."

Graber says that wasn't the only occasion in which Billy, having had a little too much to drink, regretted his actions the next day. There are other cases of clients getting their feathers ruffled only to have them smoothed the morning after. Given that his drinking may also have been the catalyst that hastened the end of his friendships with Cukor and Porter, the question needs to be asked: Did he have an alcohol problem?

"Oh, no, no," says Arch Case, "Billy wasn't a great imbiber." Most of his friends concur. Occasional excessive drinking wasn't seen as being indicative of a deeper problem in those days, as it often is today. Still, Billy's lifelong pattern of mood swings fits the profile of an alcohol or other substance abuser. He seems never to have allowed alcohol to interfere with his job performance, but there are enough stories to suggest he found a certain refuge in social drinking, especially as he got older. A man of few inhibitions anyway, he may nonetheless have found alcohol released any lingering restraints he imposed upon himself, allowing him to speak and behave among his jet-set friends the way he'd once cavorted with Cukor and the boys—with his own brand of campy candor. When it went too far, there were always flowers—tons of them—to patch things up.

In the end, Francie Brody gave Billy another chance. The Brody house in Holmby Hills was a dramatic departure for him, as the design was extremely contemporary. "That house is still by far the best-looking modern house of that type," says Michael Morrison, who tackled the commission as his first job with Billy. He designed much of the furniture in the stark, ultramodern, highly functional house, including an ingenious dining table that could accommodate three or thirty-one, and bookshelving that concealed storage cabinets inside the shelves.

"In modern architecture," says Francie Brody, "the rooms are all designed on angles. You simply can't go into Macy's and buy your furniture."

The house, with its spacious, angled rooms, was designed by noted architect A. Quincy Jones. It was Billy's first job with perhaps his best-known collaborator. Like James Dolena, Jones had considerable influence on Billy's work, and despite some superficial differences, they formed an expert, productive relationship. Jones, then thirty-seven, was no more than five-foot-seven and quite plump; Billy, now in his fiftieth year, still stood a towering six feet. Jones was reflective; Billy was outrageous.

Still, they meshed well. Billy had nothing but admiration for Jones. Called a "great humanist" in the development of California architecture, Jones was part of a group of young Modernist architects that flourished after the war. The streamlined style of their work replaced the opulence of Art Deco as the Hollywood "look." Jones taught at the School of Architecture at the University of Southern California. (He later served as dean.) According to architectural historian G. E. Kidder Smith, he "inspired young practitioners with a vital concern for creating a better environment and a better, more human shelter for all." His chief legacy, beyond all the fancy houses he designed for Hollywood's aristocracy, was improved tract housing—several thousand individual homes—that utilized natural land instead of the bulldozed sites that had so blighted the California landscape.

Francie Brody was delighted by Billy's down-to-earth advice as well as his sense of style. "It was the most pleasant experience my husband and I ever had," she says. "We worked every Wednesday night, every Saturday afternoon, and a case of whiskey a week." All in all, it took a year to plan, a year to build. The Brodys moved into their new home on Valentine's Day 1952. "Most people are supposed to have a miserable time building a house. We had a great time—and everything has lasted." She still boasts a William Haines decor today, although it was spruced up by Ted Graber several years ago.

The Brody house inaugurated Billy as a modern decorator. Although he'd continue to use antiques as part of his designs, most of his commissions now were contemporary; Lucite and Plexiglas became as frequent as mahogany and crystal. The late 1940s through the mid-1950s was really his busiest period. He did work for Barbara Stanwyck and Robert Taylor, the producer Nunnally Johnson, and the director William Seiter, whose brother Bob may have once been a trick shared by Billy and George Cukor. There was also a specially decorated yacht for Leila Hyams and a bus for her husband Phil Berg. (Now retired from agenting, Berg lived in his bus when he'd go off on architectural digs.)

One of Billy's most outstanding projects was the Mocambo nightclub. He was still a frequent patron of Hollywood's clubs: the Vendome, Chasen's, Ciro's, and now Mocambo. A Venetian carnival motif ruled throughout, with dozens of birds behind glass and a nearly pitch-black lighting scheme. Much of the artistic design was done by another young Haines protégé, the artist Tony Duquette. Duquette was also being sponsored by Elsie de Wolfe, who'd spotted a centerpiece of his at a Jimmy Pendleton party. She pronounced Duquette a genius, hired him to design furniture for her, and launched him on a successful decorating career that continues to this day.

Then there was Kitty LeRoy. The wife of the producer-director Mervyn LeRoy, she'd call the studio and brainstorm with Billy, then do the work herself and claim it was a "Bill Haines original." Even years later, the association was perpetuated. Michael Morrison, who actually *did* do LeRoy's house after he left Billy, says that when her furniture went up for auction recently, "people were still saying it was a Bill Haines design."

Later in the decade, Billy decorated the home of George Burns and Gracie Allen. Gracie had always wanted a house designed by Billy Haines; after she got it, Mary Benny (as usual) followed her lead and hired Billy to do some rooms for her and Jack. Then there was an office for Frank Sinatra, and a suite for Jack Warner at the Sherry Netherlands Hotel. And, in the most sublime of ironies, Billy did the home of Lorena Mayer, the widow of Louis B., after her remarriage. One can only imagine the titillating conversation that took place under that roof.

In 1949 Billy had been approached by the director Billy Wilder, who asked him to appear in the "waxworks" scene of his upcoming *Sunset Boulevard*, a black comedy about an aging, demented silent-screen star to be played by Gloria Swanson. As Wilder envisioned it, Swanson would be seen playing cards with a gathering of her contemporaries, a quiet but revealing moment of broken dreams and lost lives. Buster Keaton, Anna Q. Nilsson, and H. B. Warner agreed to take part, but Billy Haines turned Wilder down.

His reasoning was obvious: He was hardly a waxwork. "I'm content with my work," he told the columnist Ezra Goodman. "It's clean, no mascara on the face." He added: "It's a rather pleasant feeling being away from pictures and [also] being part of them because my friends are. I can see the nice side of them without seeing the ugly side of the studios."

Clearly his treatment by Mayer still rankled. It was reported at the time that he was working on an autobiography in the form of a novel, *The Silents Were Golden*, depicting, in his words, "an actor's rise and fall." Whether this is the same manuscript his friends recall him writing is unclear. Henry Haines remembers Billy working on a memoir with the help of screenwriter Frances Marion. At one point,

they toyed with the idea of writing it from the point of view of an antique chair at San Simeon, observing all the comings and goings. "It
wasn't very good," Henry admits.

Michael Morrison also read parts of it. "I tried as tactfully as I
could to get Billy to find an editor for it. There was just too much
Victorian flamboyance to it. But it was fascinating, described everything about San Simeon. It could've been a very good book."

The project eventually went nowhere. Friends believe a copy may
still exist, but no one quite knows where. It's intriguing to think how
Billy might have described his "rise and fall." While he apparently
still held some bitterness about the experience, he wasn't letting it
prevent him from leading a rich and rewarding life.

He escorted Joan Crawford to the premiere of *Sunset Boulevard* in
the summer of 1950. He adored the picture, its peeling back of the
Hollywood myth, and congratulated Gloria Swanson roundly.
When someone complained afterward that movie stars were never
that loony, that silent-film mansions were never that ostentatious,
Billy quickly defended Wilder's interpretation. "Bebe Daniels,
Norma Shearer and Pola Negri all had homes with ugly interiors
like that," he said. "I went through that period with all of them. Gold
lace shawls draped over pianos and fancy vases filled with pussy wil-
lows. Our homes gave off the odor of milk and ashes."

Billy Haines had played a large part in changing that. Now he
was on the edge of contemporary style, with an increasing amount of
work being done in Palm Springs, the new fashionable getaway for
the Hollywood set. He and Jimmie bought a house there, done over
in "wormwood," or "wormy" chestnut: a beautiful wood paneling of
variegated color and tiny holes. In Palm Springs, Billy occasionally
socialized with Charlie Farrell and Virginia Valli; Jack and Ann
Warner were frequent guests at his house.

Of all his remaining movie connections, however, only Joan
Crawford was as constant as in the past. In the 1950s she was defiantly clinging to the stardom Billy had put behind him. She was desperately unhappy: Her third marriage had failed, her two oldest

children were acting out against her rigid authority, and she was drinking more heavily than ever. Moreover, her films were infrequent and undistinguished. Four years younger than Billy, she turned fifty in 1954 (although she claimed to be just forty-six). She was fiercely proud of her still-taut, shapely body, especially her legs, but her features had hardened into the familiar mask of her later career. She was a formidable presence to most, but to Billy she remained just Cranberry.

During the filming of *Torch Song* in 1953, her first film back on the MGM lot in a decade, Joan insisted Billy visit the set. She'd been dazzled by Howard Strickling's publicity marking her return; WELCOME BACK JOAN read the banner over the MGM studio gate, and her dressing room overflowed with flowers. It must have been intriguing for Billy to venture back onto the lot himself. It was two years since Mayer's unceremonious resignation, hounded out, from the studio he'd founded, by pressure from East Coast shareholders. Billy was unimpressed by the whole experience of being back on the lot. A guard, not recognizing his name, asked him for identification. Later, growing bored as he watched Crawford perform a strenuous dance number, Billy began reading a newspaper. She threw a shoe at him.

"Cranberry," he told her, marveling at her endurance, "you amaze me."

"God must have his hand on my shoulders, Willie."

"I don't know about the shoulders, Cranberry," he cracked. "But only God could get your legs up that high."

He was bemused by her fierce attachment to her star status. Their mutual friend Betsy Bloomingdale recalls during the filming of *Johnny Guitar* in 1954 that Joan showed up at Billy's house for a swanky dinner party "still in her cowgirl outfit, the guns still on her hips." Crawford explained she'd just come from the studio. Billy laughed. "I know you, Cranberry. You just wanted to come to dinner dressed in that outfit, whether you just came from the studio or not."

Billy would tell friends, "The Princess is coming to dinner," and they knew he meant Crawford. Sometimes he called her the "empress of emotion." Possibly because he'd helped shape it, he remained amused by the fierce Crawford persona of which so many others were terrified.

They spoke at least three times a week. When she was working, she sometimes had her devoted secretary, Betty Barker, call Billy with jokes she'd heard on the set. Even after she moved to New York, she would call Billy for advice and ideas; he was still her arbiter of good taste. "Joan valued his opinions very much in all ways," says Betty Barker. "Whenever Joan gave a party, she would contact Billy and ask about what wines to serve with the dinners. He had taught her how to live graciously through the years. She depended upon him for guidance. She said he was 'well brought up' and 'knew everything.' "

For her part, Barker struck up a particular friendship with Jimmie. "It seemed sort of that Joan and Billy were the top echelons and we were the minions, which didn't bother us a bit," she says.

Joan's move to New York was prompted by her fourth marriage, to Pepsi-Cola magnate Alfred Steele. Squat, middle-aged, and homely, Steele nonetheless appealed to Joan because he was her equal: a star every much as important in the business world as she was in Hollywood. "He loves me even without my makeup," Joan gushed to Billy, "and in the sack, he's a tiger!" They eloped to Las Vegas and were married on May 9, 1955.

Billy had his reservations about Al Steele, whether he was good enough for Cranberry. Still, he couldn't deny or begrudge his friend's obvious happiness. He insisted that she needed some kind of reception, that an elopement took all the fun out of marriage. So he and Jimmie hosted a gala party at their home on Lorna Lane upon the Steeles' return from their honeymoon in Capri.

"It was an extremely elaborate party," remembers Bob Shaw. "Two, three hundred people, with drinks out around the pool. *Everyone* was there."

That included another old female pal from the past: Marion Davies. Hearst had died in 1951; Marion had given him constant care in his last years. Billy had gone out to see Hearst just once during that time; the old man was not usually up for receiving visitors. He'd always liked Billy, and Billy remained tremendously fond of him. Hearst came out of his room and waved at Billy from the end of a very long gallery in Marion's Beverly Hills house. "It was like looking through the wrong end of a telescope," Billy recalled. "There was this little old man. . . . Originally he was a really big man, a giant, I think six feet five or something like that. He came towards me and I said, 'Oh, how nice to see you,' and he said, 'Oh, I'm a very old man.' It was rather destroying for me."

After Hearst died, Marion drove up to San Simeon for solace, but found her entrance barred. The bitterness of the Hearst family was finally made manifest: "We just heard that Cousin Willie is dead," said Hearst's cousin, locking the gates in Marion's face.

It was a tragic end to a glamorous life. She married Captain Horace Brown just ten weeks after Hearst's death, but it was a stormy union, and many of Marion's old friends didn't care for Brown. She descended further into alcohol. "Everyone deserted Marion," Billy said bitterly. "Even her old patron, Louella Parsons. Every single one of them."

He insisted that Marion be invited to Joan's reception. Crawford, never overly fond of Marion but gracious to her in public, agreed. Billy called Marion and prepped her. "Listen, honey, go down to the bank and get all your jewels, everything Hearst gave you. You put 'em all on, kid, because this is going to be a big one."

Billy set up a receiving line for Mr. and Mrs. Steele just inside his front door; as guests arrived, they moved through the line, shaking the hands of the honored couple and their hosts, Billy and Jimmie. Everyone looked fabulous: Joan in pearls and a strapless dress, the men in snappily tailored tuxedos. It was Marion who stole the show, however (certainly to Joan's displeasure). She arrived in a full-length silver lamé gown down to the floor, bedecked in all her jewels, including her tiara. She was just this side of tipsy.

According to Bob Shaw, she made her way through the receiving line, congratulating Joan effusively and receiving a warm kiss from Steele. Whether or not a decades-old rivalry for their mutual pal

Billy was on her mind is unknown, but instead of moving past the receiving line, she joined it, gradually edging her way up next to Billy.

"Billy looked over at her and thought, 'I think she's shrinking,'" Bob Shaw says with a laugh. "The more he looked at her the more he was convinced she was shorter than she used to be." So he leaned down and lifted the hem of her dress. There, under her silver lamé, the elegant, bejeweled Marion Davies was wearing tennis shoes.

The new Mrs. Steele commissioned Billy to design their recently purchased New York penthouse at 2 East 70th Street, on the corner of Fifth Avenue. Beginning in 1956, this would become Joan's chief residence. To pay for it, she sold her house in Brentwood, announcing she was retiring from motion pictures. From the beginning, she told the *Hollywood Reporter*, all she'd wanted to be was the "best wife in the world." She now threw herself into her new role as Pepsi-Cola ambassador.

Steele spoiled her, and she loved it. The Fifth Avenue apartment was actually two entire units so that Joan could re-create her Hollywood home in the heart of New York. It was an exciting assignment for Billy and his two protégés; they arrived in New York brimming over with ideas. When Steele started giving orders, Billy snapped at him: "You fucking tycoons. You make a few bucks and you think you can start building things with no taste. Nothing gives you the privilege to do that." Steele, chastened, not used to being spoken to in that way, backed off.

It was a formidable challenge reducing eighteen rooms to eight. Billy sparred with Joan, too, but that was not unusual. She was obsessed about her closet space, needing a separate room for her 304 pairs of shoes. Billy must have looked upon the work with some measure of personal satisfaction; more than thirty years before, he'd been a young man dazzled by his patroness' Fifth Avenue apartment, determined to find his way into that world.

The finished job was a spectacular triumph of modern design: deep, luxurious rooms, a diamond-shaped dining table, a whirlpool, and the bedroom painted in geranium pink. It was promptly dubbed "Taj Joan."

"Joan threw a small, intimate party for several hundred to christen it," recalls Bob Shaw. He'd come out east with Billy and Jimmie and was staying with them at the St. Regis Hotel. "Billy finished putting the final touches on the place at 5 o'clock and then met us back at the hotel. We went back to Joan's at 7 for cocktails. When we got back she had covered every single piece of furniture in the apartment in plastic. Billy wanted to kill her."

In the end, the bill was reported to be $387,000, but it's believed it was closer to half a million. Joan had told Billy to spare no expense; it was assumed that Pepsi would pay the costs. The company did, but the Steeles were thunderstruck to discover it was a loan. They had to borrow against Joan's life insurance to pay it back.

When Joan awoke one morning four years later to find Steele sprawled out on the bedroom floor, dead from a heart attack, it was to Billy Haines that she turned for consolation. Once Billy had been just around the corner; now three thousand miles separated them. Still, "he was the first person she called," says Jean Mathison. "I remember they were on the phone for over an hour. He was there for her. Just as he always was."

In California, Billy's clients remained largely the merchant princes. He developed his most significant relationship, however, with one particular merchant *princess*.

Betsy Bloomingdale was the wife of Alfred Bloomingdale, whose name was synonymous with more than just his family's department-store chain. Alfred Bloomingdale was the personification of how corporate wealth wielded influence. He, too, could be said to be a self-made man.

In the 1950s, Bloomingdale's was not yet the classy retail giant it later became. Instead, it was a "second-tier New York department store where the city's domestic help bought their uniforms," according to Marvin Traub, who took over the business from Alfred's family. Alfred was determined to make an independent name for himself. He was a big guy who played tackle on the football team at Brown

University, a loud, blustery carouser. After graduation, he got a job at the store making $18 a week but, finding himself bored, turned to Broadway. He produced a few plays, with only *The Ziegfeld Follies of 1943*, in collaboration with Lee and J. J. Shubert, standing out.

Alfred hit his stride with a novel idea: credit cards. He launched a fledgling credit-card company after the war by getting fourteen Manhattan restaurants to honor his cards; from there it was a short step to merging with Diners Club, of which he was named president in 1955. "The day will come," he predicted, "when the plastic card will make money obsolete."

Not a very wealthy man, Alfred Bloomingdale saw his assets suddenly skyrocket. Until the advent of American Express a decade later, Diners Club was far and away the most successful credit-card company in the world, and Alfred was suddenly thrust into a world of extreme wealth and social privilege.

His wife, whom he'd married in 1946, was the former Betty Lee Newling of Beverly Hills. She'd latched on to Alfred in the belief he'd make good; it was her constant prodding that pushed him along to ever-greater heights. The daughter of an Australian immigrant who'd served as dentist to Beverly Hills' affluent families, Betty Lee had watched her father's wealthy clients with envy and ambition. She tried acting for a while in the hopes of making it big, but realized marriage to Alfred Bloomingdale held more promise. Within a decade, Betty Lee—now rechristened with the more patrician-sounding Betsy—had achieved her goal: standing at the pinnacle of Los Angeles society.

Betsy took her regal consort role very seriously. "In a world where money alone conferred social standing," writes author Kitty Kelley, "Betsy Bloomingdale reigned supreme." Betsy wore cashmere trench coats with collars and cuffs of mink. Her gardeners grew the rarest orchids on the west coast. She adored wearing an eighteen-karat gold belt studded with fifty carved emeralds. Besides Los Angeles, she and Alfred had homes in New York and Paris.

When Billy first met her, she was still a young mother and not yet the anointed arbiter of society she'd become. In 1953 she and her husband hired Billy Haines to redesign their library; in the process, he'd begin redesigning Betsy as well. Just as he had been with Crawford, Billy Haines was a guide for Betsy Bloomingdale, helping shape her public image and private habits.

"Billy Haines became one of the great influences of my life," she says today. What Billy helped cultivate in her—as well as in so many of the other Los Angeles "girls"—was an appreciation for the trappings of their class.

"I remember as a very young girl, long before I knew Billy or Alfred, I went to a dinner party at the Jack Warner house," she says. "After dinner, Mrs. Warner and Mrs. Zanuck and all the ladies retired to the oval sitting room, where coffee was served. I remember there were four of these wonderful, marvelous black lacquered chairs of Billy Haines' design. I remember everything about that night—the servants, the dinner. What's been so wonderful for me is that eventually in *my* life, Bill Haines did a house for *me*, too. I got a Crown Derby dinner service, just like there was on the table at the Warners' that night. And when the Warner furniture went up for auction, I bought those four black lacquered chairs and have them now in my house."

At the same time, Billy teased her mercilessly about her social aspirations. He called her "little girl," or, in a dig at her more humble origins, "Miss Newling." She called him "Willie Lump Lump"—"why," she says, "I don't know. But I did." They were incredibly campy together, enjoying low-brow jokes and gossip. "They'd certainly carry on," says Arch Case.

They met through Joan Crawford. It was before Joan's marriage to Steele, when she was dating Greg Bautzer, Alfred Bloomingdale's lawyer. "I wanted a dining room just like Joan Crawford's," Betsy Bloomingdale says. "I *had* to meet Billy Haines."

During a visit to his studio, she took a particular liking to two eighteenth-century carved mahogany chairs. "Those two chairs were the beginning of my romance with Billy Haines," she says. "I told him I couldn't live without them and to please hold them for me. When I went back a few days later, he told me they'd been sold. 'Forget about them, little girl,' he said, 'they're gone.' I went sobbing home to my husband, wondering why Billy would sell the chairs when he'd promised them to me. Finally, to put me out of my misery, my husband said he had bought them for me as a surprise for my birthday. After that, I belonged to Billy."

She and Alfred hired him to redo the library in their home in Bel-Air, taking off for Europe while he started the project. "Suddenly, sitting on the plane," Betsy remembers, "I said, 'Did he say the floor was going to be *black*? And something else was going to be *red*? I was certain we shouldn't go ahead with it.'" Of course, upon their return, Billy's work was "so sensational that he had to then do every other room in the house."

A few years later they moved into a larger house, a typically Spanish, red-tiled-roof mansion in Holmby Hills. Betsy had Billy transform it into an Italian palazzo, filled with sun and flowers. The house has its modern elements, but is far less contemporary than the Brody residence. Billy used his trademark hand-painted Chinese wallpaper and Chinese Chippendale-style furniture. "What's wonderful about Bill Haines is that I've lived in this house for more than thirty-five years," Betsy Bloomingdale says today, "and so little has had to be redone. The fabrics have held up — but it's more than that. Bill's eye, his taste — *that's* what's held up."

Billy's reputation sprang from not only his (and Graber's and Morrison's) talent. In large part, it was due to the sheer force of Billy's personality — still blazing after all these years.

"He could be mean, but in a funny sort of way," says Michael Morrison, who left Billy's employ in 1960. The ten-year rivalry between him and Ted Graber had come to a head; after a series of conflicts among the three of them, Morrison believed he'd be better off on his own. "Bill agreed I should go," Morrison says today, "but he said, 'You should've given me a year's notice.'" After that, they never really spoke. "I'd run into him a few times and he'd just say, 'Hello, Mike,' shake my hand, and go on."

Billy could hold a grudge; he could be hostile if he chose, without any mitigating humor. One time a client was carrying on about his bathroom, wanting all sorts of mirrors. Finally Billy snapped, "Why don't you just put one in the toilet so you can look at your quilted ass?" When another client balked at the price of fabric, Billy sniffed, "Madam, if you want *yardage,* go to Penney's."

"But he got away with it," says Francie Brody. "Because he was so charming. Because you expected him to be a little racy, a little irreverent. It was part of his character."

Betsy Bloomingdale says, "Alfred once gave me a diamond necklace and Billy thought it was much too small. He had absolutely no compunction saying to Alfred, 'Oh, what a *wee* diamond necklace for such a *big* man to give.'" Billy was known to tell his lady friends that if they could lift their hands, then the diamond rings their husbands had given them weren't big enough.

Only occasionally would a particularly uptight client (or friend) storm out on her heels. These stories are few, and sketchy—no one admits to holding a grudge against Billy Haines—but they happened. "He had too strong a personality for *everyone* to like him," says Francie Brody.

Some used his boisterous personality merely as an excuse, however. Among movie folk, homosexuality was almost a given; at any particular gathering there were always a few gay men and lesbians present. Among the Los Angeles parvenu, a world of rugged, cigar-chomping, self-made men, there was a greater unease.

"Don't forget, this was the 1950s," says Francie Brody. "People did not approve of homosexuals. I think there were quite a few people who disapproved of Bill for that reason and that reason alone. They just weren't going to have anything to do with him."

It's significant that most of Billy's clients weren't "old money." "He hit the people who were new rich," says Mary Anita Loos. "They were willing to pay whatever he charged so they [might be seen as] old money."

His clients were people who, despite their wealth and social prestige, also felt a bit outside, as if they, too, still had something to prove. When a blue-blooded easterner like Jacqueline Bouvier Kennedy or, even more threatening, British royalty, came through town, the Los Angeles "girls" would flutter about, trying to remember the proper etiquette and protocol. Billy told them to relax, that the airs of the old-money families simply weren't worth it. "Of course, Bill wasn't a part of the country club set," says Michael Morrison.

A few of Billy's clients were—the Mays, for example—but not the Salvatoris, the Deutsches, the McMartins, or even the Bloomingdales, for that matter. Henry Salvatori was an Italian Catholic immigrant who'd made his money in oil, serving as a director of the Transamerica Corporation. Armand Deutsch's family had founded Sears Roebuck, considered (like Bloomingdale's) a working-class store; besides, he was Jewish. So was Alfred Bloomingdale, until Betsy converted him to Catholicism. In the Protestant-dominated country-club set, no amount of wealth could erase the "stain" of Judaism or, for that matter, Catholicism.

Still, they were all men of bluff and swagger. They might be looked down upon by the blue bloods, but they had their own intolerances, and "fairies" were a big target. Someone like Armand Deutsch is a fascinating example: A liberal among conservatives, he tried to change Ronald Reagan's positions on gun control and abortion. A former producer at MGM and RKO, Deutsch was well-known and well-liked throughout the movie industry, and knew his share of homosexuals. Yet there was that curious dichotomy often found among "friendly" straight men: He could be friends with gays, but they were still a breed apart, something inferior. He was close with Robert Taylor, but like most people, adamantly "defended" Taylor as strictly heterosexual. As a boy, Deutsch—as the Sears Roebuck heir—had been the original intended victim of the infamous murderers Nathan Leopold and Richard Loeb. In his autobiography, Deutsch considers their homosexuality "a shocking piece of the total fabric of their crime." In another place, he casually uses the word "fag."

Among the wives of such men, the feeling was a bit different. Homosexuals might not be "real men," but they were invaluable to have around. Most of these women were originally actresses or showgirls; their (invariably gay) hairdressers, dress designers, society escorts ("walkers"), and interior designers taught them the finer points of taste and culture. Among Billy's client circle—all of whom he counted as friends—Harriet Deutsch was once a salesgirl, Grace

Salvatori a middle-class housefrau, Betsy Bloomingdale a dentist's daughter, and Lee Annenberg the orphaned niece of Columbia chief Harry Cohn. They enjoyed the company of gay men and eventually brought a few of them into accepted status within their clique.

"In those days, nobody was *really* accepted if they were homosexual," says Betsy Bloomingdale. "Billy wasn't particularly accepted among all our friends. But Alfred adored him. What he adored was the fact that this gung-ho, solid, really kind of macho fellow was, in fact, homosexual."

Then there was Jimmie. "Billy and Jimmie would come over to the house," Betsy says, "and Jimmie would be wearing some big gold something or other. We'd think, 'Gee, we'd really like to invite them for dinner, but how do we explain them to our *friends*?' "

Eventually, she says, it was Billy's manner ("so fun and so wonderful") that brought many people around. He was also older by about a decade than most of the Los Angeles parvenus; a younger, more contemporary gay figure might have been more threatening. He and Jimmie were really the only gay people to move in that set — at least the only ones who were out about it.

Except, of course, for Jerry Zipkin. The heir to his father's New York real-estate fortune, Zipkin had never worked in his life and was proud of that fact; had he not been Jewish, he'd have been nearly a clone of the Brahmin Lucius Beebe. He spent "a lifetime of taking seriously what others considered frivolous," says the writer Laurence Leamer. He could be terribly charming, but also bitingly arch and pompous. In 1949 he lived for a time with Somerset Maugham in Europe; many believe Maugham based his snobbish, acerbic character Elliot Templeton in *The Razor's Edge* on Jerry Zipkin.

His chief claim to fame, however, was as a "New York walker." As Andy Lawler had done for the Hollywood wives of the 1930s and 1940s, so Jerry Zipkin did for the wives of corporate America in the 1950s and 1960s. He was their reliable escort when their husbands were away, or simply too bored by a particular social function. Zipkin was the perfect date: sexually nonthreatening, eternally witty, terribly cultured, but with a jaded air of having seen it all. He made his lady friends feel worldly and sophisticated; on Jerry Zipkin's arm, they were far more entranced than they ever were with their own husbands.

He was not a very pleasant man, except to the few ladies who idolized him. He was quite open about his homosexuality, yet remained conflicted about it. In his New York apartment, he eschewed anything that might be considered "too feminine" or "too gay." There were no flowers, no floral prints. Instead, he used a snake motif, with patterns of cobras and vipers on his couch and even stuffed snakes adorning his tables. Billy, as might be expected, found the decor repulsive.

They had a sparring relationship. Billy, not one known for his subtlety, found Zipkin's humor cruel. They'd often get into verbal dueling matches; while each could both make the other laugh, there was a rivalry that bordered on animosity. In this, Billy was more like the husbands in the group. The men tended to avoid Zipkin, leaving him to escort their wives. Billy, on the other hand, with Jimmie in tow, socialized in the company of both husbands and wives. Zipkin, when he did turn up at gatherings, never brought a male partner; usually some socialite between marriages was on his arm.

"It was very, very unusual for the time that Billy didn't try to hide," says Francie Brody. "I don't ever remember seeing him without Jimmie."

Michael Morrison says "not hiding" his relationship with Jimmie "is putting it mildly." No hostess worth her social standing would have thought to invite Billy without Jimmie. It was tried, at least once, but by whom no one seems to recall anymore. Whoever she was, "Billy told her what to do with her invitation," says Arch Case. "If you didn't invite Jimmie, Billy wouldn't come."

Still, there was a certain protocol of the times that Billy followed. "It was never discussed," says Case, referring to homosexuality. Occasionally, in an unguarded moment with people he trusted, Billy would let an innuendo slip. One friend recalls a gathering in which Ed Lasker, Francie Brody's movie-producer brother and also a client of Billy's, jokingly called someone a "cocksucker." Billy rejoined, to a round of laughter, "And what would *you* know about sucking cock?"

He would never be as outrageous as he had been at George Cukor's or Cole Porter's. Neither would Jimmie, who was even more finely attuned to the proper rules of decorum among the society set. Their humor at these gatherings was circumspect, their allusions to their life together rare and unspecific.

And yet, simply by being there, by showing up and leaving together, by hosting parties for these people *as a couple,* the reality of their lives was implicit and unavoidable. Billy found no contradiction in living his life openly but then never discussing the essentials of that life, or of his relationship with Jimmie. That was how it was.

Even their anniversaries—which marked milestones considerably longer than most of their friends'—were never mentioned, let alone celebrated. Among their gay acquaintances—Ted and Arch, Mitt and Larry, Clifton Webb, Orry-Kelly—it was different. With Crawford, too, there was acknowledgment of the particular circumstances of their lives. Among the rest, however, nothing that would ever make them uncomfortable was ever broached.

Billy insisted, too, that he and Jimmie were never to be seated directly next to each other at parties. "It just wasn't done that way," says Michael Morrison. "At a formal party, it's supposed to be boy, girl, boy, girl. And Billy and Jimmie were sticklers on formalities." Once, when a well-meaning hostess erred and placed their name cards beside each other, Billy and Jimmie left in a huff. To their way of thinking, it was a terrible insult.

One can't pass judgment on them from the space of forty years. This was before the rise of a significant gay political movement, before some understanding of gay identity and gay oppression had been fully articulated. Billy and Jimmie hardly saw themselves as oppressed, and who can blame them? They were extraordinarily privileged men and saw no contradiction in that privilege and the fact of their homosexuality. A consciousness of identity politics—a sense of common cause among people who share similar characteristics (race, gender, ethnicity, religion, sexual orientation)—was not as prevalent then. Billy identified as homosexual, to be sure, and he was content with that fact. He also saw himself as a Virginian, as a decorator, as a longtime Hollywood resident. Yet he had as much in common with a Mexican or Chinese longtime Hollywood resident as he did with the working-class drag queens in the bars on the Strip.

Still, there had to be some conflict, some inner struggle, especially during the McCarthy period and then the turmoil of the 1960s. Billy was never a political person: He loathed partisan politics, despised politicians, and claimed to care not a whit about the positions of either the Democrats or the Republicans. Certainly he had friends in both camps. George Cukor and Tallulah Bankhead were strong Democrats. So were the Deutsches, Frank Sinatra, and, significantly, Edie and Bill Goetz. The Bloomingdales were also Democrats before they—with their friends the Reagans—switched allegiance. Most of Billy's clients were Republican, however, and some were ardently conservative: Henry Salvatori was practically a reactionary.

The first twinge of conflict between personal realities and public policy came during the late 1940s. Hollywood had been under investigation for Communist infiltration since the spring of 1947, when the House Un-American Activities Committee (HUAC) began calling witnesses. Robert Taylor, Adolphe Menjou, and others were quick to name names of suspected Communist Party members. During the next four years, scores of Hollywood actors, directors, and writers were called before the committee; in the end more than three hundred were fired and blacklisted against working in the American film industry. Billy knew many of them, including screenwriter Donald Ogden Stewart, whose friendship dated back to *Brown of Harvard*; Karen Morley, his costar from *Are You Listening?*; and John Garfield, who'd rented his house on North Stanley.

When the Republicans won control of Congress in 1953, Wisconsin Senator Joseph McCarthy was named chairman of the Senate permanent investigations subcommittee, launching a notorious period of further accusations and counteraccusations. McCarthy (along with his gay henchman, Roy Cohn) claimed an unholy alliance be-tween homosexuality and Communism. The Federal Bureau of In-vestigation, headed by J. Edgar Hoover, intensified its checks into the personal lives of Hollywood figures, especially those suspected to be liberal or gay. In some cases, even homosexual conservatives who supported the HUAC purges were investigated. As he was no longer a part of the film industry, Billy was spared this indignity; but it's known Hoover kept a file on such a benign figure as George Cukor.

That many of Billy's clients and the people with whom he social-ized supported HUAC and McCarthy must have given him pause — if not out of any altruistic concern, then out of, at the very least, a desire for self-preservation. No one had ever really forgotten the El Porto headlines; they were always there, lingering in the back of people's minds. Might they be revived now and used against him?

One of the fiercest McCarthy supporters among their friends was Nancy Reagan.

"Nancy desperately wanted a house designed by Billy Haines," says a friend who knew them both. "But she just couldn't afford him."

Until her husband became the darling and the promise of Holly-wood's right wing in the early 1960s, Nancy Reagan was on the so-cial second tier, the B list, just as she'd been an actress in B pictures. Ronald Reagan's movie career faltered in the 1950s, and Nancy found herself little more than a suburban housewife in Pacific Pali-sades, a distinctly middle-class enclave.

Nancy was, however, a staunch Republican and rabid anti-Communist, which brought her into particular circles. The Reagans were friends with Robert Taylor and his second wife, Ursula; the Robert Montgomerys; and George Murphy, the hoofer friend of Billy's who in 1964 became the junior (Republican) senator from California. During the 1960 presidential campaign, the Reagans were solidly behind Richard Nixon while most of the rest in the movie community backed John F. Kennedy. It's not known who

Billy voted for, or if indeed he voted; but friends say he never cared for any of the Kennedys. ("What?" asked one. "Those shanty Irish?")

During the Kennedy years, conservative politicians in southern California began nurturing Ronald Reagan for political office. His rejection of his former liberalism, his strong support and leadership during the HUAC and McCarthy years, and his eloquence as a public speaker made him an extremely attractive candidate. There was a sense that the Reagans were headed somewhere, and many in the Los Angeles jet set—even some who were relatively apolitical—began linking themselves to the star of television's *GE Theater* and his wife.

Nancy, too, sensed a rendezvous with destiny. She'd wanted all her life to be considered among the elite, and now needed a role model. Betsy Bloomingdale proved the perfect choice. "Betsy Bloomingdale was her idol, her goddess," says Jody Jacobs, the former society editor of the *Los Angeles Times*. "She was everything Nancy wanted to be."

It's interesting to note that if Billy Haines was a major influence in shaping Betsy's style, then his style and sensibility were part of what molded the now-famous Nancy Reagan image. Everything Betsy did, Nancy did her best to copy. She had her hair done by Betsy's hairdresser, Julius Bengtsson; she insisted that Betsy's favorite designer, Jimmy Galanos, design gowns for her as well; and suddenly Nancy was photographed all over town and in New York on the arm of Jerry Zipkin. She also became chummy with Roy Cohn. She became as surrounded by gay men as Betsy was. Nancy's friend, the screenwriter Leonard Spigelgass, would say, "There is this crazy 'faggotage' around her."

Nancy had known many gay men and lesbians during her career in Hollywood. A close friend of her mother's had been Alla Nazimova, who'd served as Nancy's godmother. She was friendly with Claudette Colbert; even if the Reagans never suspected their good pal Robert Taylor had homosexual inclinations, they had to know about Colbert. It was really only upon becoming close with Betsy

Bloomingdale, however, that Nancy's social circle became densely populated with gay men.

Nancy adored the Bloomingdales' home, which, of course, had just been decorated by Billy Haines. "Nancy was determined to get her house done by Billy Haines," says their mutual friend. "That is, when she had a house worth decorating." In the meantime, she got to know Billy and Jimmie socially, both at the Bloomingdales' and at Billy's own home on Lorna Lane, where the Reagans attended several parties.

Nancy Reagan confirms that she and her husband were frequent guests of Billy's and Jimmie's. "Bill Haines was a marvelous host, simply marvelous," she says. "That style of living and entertaining has long since disappeared."

During the 1964 presidential campaign, Ronald Reagan delivered a stirring, eloquent speech in support of the Republican candidate, Barry Goldwater. Immediately he was approached by conservative kingmakers—chief among them Billy's client Henry Salvatori—to run for governor. Reagan campaigned on a platform of bringing down taxes, cutting state spending, and ending "moral decay." In 1966 he was elected; Billy and Jimmie hosted a gala party to celebrate his victory at their home, probably as a favor to Salvatori or Betsy Bloomingdale.

"There were tons of flowers and extra staff," recalls Frank Lysinger. "Everything had to be just right." Billy broke convention by offering all his servants a drink before the party. "He tipped his glass with them," says Lysinger. "He said, 'Now do your best. Make me proud.'" Photographs show tables set up around the pool in the back of the house, the Bloomingdales, Deutsches, and Salvatoris gathered victoriously around the governor and California's new, Galanos-gowned first lady.

"Billy had a wonderful sense of humor," Nancy Reagan recalls of her host. "A very kind man. He had an elegance, a style. I certainly admired him."

She finally hired him to do some work in their Pacific Palisades home, but the commission was nothing elaborate—maybe a piece of furniture or two, friends believe. The Reagans simply didn't have the kind of money their acquaintances did; the Salvatoris and Deutsches had to donate furniture to spruce up the Governor's Mansion in Sacramento, which Nancy despised. Nancy returned to Beverly Hills as often as she could to shop, and her frequent companion was Jimmie Shields. "I used to see Jimmie all the time," she says. "We'd go the country mart and he'd point out all sorts of things to buy."

Was there ever any talk, any concern, about her socializing with a gay man? "There was never a problem," she says simply. And that's all she'll say on the topic.

Her husband had campaigned on a theme of reversing the "moral decline" in the state, with members of the John Birch Society among his most ardent and vocal supporters. Billy knew only too well the attitudes of right-wing groups like these toward homosexuals; all he had to do was recall the White Legion headlines from El Porto beach. He had to have considered the irony of his association with people who were building careers on philosophies aligned with such groups. For a man whose life had so far been so straightforward in its integrity, it's difficult to reconcile this connection.

Yet not impossible. Politicians and their supporters are expert at making rationalizations and exceptions. If the subject had ever been broached—and it most certainly never was—Nancy Reagan or Henry Salvatori or even Betsy Bloomingdale might well have reassured Billy, "Well, we don't have a problem with *you*." Or—they might have added—with Jerry Zipkin, or Jimmy Galanos, or Julius Bengtsson, or Cesar Romero. Or, for that matter, Claudette Colbert (who officially "came out" to her friends as a lesbian upon her husband's death in 1968).

For his part, Billy, too, would have made excuses for his powerful friends. Bob Wheaton, who reestablished his friendship with Billy and Jimmie in the mid-1960s, says that one always wanted to believe the best about a person, and unless someone was militantly anti-gay—like a Clark Gable or a Louis B. Mayer—he or she was considered a friend. "This was before all the political changes that came later, you must remember," he says. He has a point: The stakes had yet to be raised. Simple acceptance was victory enough. The warm welcome Billy and Jimmie found with the Bloomingdales and others was terribly affirming. Such is not meant as an *excuse* for the association, but it is, at least in part, an explanation.

Besides, it was largely these people who now made up Billy's client list. Billy knew what side his bread was buttered on. The movie folk had their own, less expensive decorators now. "The motion-picture queen is dead," Billy told columnist Ezra Goodman. "The present run of stars don't have the knowledge and interest in homes that the older ones had. They're a beatnik group of actors with no interest in it at all." Billy depended on the Bloomingdales, the Salvatoris, and the rest to make his living, to maintain the standard of living to which he and Jimmie had become accustomed.

In the mid-1960s, Billy and Ted Graber received their most prestigious commission yet: the Palm Springs home of publishing magnate and close Reagan adviser Walter Annenberg and his wife Lee. The *Hollywood Reporter* disclosed on December 10, 1964: "William Haines, one time big cinema star and now a desert decorator, has been commissioned to do the interior of the $3 million Walter Annenberg spread. No matter what the colors, the desert will definitely be greener."

Sunnylands, the name the Annenbergs bestowed upon their sprawling estate, was finished in 1966. Starkly modern, the concept behind the house was a "great tent," imagining Annenberg as an Arabian sheikh holding court in the desert. Sunnylands even had its own flag, a yellow-and-white crest, which flew under the U.S. flag when the Annenbergs were in residence. A thirty-foot Mayan column—a replica of the one at the National Museum of Anthropology in Mexico City—greeted visitors, with waterfalls cascading onto a series of smooth, flat stones. Walls were cut from rust-colored volcanic rock; huge windows overlooked man-made lakes and the golf course that surrounded the home.

Billy made a fortune from the Annenberg commission; he also became a frequent guest of the Annenbergs, meeting Richard Nixon and other powerful Republican politicians at Sunnylands. In some ways, Annenberg was a younger recast of William Randolph Hearst, although the two ended up hostile to each other. Both were big men who ruled over publishing empires with an ironclad grip. Annenberg published the *Philadelphia Inquirer*, *Seventeen* magazine, and *TV Guide*. It was an empire founded by his father, Moses Annenberg, who'd served a prison term at the height of his career for income-tax evasion. It was a scandal his son spent his life trying to live down.

Billy and Jimmie genuinely *liked* these people, particularly the women. Although they had their reservations about Ronald Reagan ("They knew he didn't have goodwill toward homosexuals," says Bob Wheaton), Billy and Jimmie seem to have liked Nancy very much. She and Lee and Betsy and the rest of "the girls" were fun. They were doting. They were young and lively. There was no personal bias against homosexuals among them. For political and social advantage, however, many of them knowingly associated with people who would have considered their friendships with gay men to be part of the "moral decline."

Such hypocrisy, of course, wasn't reserved solely for homosexuals. While he poured money into Ronald Reagan's campaign, Alfred Bloomingdale was involved in a string of sadomasochistic affairs with women, a fact that Nancy Reagan discovered and concealed from her best friend, Bets. (His mistress, Vicki Morgan, was also known to spend time with Cary Grant, although her biographer describes their relationship as curiously nonsexual). A number of "the girls" themselves had extramarital affairs; Jimmie Shields and Jerry Zipkin were their most frequent confidants on the details. During Reagan's campaign for governor, says Reagan biographer Laurence Leamer, many of his aides worried that his wife's "shady" friendships might offend voters.

The storm that they all feared broke in the fall of 1967. Governor Reagan's top aide, Lyn Nofziger, discovered (in his words) a "homosexual clique" in the administration. Apparently a number of Reagan staffers were gay, including two of his top aides (not coincidentally, rivals to Nofziger). They'd gather for private parties at a house on Lake Tahoe, owned by one of the aides. (The house was co-owned by Buffalo Bills quarterback—and later Republican vice presidential nominee—Jack Kemp, although he insisted he never visited it.)

Reportedly, there were a few sex parties arranged at the house, and some of the guests may have been underage.

Certainly Billy and Jimmie could not have been outraged by such revelations; how many sex parties had *they* thrown in their lives? They may even have known some of the accused men socially. Most of the men were married; in respect for their wives and children, Nofziger told the press, he wouldn't release their names (and, in a sign of how differently the press behaved in 1967, no one tried to discover their identities, either).

Nofziger had leaked the story to the press himself in an attempt to control the damage. He made it clear that Reagan had promptly fired all of the men involved. That purging could not have sat well with Billy Haines, for whom memories of 1933 must have resurfaced.

Billy's friends claim they cannot recall his specific reaction to the Reagan purging. "He wouldn't have discussed politics," says Arch Case. Yet "politics" had now gone to another level: This wasn't merely an "expedient" political alliance with the John Birchers, whom the Reagans, Salvatoris, and Bloomingdales could—and did—ridicule behind closed doors. This was worse: For Billy and Jimmie, this was their *friends*—people who had been guests in their home—making public denunciations of their lives.

Homosexuality, said the governor, was "an abomination in the eyes of the Lord." Reagan, widely expected to seek the 1968 Republican presidential nomination, put as much distance between himself and his purged staffers as possible. Truman Capote visited his office not long after to plead for the men on California's death row. Reagan responded to a question of whether his purge of homosexuals was complete by saying, "Perhaps we should trawl Truman through the halls to see if there are any of them left." Later, asked by reporters if homosexuals had any place in government, the governor quipped: "Well, perhaps in the Department of Parks and Recreation."

Even more distressing must have been *Nancy's* comments to the press, calling homosexuality a "sickness" and an "abnormality." This just days after being escorted by Jerry Zipkin, having her hair done by Julius, and enjoying dinner with Billy and Jimmie. The "crazy faggotage" appear to have simply moved with the flow, rationalizing in their own minds the "necessity" of their friend saying such things. Today Nancy Reagan chooses not to comment on her remarks of thirty years ago.

Billy and Jimmie may not have shared the particulars of their relationship with their jet-set acquaintances, but among their gay friends it was something that was celebrated. In 1951 they'd marked their silver anniversary—twenty-five years—with an intimate gathering at Lorna Lane. Clifton Webb was there, and Orry-Kelly, and, of course, Crawford and Eleanor Boardman. The story that they sent an invitation to Louis B. Mayer (then in his last months at the helm of MGM) with the postscript, "And you said it wouldn't last," may be apocryphal, but friends believe it to be true.

In any event, they celebrated with a trip to Europe. They started as usual in London and continued on to Paris, where they hooked up with Bob Wheaton, who was then studying at the Sorbonne. "I turned my cleaning lady into a chef for a day and threw them a party," Wheaton says. He remembers the week they spent with him very well: One night, after the opera, they waited so long for a table at a Parisian restaurant they all got smashing drunk on martinis. Billy coaxed Bob into trying the "specialty of the house," which Wheaton says he ate with gusto. When he found out they were snails, he was shocked, and Billy had a terrific laugh.

They continued on to Amsterdam, where they discovered the gay nightlife scene. At one club, Billy mentioned to the manager that he and Jimmie were marking twenty-five years together. Impressed and touched, the manager announced over the mike that two Americans were celebrating a special milestone, and called them out. The spotlight was turned on them, and to the applause of patrons, Billy and Jimmie, in each other's arms, twirled slowly around the dance floor. It was one of the rare moments in their lives when their marriage was celebrated publicly—the spotlight this time on the *both* of them.

They were still finely attired men, but Billy had increasingly put on weight. He was particularly bothered by the loose skin under his chin, and had some minor surgery to correct it. Betsy Bloomingdale recalls the day he came to her house and said, quite matter-of-factly, "Well, little girl, I've had my gobbler cut out."

By now, he was also completely bald on top, and the vitiligo on his hands and scalp had only gotten worse. By the middle of the decade he'd taken to wearing a toupee occasionally; Jimmie followed suit. Their friends are unanimous in expressing the shock they felt the first time they encountered Billy and Jimmie in their toupees. "Billy decided to use the funeral of Claudette Colbert's husband Dr. Joel Pressman as an opportunity to introduce his toupee to the world," says Bob Shaw. "I couldn't take my eyes off it. I trust someone told him how silly it looked because after that he didn't wear it very often."

When the author Fred Lawrence Guiles interviewed him in 1969, he recalls thinking Billy had a "full head of hair," so convincing was the toupee.

By the late 1950s, both Billy and Jimmie had settled down. Bob Shaw says that by the time he knew them, they rarely went out to the clubs. "Billy was in bed by ten every night," says Shaw. "If he gave a party and people stayed too late, he'd change into his pajamas and start getting ready for bed."

The "daisy chain" parties were a thing of the past. Billy and Jimmie's own sex life gradually dissipated as well; by this time, they each had their own bedroom. Still, it was a committed, even exclusive relationship. Their monogamy was by now de facto, but even when they'd been sleeping with others, they remained more committed than most of their friends in conventional heterosexual marriages. "There were never any affairs," says Arch Case. "Tricks are different than affairs."

Bob Shaw recalls having Billy and Jimmie to dinner in the mid-1960s. Also invited were several younger gay male couples. Billy didn't often socialize with Hollywood's younger gays, but Shaw, as a television writer, was well connected in that world. "The younger men were boasting about how long they'd been together," says Shaw. "Five, six, eight years. Then Billy spoke up, in a deep, growling voice: 'Anybody like to try for *thirty-nine*?'"

Their anniversaries—thirty, thirty-five, forty—were celebrated in

due course. They traveled to Europe frequently still, and Jimmie became, if possible, even more "piss elegant," as one friend describes
him. He adored cashmere jackets with solid-gold buttons, and his
collection of Cartier gold watches numbered in the dozens. "Jimmie
came to my house one night and told me he was just *furious* with
Gary Cooper," says Bob Shaw. "Cooper was going to Paris the next
day and Jimmie wanted him to take one of his watches to Cartier's
in Paris. He sniffed, 'I wouldn't let Cartier's in New York *touch* it.
They don't know *what* they're doing.' But Cooper turned Jimmie
down. He said he was too busy, and Jimmie was simply *beside*
himself!"

Jimmie was often identified as Billy's "partner" in the decorating
business, and it was technically correct, as he owned a large share of
the stock. Friends today laugh at the idea of Jimmie doing any
work. "Oh, sure, he had responsibilities," says Michael Morrison.
"He'd go out and pick out the finest avocados for our lunch."

Jimmie's nephew Charlie Conrad, the son of his sister Virginia,
was a young man in his teens and early twenties during the 1950s. He
came out from Florida a few times to stay with Billy and Jimmie,
and each time they treated him regally. He adored both of them. At
first he was a bit puzzled by his uncle's personality. "I asked my
mother, 'Is Jimmie a little effeminate?'" She laughed. "Son, you've
just had your first indoctrination into the world of interior designers."

Conrad says Billy and Jimmie were "two peas in a pod." They
were deeply committed, he said, and their differences only made
them fit that much better. "Billy had this deep, powerful voice," Conrad says. "Very masculine. He was very nonchalant about things,
didn't give a shit. Jimmie was all protocol. He was forever keeping
Billy in line." Conrad recalls a party at Chasen's in which Billy,
dressed in a tuxedo, discovered the seam down his leg was ripped.
"I'm going to have some fun," he said, attending the party with a slit
up his pants, flashing skin to the startled guests around him. Jimmie
just stood in the wings with his martini, shaking his head and shrug-
ging. "You see what I put up with?" he sighed to Betsy Bloomingdale.

Jimmie's connections were important, however. He was the one to go shopping with Nancy Reagan and Lee Annenberg. He was the one who adhered to the protocol of the smart set, and in so doing, brought many clients Billy's way. Billy knew that Jimmie's sense of propriety served him well, providing a balance not only in their social lives but in the way they lived at home as well.

That home front went through some changes as the years went by. Billy's father had died on September 22, 1950, at the Southern California Sanitarium at the age of seventy-four. George Haines had suffered a cerebral thrombosis on September 18; he died a week later and was buried beside his wife in Forest Lawn Cemetery.

In 1957 James Stone, husband of Billy's sister Lillion, died back east. Lillion then came to Los Angeles to join the rest of her family. She lived in the apartment next to Billy's studio in Beverly Hills and became a frequent guest, along with their sister Ann Langhorne, at Billy's soirees.

Among Billy's friends, too, there were the natural shifts. Polly Moran died in 1952. She and Billy had drifted apart after her marriage to former prizefighter Marty Malone. She'd finally found her man, but he often beat her and threatened to kill her. She had him arrested a few times, but clung desperately to him, even telling the judge once she'd deserved the beating because of her "nagging." There was no room for her old "boyfriend" Billy Haines in her life any longer.

Billy saw less of Fanny Brice and Roger Davis, too. Davis was a habitué of Cukor's parties, to which Billy had stopped being invited. Brice had taken a liking to Ted Graber; she considered Billy competition for Ted's attentions. There was other competition, too: Fanny had started decorating friends' homes, eventually turning her hobby into a sideline business, although she reportedly took no fee. She decorated houses for Katharine Hepburn, Ira Gershwin, Dinah Shore, and Eddie Cantor. Mary Anita Loos says she still has a couple of chairs she calls "Early Baby Snooks." Much of Fanny's work, she says, was inspired by Billy.

The only original Hollywood friends — dating back to the 1920s —

with whom Billy maintained any regular contact were Crawford, Eleanor Boardman, Orry-Kelly, Carmel Myers (with whom he'd appeared in *Tell It to the Marines*), and Hedda Hopper.

Marion Davies wasn't among them. Her descent into alcoholism was tragic, and Billy saw her infrequently. When she died in 1961, Jean Mathison recalls, Billy was deeply saddened. "One of the magazines ran a spread of photos on the glory days of San Simeon," she says. "Billy saw that, and turned off all the phones." His employees spent the day listening in rapt attention to his stories of the great Hearst castle and the fabulous parties he'd been to there.

As happens in any life lived long enough, Billy watched as old friends passed away before him. Each time, he mourned a piece of his life. His chum from the Cukor days, Jimmy Vincent, was found dead in 1953, floating in the Hudson River in New York. George Cukor went down to the morgue to claim the corpse of his friend. In 1959, two more names from that era—Louis Mason and Andy Lawler, survivors of the El Porto scandal—also died.

On September 13, 1963, Mitt Foster died at the Veterans' Administration Hospital in West Los Angeles. Billy was heartbroken. Mitt had been his mentor, his teacher, his champion, and one of his dearest friends. In his later years, after dissolving Haines-Foster, Inc., Mitt had worked as an antiques buyer for Bullock's Department Store. Larry Sullivan had taken a position as a salesman at Saks Fifth Avenue. Mitt remained a heavy drinker; after an operation for kidney failure, he quickly developed pneumonia and died. He was seventy-three years old. Larry Sullivan, Mitt's lover of some forty years, died of a cerebral thrombosis almost three years later to the day, on September 2, 1966.

Hedda Hopper, whose extreme right-wing views embarrassed even some of her supporters, nonetheless remained close to her homosexual friends until her death. Orry-Kelly was perhaps her dearest friend; when he hosted a party in 1962 to honor Mrs. Oscar Hammerstein—whose liberal politics were well-known—he told Billy he worried Hedda would make a scene. She was perfectly gracious to Mrs. Hammerstein, however.

That Orry would host a party for a big-time liberal and be tight with Hedda at the same time reflects the basic apolitical nature of many in the older Hollywood gay circles. Orry-Kelly saw no contradiction in living life as an openly gay man while at the same time encouraging Hedda to go on the offensive against Elizabeth Taylor's former husband, Michael Wilding, for allegedly having an affair with another male star. "Don't be a fart in a bandbox, Hedda," Orry told her. "Go out and scare them. Nobody paid any attention to you until you started attacking people." Hedda printed the story and was promptly sued by Wilding; she eventually settled out of court.

Billy couldn't have been comfortable with such an "outing," as he was known to never reveal the sexual orientation of any celebrity even to his friends. The closest he'd come was mild innuendo. When the Jack Bennys hosted their daughter's wedding, Billy and Jimmie were invited. So was Orry-Kelly, but Orry and the Bennys were in the midst of a feud. "I wouldn't attend that wedding now for anything," sniffed Orry. "I'm going to call Jack and tell him."

Billy insisted the only proper way to decline an invitation was to write a letter. And it must be done formally, addressing Jack and Mary as "Mr. and Mrs." Orry huffed. "I have to call him *Mr.* Benny? I've known him thirty years!"

"Well, for heaven's sake, Orry." Billy smiled, his eyes getting large. "Don't call him *Miss*."

Billy remained close with Hedda until her death in February 1966. He was one of her honorary pallbearers, and arranged for her ashes to be sent back to her hometown in Pennsylvania, where she'd been born Elda Furry eighty-one years before. "We're sending Elda back home to Altoona in a box," Billy told their mutual friend Bob Shaw.

He was particularly struck by Orry-Kelly's death in 1965. Orry had reached his peak as a Hollywood costume designer in the 1950s, winning Oscars for *An American in Paris* (1951); *Les Girls* (1957), directed by George Cukor with music by Cole Porter; and *Some Like It Hot* (1959), a comedy about men in drag. Jean Mathison recalls Orry-Kelly as a frequent visitor to the Beverly Hills studio. "The two of them together was madness," she says. "The jokes would be bouncing off the walls." Shortly before his death, Orry taught Billy and Ted Graber some basics in costume design. Billy designed a few gowns; Jean Mathison recalls he made her one out of black lace, silk, and taffeta.

"Orry-Kelly was probably his best male friend," says Bob Shaw. The friendship even predated Hollywood, harking back to those heady, lusty days in Greenwich Village. When Orry died, a little part of Billy went with him.

Although Billy and Jimmie rarely went out to the clubs anymore, exceptions were made for important parties at Chasen's or for dinner at Romanoff's. Billy had become close with Michael Romanoff's wife Gloria, and was often spotted sitting with her at her husband's restaurant. He was also seen around town frequently with Marie "Stevie" Collier, wife of his old San Simeon buddy and costar Buster Collier (ironically, they'd also been close friends with Gable and Lombard). Billy and Stevie had a delightfully flirtatious relationship; Billy adored her campy sense of humor and the two of them would joke over lunch that they were having an affair.

It was through such venues as Chasen's and Romanoff's that Billy maintained some connection to the newer faces in the movie community. Romanoff's was a popular gathering place for the Hollywood elite, from Bogart and Bacall to Frank Sinatra, Dean Martin, and the rest of the "Rat Pack." Charlie Conrad recalls a party in the late 1950s at Chasen's, to which he accompanied Billy, Jimmie, Clifton Webb, and Webb's good buddy Lauren Bacall. This was a more liberal, more Democratic group than the merchant princes; Billy moved easily in either realm.

Conrad's visit to Billy and Jimmie in 1958, neatly detailed in his scrapbooks, provides a glimpse on their world. Charlie's first day was spent playing golf at the Hillcrest Country Club as a guest of Tom and Anita May; they provided an access Billy could not. Charlie's stay was a whirl of social activity: Billy and Jimmie took him to parties at Jack Benny's and the Bloomingdales' and to galas at Chasen's and Romanoff's. Charlie met many in their circle: George Burns and Gracie Allen, Bill and Edie Goetz, Claudette Colbert,

Swifty Lazar, Lauren Bacall, Frank Sinatra, Gary and Rocky Cooper, Jules Stein.

Charlie was given the royal tour. Sinatra took him around MGM; radio actor Freeman Gosden, the voice of Amos on *Amos and Andy*, invited him to play golf at the Bel-Air Country Club. There Charlie also played with Randolph Scott and the tire company executive Leonard Firestone, for whom Billy had done some design work. Poolside at Jack Benny's, Charlie innocently asked, "Where's Rochester?" Billy got a big laugh out of that, telling Charlie that Eddie "Rochester" Anderson's house was "twice as big" as Benny's. Hedda Hopper even wrote the comment up in her column the next day.

Billy held several dinner parties while Jimmie's nephew was in town. His parties were known for their simple elegance, for being formal without being stuffy. Conrad still has the menu from a dinner honoring famed Mexican socialite and businesswoman Carmen Figueroa. The dinner began with cold salmon as an appetizer, with an entrée of poached chicken breasts with mushrooms and peas. This was followed by a bean-shoot-and-lettuce salad, along with Brie and Gruyère cheeses. For dessert there was a chocolate roll and strawberries fondant. Two different French wines, their years carefully noted on the menu, were served with dinner. Jimmie would plan the menus, then write them out and place them on the plates. Gracie Allen, upon seeing one of Jimmie's carefully inscribed menus for the first time, turned to Bob Shaw and whispered: "Does this mean I get a choice?"

Billy's reputation as a classy, elegant host persisted into his (and the century's) sixties. His reputation as a cutup continued as well. There is a delightful series of photographs taken by Jean Howard at a party thrown by Joseph Cotten in 1955, in which Billy, fully dressed, leads a conga line straight into the pool.

Despite being photographed with Jennifer Jones and the occasional socializing with Lauren Bacall, Billy wasn't much connected with the "new Hollywood." He certainly didn't know the new batch of stars that appeared in the 1950s: Montgomery Clift, James Dean, Rock Hudson, Marlon Brando. He heard the whispered stories about their affairs with men, but he had no direct knowledge.

His contacts remained with the old crowd. Joan Crawford threw a huge party at the Papillon Restaurant for Noël Coward, hiring Billy to turn the place into a shimmering garden of Versailles. Showers of pink gardenias hung throughout. The guest list included the usual faces: Barbara Stanwyck and Robert Taylor (before their divorce); Marlene Dietrich; Clifton and Maybelle Webb; Jack and Mary Benny; and Claudette Colbert and Joel Pressman. Later, Crawford threw another party for Coward, this time at "21" in New York, after he was knighted by the queen. Billy was there to toast his old friend, and invited him out to visit him in Hollywood.

"I remember Noël Coward coming out and staying at Billy's," says Bob Shaw. "Billy and Jimmie had a small dinner party, Noël, myself, and Clifton Webb." Webb's mother Maybelle had died a few years before; he still mourned her tremendously. Coward's famous quip about Webb — "the world's oldest living orphan" — was actually spoken at Billy Haines's, and it came out this way: "Noël wanted to go see a hypnotist who was performing in town," Shaw says. "But Clifton just didn't want to go out. 'It's too soon for frivolity,' he said. Of course, Maybelle had been dead for a few years by this time. Billy tried to coax him, but he wouldn't go. Finally Noël said: 'Clifton, *sixty-six* is not a bad age to be orphaned."

Webb was one of the perennials around 601 Lorna Lane. Charlie Conrad recalls napping in a chaise longue by the pool during one of his visits, only to be awakened by the crack of Clifton Webb's cane on his head, demanding to know where Jimmie was. Both Billy and Jimmie adored the sometimes crotchety old man, who was in cranky, ill health the last few years of his life. His death in 1966 was one more loss to Billy's circle.

Gradually, relations with his tenant, Cole Porter, thawed, although the composer pointedly hired the East Coast decorator Billy Baldwin to do his New York apartment about the same time Billy was doing Joan Crawford's. Don Bachardy recalls that Porter wasn't the easiest man to get along with; he'd also iced out Bachardy's lover,

Christopher Isherwood, during this period. Billy and Porter had to deal with each other at least twice a year—when the rent was paid and when notice was given to stay on for another year—so tensions eased somewhat. Charlie Conrad recalls being a student and writing a term paper on Cole Porter's music. Jimmie brought him over to Porter's house, and Porter read the piece and autographed the last sheet. "I got a B." Conrad laughs. "I thought with Cole Porter's signature I might have done better."

Porter died in 1964. After his death, Billy rented out the house to Robert Mitchum, then to the director Mike Nichols, a rare connection to contemporary Hollywood.

Beginning in the middle part of the 1960s, Billy considered himself semi-retired, going into the studio less often and leaving most of the decisions up to Ted Graber. He and Jimmie also socialized less. It was now Ted Graber who often had dinner with the Deutsches and the Salvatoris and the Annenbergs. "I think in some ways," says one friend, "[Billy and Jimmie] were a little world weary. They still liked to travel, and put on airs, especially Jimmie—but they seemed to enjoy quieter times with friends who were primarily gay, not people in the movies, and certainly not their clients."

With such old friends as Tom Douglas, who dated back to the Cukor days, and Sholto Bailie, an Englishman who was also close with Clifton Webb and Noël Coward, there was no need to guard what was said, no need to worry that someone was going to make hostile public pronouncements about their lives.

Perhaps their best friend was Harris Woods. Jimmie was especially close with Woods, an independently wealthy man-about-town who had no connection to the movies except as a walk-on in George Cukor's *Camille*. "Harris was a friend to everyone, a very decent man," recalls Bob Wheaton. "At the end of their lives, Billy and Jimmie were very close to him."

Woods was a hillside neighbor of Cukor's and was friendly with the director as well. There were enough overlapping friends— Wheaton, Douglas, Bailie, Woods—that Billy found himself reconnecting with Cukor. Cukor's good friend Charles Williamson recalls seeing Billy occasionally at Cukor's on Sunday afternoons in the late 1960s. In a letter dated 1972, Billy addresses Cukor as "Boo Boo" and updates the director (who was off filming a picture) on the goings-on among their shared circle of friends. "All's well here, the usual ones for dinner, the lower colonies of Doheny [Drive]. . . . We speak of you often and exchange reading your letters. We speak with love, respect and a somewhat lonesome laughter."

The tone of their later letters suggests two old men who were enormously fond of each other and pleased to once again be a part of each other's lives. "There had always been an enormous amount of reserve affection," Bob Wheaton says. "The old friendship meant something."

The mutual friendship of Harris Woods was a strong bond between them. Billy and Cukor would joke about Woods's tendency to dye his gray hair black but never take the time to make sure it was even. "Dear [Harris] appeared the other night with black hair," Billy wrote to Cukor. "He looked like Pola Negri in the front but in the back the *sheitel* looked like a patch on grandmere's quilt."

Billy teased Cukor about being a year older than he was. "Dear director," he wrote after reading a press report of Cukor's age in 1972. "Why do you lie about your age? Joyce Haber said you were only 71. Now, now, you know darn well that you are my elder, that's why I respect you so. I am going to order some Pablum [a baby food] for both you and Harris." Billy signed his letter, "Buenas noches amigo, your shtuck goy friend, Willie Haines," adding parenthetically, "late of MGM and *Brown of Harvard*."

Cukor had a fondness for the old gay Hollywood set. He found small parts for Roger Davis in a number of his films; in 1960, he cast Edmund Lowe and Ramon Novarro in small but juicy supporting parts in *Heller in Pink Tights*. Eight years later, Novarro — Billy's gentle friend and lover from more than forty years before — was murdered by two hustlers he'd picked up on the street. They beat him savagely; Hollywood's great Ben Hur finally suffocated on his own blood and died.

Novarro's death stunned Hollywood, especially since it was followed so soon by the shocking brutality of the Charles Manson murders of actress Sharon Tate and her friends. Hollywood, the land of magic and make-believe that Billy had so fortuitously stumbled upon in 1922, a wonderland of crystal-clear air and sunny skies, was now a town of violence, blood, smog, and fear. "Sometimes I'll see an old film on television," Billy told a friend, "and I'll catch a glimpse of something, something of Hollywood I think I recognize from long ago. But then it's gone, and I'm not even sure if it was really there."

10

TELLING THE WORLD

1969-1974

In the late 1960s, the world seemed to bounce off its axis. Billy told one friend he felt as if the world were simply standing still, that everything had been "pulled up, knocked over, uprooted." The country was torn by a bloody, senseless war in Southeast Asia. College campuses were on fire, literally and figuratively, and Martin Luther King, Jr., and Robert Kennedy were assassinated just months apart in 1968. Thirty-four people had been killed—and a thousand more injured—in fiery race riots in the Watts section of Los Angeles, not twenty minutes from Billy's elegant, ordered home in Brentwood. The civil-rights movement had brought the racial divide in America to the forefront of the nation's consciousness. Now women—and homosexuals—were marching for their own liberation.

"Billy never could fathom all the changes going on in the world," says one friend. "He wasn't comfortable with all of what was going on—the hippies with their long hair and dirty clothes, their lack of manners. It went against how he'd always lived his own life. But when you think about it, he'd been marching to his own drummer all along. I'm not sure he made the connection, though."

Billy Haines—that true child of the twentieth century—was having a hard time keeping up. In his own youth, he'd been the rebel, daring to create a life for himself beyond the vision of his parents or society. He'd been part of the generation to shape the bohemia of Greenwich Village, part of the wide-eyed Flaming Youth of the Roaring Twenties. In pre-Code Hollywood, he'd set the trend for living openly with a lover of the same gender. He'd reveled in his own counterculture.

For his generation, however, acceptance—not transformation—had been the goal, and acceptance was a dream Billy had largely achieved by the late 1960s. He'd done it by proving he was as good as anyone else—or better, in some cases. He'd made the world *want* what he had to offer, turned his society around to his way of thinking, even if it meant redefining himself to fit the ever-changing views of the times.

So there was little empathy for the barefoot, long-haired boys and the topless, short-haired girls marching in the Christopher Street West Parade—Los Angeles' first gay-pride march—in June 1970. Held in commemoration of the Stonewall riots in New York the year before (generally considered to be the flashpoint of the contemporary gay movement), the Christopher Street West Parade drew twelve hundred brave souls down Hollywood Boulevard. Police Chief Ed Davis had attempted to block the march, saying that giving the marchers a permit would be like "permitting a parade of thieves and burglars." The march, however, went on as scheduled, with a six-foot transsexual waving from an open convertible, an eight-foot Vaseline jar with the sign "Ain't Nothin' So Good Without the Grease" swaying in a pickup truck, and a hundred drag queens blowing kisses to startled (and sometimes hostile) onlookers. It was like nothing the city had ever seen. Lesbian-rights activist Karla Jay, who was present, called it all "*so* Hollywood."

"It *was* quite tacky," says one longtime Los Angeles resident and a gay friend of Billy's. "It made me shudder. Billy didn't go, of course. None of us did. But we *were* curious to hear about it, nonetheless."

Much like Billy, this is a man who lived openly with his lover and never hid his orientation to his wealthy heterosexual friends. This is a man who finally attended his first gay-pride parade in 1996, and still felt it to be "terribly tacky." In the end, he admits, he "had an enjoyable time."

Might Billy, had he lived, come to the same conclusion? This friend says it's possible, but the very idea of it makes many of Billy's other friends laugh out loud.

"He would've hated it," says Arch Case. "He would have despised the behavior. I think that's our era. We like it being sort of naughty, sort of hidden."

Ted Graber says Billy viewed the gay-liberation movement with a sense of detached bemusement. "He said it gets it out of their system. Let them have their fun."

"He would've had no part of it," says Bob Shaw. "It just didn't exist. That concept of being gay, being part of something bigger based on that. In those days, it didn't come up. You have to understand that. I never even heard Billy say so-and-so was gay. In fact, you could be with Billy all night and, if you didn't know, you'd never know *he* was gay."

Despite his love of camp humor, Billy saw little in common between himself and the marchers in the Christopher Street West Parade. For one thing, they were mostly young, and he was, after all, now seventy years old. Although he'd elbow Arch and Ted in restaurants and suggest that their waiter was "a friend of Bertha's," he saw little union among himself and the wider gay population.

Especially those who pushed at the edges of gender. He may have befriended Jean Malin and applauded Karyl Norman's act three decades earlier, but those were *performances.* "He liked men to be men and women to be women," Ted Graber says simply. Indeed, in a letter to George Cukor in April 1972, he commented on a black actor he'd seen on television being "male (debatable), swathed in ermine and black sateen looking exactly like a black Bunny from the Club Goliath."

Michael Morrison says, "I can't *imagine* Billy at a gay-pride parade. But that doesn't take away from his courage. He'd always done what he wanted to do."

"He was out—he made no bones about that," says Bob Wheaton. "He just saw no need to march in parades and tell the world."

In 1969 he was telling the world something else: That taste and style and refinement still had a place in an era that seemed to repudiate beauty and culture—at least the kind that had been Billy's life pursuit.

Late the year before, President Richard Nixon, following his election in November, asked Walter Annenberg to take the post as ambassador to Great Britain. It was a tremendous honor, but not entirely unexpected; Annenberg had been one of Nixon's chief campaign boosters. It was an opportunity, Annenberg felt, to finally and permanently redeem his family's name, but with it came considerable risk. Like many in Billy's privileged set, Walter and Lee were painfully aware of their lack of social pedigree. The nomination had caused considerable consternation within the ranks of the "Protestant Establishment." This wasn't just any ambassadorship, after all: It was the embassy to the Court of St. James's.

Annenberg's discomfort was only exacerbated by the popularity of the man he was replacing, Ambassador David Bruce. He was a career diplomat, part of the established, old-money order. He was both highly skilled and highly regarded, and his wife, the stately Evangeline Bruce, was considered to be the finest hostess in the diplomatic corps. The Bruces' gentility and culture had charmed the British, and nearly everyone was very sorry to see them go.

"Lee Annenberg approached Billy and me and asked us to help," recalls Ted Graber. "She wanted the very best. She wanted to show them a thing or two."

Billy was roused from his semi-retirement to participate in the job. He and Ted were more like partners than employer-employee at this point, but Billy's years of experience would prove beneficial. There was no way he could have sat this one out: This was the culmination of his life's work, the pinnacle opportunity to express himself. All other jobs would be put on hold; he and Graber stood to make an enormous sum of money from the Annenbergs. From early 1969 on, they became, in effect, the American ambassador's personal interior decorators.

Even before Walter had been confirmed in the post, Billy flew

with Lee and Ted to London to tour Winfield House, the grand
manor in Regent's Park where the American ambassador lived. Lee
had heard stories it was in disrepair, and she wanted her decorators'
advice—as well as their companionship and support, given Evangeline Bruce's barely concealed hostility toward her. The Bruces were
still in residence, and Mrs. Bruce had told friends she'd "never even
heard of these strange people" until Walter had been nominated.
Lee, then a svelte blonde, laughs when she recalls her first meeting
with Evangeline Bruce. "I believe she thought she was going to meet
a dumpy little Jewish matron. Instead, she got me!"

Most people considered Lee's insistence on touring the residence
with Billy and Ted arrogant, presumptuous, and insensitive. After
all, she was implying that what the Bruces had settled for wasn't going to be good enough for her.

"The truth is, the place was *horrible*," remembers Graber. "Simply
horrible." The three-story, thirty-five-room Georgian mansion had a
leaky roof, cracked plaster, and faulty wiring. Very little maintenance had been done since the house was built in 1937. Its original
owner was Barbara Hutton, American heiress to the Woolworth fortune, who deeded it over to the U.S. government in 1946. Lee was
aghast at the house's condition. Not only was it physically deterio-
rating, Evangeline Bruce had even allowed water stains on the tables under her plants!

As Mrs. Bruce watched in stony silence, Lee walked through the
house with Billy and Ted, listening to their advice on what needed to
be done. It seemed overwhelming. Finally she started to cry. Ted
suggested they do it later, but Lee insisted they continue. By the time
they were finished taking notes and snapping photographs, Mrs.
Bruce had had enough.

Within days, the British papers were filled with sarcastic asides
about the "Hollywood decorators" who would be redoing Winfield
House. Meanwhile, back at home, the American press was sniping
over whether Walter was fit for the job, reviving the scandal over his
father's prison term. One magazine called Walter's nomination a
"monumental joke." Lee insisted to Billy that it was simply the last
gasping breath of the "Establishment."

To others, however, the Annenbergs represented that very establishment, the elite, the oppressor class. Walter railed against the rioting students in speeches and editorials, chastising them for not being grateful for the opportunities before them and for disregarding the civilities of society. Yet to the blue-blooded "Establishment"—as Lee called it—they were usurpers, gauche and uncouth. Walter and Lee were terribly nervous undertaking their new assignment. Walter had become comfortable in the world of business and politics; he had found himself easily at the apex of the Palm Springs–Hollywood set. "But the universe of high society still intimidated him," Annenberg biographer John Cooney writes, "and both he and Lee were walking on eggs, so intent were they upon doing what was right, what was proper."

In this, Billy could understand. He could also help. Lee turned to him repeatedly for advice, on what to say, what to wear, how to act. Billy and Ted began work on Winfield House almost immediately. They had suites at the Ritz and a Princess limousine with a driver to carry them back and forth to Regent's Park. According to Billy's British friend Geoffrey Toone, Billy even redecorated his rooms at the Ritz for the duration.

In March, Walter was confirmed by the Senate. Then, on April 29, Billy and Ted were present to witness him present his ambassadorial credentials to Queen Elizabeth II. "It was simply unimaginable to me that we should have come this far," says Ted Graber. "To Billy, too. What a wonderful, wonderful life."

It was typical British pomp and circumstance. From the American Embassy, Walter was taken in a gilded coach led by a pair of bay-colored horses to Buckingham Palace. The ceremony was being filmed by the BBC for its documentary *The Royal Family*. Walter was led into the reception chamber overlooking the palace gardens and presented to the queen. The formal presentation went smoothly, but when the queen, in the presence of the rolling cameras, tried to exchange small talk, Walter grew stiff and awkward. She was aware of the renovation work Billy and Ted were doing, so she asked, "You aren't living at the embassy at the moment, are you?"

Walter's reply became famous for its stilted preposterousness. He said, "We're in the Embassy residence, subject, of course, to some of the discomfiture as a result of a need for, uh, elements of refurbishment and rehabilitation."

The queen gazed at him uncomprehendingly. Then she smiled, struck, as Cooney says, by the "obvious effect her presence had on the rich and powerful man before her."

To most, the new ambassador seemed pretentious, desperate to prove himself as erudite and sophisticated as his predecessor. Those more sympathetic to him said he was merely nervous. He was derided for months in both the British and American press for the remark. Billy soothed Lee's feelings, who felt their treatment ever since the nomination had been unfair.

For his part, Billy found Walter could be something of a boor, not as consistently warm or friendly as Alfred Bloomingdale or some of the other husbands among the merchant princes. During the next several months, as Billy and Ted captained the team of workmen who took over Winfield House, Walter's frustration and rage were often targeted at his decorators. There was a cutting, condescending vindictiveness in his voice. Under his breath, he'd curse the "men" who told him where he could sit, what rooms he could enter, which fixtures were staying and which were going. Lee would always intercede on Billy's and Ted's behalf, ordering her husband to apologize.

It was all worth it, however. For Billy, Buckingham Palace was a long way from Staunton. Nothing symbolized better the journey Billy had taken than this. He'd conquered the giants of Hollywood—Jack Warner, Bill Goetz—and the titans of American capitalism—Alfred Bloomingdale, Walter Annenberg. Now he dared to stand before royalty itself—and not a "second-rate" monarchy like Belgium this time. This was the House of Windsor and its attendant aristocracy, the pinnacle of social prestige. Ambassador Annenberg might worry how the British would receive him, but Billy Haines had something to prove, too. For all his devotion to European culture and style over the years, now his work would be judged not by Los Angeles, but by London. This was his last big, important job—the most important ever—and, at seventy years old, he knew that. The dreamer from Staunton stood once more in the wings, waiting for his chance to prove his stuff.

Billy and Ted traveled back and forth to London a total of eight times in nine months. They had a November deadline and often worked twelve-hour days. It was an enormous task, but never daunting. "Large size has never frightened me," Billy explained. "Only the small."

They were frustrated by the different working methods of British tradesmen, who insisted on breaking for tea in the middle of the afternoon. When Ted discovered a pack of carpenters playing cards, he says he "lined them up and chewed them out, just like a drill sergeant."

Billy was pleased by the blossoming of his protégé and his take-charge attitude. "He runs the business," he candidly told reporters. Billy relished the newfound sense of partnership with Ted, finding it a perfect balance. He told a British newspaper, "You get the courage from youth, the simplicity from age, and the mixture makes a good noise."

Despite some initial barbs about the "Hollywood decorators," the British press was, on the whole, respectful of Billy. Although they noted he was once a star of the silent screen, few reporters seemed to know much about him. He was from a time long ago, a time many had never lived through. When one young reporter asked Billy his age, he snapped, "Eighty-four!" The scribe dutifully reported that an "octogenarian" decorator was working at Winfield House. Billy commented, laughing, "He didn't even say, 'My, you are well-preserved.' "

Despite Graber's growing influence, the house's decor clearly carries Billy's imprint: Chippendale furniture, George III wine coolers, Ming chests, lotus-patterned Lowestoft china. As he had with other clients who were art fanciers, Billy utilized the Annenbergs' impressive collection of paintings and sculpture to good effect, with Renoirs, Gauguins, Toulouse-Lautrecs, and Monets placed strategically throughout. The Annenbergs made it a point to tell their British visitors these were part of their private collection; they'd take the artwork with them when they left.

Ted Graber says he and Billy knew they had to be faithful to the architectural integrity of the house. This could not be a modern house like Sunnylands. Instead, Regency-style wall lamps were maintained; the eighteenth-century French furniture originally bought by Barbara Hutton was renovated and reused. "The only difference between Winfield House today and the way it might have been in the eighteenth century is that there's more furniture now," Graber said. "In those days they had grand salons, which required lots of space."

There was one major structural change: The front staircase was rebuilt in a more sweeping style, as befits a Georgian house. It's the first thing one sees upon entering the entrance reception hall, the first real image one gets of Winfield House, and Billy felt it important that the grandeur of the place hit a visitor immediately.

His favorite room, however, was the garden room, facing the lush rear garden. Its fourteen-foot-high walls were covered in Billy's signature Chinese hand-painted wallpaper. This particular specimen had been dear to his heart ever since he'd discovered it in an antique shop in London in 1959. It was more than one hundred years old, having originally decorated a hall at Trinity College in Dublin. "It was exquisite," Billy said of the pale green paper, depicting delicate birds and butterflies among leafy Chinese trees. It was also very, very expensive. He didn't buy it at that time, yet he would think of it often when he'd be choosing wallpaper for various houses.

When Lee Annenberg showed him the garden room, Billy knew he'd found a home for the paper. They hurried down to the antique shop early the next morning; to their delight, the paper was still there. Lee adored it and bought it on the spot. They had it shipped to New York, where it was painstakingly cleaned and pressed. Then it was sent to Hong Kong, where Chinese artists fixed faded areas and filled in colors. It was mounted on canvas and sent back for installation at Winfield House. It was the pièce de résistance, and everyone who saw it raved about it. To complement it, Nancy and Ronald Reagan gave the Annenbergs a jade tree when they visited that fall.

The final bill for the house topped $1 million. The U.S. government contributed just $50,000; Annenberg paid the rest as a nontaxable gift to the government. (No wonder he insisted the artwork wasn't part of the deal.)

On November 21, the residence was officially opened to reporters; Billy led a couple of tours. "It took nine months to finish, to the *hour*," he told reporters. "Well, we were five minutes late." The last cushion, he said, had been plumped five minutes after five o'clock on November 1.

All animosities were forgotten as Annenberg publicly thanked his decorators. "We operated as a team under the Haines flagship," he said. For his part, Billy defended Annenberg against charges of opulence. "The United States government has not kept its properties in proper condition," he told the *Times* of London sternly. "Much furniture had to be bought." Ninety-five percent of Winfield House's collection, he pointed out, was authentic antiques.

The British press had clucked over the expense; many felt the extravagance excessive. Philip Howard of the *Times* of London, following Billy through the house, was particularly snide in his coverage, unable to resist jabbing Annenberg's by-now-infamous response to the queen. "The American ambassador's residence was opened yesterday for an awed walk-through by the press," Howard wrote. Annenberg's "little gray house," Howard wrote, "has been requixed, replumbed, reroofed, regilded, painted inside and out, and refurnished with a spectacular splendor that justifies Mr. Walter Annenberg's sesquipedalian orotundity." Howard observed that "Niagaras of crystal chandeliers cascade, Chippendale fireplaces brood . . . [and] genteel Louis XV settees turn their elegant backs on the Regency lacquer tables, the yellow glaze Ming, and the framed picture of President Nixon."

Other British tabloids were more direct. "Walter Annenberg has hired a Beverly Hills decorator who has turned Winfield House into a movie mogul's palace," said one. Billy sniffed to the *Los Angeles Herald-Examiner*, "Those English journalists should *see* a few of our movie moguls' palaces over here—at least the way *I* design them." The newspaper observed: "Were Haines less charitably disposed he could grind the ladies who wrote the decorating reviews into pâté and serve them with this afternoon's cocktails. He is as well known in this city for his wit as for his way with decor."

On November 25, a gala party was held to unveil the redesign of Winfield House. A select thirty-six were invited to dinner, Billy and Ted among them. Princess Margaret went out of her way to tell reporters how splendid she found the renovation. Afterward, 450 people attended a party in the great hall. Jimmie came over with his sister Virginia and nephew Charlie Conrad. Londoners who had once been loyal to the Bruces couldn't help but admit that Billy and Ted had worked wonders with Winfield House. The sniping stopped in the British press; Annenberg's reputation was markedly enhanced by the job his decorators had done on his house.

In the United States, there was even more praise. Billy became the darling of the house-decorating magazines. His pithy comments and witty observations made good copy for a new generation of reporters. *Architectural Digest* featured several spreads of his work; editor Paige Rense, with whom he became friendly, ran a lengthy interview with him after the unveiling of Winfield House.

"I wanted it to be the best of two countries — England and America," Billy said of his London triumph. He could have been speaking of himself. He needn't have worried. Once again, in the end, Billy Haines had triumphed.

After Winfield House, Billy made a point to keep abreast of work being done at the studio. "It keeps me in practice," he told a reporter. "It calls upon every emotion, even from silent pictures. My last job is always the most important job we have ever done."

In truth, Winfield House *was* his last job. Ted Graber ran the show now, much to Billy's pleasure. Billy was allowed to enjoy his last years of health with considerable leisure.

Charlie Conrad recalls a trip back to Virginia around this time. Billy and Jimmie visited Charlie, now married with children and living in Harrisonburg, about half an hour north of Staunton. Billy was determined to make the drive down to his hometown. Although he'd visited a few times over the years, he hadn't been there in some time. "So we all went down," Conrad remembers. "Billy was full of life that day. He walked into the bank, where he knew the teller. But she didn't recognize him. He went up to her, wrote a check for one million dollars, and pushed it through. She was stunned. She said, 'Mr. Haines, it'll be just a minute—' Then she turned and said really slowly, *'Billy Haines?'* And we all got a big laugh out of that."

He had indeed become a millionaire by the late 1960s, and certainly after Winfield House. There was a particular delight returning to the middle-class streets of Staunton and writing a check for a million dollars, even if he had no intention of cashing it. In case there was anyone who hadn't heard—the classmates who'd taunted him, the teachers who'd despaired of him—he wanted word to get around that Billy Haines had *made it.*

It was with a keen sense of satisfaction that Billy now looked back upon his life. Despite the turmoil and trauma, he enjoyed the luxury—rare among so many—of having achieved his dreams.

He and Jimmie traveled to Europe a number of times during their last years, socializing with Noël Coward and Alan Searle, Somerset Maugham's lover, who was still depressed over the novelist's death in 1965. Cukor wrote Searle in 1970: "[Bill Haines] is talking about you and would love to see you. I'm telling him to look you up at the Dorchester. He's full of pep and you'd have an enjoyable time together." Billy may have been full of pep, but he and Jimmie found Searle sad and lonely.

Billy also met up with Joan Crawford in London in 1970, who was there making what turned out to be her last film, a sad horror mess called *Trog*. Billy simply looked at her and said, "Cranberry, why do you persist?" She told him it was all she had left; her marriages had failed, her relationships with her children had disintegrated. And besides, Al Steele had left her deep in debt.

Still, the three old friends managed to have at least one night out on the town together. They'd taken adjacent rooms at the Dorchester and made reservations at a posh London eatery, Les Ambassadeurs. Although the restaurant was not far from the hotel, none of them knew quite where it was, so they hired a chauffeur. Billy told friends how Joan affected a British accent and told the chauffeur the name of the restaurant. They got horribly lost and missed their reservations, but the three of them, laughing in the backseat of that Rolls-Royce, were as gay and giddy as they had been nearly fifty years before.

They had no way of knowing it would be the last time.

"I have never been bored in my whole life," Billy told an interviewer. "If I was ever bored, it was my own fault."

His life had been a continual quest for the new and different, a constant challenge to keep topping what came before. As such, he had precious little time for retrospection. He told a reporter in 1970 that he'd kept not one clipping or photograph from his days in the movies. To a British fan who wrote telling him silent films were making a comeback in England, Billy replied: "I can't say I'm wholly sympathetic to your hobby . . . I am one that has not wanted ever to look over my shoulder at Lot's wife."

He viewed his twelve years as a movie star—now nearly four decades in the past—as a youthful adventure and little more. Indeed, he liked to poke fun at those days. When Billy would call Bob Shaw at his office, he'd say to Shaw's secretary: "Tell him it's Brown of Harvard on the phone" or "Slide Kelly Slide wants him to return the call."

He had little remaining connection with Hollywood. Those he stayed in contact with—Crawford, Eleanor Boardman, even George Cukor—had themselves been largely displaced. In a telling letter to Cukor after watching the Academy Awards on television in April 1972, Billy comes across like a bemused, out-of-touch alumnus. It's a bitingly bitchy, campy assessment of the Hollywood that had supplanted his own, and his contemporaries were among the first to be skewered.

"We thought it was very entertaining and handsomely mounted and praise to our merciful Father—no Bob Hope," Billy wrote. He wisecracked about Tennessee Williams's ruffled pink shirt and Alan King's nose job. "All of this," he wrote, "led up to the climax of that talented lady of song, Miss Debby [*sic*] Reynolds, who sang a sad ballad in Ethel Wales' wedding dress [that] she wore in *The Covered Wagon*." (Ethel Wales was one of the busiest character actresses of the 1920s and played the mother in James Cruze's *The Covered Wagon*.)

Billy continued, "Now behold, dear reader, the next to appear was Miss Helen Hayes, known as Miss Cyclamate of 1972 (the Artificial Sweetener). She never looked lovelier with little corkscrew curls falling in front of her ears but, alas, what came out of her mouth was another story. She was lip lazy, tongue tripping, and hand wringing—a reject practitioner from the Mother Church in Boston."

His most stinging observations were reserved for Charles Chaplin, who was presented with an honorary Oscar that night. Over the years, Billy had found his old fellow court jester from San Simeon increasingly distant and mercenary. It wasn't allegations of Communism that Billy held against him; what was more outrageous was his latter-day air of self-conscious superiority. "He appeared completely huffed, puffed, stuffed, and bewildered," Billy wrote to Cukor of Chaplin's appearance on the awards program. "He didn't know where the hell he was. I still contend greed and masturbation takes its toll."

In between his humor, one can still detect some lingering bitterness for his long-ago expulsion from the ranks. "The old ones (actors that is) never know when to quit," he wrote. Newer stars didn't escape his jabs, either. "The whole evening was an entertaining farce swathed in forgetfulness and insincerity, played in front of a background of Reynolds Wrap, long hair, beards, and a few exposed wayward tits—those of Miss [Raquel] Welch. She was the only beauty there, besides Dick Chamberlain."

Still, for all his disdain, he had moments of nostalgia for his Hollywood days. In early 1972 he saw *Show People* at a King Vidor revival at the Los Angeles County Art Museum and was pleasantly surprised by how well it held up. He was also pleased by his own performance, grateful after all these years for Vidor's insistence on restraint. "I felt I was looking at an ectoplasm on the screen," he told the *Los Angeles Herald-Examiner*. "I felt sorry for us because I was part of something that no longer exists. Almost everybody in the film with me had gone on." The newspaper noted he seemed visibly touched by all the young people asking for his autograph.

Filmograph magazine asked him in late 1972 which was his favorite among all his films. His response showed he was very much living in the present but could also be reflective about his past. "Selecting a favorite picture from amongst the films I have made is somewhat like picking a favorite egg out of a large crate of eggs," he said. "They all look alike in memory. I can only look back over those glorious and wondrous years as being part of the early spring of a very rewarding career, recalling the excitement, the camaraderie, and joy of working in an art medium that none of us realized was being created at the time."

In the summer of 1973 he was diagnosed with lung cancer. He'd been feeling weak, suffering from a shortness of breath and nausea.

Friends say Billy was never a heavy smoker, yet he had consistently smoked since his days working in his father's cigar factory. Until his diagnosis, he'd enjoyed a long run of bullish good health. Just the year before, he and Jimmie had taken what turned out to be their last trip to Europe; they spent several months traipsing over the Continent, from London to Venice. Now friends were shocked to see Billy, usually so strong and robust, weakened and dizzy.

In fact, it had been Jimmie whose health had been more worrisome. He'd had a bout with skin cancer a few years before, having a growth removed from his nose. There was also a throat operation, after which he couldn't speak for several months. He was just sixty-five in 1970, but had declined much faster than Billy.

Bob Shaw believes Jimmie may have begun showing early signs of Alzheimer's disease by 1971 or 1972. He'd forget simple tasks and people's names. Once, at a dinner party at Lorna Lane, Jimmie suddenly announced: "We should have invited Polly Moran. We haven't seen her in so long."

Billy let out a long sigh. "The reason we haven't seen her," he said, slightly exasperated, "is because she's been *dead* for twenty years."

What made it even more difficult was that Jimmie was still lucid enough to recognize his trouble. "It was very disconcerting for him," says Shaw. Understandably, Jimmie counted more and more on Billy's continued good health and vitality.

Friends say Jimmie was devastated by Billy's diagnosis, and throughout the fall, despite Billy's growing weakness, refused to believe the worst. Everyone had assumed Billy would survive Jimmie, including Billy himself. Now Billy worried what might happen to his partner of forty-seven years after he was gone.

"You've got to promise you'll take care of Jimmie," he told Ted Graber and others, including his sisters Ann and Lillion. Billy had provided well for Jimmie in his will: He'd continue to own shares in William Haines, Inc., which was willed to Ted, and he'd have the house and all their possessions for the duration of his life. Jimmie would need more than that, however: Billy feared that without his being there to constantly reassure him, Jimmie's mind would deteriorate even faster.

Meanwhile, Billy's own health rapidly declined. He lost an enormous amount of weight and within months was confined to a wheelchair. He no longer had even a nominal involvement in the work of the company: Ted was on his own. During Billy's illness, Ted designed (in collaboration with architect Harry Saunders) the house of insurance industry mogul Joe Bain. It was a monument to opulence, with antique floors, grand pillars, and ceilings imported from England. Billy had little, if any, input into the job, although his name remained on the contract. When it was completed, Ted took Billy to see it, pushing him through the elegant rooms in his wheelchair. Billy was quiet for much of the tour. Finally he looked up at Ted, the pride catching in his voice, and said, "The student has surpassed the master."

After that, he rarely went out. He didn't even allow close friends like Betsy Bloomingdale in for visits; instead, he spoke to her regularly every Sunday on the phone. Joan Crawford, too, called several times a week; Billy was only occasionally able to speak with her, so she got most of her updates from Jimmie. His sisters took turns sitting at his bedside; Jimmie often fell asleep in the chair next to him, refusing to leave Billy's room.

"I remember one Sunday, right near the end," says Betsy Bloomingdale. "I called on Sunday as usual, and Billy said, 'Well, little girl, I think this is the last Sunday we'll speak.' And I just said, 'Oh, Billy,' and started to cry."

In late November Billy learned his old friend Constance Talmadge had died. Like Marion Davies, Dutch had become a hopeless alcoholic and Billy had lost touch with her. Her death nonetheless depressed him.

In early December his physician, W. L. Marxer, who'd treated him since 1952, ordered him moved to St. John's Hospital in Santa Monica. Bob Shaw surprised him with a visit. "He was very affable and pleasant," Shaw recalls. "But after about two or three minutes he said, 'Bob, I really need my rest.' I suppose I should've let him know I was coming. He was trying to be nice to me, but he just couldn't keep up the conversation. He only lasted a few weeks after that."

They celebrated Christmas in Billy's room, with small gifts that Billy seemed not to notice. He managed to smile and briefly clasped Jimmie's hand. The next day, December 26, 1973, at 6:45 P.M., with Jimmie sitting in the chair beside him, he suffered a sudden cardiac arrest and died. William Haines was just one week short of his seventy-fourth birthday.

When he left his house for the last time, he'd told Ted Graber to pause. He asked that he be turned around in his wheelchair so that he could see into the house. His eyes passed over the George III mahogany chairs, the Regency dining table, the black-lacquer longcase clock, the giltwood wall mirror, the marble bust of Clinus, the equestrian figure by Narino, the "Les Incas" wallpaper, the red Turkish carpet.

Billy choked back his emotion. "To hell with all this beauty I leave behind," he said. Then he gestured that he was ready to go.

"He did everything with style, including dying," says Ted Graber. Billy died quickly, with as much dignity as he had lived.

Among his friends—and they were many—there was considerable grief at Billy's death. Betty Barker says Joan Crawford was "devastated" when Jimmie called to tell her Billy had died. Yet the world at large had long since forgotten William Haines. *Variety* didn't get around to running an obituary until January 16, 1974. His death merited just a small announcement in the *New York Times*, which traditionally had given large play to the deaths of old movie stars. The *Times* simply reported he'd been "a film comedian of the 1920s." No mention was made of the El Porto beach scandal, or the rumors that had followed his career in pictures; in fact, the *Times* said that Billy had "specialized in the role of the wisecracking character who wins the girl just before the fadeout."

Yes, but how much more was left unsaid.

Only his brothers and sisters were listed as survivors in the *Los Angeles Times*; perhaps not surprisingly, given the era, there was no mention of Jimmie. Certainly their friends considered Jimmie the "widow," and most of the flowers—from Crawford, the Annenbergs, the Bloomingdales, the Reagans—came addressed to him. He sat like a stunned child, or a little old man, hardly moving from the sofa, not even to receive guests.

Billy had requested there be no service. "He said he didn't want everyone standing around with their fingers up their noses," Jean Mathison says with a laugh. He was cremated on December 28, and a small urn containing his ashes was placed on a shelf at the Woodlawn Mausoleum in Santa Monica. There was a space reserved next to him for Jimmie.

He left an estate worth several million dollars. He'd named both Jimmie and Ted Graber as executors, but Jimmie was in no state to carry out his duties, so Ted took charge. Billy had bequeathed fifty-one percent of the shares in William Haines, Inc., to Ted, effectively leaving him the business. He'd set up a trust fund to take care of Jimmie; upon Jimmie's death, the trust would be divided in four for each of Billy's siblings. As he had all his life, he was ensuring the welfare of his family.

He also left cash bequests to Jean Hayden (Mathison); his longtime maid, Andrée Cordier; the Haines family maid, Buffy Braxton; and his cook, Marguerite Agnesse. In addition, clearly thinking Jimmie was likely to die before him, Billy inserted a clause leaving money to Jimmie's sister, Margaret Lawson. His generosity, so evident in life, remained apparent in death.

So did his sense of humor. He left special mementos to some special friends. At the reading of the will, there was much laughter amid the tears. "To Ted Graber," Billy wrote, "my longtime associate and friend, who over these many years has become part of my mind and an added strength to my ego. It has been seldom that he has not rewarded me with laughter at one of my bum jokes." He bequeathed to Graber two Chinese figurines of seated ladies dating from the T'ang period, one playing with a dog and the other with a drum. "Let's hope they don't end up playing with something else," Billy wrote.

To Gloria Romanoff, "who has always brought joy and news through the dreary windows of my Sundays," he left two Lowestoft platters, circa 1760. Stevie Collier, "a warm and glorious friend besides being a refreshing and capable camp," received a bronze spread-eagle clock on a marble base. Billy wrote the clock "has always been in my bedroom where she would never come. Alas!"

It was Betsy Bloomingdale who received the most touching gift. For years she had loved one of the most eccentric pieces in Billy's house: a twelve-piece porcelain band of monkeys, made in Germany, with each monkey in period costume playing a different instrument. Of all the elegant pieces in Billy's house, this was the one he left his "little girl." Betsy, he wrote, "has taken more abuse from me, although wrapped in love, than any kind lady should."

It was one last wisecrack from Billy Haines.

Jimmie went through the motions, signing executors' forms whenever Ted asked him, but he was silent and withdrawn, as if he weren't quite sure what to do or what to say without Billy at his side.

On New Year's Eve, he attended a party at the Bloomingdales'. It had been just a week since Billy's death; Betsy insisted Jimmie not spend the holiday alone. He remained somber and reticent all evening, sitting off by himself and staring into space. People went out of their way to try to engage him, but he remained blank-eyed and unresponsive.

Finally Ronald Reagan approached him. He'd never been all that fond of Jimmie; he felt him too effeminate and self-absorbed. Now he took him by the elbow for a walk. Jimmie would tell friends that Reagan was warm and supportive. "Jimmie," he said, "you loved Billy, and he was a wonderful person, and it's very hard to go on. But Billy would want you to. He wouldn't want to see you like this."

Nancy Reagan confirms the story. "Yes, I recall that happening. That's my husband's nature. He felt sorry for Jimmie. We all did."

For a few days, Jimmie's spirits lifted as he told the story to friends. "We were all amazed," says Bob Wheaton. "Jimmie called it unbelievable. Reagan wasn't known to be all that friendly to gays. But my opinion of him changed a little after hearing that."

A few days later, Harris Woods arranged a dinner to get Jimmie out of the house. Bob Wheaton drove Jimmie to the restaurant. "He was still grieving," Wheaton recalls. "There were tears in his eyes the whole time. He said he just missed Billy terribly."

He couldn't bear to read the many notes of condolence; they simply confirmed the truth that Billy was gone. When Laura La Plante and her husband Irving Asher stopped by to see Jimmie, she noticed her card—and dozens of others—remained unopened on the table. Jimmie told his old friend Carmel Myers, "It's no good without Billy."

Looking back, Jimmie's grief seems to have only exacerbated his already weakening mental condition. He'd sit for long periods without speaking; often he'd enter a room carrying a piece of sculpture or a book, yet couldn't explain what he was doing with it. In February he walked to the market, as he'd done countless times. He greeted the clerks and then slipped a pound of bacon under his jacket. When he attempted to walk out of the store, he was stopped and the police were called.

"Poor Jimmie," remembers Ted Graber. "He was terrified." Ted was summoned to the store, where he convinced the police to let Jimmie go. "I asked Jimmie, did he know what he'd done? He didn't. He was just terrified. He didn't need to steal. He could've bought the whole store if he wanted to."

The one thing Jimmie *couldn't* forget, however, was Billy's death.

His nephew, Charlie Conrad, came to visit him in late February. "He told me he was having a hard time," Conrad remembers. "I didn't realize how hard."

Billy's sisters and Ted Graber all encouraged Jimmie to get out more and socialize. On the night of March 4, he accepted an invitation to a small dinner party given by Count Maximillian de Henckel, who had a house in Mandeville Canyon. Frank Lysinger was there, and recalls his host's attempts to cheer Jimmie up. It was a thankless task. "I just can't go on without Billy," Jimmie told them. Lysinger says they managed to make him laugh a couple of times, but when he left, Jimmie had "such a sad look on his face."

He suffered through the next day. The house was eerily quiet; without Billy's booming voice echoing across the marble, every sound seemed jarring and unexpected. The maid and the cook retired early that night; there were no guests. Jimmie was alone with his thoughts and his memories.

Around eight o'clock he started making phone calls. He called his sisters. He called George Haines. He called Harris Woods. "People thought he was a little drunk," says Arch Case. He may have been. At some point he also swallowed an entire bottle of sleeping pills that had been prescribed for him following Billy's death. He taped a note to his door, telling the maid not to come inside, instructing her to call Ted Graber instead. Then he locked the door behind him.

Taking out a pen, he wrote a letter on his legal-size personal notepad, the name "Jimmie" inscribed across the top. "Goodbye to all of you who have tried so hard to comfort me in my loss of William Haines, whom I have been with since 1926. I now find it impossible to go it alone — I am much too lonely." He went on to ask Ted Graber to ensure the distribution of his possessions to his sisters, brother, and one of his nephews. "I have money in my bathroom to send everything," he wrote.

With that, he removed his clothes, lay down upon the bed, and fell asleep. He never woke up. Jimmie Shields was two weeks shy of his sixty-ninth birthday.

The coroner's report said Jimmie had died around 9:45 P.M. on the night of March 5 of acute barbiturate intoxication. The maid, Marguerite Agnesse, had indeed found Jimmie's door locked around 7 o'clock that following morning, and read the note to call Ted Graber. Graber arrived around 8:15, forced open the door, and discovered Jimmie's body. Again, there was no service. This time, there was not even a notice in the paper of Jimmie's death. His ashes were simply placed beside Billy's in Woodlawn Mausoleum.

"I was stunned," says Bob Shaw. When Ann Langhorne called him to tell him the news, she began by saying, "I have something very sad to tell you." Shaw assumed she was distraught, forgetting she'd called him about Billy's death two months before. When she told him Jimmie had committed suicide, he was thunderstruck. "I knew he was depressed, but not to the point of that."

Betty Barker says she and Joan Crawford were both struck with a sense of guilt. Jimmie had asked them to visit after Billy's death, but they hadn't yet made the trip. "I always told him that I would 'very soon,'" she says, "but to my great regret I put it off for too long." Still, it had been just two months since Billy's death.

Bob Wheaton had been convinced Jimmie was rallying. No one suspected that Jimmie would take his own life, except perhaps for Harris Woods, who'd become Jimmie's closest confidant. He later told friends that Jimmie had seemed quite sublime when he spoke of joining Billy. It was not an act of a disturbed mind, Woods insisted, but rather of a man determined to continue a love story begun nearly half a century before.

"The impression I always got from Harris Woods," says Charles Williamson, "was that Billy and Jimmie loved each other very deeply and profoundly." So profoundly that suicide, in a way, made sense. Jimmie viewed taking his life not so much as an escape from depression—although it was surely that—but as an act of love.

His nephew, Charlie Conrad, returned to California to put Jimmie's estate in order. Jimmie wasn't worth nearly as much as Billy, with a clear market value of his property just under $400,000. His shares in William Haines, Inc., were divided among his sisters and brother, and he left cash gifts to Marguerite Agnesse and Andrée Cordier, as Billy had done. He also bequeathed a solid-gold cigarette case to Harris Woods. His jewelry collection, worth over $13,000, was divided among his siblings. To them went his platinum cuff links set with diamonds and sapphires, his jade and gold rings, his elaborate gold bracelets. His fabulous collection of eleven Cartier and Piaget gold watches, including the one with the seven sapphires, was given to his nephews. Charlie Conrad treasured one for years, until a thief broke into his house and made off with it. Who knows how much he got for it, or where it is now.

The rest of their worldly goods went up for auction. Sotheby Parke Bernet of Los Angeles held the first of eight auctions on October 20, 1974. This auction was mostly of the porcelain dish and tea service collections, raising $13,215 for the estate. A full $9,000 of that total came from the sale of an antique pair of glazed warrior figurines.

The main event was held over the course of three separate evenings, on October 29, November 4, and November 11. This time Billy's magnificent furniture went on the block. Camilla Snyder, writing for the *Los Angeles Herald-Examiner*, called the auction preview "a gay and tasteful memorial to Billy Haines." The way of life represented by the pieces, Snyder wrote, "is all but extinct. It went out when full-time staffs of live-in servants became too costly and when rooms with grand proportions could no longer be accommodated by modern architects." Still, she reasoned, most everyone could find room for one or two great pieces "in their home or — we shudder at the word — condominium."

One old friend observed, "Billy would have loved to see his things here at Sotheby in these simulated room settings, his clock next to Mrs. [Charles] Blyth's red lacquer cabinet. I think he would have stood in a corner watching to see who came and trying to overhear what his friends really thought of his pieces." Among the four hundred guests who attended the preview buffet were Betsy and Alfred Bloomingdale, Paige Rense of *Architectural Digest*, Clifford May, and Lorena Nidorf, the widow of Louis B. Mayer.

Those great pieces did indeed find homes. A black-lacquer cabinet sold for $19,000; a set of twelve George III mahogany chairs went for $9,500; a Regency painted and giltwood armchair brought in $4,300; and the beloved black-lacquer longcase clock, designed by Peter Garon with a twenty-two-bell musical train, sold for $12,000. There was also artwork sold here, including the equestrian figure by Narino ($4,000) and Narino's acrobat oil on canvas ($14,000). The three-part sale raised $115,825.

Four more auctions, each smaller than the last, were held over the next three months. Altogether they raised over $150,000 for Billy's estate. The last, held in February 1975 and in which a pencil sketch by Toulouse-Lautrec sold for $1,500, paid off taxes and the costs of administering the estate.

The house on Lorna Lane was sold in March 1975 for over $200,000 to a husband and wife, both physicians. Included in the sale was the magnificent Austrian Empire six-arm giltwood and gesso chandelier that had hung over many of Billy's parties. It's not known whether the new owners kept it or sold it. In time, they paved over the swimming pool out back and erected a tennis court, making the house their own. With the exception of a few Roman statuaries peeking out from among the cypress trees, there was no trace left of Billy Haines or Jimmie Shields.

"Many years ago," remembers Bob Shaw, "I approached Billy about writing his biography. I really wanted to do it. I told him, 'You've lived an incredible life. Your story is worthwhile.' But he just laughed. He'd have none of it."

Billy Haines knew his story was worth telling. He just didn't think it *could* be told. He knew he'd lived an incredible life—and not just because of the glittery company he kept and the expensive things with which he filled his home.

When he sat there in his wheelchair in the doorframe of his house, consigning to hell the beauty he left behind, he was lamenting the fact that no one would ever fully understand his special good fortune—a particularly damnable realization. For in truth, the beauty he left behind was not just the chandelier overhead and the paintings

on the walls. It was all the hundreds of gatherings—big and small—
under that chandelier, and the intimate conversations he'd held beside
those paintings. Conversations with people—influential, powerful
people—who were guests in his home, the home he shared openly
with his lover of nearly half a century.

That was the true beauty of his life, the beauty he left behind. *That*
was what he assumed no one would ever understand. How he'd
made his way into a world of fame and riches, how he'd won the respect of those in high places, how he'd overcome obstacles ever since
he was a young boy, and how he'd gone off to achieve his dreams—
all without ever surrendering who he was. All without ever compro-
mising his sense of integrity. All without ever abandoning the man
he loved.

Part of Billy's legend has always been his relationship with Jimmie Shields—how Billy refused Louis B. Mayer's demands to dump
Jimmie, how they stayed together for almost half a century, how
Jimmie took his own life after Billy had died. When I began this
project, I considered Billy's relationship with Jimmie little more
than a romantic dressing in which to wrap the "real" story—the
story of Hollywood's great cultural shift in the early 1930s and how
that impacted the gay subculture.

And yet, the moment I discovered Jimmie's suicide note, my pulse
quickening and my eyes growing wide, I knew this was as much a
love story as anything else. Regrettably, very little testimony to the
particular dynamics of their relationship could be uncovered, other
than the superficial: Billy as provider, Jimmie as materialistic, status-
conscious provi*dee*. A few of their friends spoke to the working partnership between them—Jimmie as the monitor of protocol and
Billy's social "hostess"—but few seemed privy to any emotional details. To their affection. To their *love*. For, in the end, what else could
have kept them together for fifty years?

There are few stories in this culture of enduring love, of love that
survives the fires of early passion and becomes something else—
fewer still of enduring gay love. In a society that still views gay relationships as fleeting and inconsequential, Billy Haines and Jimmie
Shields stand out. That Billy and Jimmie owned the house on Lorna

Lane together—both names on the deed—is an unusual symbol of commitment for the times, especially since it was Billy's money that bought and maintained the house. Yet Billy's money was Jimmie's, too; Jimmie's contributions to the relationship were apparently significant enough to balance things out.

Still, even after all the interviews and research, it remains difficult to say just what that relationship was. They were, essentially, very private people (the rare but infamous episodes of misbehavior notwithstanding). There are precious few photographs of them together. They were taught by the prevailing culture that their personal situation was not part of polite conversation. When I'd ask their friends what kept them together—despite Jimmie's materialistic demands, despite El Porto beach, despite Billy's tricks and the loss of his movie career (all things that would have ended many another relationship, gay *or* straight)—I was met most often by blank stares. "It just worked, I guess," said one friend. But what does that mean? I asked. *What* worked? Finally, another friend surmised, "I suppose it just came down to the fact that they loved each other. What else could it be?"

Indeed. Had Harris Woods still been alive when I began research for this book, perhaps he—Jimmie's closest friend—might have been able to shed some light on their love. It would have had to have been one of their close gay friends to do so; even heterosexual friends as close as Betsy Bloomingdale weren't always privy to the emotional side of their relationship. Crawford, maybe—but she, too, was gone by the time I started this project.

In the end, reading the note Jimmie left, hearing how Billy worried what would happen to his mate after he was gone, viewing the evidence of fifty years together, I came to the conclusion that whatever else Billy's story is—and it is many things—it is a love story. Pure and simple.

Years pass, and Billy Haines's story gradually takes on a significance few could have appreciated at the time of his death. He was right to believe his struggles and triumphs were left to hell rather than posterity; such was the state of the world is 1973. Twenty-five years later, the world is a far different place; Billy's story emerges, not from hell, but from the memories of those who loved him, who have moved along into more contemporary ways of thinking, who understand now, finally, just why his story is worth telling.

There are precious few left. When I first began research for this book, I was warned that no one was left alive, and if I *could* manage to locate anyone, they'd certainly never agree to talk. "Don't mention the 'gay' word to them," I was told. "Let them bring it up first."

I did as they suggested. I found several men willing to talk, and almost immediately upon telling them I was writing the life of William Haines, they raised the subject themselves, without any coaxing from me. "Of course, he was so courageous about not hiding his homosexuality," I heard time and again, and these old men went on to share stories with me that I'd been warned would never be told.

Might the times have changed these men, many of whom, a decade before, had turned historians and biographers away from their doors? Might the deaths of some of the more prominent figures—Cukor, especially—have freed them enough to speak? "I think it's important that somebody, somewhere, get some of these stories down," said one man. Might such a duty to posterity have finally convinced them to tell their tales? Some were forthright about using their names; others remained reticent, requesting anonymity. No one slammed the door in my face or hung up the phone, however, as Grady Sutton had been known to do several years before.

It wasn't just gay men who were eager to talk, either. Even Billy's friends among the society set were quick to impart to me their realizations of just how brave Billy was. "Being so up-front—that was terribly, terribly courageous," says Francie Brody. "Looking back, especially, I can see how unusual that was."

What was once considered unmentionable—and certainly not appropriate material for a biographer—was now the impetus to speak. Yes, there were many other qualities of Billy Haines his friends wanted to get across—his generosity, his taste, his style, his sense of humor—but over and over again, it was his courage that they came back to. "Yes," Anita Page had said at the start of all this. "Courageous he certainly was."

Among Billy's circle of friends, Bob Wheaton, Bob Shaw, Geoffrey Toone, and Frank Lysinger are still active. Michael Pearman has retired to Florida. Roger Davis died at age ninety-six in 1980; Harris Woods died in 1989.

George Cukor grew more sentimental about his old friend as the years went on. Although he would play the air violin when Harris Woods got weepy over Jimmie's death, Cukor nonetheless had a soft spot when it came to Billy. "When George had his house re-done," says Charles Williamson, "it was done exactly the way Haines had originally done it. George was insistent about that. Even about where things were placed. An ashtray could still be on the table twenty years later. 'Bill placed it there,' George would say, 'and that's where I want it to stay.' "

Cukor died in January 1983. His house was bought soon after and gutted. Many of those who remembered Billy's exquisite decors shuddered, but they were even more distressed by David Geffen's purchase of the Jack Warner house after Ann died in 1990. "He *ruined* it," Ted Graber says, cringing. "That magnificent house. He tore everything out and started from scratch. That was one house that should have been left alone."

Billy's two sisters have passed away, Ann Langhorne in 1986 and Lillion Stone in 1993. At this writing, both brothers are still alive: George, who was handsome enough to have been a movie star but lacked Billy's outgoing nature, was eighty-nine in 1997; and Henry, the baby of the family and an engaging, charming man, was eighty.

Joan Crawford, in the years after Billy's death, became reclusive, never leaving her New York apartment. Billy had been one of the few constants in her life, and in her last years, she had few confidants. She died in May 1977, just a little more than four years after Billy's death. When daughter Christina's book *Mommie Dearest* was turned into a movie in 1981, William Haines, Inc., still flourishing under Ted Graber, was consulted for the set designs of Joan's New York apartment.

Graber carried on Billy's legacy with panache. Shortly after Billy's death he decorated the Pacific Palisades home of Ronald and

Nancy Reagan. So happy was Nancy with his work that she commissioned him to redesign the upstairs private quarters of the White House when her husband was elected president in 1980. Had Billy lived, he'd have done the job with Graber just as they had done Winfield House. There was much banter in the press about the cost, but all agreed the results were spectacular. Graber was referred to in the press as the "First Decorator," since he actually lived in the White House for a time; he appeared with Nancy at nearly every state party. Jerry Zipkin, who was likewise a frequent presence, was called the "First Fop."

Graber retired soon after the White House assignment; the studio was sold in November 1985. Today, in his late seventies, he lives quietly with Arch Case in a lovely home on the California coast near Mendocino. "I have had a wonderful life," he says. When he speaks of Billy, he grows wistful. "I loved him dearly. It isn't often that one loses a father only to have another one step in to fill the void."

"I believe if you talk about people, they're around," says Betsy Bloomingdale. "Sitting here, talking about Billy, I believe he's around in the house right now. I like that. I like to talk about him and feel him around me. Every once in a while, he still gives me a kick in the pants."

On a warm spring day, I picked up one of Billy's old friends at his apartment in West Hollywood. He'd never been to Billy's grave. I told him I'd drive him out to Santa Monica. "I'd like that," he said. "I didn't know that he and Jimmie were together. I'd like to see that."

This is a man who was married (to a woman) for many, many years, who lived his life in the shadows of Hollywood society, his story whispered about and winked over, but never fully known. "Billy and Jimmie were different," he said as we drove. As different as could be found in the shadowy world of pre-Stonewall Hollywood, when lovers (like this man's) were kept in separate homes, marriages were arranged, and lies were told again and again and again.

Anita Loos wrote, "As a love-and-success story, Bill's legend was far more thrilling than any he ever filmed for L. B. Mayer." And it was true: In the end, Billy Haines is remembered not for any great picture, nor even for any great house—as great as many of them were. He is remembered instead for the life he lived, for playing no game but his own.

We stopped just outside the mausoleum. I helped this old friend of Billy Haines's out of the car and took him gently by the elbow as we approached the entrance. Inside, it was considerably cooler than the mounting warmth of the late morning. We were surrounded by walls of glassed-in shelves, behind which stood urns of various shapes and sizes. Small metal plaques graced each compartment, the name and dates of their occupants carefully inscribed. We searched for a while, and then discovered what we came to see.

There, about a quarter of the way up from the floor, was the legend WILLIAM HAINES, 1900–1973. And beside it, JAMES SHIELDS, 1905–1974.

Billy's old friend let out a long sigh and didn't say anything for several minutes. Finally he touched the glass with one finger. "Yes," he said. "That's the way it should be."

Filmography

The following are confirmed assignments, arranged in order of release. William Haines played uncredited bits in a number of other pictures in the 1922–1923 period. The director's name follows the release date.

BROTHERS UNDER THE SKIN. Goldwyn, 1922. *E. Mason Hopper.* Cast: Pat O'Malley, Helene Chadwick, Mae Busch, Norman Kerry, Claire Windsor, WH (unbilled).

LOST AND FOUND ON A SOUTH SEA ISLAND. Goldwyn, 1923. *Raoul Walsh.* Cast: House Peters, Pauline Starke, Antonio Moreno, Mary Jane Irving, Rosemary Theby, George Siegmann, WH (unbilled).

SOULS FOR SALE. Goldwyn, 1923. *Rupert Hughes.* Cast: Eleanor Boardman, Richard Dix, Mae Busch, Barbara La Marr, Lew Cody, Frank Mayo, Aileen Pringle, Dale Fuller, WH.

THREE WISE FOOLS. Goldwyn, 1923. *King Vidor.* Cast: Eleanor Boardman, Claude Gillingwater, William H. Crane, Alec B. Francis, WH, ZaSu Pitts, Creighton Hale.

THREE WEEKS. Goldwyn, 1924. *Alan Crosland.* Cast: Aileen Pringle, Conrad Nagel, WH.

TRUE AS STEEL. Goldwyn, 1924. *Rupert Hughes.* Cast: Aileen Pringle, Eleanor Boardman, Norman Kerry, WH.

THE MIDNIGHT EXPRESS. Columbia, 1924. *George Hill.* Cast: Elaine Hammerstein, WH, George Nichols, Edwin Booth Tilton.

THE GAIETY GIRL. Universal, 1924. *King Baggott.* Cast: Mary Philbin, WH, Joseph J. Dowling, Grace Darmond.

WINE OF YOUTH. MGM, 1924. *King Vidor.* Cast: Eleanor Boardman, Ben Lyon, WH, William Collier, Jr., Eulalie Jensen, Pauline Garon.

THE DESERT OUTLAW. Fox, 1924. *Edmund Mortimer.* Cast: Buck Jones, WH, Evelyn Brent.

CIRCE THE ENCHANTRESS. MGM, 1924. *Robert Z. Leonard.* Cast: Mae Murray, James Kirkwood, Tom Ricketts, WH, Lillian Langdon.

WIFE OF THE CENTAUR. MGM, 1924. *King Vidor.* Cast: Eleanor Boardman, John Gilbert, Aileen Pringle, WH.

A FOOL AND HIS MONEY. Columbia, 1925. *Erle Kenton.* Cast: Madge Bellamy, WH, Stuart Holmes, Alma Bennett, Charles Conklin.

WHO CARES? Columbia, 1925. *David Kirkland.* Cast: Dorothy Devore, WH, Lloyd Whitlock, Beverly Bayne.

THE DENIAL. MGM, 1925. *Hobart Henley.* Cast: Claire Windsor, Bert Roach, WH, Lucille Rickson.

FIGHTING THE FLAMES. Columbia, 1925. *Reeves Eason.* Cast: Dorothy Devore, WH, Frankie Darro, David Torrence.

A SLAVE OF FASHION. MGM, 1925. *Hobart Henley.* Cast: Norma Shearer, Lew Cody, WH, Mary Carr, James Corrigan, Miss Du Pont.

THE TOWER OF LIES. MGM, 1925. *Victor Sjostrom.* Cast: Lon Chaney, Norma Shearer, WH, Ian Keith, Claire McDowell, David Torrence.

LITTLE ANNIE ROONEY. United Artists, 1925. *William Beaudine.* Cast: Mary Pickford, WH, Walter James, Gordon Griffith.

SALLY, IRENE AND MARY. MGM, 1925. *Edmund Goulding.* Cast: Constance Bennett, Joan Crawford, Sally O'Neil, WH, Henry Kolker, Douglas Gilmore, Kate Price.

MEMORY LANE. First National, 1926. *John M. Stahl.* Cast: Eleanor Boardman, Conrad Nagel, WH, John Steppling, Eugenie Ford, Frankie Darro.

THE THRILL HUNTER. Columbia, 1926. *Eugene DeRue.* Cast: WH, Kathryn McGuire, Alma Bennett, E. J. Ratcliffe, Bobby Dunn, Frankie Darro.

BROWN OF HARVARD. MGM, 1926. *Jack Conway.* Cast: Jack Pickford, WH, Mary Brian, Francis X. Bushman, Jr., Mary Alden, David Torrence.

MIKE. MGM, 1926. *Marshall Neilan*. Cast: Sally O'Neil, WH, Charlie Murray, Ned Sparks, Ford Sterling, Frankie Darro, Junior Coghlan.

LOVEY MARY. MGM, 1926. *King Baggott*. Cast: Bessie Love, WH, Mary Alden, Vivia Ogden, Martha Mattox, Jackie Coombs.

TELL IT TO THE MARINES. MGM, 1926. *George Hill*. Cast: Lon Chaney, WH, Eleanor Boardman, Eddie Gribbon, Carmel Myers, Warner Oland.

A LITTLE JOURNEY. MGM, 1927. *Robert Z. Leonard*. Cast: Claire Windsor, WH, Harry Carey, Claire McDowell, Lawford Davidson.

SLIDE KELLY SLIDE. MGM, 1927. *Edward Sedgwick*. Cast: WH, Sally O'Neil, Harry Carey, Junior Coghlan, Warner Ricmond, Paul Kelly, Karl Dane.

SPRING FEVER. MGM, 1927. *Edward Sedgwick*. Cast: WH, Joan Crawford, George K. Arthur, George Fawcett, Eileen Percy.

WEST POINT. MGM, 1927. *Edward Sedgwick*. Cast: WH, Joan Crawford, William Bakewell, Neil Neely, Ralph Emerson.

THE SMART SET. MGM, 1928. *Jack Conway*. Cast: WH, Alice Day, Jack Holt, Hobart Bosworth, Coy Watson, Jr., Constance Howard, Julia Swayne Gordon.

TELLING THE WORLD. MGM, 1928. *Sam Wood*. Cast: WH, Anita Page, Eileen Percy, Frank Currier, Polly Moran, Bert Roach, William V. Mong.

EXCESS BAGGAGE. MGM, 1928. *James Cruze*. Cast: WH, Josephine Dunn, Neely Edwards, Kathleen Clifford, Greta Granstedt, Ricardo Cortez.

SHOW PEOPLE. MGM, 1928. *King Vidor*. Cast: Marion Davies, WH, Dell Henderson, Paul Ralli, Tenen Holtz, Harry Gribbon, Sidney Bracy, Polly Moran.

ALIAS JIMMY VALENTINE. MGM, 1929. *Jack Conway*. Cast: WH, Lionel Barrymore, Leila Hyams, Karl Dane, Tully Marshall, Howard Hickman, Billy Butts.

THE DUKE STEPS OUT. MGM, 1929. *James Cruze*. Cast: WH, Joan Crawford, Karl Dane, Tenen Holtz, Edward Nugent, Jack Roper, Delmer Daves.

A MAN'S MAN. MGM, 1929. *James Cruze*. Cast: WH, Josephine Dunn, Sam Hardy, Mae Busch, Gloria Davenport. Cameos by Greta Garbo and John Gilbert.

THE HOLLYWOOD REVUE OF 1929. MGM, 1929. *Charles Reisner*. Cast: John Gilbert, Marion Davies, Norma Shearer, WH, Joan Crawford, Buster Keaton, Bessie Love, Marie Dressler, Anita Page, Jack Benny.

SPEEDWAY. MGM, 1929. *Harry Beaumont*. Cast: WH, Anita Page, John Miljan, Ernest Torrence, Karl Dane.

NAVY BLUES. MGM, 1929. *Clarence Brown*. Cast: WH, Anita Page, Karl Dane, J. C. Nugent, Edythe Chapman, Gertrude Sutton, Wade Boteler.

THE GIRL SAID NO. MGM, 1930. *Sam Wood.* Cast: WH, Leila Hyams, Polly Moran, Marie Dressler, Francis X. Bushman, Jr., Clara Blandick, William Janney, William V. Mong, Junior Coghlan.

FREE AND EASY. MGM, 1930. *Edward Sedgwick.* Cast: Buster Keaton, Anita Page, Trixie Friganza, Robert Montgomery, Fred Niblo. WH had cameo.

WAY OUT WEST. MGM, 1930. *Fred Niblo.* Cast: WH, Leila Hyams, Polly Moran, Cliff Edwards, Francis X. Bushman, Jr., Vera March, Charles Middleton.

REMOTE CONTROL. MGM, 1930. *Malcolm St. Clair and Nick Grinde.* Cast: WH, Charles King, Polly Moran, John Miljan.

A TAILOR-MADE MAN. MGM, 1931. *Sam Wood.* Cast: WH, Dorothy Jordan, Joseph Cawthorn, Marjorie Rambeau, William Austin, Ian Keith, Hedda Hopper.

THE STOLEN JOOLS. National Variety Artists two-reeler, distributed by Paramount, 1931. *William McGann.* Cast: Wallace Beery, Maurice Chevalier, Gary Cooper, Joan Crawford, Bebe Daniels, Irene Dunne, WH, Buster Keaton, Laurel & Hardy, Our Gang, Edward G. Robinson, Norma Shearer, Lowell Sherman, Barbara Stanwyck, Wheeler & Woolsey.

JUST A GIGOLO. MGM, 1931. *Jack Conway.* Cast: WH, Irene Purcell, C. Aubrey Smith, Lillian Bond. WH also served as art director, but went uncredited.

THE NEW ADVENTURES OF GET-RICH-QUICK WALLINGFORD. MGM, 1931. *Sam Wood.* Cast: WH, Leila Hyams, Ernest Torrence, Jimmy Durante.

ARE YOU LISTENING? MGM, 1932. *Harry Beaumont.* Cast: WH, Madge Evans, Anita Page, Karen Morley, Neil Hamilton, Wallace Ford, Jean Hersholt.

FAST LIFE. MGM, 1932. *Harry Pollard.* Cast: WH, Madge Blake, Conrad Nagel, Cliff Edwards, Arthur Byron.

YOUNG AND BEAUTIFUL. Mascot, 1934. *Joseph Santley.* Cast: WH, Judith Allen, Joseph Cawthorn, John Miljan, Vincent Barnett, Franklin Pangborn, Edward Hearn.

THE MARINES ARE COMING. Mascot, 1934. *David Howard.* Cast: WH, Esther Ralston, Conrad Nagel, Armida, Edgar Kennedy, Hale Hamilton, Dell Henderson.

CRAIG'S WIFE. Columbia, 1936. *Dorothy Arzner.* Cast: Rosalind Russell, John Boles, Billie Burke, Jane Darwell, Thomas Mitchell. WH served as set designer, although he is not credited.

William Haines may also have played a bit part in *Married Flirts* (1924), directed by Robert Vignola for MGM, starring Pauline Frederick and Conrad Nagel. His appearance is uncomfirmed.

Acknowledgments

In my search for Billy Haines, it is the small moments that stand out, for in them lie great revelations: Meeting Billy's gracious younger brother, Henry Haines, and marveling at the resemblance between them. Walking up the front steps of Billy's childhood home in Staunton, Virginia. Having a few beers with Jimmie Shields's nephew, Charlie Conrad, and finding the stories funnier — and racier — as the evening went on. Sitting in the Palm Springs sun with Bob Wheaton and his lover, discussing the gay circles of Hollywood's Golden Age. Discovering, quite unexpectedly, Jimmie Shields's suicide note — the original, in his own handwriting — tucked away among the pages of his probate file. And, of course, having lunch at the Hollywood Roosevelt Hotel with Anita Page.

But none was more memorable than the two days I spent in the home of Ted Graber and Arch Case, two warm, witty, admirable gentlemen who showed by example — still together, in sickness and in health, after forty years — why Billy's (and Jimmie's) story holds particular relevance today.

I began this project with great respect for Billy Haines. I finished it with even more. Politically, I'm not sure he and I would have always seen eye-to-eye. I was prepared to be critical about his friendships with right-wing politicians and their supporters; criticism is healthy — even necessary — for any biography. Yet I came away with a better understanding, a greater appreciation for the times as Billy lived them, for the stands he took and didn't take, for the (bottom-line) integrity from which he never wavered. Just as I was asking his friends and acquaintances to move along with me toward a more contemporary way of thinking, I realized I needed to travel back in time with them. I needed to leave my political assumptions and definitions in the 1990s where they belong, where they fit, where they make sense. It hardly needs to be said that such convictions often have less application to previous decades.

I must thank those who trusted me enough to share their stories. Some may question a particular focus I give to their recollections; some may wonder why I've emphasized one thing—Billy's connections to the gay world, for example—over another—his innovations in the design field, perhaps. I hope they understand my reasons better after reading this book. The responsibility for the conclusions drawn is mine.

In particular, I must thank Ted Graber and Arch Case, for their generosity and hospitality, as well as their spirited recollections; Jean Hayden Mathison, for her sharp memory and for opening other doors for me; Henry and Margaret Haines, for their graciousness and willingness to answer my continual questions, faxed over in the wee hours of (their) morning; Charlie Conrad, for his enthusiasm and generous assistance; Sergei Troubetzkoy, for his devotion to the project and his tireless skills as a researcher; Jim Walker, for his courage and candor in speaking publicly for the first time; and Bob Wheaton, for his keen memory, his helpful connections, and his warm embrace of the ambitious goal of my book—to begin documenting the gay circles of the Golden Age of Hollywood.

The personal interviews with Billy's friends and colleagues form the heart of this book. I was warned few would be living who remembered Billy from his movie days. It was true. Most of his costars have passed on; all of his directors are gone. I just missed MGM studio executive J. J. Cohn by a matter of weeks; he'd been on the lot from the 1920s through the 1950s. He died shortly before my first research trip to Hollywood.

I was both surprised and delighted when former First Lady Nancy Reagan graciously consented to an interview about her friendship with Billy. She was just getting over pneumonia but couldn't have been more friendly—or guarded in what she said. Still, I am tremendously grateful for her input.

There were some, however, who chose not to respond. Lee Annenberg never answered my letters requesting an interview. Mary Brian, one of Billy's few surviving costars (and from *Brown of Harvard* yet!), declined an interview after I'd left several telephone messages. And I never got to speak with the elder of Billy's surviving brothers, George Haines.

I was extremely fortunate to encounter many helpful archivists, historians, and librarians along the way—especially Charles Silver and Ron Magliozzi of the Film Studies Center at the Museum of Modern Art in New York, who were early and enthusiastic supporters. It is because of their efforts that I viewed as many William Haines films as I did. They both have my deepest thanks. I must also express my gratitude to Sam Gill of the Margaret Herrick Library of the Academy of Motion Picture Arts and Sciences, a truly kind, generous man whose vast knowledge of Hollywood history and the resources available to historians proved invaluable not only during my research at the library but often later, on the phone from the East Coast.

I also want to acknowledge the help of Mary Corliss of the Film Stills Archive of the Museum of Modern Art; Briggitte Kueppers at the UCLA Arts Library Special Collections; Gladys Irvis at the American Film Institute; Sarah Huggins at the Library of Virginia; Elaine Jackson-Retondo of the Documents Collection at the University of California Library, Berkeley; Roberto Landazurai of the San Francisco History Project at the San Francisco Public Library; and Julie Franklin of the Treasure Island Library.

I owe a deep and lasting debt to my fellow biographers and journalistic colleagues. Fred Guiles was an early and generous supporter. My interview with Charles Higham proved fascinating, witty, and extremely helpful. Lawrence Quirk helped confirm anecdotes while providing enormous enthusiasm. Patrick McGilligan offered many leads; his biography of George Cukor was an inspiration. I also thank Kevin Thomas of the *Los Angeles Times*, Kitty Kelley, Kevin Brownlow, Cari Beauchamp, Gavin Lambert, Emmanuel Levy, Kelly Vencill at *Architectural Digest*, Christopher Bram, Anthony Slide, Michael Ankerich, Axel Madsen, Jan Dennis, and Richard Reinhardt.

Special thanks go to Ed Sikov, who was the first to encourage me in the idea of a biography of Billy Haines. Ed's detailed knowledge of Hollywood and where to go to find answers proved invaluable to me as a novice biographer. Our camaraderie in exploring the bowels of the Los Angeles Hall of Justice, growling over inefficient service and then exclaiming in delighted surprise upon finding the records we sought, is an experience I won't soon forget.

Also, my thanks to Monica Trasandes of *Frontiers* newsmagazine and Robert David Sullivan of the *Boston Phoenix*, for early on recognizing the worth of Billy's story and running my articles on him; Tom Barnes, a good friend and invaluable last-minute researcher; Michael Yakaitis; Dale Vandergriff, Randall Monroe, Neil Mitchell Cowan; the late Larry Austin of the Silent Movie Theater; Robert Smith; Lesléa Newman; Michael Cohen; Susan Gluck; John Bonelli; Judi Floyd; Surina Khan; and last but never least, Brendan Stephens, for everything.

My editor, Ed Iwanicki, has been a source of inspiration and encouragement from the very beginning. He has been consistently insightful, thought provoking, and supportive. I am deeply grateful. I also want to thank my ever-resourceful agent, Malaga Baldi, for her tireless advocacy and sustaining friendship.

And finally, as always, my gratitude and love to Tim and Victor.

Interviews: Don Bachardy; Betty Barker; Betsy Bloomingdale; Francie Brody; Arch Case; Frank (Junior) Coghlan; Charlie Conrad; Douglas Fairbanks, Jr.; Tucker Fleming; Ted Graber; Henry Haines; Margaret Haines; Emily Haselden; Harry Hay; Jean Howard; Jody Jacobs; Mary Anita Loos;

Frank Lysinger; Jean Mathison; Michael Morrison; Anita Page; Michael Pearman; Nancy Reagan; Bob Shaw; Geoffrey Toone; Jim Walker; Bob Wheaton; Miles White; Charles Williamson. Several of Billy's friends spoke with me on the condition their names not be used.

Correspondence: Betty Barker; Christina Crawford; Douglas Fairbanks, Jr.; Curtis Harrington; Katharine Hepburn; Joan Fontaine; William Kizer; Lon McCallister; Geoffrey Toone. Before her death, I had enjoyed an irregular correspondence with Eleanor Boardman. At the time, I never had reason to ask her about Billy Haines—a missed opportunity I continue to waste time regretting—but her letters served as background for the period.

Archives and organizations: Margaret Herrick Library, Academy of Motion Picture Arts and Sciences, Beverly Hills; the Film Studies Center, the Periodicals Library, and the Film Stills Archive at the Museum of Modern Art, New York; New York Public Library for the Performing Arts, Lincoln Center, New York; Motion Picture Division and Periodicals Department, Library of Congress, Washington, D.C.; American Film Institute Library, Los Angeles; the Special Collections department of the UCLA Arts Library; the Bettmann Archive; World's Fair Collectors Society; the National Archives, Washington, D.C., and Waltham, Massachusetts; Vital Statistics Branch, Department of Health Services, State of California; National Personnel Records Center, St. Louis; the Library of Virginia, Richmond; the Staunton, Virginia, Public Library; the Boston Public Library; the New York Public Library; the Hopewell, Virginia, Public Library; W. E. B. DuBois Library at the University of Massachusetts, Amherst; Olin Library at Wesleyan University, Middletown, Connecticut; the Massachusetts State Archive; the Documents Collection at the University of California Library, Berkeley; and the Treasure Island Library.

Notes

In most instances I have referenced the source of a quote or information within the body of the text, especially if it came — as so much of Billy Haines's story does — from the fan magazines of the 1920s and 1930s. *Photoplay*'s September–October 1929 article "The Wisecracker Reveals Himself" is cited as "WRH" throughout the notes.

CHAPTER 1
Wine of Youth:
1900-1915

All quotes from Billy Haines in this chapter come from "The Wisecracker Reveals Himself."

Details on his family history come from the U.S. Census records for Augusta County (1870, 1880, 1900, and 1910); the records of Trinity Episcopal Church, Staunton, Virginia; the vital records of Staunton; back issues of the *Staunton Leader*; the Staunton Public Library, History and Genealogy Room; and an interview with Henry Haines. I am especially indebted to local historian Sergei Troubetzkoy, who proved a treasure trove of information.

Charles Haines's Civil War military records were located at the National Archives, Washington, D.C.

The stories of Billy's childhood are culled from interviews with several friends and his brother, Henry Haines, as well as from WRH and another article, "Hometown Stories of the Stars," an undated clip from *Photoplay* in the Billy Rose Theater Collection at the New York Public Library of the Performing Arts. Back issues of the *Staunton Leader* also provided information. I am indebted also to Sergei Troubetzkoy for the anecdote about "Miss" Willie Teagle.

Information on Hopewell and Billy's time there comes from WRH; the *Staunton Leader*; the *New York Times*; the Library of Virginia, Richmond; *The Hornbook of Virginia History*, edited by Emily J. Salmon and Edward D. C. Campbell, Jr. (Library of Virginia, 1994); *The Prince George-Hopewell Story*, by Francis Earle Lutz (William Byrd Press, 1957); *The History of the Explosives Industry in America*, by Arthur Pine Van Gelder and Hugo Schlatter (Columbia University Press, 1927); *Du Pont: Behind the Iron Curtain*, by Gerard Colby Zilg (Prentice-Hall, 1974); and E. I. du Pont de Nemours's *Autobiography of an American Enterprise* (distributed by Charles Scribner's Sons, 1952).

CHAPTER 2
The Thrill Hunter:
1916-1922

Unless otherwise noted, all quotes from Billy in this chapter come from WRH.

George Chauncey's *Gay New York* provided invaluable background material, helping put Billy's experience in Greenwich Village in perspective. Other information comes from the U.S. Census records for New York City (1920), New York city directories, and interviews with Ted Graber, Arch Case, Michael Pearman, Bob Wheaton, and Henry Haines.

Information on George Haines's bankruptcy comes from the records of the probate court in Staunton, Virginia. Details of the sale of the Haines home come from the book of deeds, Staunton Town Hall, as well as from an interview with Staunton historian Sergei Troubetzkoy. The Richmond city directories provided data on the years Billy and his family lived there.

The Orison Swett Marden connection is mentioned in early Goldwyn publicity, found in the *Photoplay* collection at the Museum of Modern Art Film Studies Center in New York. Biographical details on Marden come from the U.S. Census for New York (1920), the Contemporary Authors series, and *Who's Who 1922–1923*.

Details on the firm of S. W. Straus come from WRH and New York city directories.

Biographical data on Mitchell Foster and Larry Sullivan are derived from various sources: interviews with Michael Pearman, Ted Graber, and Henry Haines; the U.S. Census for Massachusetts (1900, 1920); Massachusetts vital records at the Massachusetts State Archive; Boston city directories; and the *Brookline Chronicle*.

The description of Billy's physical appearance is culled from several early (1922–1924) magazine articles. The meeting with Malin in New York was discovered in clippings dating from Malin's period in Hollywood. The New York connection with George Burns, Jack Benny, Orry-Kelly, and Cary Grant (then Archie Leach) comes from interviews with Charles Higham (who discussed the period with Burns), Henry Haines, Michael Pearman, Bob Shaw, and Ted Graber. His longtime friendship with Kelly was confirmed by Jean Mathison. "Gone were the funny clothes . . ." comes from Martin Gottfried, *George Burns and The Hundred Year Dash*. Details on Grant's and Kelly's early life come from Higham's *Cary Grant: The Lonely Heart*. The account of George Cukor circa 1921 comes from Patrick McGilligan's biography.

Details on the woman from Fifth Avenue come from WRH. "I was kept by . . ." comes from an unpublished interview conducted by the author Fred Lawrence Guiles in 1969, the tape of which was heard by this author.

Dozens of accounts in Billy's files at the Academy of Motion Picture Arts and Sciences Library (AMPAS), the Museum of Modern Art (MoMA), and the New York Public Library for the Performing Arts at Lincoln Center (NYPL) provide information on the New Faces contest and how Billy was "discovered" by Bijou Fernandez. These have been analyzed and synthesized here. Arthur Marx's biography of Sam Goldwyn provided background information on the Goldwyn studios. Details on Eleanor Boardman's career come from her file at NYPL and my correspondence with her. The description of Billy's meeting with Goldwyn comes from Herbert Howe, "Bullied into Pictures," *Photoplay*, October 1924.

The quotes on House Peters and the making of *Lost and Found on a South Sea Island* come from *Filmograph*, Vol. 3, No. 3, 1972.

CHAPTER 3
The Gaiety Girl:
1923-1926

If not specifically indicated otherwise, Billy's quotes are from WRH.

Most of the details of Billy's early screen career come from his files at AMPAS, MoMA, and NYPL, as well as from various published interviews in movie magazines and newspapers. In addition, a lengthy unpublished interview with Billy conducted by Fred Lawrence Guiles in September 1969 provided much valuable information and insight. I am deeply indebted to Guiles for allowing me access to that interview.

The story of Billy and the tailor comes from Charleson Gray, "The Real William Haines," *Modern Screen*, July 1931.

Details of Barbara La Marr's life come from her files at AMPAS, MoMA, and NYPL. Billy's comments about their friendship come from WRH. Other details of their relationship came from an interview with Ted Graber and press clippings in the files of both Billy and La Marr.

"I had to wear . . ." and "I can't be . . ." come from *Filmograph*, Vol. 3, No. 3, 1972. His quote on his salary at the time is taken from WRH.

The Gloria Swanson quote on Elinor Glyn comes from her autobiography, *Swanson on Swanson*. The Baby Peggy quip comes from *Photoplay*, October 1924.

Billy's reaction to *Midnight Express* is remembered in *Filmograph*, Vol. 3, No. 3, 1972.

The Peggy Hopkins Joyce anecdote comes from various clippings; Billy's quotes are taken from WRH. The *Photoplay* quote on Joyce appeared in May 1933.

I am indebted to Charles Higham's masterful biography of Louis B. Mayer, *Merchant of Dreams*, for the details of the MGM merger. Mayer's speech is quoted from *Merchant of Dreams*.

Details on *Wine of Youth* come from the various Vidor biographies noted in the bibliography. Billy's quotes on the film come from WRH and *Filmograph*, Vol. 3, No. 3, 1972.

Billy's addresses on Ingraham Street and North Western Avenue were determined through the Los Angeles city directories, 1923–1926. Both residences are still standing. "I like the domestic life . . ." comes from Helen Ludlam, "Billy Gets Wise," *Picture Play*, February 1932.

An interview with Frank (Junior) Coghlan provided details on the filming of *Mike*. Coghlan's autobiography, *They Still Call Me Junior*, was also helpful.

The Billy Haines–Norma Shearer affair comes from Lawrence Quirk's *Norma: The Story of Norma Shearer*. Further details are from an interview with Quirk.

Details of the Billy Haines–Ramon Novarro friendship come from interviews with several sources, including Lawrence Quirk, and the files of both stars at AMPAS, MoMA, and NYPL. Jane Ellen Wayne interviewed a former MGM technician about Billy for *Gable's Women*. The bordello incident derives from Anita Loos, *A Girl Like I*.

I am very grateful for the wise and informative counsel of Harry Hay, whose memory of the early Los Angeles gay scene was vital in establishing the context of Billy's nightlife.

Billy's comment about Victor Sjostrom comes from *Filmograph*, Vol. 3, No. 3, 1972.

Salary figures come from the payroll ledgers kept by Eddie Mannix as part of the Howard Strickling Collection at AMPAS.

Details on the life of Joan Crawford are taken from the various Crawford biographies. "Let me give you some advice . . ." comes from Bob Thomas, *Joan Crawford*. Christina Crawford's quote about her mother's friendship with Billy is from a letter to this author.

Details on the life of Hedda Hopper are taken from George Eels's *Hedda & Louella*.

Billy's relationship with Thalberg comes from various Thalberg biographies and from an unpublished interview Billy gave to Fred Lawrence Guiles in September 1969. "Looked down our noses . . ." comes from the same source. "Every night Irving . . ." is taken from Anita Loos, *The Talmadge Girls.*

Billy's comments about Mary Pickford come from *Filmograph*, Vol. 3, No. 3, 1972. Billy's quote on *Memory Lane* also comes from *Filmograph*.

Details on the production of *Brown of Harvard* come from the files at AMPAS, MoMA, and NYPL, as well as various published interviews with Billy Haines, especially WRH. The Thalberg screening anecdote comes from Samuel Marx, *Mayer and Thalberg: The Make Believe Saints.* Production costs and profits are taken from the MGM ledgers at AMPAS.

Those interviewed for this chapter include Frank (Junior) Coghlan, Charles Higham, Michael Pearman, Ted Graber, and Henry Haines.

CHAPTER 4

Free and Easy:
1926-1928

All of Billy's quotes are taken from WRH, unless otherwise indicated.

The story of Billy's trip back to Virginia comes from his file at NYPL, where an unsourced clipping describes the visit. Other information comes from interviews with Henry Haines and Sergei Troubetzkoy, as well as WRH and "Hometown Stories of the Stars," *Photoplay*, 1926.

Details on Billy and Jimmie's relationship come from interviews with Arch Case, Ted Graber, Bob Wheaton, Bob Shaw, Michael Pearman, and others. Biographical information on Jimmie Shields comes from the U.S. Census for Pennsylvania (1910) and from his nephew, Charles Conrad.

"I still put my fingers . . ." comes from *Filmograph*, Vol. 3, No. 3, 1972.

For some of the information on the production of *Tell It to the Marines*, I am indebted to Michael Blake's excellent biography of Lon Chaney. Other information comes the production files at AMPAS and clippings files at MoMA and NYPL. Billy's quote about Lon Chaney comes from *Filmograph*, Vol. 3, No. 3, 1972.

The quotes from Hal Elias come from an oral history conducted by Douglas Bell and located at the Margaret Herrick Library of the Academy of Motion Picture Arts and Sciences.

The interview with Dorothy Spensley appeared in the October 1926 issue of *Photoplay*, in an article entitled "The Kidding Kid." "You can cut . . ." comes from the *Evening World*, March 16, 1929. The exchange with Samuel Richard Mook comes from "Random Notes on Billy," *Picture Play*, July 1930.

Although I have not been able to locate the exact interview with the Boston reporter, the Polly Moran story was repeated by numerous Hollywood writers.

This account of Billy's exchange with the Boston reporter comes from Samuel Richard Mook, who was present. Mook wrote about it in *Picture Play*, July 1930.

Polly Moran's "Me and the Boyfriend" appeared in *Film Fun*, January 1930. Details of her friendship with Billy come from her files at AMPAS, MoMA, and NYPL, as well as from interviews with Ted Graber, Arch Case, Henry Haines, Bob Wheaton, and others.

"You know, my dear . . ." comes from Dorothy Spensley, "The Kidding Kid."

Details on Billy's relationship with Mayer are drawn from several sources, including the Mayer biographies; Anita Loos's several books; Norman Zierold's *The Moguls*; interviews with Arch Case, Ted Graber, Bob Wheaton, Bob Shaw, Anita Page, and Charles Higham; and an unpublished interview Billy gave to Fred Lawrence Guiles in September 1969.

"I always longed for the day . . ." comes from an unpublished interview with Billy Haines from the *Photoplay* Collection, dated 1930, at MoMA.

Billy's home on North Stanley Drive was described in several magazine articles in 1927–1929, all located in his files at MoMA and NYPL. Details of his purchase were obtained through Los Angeles County Records and Deeds, September 21, 1926, Grantee Deed Book 6370, page 185.

Details on the production of *Slide Kelly Slide* are taken from the files at AMPAS, MoMA, and NYPL, along with an interview with Frank (Junior) Coghlan. I am also grateful to Frank Coghlan for showing me a print of this film.

Financial figures for Billy's films and MGM in general were obtained from the Eddie Mannix ledgers in the Howard Strickling Collection, AMPAS.

The Garbo anecdote comes from *Variety*, October 13, 1931.

Constance Blake's observation about Billy's servants comes from "Why Billy Haines Stayed at Metro," *Movie Mirror*, January 1932.

The description of San Simeon and Billy's quotes about Hearst come from Ken Murray's *The Golden Days at San Simeon*. Further details come from an unpublished interview Billy gave to Fred Lawrence Guiles in September 1969. Other information on San Simeon is taken from Marion Davies's *The Times We Had* and Barry Paris's *Louise Brooks*. "What she did feel more than anything . . ." comes from Fred Lawrence Guiles, *Marion Davies*. "It was one of my little stays . . ." and "I'd pick up a particular piece . . ." were taken from an unpublished interview Billy gave to Guiles in September 1969.

The exchange with Mayer in which Billy says he was "kept by the best men and women" also comes from the interview with Guiles.

"The public wasn't . . ." is from the Hal Elias oral history at AMPAS.

"He had his minor league . . ." comes from Charles Higham, *Merchant of Dreams*. I am also indebted to Higham's book and a personal interview with him for insight into Mayer's character.

"Thalberg was naïve . . ." comes from Samuel Marx, *Mayer and Thalberg*.

Billy's retort to Elinor Glyn comes from the interview with Guiles.

Details on *West Point* come from the files of AMPAS, NYPL and MoMA, as well as William Bakewell's memoirs. The report of the auto accident appeared in the *New York Times*, August 30, 1927.

"You should see me strutting . . ." is taken from Constance Blake, "Why Billy Haines Stayed at Metro," *Movie Mirror*, January 1932.

I am indebted to Alexander Walker's excellent account of the end of the silent era and the beginning of sound, *The Shattered Silents*, for being able to put Billy Haines's career in context.

My interview with Anita Page provided details and quotes on *Telling the World*.

Details on *Excess Baggage* are taken from the Production Code Administration files at AMPAS.

"It was an act . . ." comes from the interview with Guiles.

Those interviewed for this chapter include Frank (Junior) Coghlan, Anita Page, Charles Higham, Henry Haines, Ted Graber, Arch Case, Michael Pearman, Bob Wheaton, Bob Shaw, Harry Hay, and others.

CHAPTER 5
Excess Baggage:
1928-1931

Again, unless otherwise noted, Billy's quotes in this chapter come from WRH.

The "lip lazy" anecdote was told by Frances Marion in her memoirs. It was also told by Billy in various versions in a number of interviews. Marion left out the sexual innuendo, but Billy recalled the details for Charles Higham and for Fred Guiles in an unpublished interview.

"Clap in a nunnery" comes from Higham, *Merchant of Dreams*. The "night of the Titanic" quote comes from Bob Thomas, *Thalberg: Life and Legend*.

"It was certainly . . ." and "It was the height . . ." are taken from the Guiles interview.

Joy's letter to Milliken about *Alias Jimmy Valentine* was dated August 27, 1928. This and other information are located in the Production Code Administration files at AMPAS.

The quote from Father Daniel Lord comes from his book, *Played by Ear* (Chicago: Loyola University Press, 1955).

For a fascinating backdrop to Billy's career troubles, I referred to Gregory Black's excellent and exhaustive account of the coming of the Production Code, *Hollywood Censored*.

Warner Baxter's contracts are located at AMPAS.

I am grateful to Cari Beauchamp for sharing information from unpublished notes to Frances Marion's *Off with Their Heads*, from which details of Billy's contracts are taken.

The story of the raid on the gay bar comes from Anita Loos, *The Talmadge Girls*.

Harry Hay provided insight and information on the gay scene in Los Angeles in 1929–1931. I am again also indebted to the masterful *Gay New York* by George Chauncey for further information.

I combed through the index for criminal arrests in the Los Angeles County Court for any reference to Billy's alleged arrests; I found none. It could be that he never was arrested, that the "incidents involving the police" while he was at MGM never went that far. Or it could be, as in the case of others—notably George Cukor—charges were dropped and records cleared.

"It's such a fallacy . . ." comes from an unpublished interview with Billy by Fred Lawrence Guiles, September 1969.

Details of Billy's family moving to California come from Henry Haines, Jean Mathison, Ted Graber, and the city directories of Richmond and Los Angeles. Details of Jimmie's mother come from Charles Conrad and undated clippings from the *Daytona Beach News Journal*.

The "take the nipple out of your mouth" anecdote comes from Bob Thomas's *Thalberg: Life and Legend*. The goosing Thalberg anecdote was told to Thomas by Billy for the same book.

For details on Billy's relationship with Thalberg, I drew upon Thomas's biography as well as Billy's interview with Guiles. Billy's quote about Thalberg comes from that interview.

Details of Billy's "dual nature" and outlandish pranks are taken from dozens of clippings in his files at AMPAS, MoMA, and NYPL. Most are from the fan magazines *Photoplay*, *Picture Play*, *Modern Screen*, and others.

Billy's affair with one of his leading ladies was told to me by Arch Case and Ted Graber.

"When you make silent pictures . . ." is from Samuel Richard Mook, "Random Notes on Billy," *Picture Play*, July 1930.

The quote from the fan comes from *Haines Gem*, August 1929.

Billy's quote about Marie Dressler comes from the interview with Guiles.

"I've always done . . ." is from the *Los Angeles Examiner*, August 3, 1930.

Billy's 1930 contract was announced in the *New York Morning Telegraph* on August 16, 1930.

Details on the opening of the shop on LaBrea Avenue come from various news clippings and magazine articles in Billy's files at AMPAS, MoMA, and NYPL. Samuel Richard Mook interviewed him extensively about his house for *Picture Play* in July 1930. An unpublished *Photoplay* article on his shop shortly after it opened is in the MoMA files. I also interviewed Ted Graber, Arch Case, and Jean Mathison.

Details on Joan Crawford's house come from correspondence with Douglas Fairbanks, Jr., as well as Crawford's *My Way of Life* and Fairbanks's *The Salad Days*.

Information on Fanny Brice and Roger Davis is drawn mostly from Herbert Goldman's *Fanny Brice* but also from various clippings in Billy's AMPAS and MoMA files. The story of Haines and Roger Davis en route to San Francisco comes from the July 1930 issue of *Picture Play*. Ted Graber, Arch Case, and Michael Pearman provided additional information on Roger and Billy's friendship.

Information on Gary Cooper's affair with Andy Lawler comes from Lawler's cousin, William Kizer, and from Larry Swindell's biography.

"Ever since I've been . . ." comes from Charles Grayson, "The Life and Times of a Wisecracker," *Motion Picture Classic*, April 1931.

Details of the filming of *Just a Gigolo* come from *Modern Screen*, July 1931. Its troubles with the MPPDA come from the Production Code files at AMPAS.

Details of Billy's European trip come from Ted Graber and various clippings in Billy's files at MoMA and NYPL.

"Not Joan, not Eleanor . . ." and "Last year I . . ." are taken from *Modern Screen*, June 1931.

"She ran her own train . . ." comes from Barry Paris, *Garbo: A Biography*. Details on Garbo's private life and relationships with Lilyan Tashman, Fifi D'Orsay, and Mercedes de Acosta come from Paris, Charles Higham's *Merchant of Dreams*, de Acosta's *Here Lies the Heart*, and the clippings files of each actress at AMPAS and MoMA. "Greta Garbo and Fifi D'Orsay . . ." comes from an unsourced clip dated February 16, 1930, at AMPAS. "Do you want . . ." comes from Mercedes de Acosta, *Here Lies the Heart*.

Details of the Nils Asther–Vivian Duncan marriage come from dozens of clippings in Asther's files at AMPAS, MoMA, and NYPL.

Details on the Clara Bow scandals and trial come from David Stenn's remarkable biography *Runnin' Wild*, as well as clippings from her files at AMPAS.

The quote from Alexander Walker on the "latent sadism" of the fan magazines is taken from *The Shattered Silents*.

Interviews conducted for this section include Anita Page, Douglas Fairbanks, Jr., Charles Higham, Ted Graber, Arch Case, Jean Mathison, Henry Haines, Michael Pearman, Bob Wheaton, Bob Shaw, Charles Conrad, Harry Hay, and others.

CHAPTER 6
The Duke Steps Out:
1931-1933

The fact that Billy and Jimmy Durante formed a baseball team during the filming of *The New Adventures of Get-Rich-Quick Wallingford* comes from the Jimmy Durante biography.

Details of Billy's demotion come from his files at AMPAS, MoMA, and

NYPL, as well as from interviews with Henry Haines, Ted Graber, and Arch Case. "I would have stayed . . ." is from Constance Blake, "Why Billy Haines Stayed at Metro," *Movie Mirror*, January 1932. The *Los Angeles Times* quote is from September 24, 1931. "I want good stories . . ." comes from the *Los Angeles Examiner*, September 21, 1931.

The Prince Charles of the Belgians story was pieced together through various clips in Billy's file at AMPAS and MoMA, including a large article in the January 11 edition of the *Los Angeles Times* magazine section. Additional details were provided by Ted Graber and Bob Wheaton. For background on Charles and his family, I consulted Theodore Aronson, *Defiant Dynasty: The Coburgs of Belgium* (Indianapolis: Bobbs-Merrill, 1968.)

The *Modern Screen* article, "The Real William Haines," was written by Charles Gray and appeared in July 1931.

Details of Billy's tour with *Wallingford* and his performance at the Capitol come from various clippings in his MoMA and NYPL files. "This business of living . . ." comes from Helen Ludlam, "Billy Gets Wise," *Picture Play*, February 1932.

The story of Billy Haines's proposal to Anita Page and their relationship comes from an interview with Miss Page as well as Michael Ankerich, "Hollywood's Dancing Daughter," *Films of the Golden Age*, Fall 1995.

Details of Laura Haines's death and illness are taken from her death certificate, various newspaper obituaries in Billy's MoMA file, and an interview with Henry Haines.

Bill's dieting and exercise schedule in 1932 was mentioned in several articles. The increasingly innuendo-ridden press Billy was getting by 1931–1932 is well documented by dozens of clippings in his AMPAS, MoMA, and NYPL files. The Douglas Fairbanks article appeared in the April 1932 issue of *Vanity Fair*.

Details of the highly charged atmosphere at MGM during Billy's last months come from studio files at AMPAS; an interview with Charles Higham; Higham's biography of Mayer, *Merchant of Dreams*; and other Hollywood histories. Most of my details of the Paul Bern suicide were drawn from *Merchant of Dreams*. Details of Garbo's trip to Europe, including the quote about the lesbian bar, come from Barry Paris's *Garbo*.

The Anita Loos version of Billy's final confrontation with Mayer comes from *The Talmadge Girls*.

The sexual tryst with Clark Gable has been detailed before, notably in Patrick McGilligan's biography of George Cukor, *A Double Life*. Several of Billy's friends—including Arch Case, Bob Wheaton, Michael Pearman, and others—confirmed that he had indeed told them of the incident. Joan Crawford also referred to it in several published interviews.

Details of Billy's first design projects come from clippings in his MoMA and

NYPL files, as well as Larry Swindell's biography of Carole Lombard, *Screwball*, various Hollywood editions of *Architectural Digest*, and Pilar Viladas, "Decorating's Leading Man," *House and Garden*, August 1990. The article on Lombard's house ran in *Motion Picture*, May 1934.

Details on San Simeon are from an unpublished interview with Billy conducted by Fred Lawrence Guiles in September 1969, as well as Ken Murray's *The Golden Days of San Simeon*, Marion Davies's *The Times We Had*, and Barry Paris's biography of Louise Brooks.

The Production Code hearings and the time frame for the late summer and early fall of 1933 are based on a detailed study of *Variety*, as well as the *New York Times*, the *Los Angeles Times*, *The Memoirs of Will Hays*, and, notably, Gregory Black's *Hollywood Censored*.

"I was kicked out . . ." and "He was a ridiculous man . . ." come from Billy's interview with Guiles. "Louis B. Mayer kicked me out . . ." is from *Architectural Digest*, September–October 1972. "A dyed-in-the-wool . . ." comes from Norman Zierold's *The Moguls*.

Details on Nils Asther come from his files at AMPAS and MoMA. The account of Ramon Novarro's later life comes from his files at MoMA and NYPL. Myrna Loy's quote comes from her autobiography, *Being and Becoming*.

I am indebted to film historian Ed Sikov for the *Modern Screen* piece on Vincent Price.

Details on the life and career of Cary Grant are drawn from his files at AMPAS and NYPL, as well as the various biographies, especially Charles Higham's *Cary Grant: The Lonely Heart*.

The account of Dorothy Arzner's life and career is drawn from Judith Mayne's superb study *Directed By Dorothy Arzner*. "Mayer put out the word . . ." is from the *Los Angeles Times*, January 24, 1975.

CHAPTER 7
A Fool and His Money:
1934-1936

"But he said . . ." comes from an interview with Michael Morrison by this author.

Background on Phil Berg comes from Leila Hyams's file at AMPAS.

"When you start . . ." comes from Bob Thomas's biography of Joan Crawford.

"When I read . . ." is taken from *Movie Mirror*, January 1932.

"What will I do . . ." comes from WRH.

Details of Billy's trip to Europe and the Near East come from various clippings from both Los Angeles and New York papers at MoMA and NYPL.

Background information on Mascot Pictures is derived from Jon Tuska's excellent history of the studio, *The Vanishing Legion*. Details of Billy's work in his last two films come from his clipping files at AMPAS, NYPL, and MoMA, as well as the *New York Times* collection of film reviews.

"There aren't nearly . . ." comes from *Picture Play*, February 1934.

Billy's nightclub activity is derived from back issues of the *Hollywood Reporter*.

The anecdote of Thalberg and Shearer at Billy's party for Mrs. Patrick Campbell comes from Lawrence Quirk's biography of Shearer and was further elaborated on in an interview with Quirk by this author.

The quotes from Mary Anita Loos come from an interview with this author.

Details on Lombard's party-giving and Billy's quote about watching her undress come from Larry Swindell's biography *Screwball*.

"It looks like someone . . ." comes from Howard Mandelbaum and Eric Myers, *Screen Deco: A Celebration of High Style in Hollywood*.

Background information on Los Angeles architecture and decoration is taken from Tim Street-Porter's superb *The Los Angeles House*. "The Hollywood Regency Style . . ." comes from John Chase's *Exterior Decoration*, also quoted in *The Los Angeles House*.

The quotes on Elsie de Wolfe's style come from Jane Smith's biography *Elsie de Wolfe: A Life in the High Style*. I also consulted Aaron Betsky's *Queer Space: Architecture and Same Sex Desire*. Betsky makes a convincing argument that gay designers like de Wolfe brought a distinct sensibility to their work, a rejection of conventional norms, definitions, and structures in favor of newer, more idiosyncratic ideas. A case could be made along these lines for Billy as well: Likely influenced by Elsie de Wolfe, he was influential in discarding Hollywood's gaudiness and inaugurating a classic yet practical look. Still, his conscious motivation was anything but radical: he wanted to bring to Hollywood the kind of elegance (and the ensuing high society respect) associated with European aristocracy.

"I contend . . ." and "I'm tired . . ." come from *Architectural Digest*, September–October, 1972. Details on Los Angeles architects, including Williams and Dolena, come from "Architects to the Stars," *Architectural Digest*, April 1994.

"He is going to supply . . ." comes from the *Los Angeles Times*, February 11, 1934. "Joan loves blue . . ." comes from Erskine Johnson's syndicated column, May 20, 1950.

Details on the Claudette Colbert redesign, as well as the quip about Garbo, come from Harriet Parsons, "He Hitches His House to a Star," *Movie Mirror*, May 1934. Details on the Barrymore redesign come from the same article.

Billy's quote about actors being more vain than actresses was reported by Ezra Goodman in *The Fifty Year Decline and Fall of Hollywood*.

"I loathe cozy . . ." comes from *Architectural Digest*, September–October 1972.

The sections on Cukor's house are taken from both the McGilligan and Levy biographies, as well as both Cukor's and Billy's files at AMPAS, NYPL, and MoMA. In addition, there is a wealth of information on Cukor's house in the Cukor collection at AMPAS. I am grateful also for the synthesis provided by Pilar Viladas in her article on Billy for *House and Garden.* "Cukor's house is like . . ." comes from McGilligan. "I'm afraid I shall . . ." comes from Levy. "You certainly know . . ." comes from a letter from Cukor to Billy in Cukor's papers at AMPAS.

Gleanings of the Hollywood gay social scene come from many sources. I am indebted first of all to Bob Wheaton, Michael Pearman, Bob Shaw, Frank Lysinger, Arch Case, Ted Graber, Kevin Thomas, Charles Higham, Lawrence Quirk, William Kizer, Patrick McGilligan, and several others who requested anonymity. They helped me reconstruct a world that was both very private and very public, a world structured in a way almost unrecognizable to us sixty years later.

Back issues of *Photoplay,* the *Hollywood Reporter, Movie Mirror,* and other fan magazines and trade publications were vital in establishing the social habits and network of Hollywood's homosexuals. Hundreds of photographs from the collections of MoMA, NYPL, the Bettmann Archive, and AMPAS were sorted through, as well as photos in private collections and at such retail sources as Eddie Brandt's Saturday Matinee. The photographic evidence also helped document who socialized with whom.

Books that, laced together, helped to establish the gay circles include (but are not limited to) Hector Arce, *The Secret Life of Tyrone Power*; Simon Callow: *Charles Laughton: A Difficult Actor*; David Chierichetti, *Mitchell Leisen: Hollywood Director*; Stephen Citron, *Noël & Cole: The Sophisticates;* Gerald Clarke, *Capote: A Biography;* Mercedes de Acosta, *Here Lies the Heart*; George Eels, *The Life That He Led: A Biography of Cole Porter;* Mark Gatiss, *James Whale: A Biography of the Would-Be Gentleman*; Herbert Goldman, *Fanny Brice*; David Grafton, *Red, Hot & Rich! An Oral History of Cole Porter*; Charles Higham, *Errol Flynn* and *Cary Grant: The Lonely Heart*; Gavin Lambert, *Nazimova*; Emanuel Levy, *George Cukor, Master of Elegance*; Axel Madsen, *The Sewing Circle* and *Stanwyck*; Patrick McGilligan, *George Cukor: A Double Life;* Joe Morello, *Genius & Lust: The Creative and Sexual Lives of Noël Coward and Cole Porter*; Barry Paris, *Garbo* and *Louise Brooks*; Graham Payne and Sheridan Morley, *The Noël Coward Diaries*; Charles Schwartz, *Cole Porter: A Biography*; Donald Spoto, *Blue Angel: The Life of Marlene Dietrich*; Karen Swenson, *Greta Garbo: A Life Apart.*

"Homosexuality in that period . . ." comes from Grafton's biography of Cole Porter.

"Cary stopped . . ." comes from an interview with Michael Pearman by this author. "Frank Horn covered . . ." and "Orry-Kelly was . . ." comes from an interview with Bob Wheaton by this author.

"Mr. Cukor has . . ." comes from McGilligan.

"Andy Lawler was . . ." comes from an interview with Bob Wheaton by this author. Information on Lawler comes from Wheaton, Lawler's cousin William Kizer, the McGilligan biography of Cukor, and the Swindell biography of Gary Cooper.

I am also grateful to Jean Howard for confirming several stories for me and sharing a few new anecdotes.

"They [the gay elite] . . ." comes from McGilligan. "At Billy's parties . . ." comes from an interview with Michael Pearman by this author. Details on Hollywood's lesbian community come from the above-referenced sources as well as the files of many of the women involved at AMPAS, MoMA, and NYPL. "When Lilyan had . . ." comes from the Paris biography of Garbo. The account of Tashman's funeral comes from various New York newspapers in her NYPL file. Information on Kay Francis comes from William Kizer, various newspaper clips and photos, *The Leading Ladies*, and George Eel's monumental *Ginger, Loretta, and Irene Who?* Details on Barbara Stanwyck come from Bob Shaw and Axel Madsen's biography. The anecdote about Claudette Colbert and her husband's death comes from Shaw. Colbert's relationship with Dietrich was established from clips and photographs in her file at AMPAS, NYPL, and MoMA. "If you want something . . ." comes from Spoto's biography of Dietrich.

The full story of the El Porto Beach incident and its aftermath was assembled from contemporary reports. There is no listing for either Billy or Jimmie in the Los Angeles County Superior Court criminal index from January 1, 1926, through December 31, 1936. There is nothing in the district attorney's files, and the police records covering Manhattan Beach are no longer extant. Possibly nothing was ever recorded after the dismissal of the case, although police reports of the riot and the Walkers' charges surely existed at some point. I have based my account, then, squarely on the newspaper accounts, particularly from the *Los Angeles Times*, the *Los Angeles Examiner*, the *Long Beach Press-Telegram*, and the *Manhattan Beach News*.

I am deeply indebted to two additional sources, both of whom proved extraordinarily helpful: local historian Jan Norris, who penned a history of the town and who shared with me her knowledge of the area and the case; and, of course, Jim Walker, who showed courage and candor in speaking about the incident for the first time. The Manhattan Beach Public Library also provided important background.

"Billy rented that . . ." comes from an interview with Anita Page by this author.

"The two police cars . . ." comes from Jan Norris's invaluable history of Manhattan Beach. Background on the town and its movie connections comes from the same book.

Bob Wheaton, Ted Graber, and Michael Pearman shared with me stories they had heard in Billy's circle of friends about the incident.

The quotes from Jim Walker come from an interview with him by this author.

Reports of child molestation cases in the Manhattan Beach area come from the back issues of the *Manhattan Beach News*.

The issue of false memories or "memory distortion" has been taken up by the American Psychological Association in a number of studies over the past decade. I am grateful to Dr. Timothy Huber, a clinical psychologist at Veterans Memorial Medical Center in Meriden, Connecticut, for enlightening me on the topic and explaining how false memories can be so compelling.

Cukor's arrest is discussed in Patrick McGilligan's exemplary biography. He writes: "Interviews with people who were in a position to know leave no doubt as to the occurrence. . . . One reliable version has it that Haines and Cukor were themselves haplessly assaulted by naval personnel in Long Beach when they became too aggressive in their flirtations, and that it was the navy men, not Cukor and Haines, who should have been arrested." McGilligan places the incident shortly after the El Porto scandal. It's hard to believe, however, that Billy would have gone out cruising—on a beach yet, and very near to El Porto—so soon after being horribly bruised by bad publicity. The account bears some striking similarities to what happened in El Porto; this might be the incident that people were recalling for McGilligan. Thus Cukor may well have been there, and MGM may have protected Billy and Jimmie to save Cukor's neck.

"I remember writing . . ." comes from an interview with Henry Haines by this author.

"Jimmie talked to . . ." comes from an interview with Geoffrey Toone by this author.

The Lili Damita–Robert Benchley story came from Bob Wheaton. It has been told before, in Patrick McGilligan's biography of Cukor, but Damita was misidentified as Tallulah Bankhead.

CHAPTER 8
A Tailor-Made Man:
1936-1945

Quotes in this chapter, unless otherwise noted, come from interviews by this author with Don Bachardy, Arch Case, Frank (Junior) Coghlan, Ted Graber, Henry Haines, Mary Anita Loos, Frank Lysinger, Jean Mathison, Michael Pearman, Geoffrey Toone, and Miles White.

Bob Thomas's observations come from his biography of Joan Crawford. Thomas had interviewed Billy in the past. The account of Crawford's 1936 Christmas party comes from the *Hollywood Reporter*. Christina Crawford's comments are taken from correspondence with this author.

The *Modern Screen* article "What's the Matter With Lombard?" was published in 1937. The "Don't you have any girlfriends?" anecdote was originally reported in Larry Swindell's biography of Lombard. Swindell interviewed Billy for the book.

Details on *Craig's Wife* and Billy's work with Dorothy Arzner come from *Variety*, the *Hollywood Reporter*, and Judith Mayne's biography of Arzner.

My account of the Jack Warner house and Billy's work on it comes from interviews with Jean Mathison, Ted Graber, Betsy Bloomingdale, and Arch Case. Background on Jack and Ann Warner comes from Jack Warner's autobiography, *My First 100 Years in Hollywood*, and *Clown Prince of Hollywood* by Bob Thomas.

Details on the Bennett sisters' houses come from the *Bennett Playbill* and *Architectural Digest*, April 1994.

I am extremely grateful to Elaine Jackson-Retondo of the Documents Collection at the University of California, Berkeley, for locating press clippings of Billy's exhibit at the Golden Gate International Exposition. My description of the expo is culled from various sources, including the *New York Times*, the *Los Angeles Times*, the *San Francisco Chronicle*, and Herb Caen's *Baghdad by the Bay* (New York: Doubleday, 1949), from which "a place of lightness . . ." is taken. I am also indebted to the Treasure Island Museum for providing important background.

Billy's gradual reemergence into society after the El Porto Beach incident was documented through clips in his files at AMPAS, MoMA, and NYPL. The account of Hearst's 1938 birthday party at Ocean House comes from Ken Murray's *The Golden Days of San Simeon* as well as interviews with Michael Pearman, Ted Graber, and Arch Case. Details on Ocean House itself were drawn from Guiles's biography of Marion Davies and *Architectural Digest*, April 1994, from which the Chaplin quote is taken. Colleen Moore's quote is from her autobiography, *Silent Star*.

The Loretta Young anecdote was told to me by Bob Shaw.

My account of the filming of *Gone With the Wind* and Cukor's conflict with Gable is drawn from both Cukor biographies (McGilligan and Levy), as well as interviews with Bob Wheaton, Arch Case, and Ted Graber. "He and Victor Fleming . . ." comes from McGilligan. My description and analysis of the "one of Billy's old tricks" episode is based on interviews with Bob Wheaton, Michael Pearman, Arch Case, Ted Graber, Kevin Thomas, Charles Higham, and Patrick McGilligan.

Details of Billy's family come from Henry Haines.

Information on the Lincoln Continental comes from Booton Herndon's *Ford: An Unconventional Biography of the Men and Their Times* (New York: Weybright & Talley, 1969).

The description of Jimmie's personality and his relationship with Billy is based on interviews with Bob Shaw, Bob Wheaton, Michael Pearman, Charlie Conrad, Arch Case, Ted Graber, Charles Williamson, and others.

Billy's and Jimmie's relationship with and split from George Cukor is derived from interviews with Wheaton, Shaw, Case, and others. Details of Andy Lawler's career come from his cousin, William Kizer.

My account of the relationship with Cole Porter is based on interviews with Bob Wheaton, Frank Lysinger, Bob Shaw, Charlie Conrad, Arch Case, Ted Graber, Jean Howard, Jean Mathison, Miles White, and others. Background on Porter and Café Society comes from the Grafton, Schwartz, and Morello biographies of Porter, as well as Jean Howard's *Travels with Cole Porter* and Lucius Beebe's *Snoot if You Must*. "My dear, I've heard . . ." and "The Porters had . . ." come from Howard.

Details on the gay circles in 1930s–1940s Hollywood were given by Bob Wheaton, Frank Lysinger, Bob Shaw, Michael Pearman, Miles White, Harry Hay, and Don Bachardy, as well as others. Also helpful were the Gatiss biography of James Whale, Axel Madsen's biography of Barbara Stanwyck, and Hector Arce's biography of Tyrone Power.

Billy's work on the Goetz house is documented in *Architectural Digest*, April 1992, from which comes Edie Goetz's quote about Cole Porter. Billy's relationship with the Goetzes comes from conversations with Ted Graber and Charles Higham, whose *Merchant of Dreams* provided important background. Details on the Jean Howard commission come from an interview with Howard as well as Tim Street-Porter's definitive *The Los Angeles House*. "Billy Haines has great . . ." comes from Howard's *Travels with Cole Porter*.

For Hollywood during World War II, I referred to various accounts of the period. Especially helpful was the overview provided by Ray Hoopes's *When the Stars Went to War*. The role played by Prince Charles of the Belgians is recorded in most standard histories of the war. Billy's reaction to Lombard's death comes from several sources, including Ted Graber and the Swindell biography. "Can you imagine . . ." comes from Ted Graber. Billy's military data were obtained through the National Personnel Records Center in St. Louis. His actual records, however, were destroyed (as so many were) in a fire in July 1973.

An interview with Frank Lysinger provided details on Club Gala and Billy's patronage of it. "Jimmie was a happy . . ." comes from an interview by this author with Francie Brody.

Details on the split with Porter were gathered from interviews with Bob Wheaton, Arch Case, Frank Lysinger, Charlie Conrad, Charles Williamson, Don Bachardy, and others.

CHAPTER 9
The Smart Set:
1945-1968

Unless otherwise indicated, all quotes in this chapter from Betsy Bloomingdale, Francie Brody, Arch Case, Charlie Conrad, Ted Graber, Mary Anita
Loos, Jean Mathison, Michael Morrison, Bob Shaw, and Bob Wheaton come
from interviews with this author.

"Bill Haines was . . ." comes from an interview with Jody Jacobs by this
author.

"They weren't to the . . ." is from Kitty Kelley's biography of Nancy Reagan.

"He took my . . ." comes from an interview with Henry Haines by this author. Billy's purchase of his home on Lorna Lane is recorded at Los Angeles
County Records and Deeds, May 22, 1944, Grantee Deed Book 20980, page
40. "I liked it . . ." comes from an interview with Margaret Haines by this author. "This is where I . . ." comes from *Architectural Digest*, September–October
1972. Charlie Conrad and Christina Crawford shared their memories of the
house in correspondence with this author. The wallpaper anecdote was told to
me by Bob Shaw.

Biographical background on Ted Graber comes from an interview with him
by this author, as well as articles in the following periodicals: *Architectural Digest*, September 1980; *Time*, December 29, 1980; *Newsweek*, January 5, 1981;
Architectural Digest, July 1981; *People*, March 1, 1982; and *Los Angeles Magazine*,
February 1983. Unless otherwise indicated, quotes from Ted Graber come
from an interview with this author. "I lean to light . . ." is from *Newsweek*, January 5, 1981.

"In the time of . . ." is taken from *Architectural Digest*, September–October
1972. Pilar Viladas's appraisal of Billy's skill was found in her article on him in
House & Garden, August 1990. The *Interiors* magazine piece on his office ran in
December 1949.

Background on Francie Brody's family comes from John Gunther, *Taken at
the Flood: The Story of Albert D. Lasker* (New York: Harper & Brothers, 1960) as
well as from an interview with her. Details on A. Quincy Jones are derived
from biographical essays.

Information on Billy's clients through the mid-1950s comes from various
newspaper clippings located in his AMPAS files as well as interviews with
Jean Mathison, Michael Morrison, Ted Graber, and Arch Case.

"I'm content with . . ." comes from Ezra Goodman, "Ring Up the Curtain on
William Haines," *New York Times*, June 8, 1949. Goodman also reported on *The
Silents Were Golden*. "Bebe Daniels, Norma . . ." comes from Erskine Johnson's
column, *Los Angeles Daily News*, May 20, 1950.

The *Torch Song* anecdote comes from *A Portrait of Joan*. Details of Billy's continued friendship with Crawford were provided by Betty Barker, Ted Graber, Jean Mathison, and Bob Shaw. "Joan valued his . . ." comes from an interview with Betty Barker by this author. Billy's feelings about Al Steele were shared by Arch Case and Bob Shaw.

"It was like looking . . ." comes from Billy's interview with Fred Lawrence Guiles. The Marion Davies tennis shoes anecdote comes from Bob Shaw.

Details on the Crawford-Steele marriage come from the various Crawford biographies. "You fucking tycoons . . ." comes from an interview with Arch Case.

Background on the Bloomingdales comes from an interview with Betsy Bloomingdale, as well as *Time*, February 23, 1968; the *New York Times*, August 24, 1982; the Joyce Milton-Ann Louise Bardach and Gordon Basichis biographies of Vicki Morgan; and Marvin Traub, *Like No Other Store: The Bloomingdale's Legend and the Revolution in American Marketing* (New York: Times Books, 1993), from which his quote is taken. "In a world . . ." comes from Kitty Kelley's biography of Nancy Reagan.

I am indebted to Kitty Kelley, Jody Jacobs, Francie Brody, Betsy Bloomingdale, Arch Case, and Ted Graber for providing background and analysis of the Los Angeles social world, its relationship with Billy, and its acceptance (or not) of homosexuality. The descriptions of and quotes from Armand Deutsche are taken from his memoir, *Me and Bogie*. Background and anecdotes on Jerry Zipkin come from interviews with Nancy Reagan, Ted Graber, and Arch Case, as well as the various Nancy Reagan biographies.

My description of the HUAC and McCarthy periods in Hollywood is drawn from the many published accounts detailing the experience.

"The motion-picture queen . . ." was quoted by Ezra Goodman in *The Fifty Year Decline and Fall of Hollywood*.

Details on the Annenbergs and the Sunnylands commission come from interviews with Ted Graber, Michael Morrison, Jean Mathison, and Arch Case, as well as John Cooney, *The Annenbergs*, and Gaeton Fonzi, *Annenberg: A Biography of Power*.

All quotes in this section from Nancy Reagan are from my interview with her. My account of the relationship between the Reagans and Billy and Jimmie is drawn from my interview with Mrs. Reagan, as well as interviews with Betsy Bloomingdale, Jody Jacobs, Ted Graber, Arch Case, Bob Wheaton, and Jean Mathison. Background on Ronald Reagan's California political career comes from the various Reagan biographies. The Spigelgass quote comes from the Laurence Leamer biography of Nancy and Ronald Reagan. "There were tons . . ." is from an interview with Frank Lysinger by this author.

Alfred Bloomingdale's extracurricular sadomasochistic activities have been written about in a number of articles and books, notably the Basichis and Milton biographies of Vicki Morgan. My account of Governor Reagan's 1967 purge of homosexual staffers, and his and Nancy's subsequent public comments, is based on the various Reagan biographies as well as interviews with Bob Wheaton, Arch Case, and Ted Graber.

The lovely Amsterdam anniversary anecdote was told to me by Frank Lysinger. Virtually everyone I spoke with had an anecdote about Billy's and Jimmie's toupees.

Details of George Haines's death are from his death certificate and an interview with Henry Haines. Polly Moran's unhappy marriage is documented in clips in her AMPAS and NYPL clips. Details of the later lives and deaths of Mitchell Foster and Larry Sullivan come from their death certificates. The Hedda Hopper anecdotes come from her autobiography, *From Under My Hat*, and George Eels's *Hedda and Louella*. The Orry-Kelly anecdote about Jack Benny was told to me by Bob Shaw. My thanks to Shaw, Bob Wheaton, Ted Graber, Arch Case, Jean Mathison, Charles Williamson, and Betsy Bloomingdale for shedding light on Billy's various friendships through the 1960s.

Charlie Conrad very generously provided his scrapbook and journals of his 1958 visit to Billy and Jimmie, filled with photos, dinner menus, daily logs, and anecdotes. This provided a fascinating window on their world.

My account of the renewed friendship with Cukor in the late 1960s is based on interviews with Bob Wheaton, Charles Williamson, and Don Bachardy, as well as letters in Cukor's files at AMPAS. Charles Williamson very graciously allowed me to see a letter from Billy to Cukor, now in Williamson's possession, dated April 11, 1972, from which the "All's well here . . ." quote is taken. The quote on Harris Woods is also from that letter.

CHAPTER 10
Telling the World:
1969–1974

Unless otherwise noted, all quotes in this chapter from Betsy Bloomingdale, Arch Case, Charlie Conrad, Ted Graber, Michael Morrison, and Bob Shaw come from interviews with this author.

My account of the Christopher Street West Parade is drawn from Martin Duberman's *Stonewall* (Dutton, 1993).

Background on the Annenbergs and Walter's nomination to the Court of St. James's comes from the two Annenberg biographies, as well as interviews with Ted Graber, Jean Mathison, and Arch Case. "I believe she . . ." comes from John Cooney, *The Annenbergs: The Salvaging of a Tainted Dynasty*. Details on Winfield House and Billy's renovation of it come from the Annenberg biographies and interviews with Ted Graber, Jean Mathison, and Arch Case, as well as dozens of newspaper and magazine accounts, including (but not limited to) the *Times* of London, the *Los Angeles Times*, the *New York Times*, the *Los Angeles Herald-Examiner*, and *Architectural Digest*. "But the universe . . ." comes from the Cooney biography. Annenberg's "discomfiture" with the Queen, his rocky reception as ambassador, and his annoyance with his decorators comes from the Annenberg biographies.

"He runs the business . . ." comes from the *Los Angeles Times*, December 14, 1969. The encounter with the young reporter who wrote that Billy was eighty-four is from the same article. "The only difference . . ." comes from *Architectural Digest*, January 1986. "It took nine . . ." is from the *New York Times*, November 22, 1969. "We operated as a . . ." is from the same article. "The United States government . . ." comes from the *Times* of London, November 22, 1969, as does Philip Howard's description of the house. "Those British journalists . . ." is from the *Los Angeles Herald-Examiner*, September 8, 1970. "I wanted it to . . ." is from the same article.

Cukor's letter to Alan Searle is dated May 18, 1970, and is in his file at AMPAS.

The anecdote of Billy, Jimmie, and Joan Crawford getting lost in London was told to me by Charles Higham, who was told the story by Billy.

"I have never . . ." comes from Billy's 1969 interview with Fred Lawrence Guiles.

Billy's letter to Cukor on the 1972 Academy Awards is dated April 1, 1972, and is in the possession of Cukor's friend Charles Williamson, who most generously allowed me to quote from it.

"Selecting a favorite . . ." is from *Filmography*, Vol. 3, No. 3, 1972.

Details of Billy's final illness were culled from his death certificate and interviews with Henry Haines, Ted Graber, Arch Case, Bob Shaw, and Jean Mathison.

Billy's probate file, which includes his will, is more than a foot high. I examined it at the Los Angeles County Probate archives. It provided details of Billy's financial worth and the bequests he left to his heirs. The amusing sentiments attached to the gifts left to Ted Graber, Gloria Romanoff, Stevie Collier, and Betsy Bloomingdale are all quoted from his will.

My account of Jimmie's life after Billy's death is based on interviews with Betsy Bloomingdale, Nancy Reagan, Bob Wheaton, Bob Shaw, Ted Graber, Arch Case, Frank Lysinger, and Betty Barker. The Ronald Reagan anecdote was first told to me by Bob Wheaton; it was confirmed to me by Nancy Reagan. Arch Case and Ted Graber shared with me the incident of Jimmie attempting to walk off with a pound of bacon. Frank Lysinger recounted Jimmie's last night out at Maximillian de Henckel's. My account of Jimmie's last hours and his suicide is drawn from conversations with Ted Graber and Arch Case as well as Jimmie's death certificate, the autopsy report, and the coroner's files. The famous suicide note is located in Jimmie's probate file as a codicil to his will.

"The impression I . . ." is from an interview with Charles Williamson by this author.

Jimmie's will is also located at Los Angeles County Probate archives. Details of his financial worth and bequests to his heirs are from this document.

The auctions at Sotheby are fully detailed in Billy's probate file. Camilla Snyder's article ran in the *Los Angeles Herald-Examiner* on November 5, 1974, entitled "An Ode to Billy Haines." The sale of the Lorna Lane house is also documented in Billy's probate file.

"When George had . . ." comes from an interview with Charles Williamson by this author.

"As a love-and-success . . ." comes from Anita Loos, *The Talmadge Girls*.

Bibliography

Pieces of Billy Haines's story turn up in numerous Hollywood narratives. I am grateful to the following published accounts for not only adding to Billy's story but also helping set it in context by providing important background. Books with more specialized content are acknowledged in the notes for particular chapters.

Anger, Kenneth. *Hollywood Babylon*. New York: Dell, 1975.

Anger, Kenneth. *Hollywood Babylon II*. New York: Dutton, 1984.

Ankerich, Michael. *Broken Silence: Conversations with 23 Silent film Stars*. Jefferson, NC: McFarland, 1989.

Arce, Hector. *Gary Cooper: An Intimate Biography*. New York: William Morrow, 1979.

Arce, Hector. *The Secret Life of Tyrone Power*. New York: William Morrow, 1979.

Bacall, Lauren. *By Myself*. New York: Knopf, 1979.

Bakewell, William. *Hollywood Be Thy Name*. Jefferson, NC: McFarland, 1982.

Baldwin, William W. *Billy Baldwin Remembers*. New York: Harcourt Brace Jovanovich, 1974.

Bankhead, Tallulah. *My Autobiography*. New York: Harper and Brothers, 1952.

Basichis, Gordon. *Beautiful Bad Girl: The Vicki Morgan Story*. Santa Barbara, CA: Santa Barbara Press, 1985.

Beauchamp, Cari. *Without Lying Down: Frances Marion and the Powerful Women of Early Hollywood*. New York: Scribner, 1997.

Beebe, Lucius. *Snoot if You Must*. New York: E. P. Dutton, 1943.

Bennett, Joan, and Lois Kibbee. *The Bennett Playbill*. New York: Holt, Rinehart & Winston, 1970.

Berg, A. Scott. *Goldwyn: A Biography*. New York: Knopf, 1989.

Betsky, Aaron. *Queer Space: Architecture and Same-Sex Desire*. New York: William Morrow, 1997.

Black, Gregory D. *Hollywood Censored: Morality Codes, Catholics, and the Movies*. London: Cambridge University Press, 1994.

Blake, Michael. *Lon Chaney: The Man Behind the 1000 Faces*. New York: Vestal Press, 1993.

Brian, Denis. *Tallulah, Darling*. New York: Pyramid Books, 1972.

Brooks, Louise. *Lulu in Hollywood*. New York: Alfred A. Knopf, 1982.

Brownlow, Kevin. *The Parade's Gone By*. New York: Knopf, 1960.

Callow, Simon. *Charles Laughton: A Difficult Actor*. London: Methuen London, 1987.

Carey, Gary. *Doug and Mary: A Biography of Douglas Fairbanks and Mary Pickford*. New York: E. P. Dutton, 1977.

Carrier, Jeffrey L. *Tallulah Bankhead*. New York: Greenwood Press, 1991.

Chauncey, George. *Gay New York*. New York: Basic Books, 1994.

Chierichetti, David. *Mitchell Leisen: Hollywood Director*. Los Angeles: Photoventures Press, 1995.

Citron, Stephen. *Noël & Cole: The Sophisticates*. New York: Oxford University Press, 1993.

Clarke, Gerald. *Capote: A Biography*. New York: Ballantine Books, 1988.

Coghlan, Frank, Jr. *They Still Call Me Junior*. Jefferson, NC: McFarland, 1993.

Considine, Shaun. *Bette and Joan: The Divine Feud*. New York: E. P. Dutton, 1989.

Cooney, John. *The Annenbergs: The Salvaging of a Tainted Dynasty*. New York: Simon & Schuster, 1982.

Crawford, Christina. *Mommie Dearest*. New York: William Morrow, 1978.

Crawford, Joan. *My Way of Life*. New York: Simon & Schuster, 1971.

Crawford, Joan, and Jane Kesner Ardmore. *A Portrait of Joan*. New York: Doubleday, 1962.

Crowther, Bosley. *Hollywood Rajah: The Life & Times of Louis B. Mayer*. New York: Holt, Rinehart & Winston, 1960.

Crowther, Bosley. *The Lion's Share*. New York: Dutton, 1957.

Davies, Marion (ed. by Pamela Phau and Kenneth S. Marx). *The Times We Had: Life with William Randolph Hearst*. Indianapolis: Bobbs-Merrill, 1975.

de Acosta, Mercedes. *Here Lies the Heart*. New York: Reynal, 1960.

Denis, Brian. *Tallulah Darling*. New York: Macmillan, 1972.

Deutsch, Armand. *Me and Bogie and Other Friends and Acquaintances from a Life in Hollywood and Beyond*. New York: G. P. Putnam's Sons, 1991.

Dowd, Nancy, and David Shepard. *King Vidor*. Metuchen, NJ, and London: Directors Guild of America and the Scarecrow Press, 1988.

Durgnat, Raymond, and Scott Simmon. *King Vidor: American*. Berkeley: University of California Press, 1988.

Eames, John Douglas. *The MGM Story*. New York: Crown, 1975.

Eels, George. *Ginger, Loretta, and Irene Who?* New York: G. P. Putnam's Sons, 1976.

Eels, George. *Hedda and Louella*. New York: G. P. Putnam's Sons, 1972.

Eels, George. *The Life that He Led: A Biography of Cole Porter*. New York: G. P. Putnam's Sons, 1967.

Eels, George, and Stanley Musgrove. *Mae West*. New York: William Morrow, 1982.

Eyman, Scott. *Mary Pickford, America's Sweetheart*. New York: Donald I. Fine, 1990.

Fairbanks, Douglas, Jr. *A Hell of a War*. New York: St. Martin's Press, 1993.

Fairbanks, Douglas, Jr. *The Salad Days*. New York: Doubleday, 1988.

Flamini, Roland. *Thalberg: The Last Tycoon and the World of MGM*. New York: Crown, 1994.

Fonzi, Gaeton. *Annenberg: A Biography of Power*. New York: Weybright and Talley, 1969.

Fountain, Leatrice Gilbert. *Dark Star*. New York: St. Martin's Press, 1985.

Franklin, Joe. *Classics of the Silent Screen*. New York: Cadillac, 1959.

Gabler, Neal. *An Empire of Their Own*. New York: Doubleday, 1987.

Gatiss, Mark. *James Whale: A Biography of the Would-Be Gentleman*. London: Cassell, 1995.

Goldman, Herbert G. *Fanny Brice: The Original Funny Girl*. New York: Oxford University Press, 1992.

Goodman, Ezra. *The Fifty Year Decline and Fall of Hollywood*. New York: MacFadden Books, 1962.

Gottfried, Martin. *George Burns and the One Hundred Year Dash*. New York: Simon & Schuster, 1996.

Grafton, David. *Red, Hot & Rich! An Oral History of Cole Porter*. New York: Stein and Day, 1987.

Guiles, Fred Lawrence. *Joan Crawford: The Last Word*. New York: Birch Lane Press, 1995.

Guiles, Fred Lawrence. *Marion Davies: A Biography*. New York: McGraw-Hill, 1972.

Guthrie, Lee. *The Life & Loves of Cary Grant*. New York: Drake, 1977.

Harris, Radie. *Radie's World*. New York: G. P. Putnam's Sons, 1975.

Harris, Warren G. *Gable and Lombard*. New York: Simon & Schuster, 1974.

Hays, Will H. *Memoirs of Will H. Hays*. Garden City, NY: Doubleday, 1955.

Hepburn, Katharine. *Me*. New York: Knopf, 1991.

Higham, Charles. *Errol Flynn: The Untold Story*. Garden City, NY: Doubleday, 1980.

Higham, Charles. *Merchant of Dreams: Louis B. Mayer, MGM & the Secret Hollywood*. New York: Donald I. Fine, 1993.

Higham, Charles, and Roy Moseley. *Cary Grant: The Lonely Heart*. New York: Harcourt Brace Jovanovich, 1989.

Hoopes, Roy. *When the Stars Went to War*. New York: Random House, 1994.

Hopper, Hedda. *From Under My Hat*. New York: Doubleday, 1952.

Howard, Jean. *Jean Howard's Hollywood*. New York: Harry N. Abrams, 1989.

Howard, Jean. *Travels with Cole Porter*. New York: Harry N. Abrams, 1991.

Johnes, Carl. *Crawford: The Last Years*. New York: Dell, 1979.

Josefsberg, Milt. *The Jack Benny Show*. New Rochelle, NY: Arlington House, 1977.

Kelley, Kitty. *Nancy Reagan: The Unauthorized Biography*. New York: Simon & Schuster, 1991.

Kern, Walter. *The Silent Clowns*. New York: Alfred A. Knopf, 1975.

Kobal, John. *People Will Talk*. New York: Alfred A. Knopf, 1985.

Kotsilibas-Davis, James, with Myrna Loy. *Myrna Loy: Being and Becoming*. New York: Donald Fine, 1987.

Lambert, Gavin. *Nazimova*. New York: Alfred K. Knopf, 1997.

Lambert, Gavin. *Norma Shearer: A Life*. New York: Alfred K. Knopf, 1990.

Lambert, Gavin. *On Cukor*. New York: G. P. Putnam's Sons, 1972.

Leamer, Laurence. *Make Believe: The Story of Nancy and Ronald Reagan*. New York: Harper & Row, 1983.

Leighton, Frances Spatz. *The Search for the Real Nancy Reagan*. New York: Macmillan, 1987.

Levin, Martin. *Hollywood and the Great Fan Magazines*. New York: Arbor House, 1970.

Levy, Emmanuel. *George Cukor: Master of Elegance*. New York: William Morrow, 1994.

Loos, Anita. *A Girl Like I*. New York: Viking Press, 1966.

Loos, Anita. *Kiss Hollywood Goodbye*. New York: Viking Press, 1974.

Loos, Anita. *The Talmadge Girls*. New York: Viking Press, 1978.

McGilligan, Patrick. *George Cukor: A Double Life*. New York: St. Martin's Press, 1991.

Madsen, Axel. *The Sewing Circle*. New York: Birch Lane Press, 1995.

Madsen, Axel. *Stanwyck: The Life & Times of Barbara Stanwyck*. New York: HarperCollins, 1994.

Mandelbaum, Howard, and Eric Myers. *Screen Deco: A Celebration of High Style in Hollywood*. New York: St. Martin's Press, 1985.

Manvell, Roger. *Chaplin*. Boston: Little, Brown, 1974.

Marion, Frances. *Off with Their Heads: A Serio-Comic Tale of Hollywood*. New York: Macmillan, 1972.

Marx, Arthur. *Goldwyn*. New York: W. W. Norton, 1976.

Marx, Samuel. *Mayer & Thalberg: The Make-Believe Saints*. London: W. H. Allen, 1976.

Mayne, Judith. *Directed by Dorothy Arzner*. Bloomington: Indiana University Press, 1994.

Milton, Joyce, and Ann Louise Bardach. *Vicki*. New York: St. Martin's Press, 1986.

Moore, Colleen. *Silent Star*. Garden City, NY: Doubleday, 1968.

Morello, Joe. *Genius and Lust: The Creative and Sexual Lives of Noël Coward and Cole Porter*. 1995.

Murray, Ken. *The Golden Days of San Simeon*. New York: Doubleday, 1971.

Negri, Pola. *Memoirs of a Star*. New York: Doubleday, 1970.

Paris, Barry. *Garbo*. London: Pan Books, 1996.

Paris, Barry. *Louise Brooks*. New York: Alfred A. Knopf, 1989.

Parish, James Robert. *The Hollywood Beauties*. New Rochelle, NY: Arlington House, 1978.

Parish, James Robert. *The Paramount Pretties*. New Rochelle, NY: Arlington House, 1972.

Parish, James Robert, and William T. Leonard. *The Funsters*. New Rochelle, NY: Arlington House, 1979.

Parish, James Robert, and Don E. Stanke. *The Leading Ladies*. New Rochelle, NY: Arlington House, 1977.

Parsons, Louella O. *The Gay Illiterate*. Garden City, NY: Garden City Publishing, 1945.

Parsons, Louella O. *Tell It to Louella*. New York: G. P. Putnam's Sons, 1961.

Payne, Graham, and Sheridan Morley (eds.). *The Noël Coward Diaries*. New York: Little, Brown, 1982.

Quirk, Lawrence. *Norma: The Story of Norma Shearer*. New York: St. Martin's Press, 1988.

Reagan, Nancy, with William Novak, *My Turn*. New York: Random House, 1989.

Robbins, Jhan. *Inka, Dinka, Doo: The Life of Jimmy Durante*. New York: Paragon House, 1980.

Russo, Vito. *The Celluloid Closet*. New York: Harper & Row, 1987.

Schwartz, Charles. *Cole Porter: A Biography*. New York: Dial Press, 1977.

Selznick, David O. (edited by Rudy Behlmer). *Memo from David O. Selznick*. New York: Avon Books, 1973.

Smith, Jane S. *Elsie de Wolfe: A Life in the High Style*. New York: Atheneum, 1982.

Spoto, Donald. *Blue Angel: The Life of Marlene Dietrich*. New York: Doubleday, 1992.

Spoto, Donald. *Laurence Olivier: A Biography*. New York: HarperCollins, 1992.

Stenn, David. *Clara Bow: Runnin' Wild*. New York: Doubleday, 1988.

Street-Porter, Tim. *The Los Angeles House*. Los Angeles: Clarkson-Potter, 1995.

Swanberg, W. A. *Citizen Hearst*. New York: Scribners, 1961.

Swanson, Gloria. *Swanson on Swanson*. New York: Random House, 1980.

Swenson, Karen. *Greta Garbo: A Life Apart*. New York: Scribner, 1997.

Swindell, Larry. *Gary Cooper: The Last Hero*. Garden City, NY: Doubleday & Co., 1980.

Swindell, Larry. *Screwball: The Life of Carole Lombard*. New York: William Morrow, 1975.

Thomas, Bob. *Jack Warner: Clown Prince of Hollywood*. New York: McGraw-Hill, 1990.

Thomas, Bob. *Joan Crawford*. New York: Simon & Schuster, 1978.

Thomas, Bob. *Thalberg: Life and Legend*. New York: Doubleday, 1969.

Timmons, Stuart, *The Trouble with Harry Hay*. Boston: Alyson, 1990.

Tornabene, Lyn. *Long Live the King: A Biography of Clark Gable*. New York: G. P. Putnam's Sons, 1976.

Tuska, Jon. *The Vanishing Legion: A History of Mascot Pictures*. Jefferson, NC: McFarland, 1982.

Vickers, Hugo. *Cecil Beaton*. London: Weidenfeld & Nicholson, 1985.

Vidor, King. *A Tree Is a Tree*. New York: Harcourt, Brace, 1953.

Walker, Alexander. *Rudolph Valentino*. New York: Stein & Day, 1976.

Walker, Alexander. *The Shattered Silents*. New York: William Morrow, 1979.

Wansell, Geoffrey. *Haunted Idol: The Story of the Real Cary Grant*. New York: William Morrow, 1984.

Warner, Jack L. (with Dean Jennings). *My First 100 Years in Hollywood*. New York: Random House, 1965.

Wayne, Jane Ellen. *Crawford's Men*. New York: Prentice-Hall, 1988.

Wayne, Jane Ellen. *Gable's Women*. New York: Prentice-Hall, 1987.

West, Mae. *Goodness Had Nothing to Do with It*. New York: Manor Books, 1976.

Zierold, Norman. *The Moguls*. New York: Coward-McCann, 1969.

Index